## Praise for Michelle Richmond's *The Marriage Pact*

"This **fast-paced nail-biter** goes in unpredictable directions. . . . With strong writing, intriguing characters, and a compelling conceit, this psychological thriller seems destined for the top of summer reading lists. Recommended **as a fresh voice for readers of Gillian Flynn or Ruth Ware.**"

—*Library Journal*

"Creepy and engrossing."

—*Booklist*

"Gripping, thought-provoking, and **irresistible.**"
—Dean Koontz, #1 *New York Times* bestselling author

"**Riveting psychological suspense!** This book will keep you up all night, while making you second-guess everything you know and everyone you've ever loved."

—Lisa Gardner,
#1 *New York Times* bestselling author of *Right Behind You*

"**A truly chilling thriller** . . . It ranks with *The Stepford Wives* and *Gone Girl* as a terrifying look at what it really means to say 'I do.'"

—Joseph Finder,
*New York Times* bestselling author of *Guilty Minds*

"This psychological thriller offers a **smart, searing and frightening** look at modern love."

—Today.com

" 'Till death do us part' takes on an entirely **scary** new meaning."

—*Family Circle*

"An undeniably creepy web of lies, deceit and consequences."

—*The Mercury News*

"So intriguing . . . a quintessential page-turner; there's an incipient sense of dread from word one. Readers will surely succumb to temptation and plunge in."

—*Criminal Element*

"Michelle Richmond is, simply put, a great storyteller. And *The Marriage Pact*, without gimmicks or tricks, is a twisting, suspenseful, keep-you-up-all-night thriller. But it's more than that, too. It's **a deep, insightful, nearly voyeuristic view into the modern marriage**. . . . A smart, engrossing, scary read!"

—Lisa Unger,
*New York Times* bestselling author of *The Red Hunter*

"With a **brilliant** premise for a novel of psychological suspense, taut plotting, and deft writing, *The Marriage Pact* shows in gripping detail just what could go wrong when we try too hard to protect the love we cherish most."

—JP Delaney,
*New York Times* bestselling author of *The Girl Before*

"Clever and original—**as smart as it is scary.**"

—Gin Phillips, author of *Fierce Kingdom*

# THE MARRIAGE PACT

# THE MARRIAGE PACT

*A Novel*

## MICHELLE RICHMOND

BANTAM BOOKS | NEW YORK

2018 Bantam Books Trade Paperback Edition

Copyright © 2017 by Michelle Richmond
Reading group guide copyright © 2018 by Penguin Random House LLC

Published in the United States by Bantam Books, an imprint of Random House, a division of Penguin Random House LLC, New York.

BANTAM BOOKS and the HOUSE colophon are registered trademarks of Penguin Random House LLC.

RANDOM HOUSE READER'S CIRCLE & Design is a registered trademark of Penguin Random House LLC.

Originally published in hardcover in the United States by Bantam Books, an imprint of Random House, a division of Penguin Random House LLC, in 2017.

Library of Congress Cataloging-in-Publication Data
Names: Richmond, Michelle, author.
Title: The marriage pact: a novel / Michelle Richmond.
Description: New York: Bantam Books, [2017]
Identifiers: LCCN 2016038793| ISBN 978-0-553-38636-3 (paperback) | ISBN 9780804179867 (ebook)
Classification: LCC PS3618.I35 M37 2017 | DDC 813/.6—dc23 LC record available at https://lccn.loc.gov/2016038793

Printed in the United States of America on acid-free paper

randomhousebooks.com
randomhousereaderscircle.com

4 6 8 9 7 5 3

*Book design by Susan Turner*

*For Kevin*

# THE MARRIAGE PACT

## 1

I COME TO ON A CESSNA, BUMPING THROUGH THE AIR. MY HEAD IS throbbing, and there is blood on my shirt. I have no idea how much time has passed. I look at my hands, expecting to see restraints, but there are none. Just an ordinary seatbelt looped around my waist. Who strapped me in? I don't even remember boarding the plane.

Through the open door of the cockpit, I see the back of the pilot's head. It's just the two of us. There is snow in the mountains, wind buffeting the plane. The pilot seems completely focused on his controls, shoulders tense.

I reach up and touch my head. The blood has dried, leaving a sticky mess. My stomach rumbles. The last thing I ate was the French toast. How long ago was that? On the seat beside me, I find water and a sandwich wrapped in wax paper. I open the bottle and drink.

I unwrap my sandwich—ham and Swiss—and take a bite. Shit. My jaw hurts too much to chew. Someone must have punched me in the face after I hit the ground.

"Are we going home?" I ask the pilot.

"Depends on what you call home. We're headed to Half Moon Bay."

"They didn't tell you anything about me?"

"First name, destination, that's about it. I'm just a taxi driver, Jake."

"But you're a member, right?"

"Sure," he says, his tone unreadable. "Fidelity to the Spouse, Loyalty to The Pact. Till death do us part." He turns back just long enough to give me a look that warns me not to ask any more questions.

We hit an air pocket so hard my sandwich goes flying. An urgent beeping erupts. The pilot curses and frantically pushes buttons. He shouts something to air traffic control. We're descending fast, and I'm clutching the armrests, thinking of Alice, going over our final conversation, wishing I'd said so many things.

Then, suddenly, the plane levels out, we gain altitude, and all appears to be well. I gather the pieces of my sandwich from the floor, wrap the whole mess back up in the wax paper, and set it on the seat beside me.

"Sorry for the turbulence," the pilot says.

"Not your fault. Good save."

Over sunny Sacramento, he finally relaxes, and we talk about the Golden State Warriors and their surprising run this season.

"What day is it?" I ask.

"Tuesday."

I'm relieved to see the familiar coastline out my window, grateful for the sight of the little Half Moon Bay Airport. The landing is smooth. Once we touch down, the pilot turns and says, "Don't make it a habit, right?"

"Don't plan to."

I grab my bag and step outside. Without killing the engines, the pilot closes the door, swings the plane around, and takes off again.

I walk into the airport café, order hot chocolate, and text Alice. It's two P.M. on a weekday, so she's probably embroiled in a thousand meetings. I don't want to bother her, but I really need to see her.

A text reply arrives. *Where are you?*

*Back in HMB.*

*Will leave in 5.*

It's more than twenty miles from Alice's office to Half Moon Bay. She texts about traffic downtown, so I order food, almost the whole left side of the menu. The café is empty. The perky waitress in the perfectly pressed uniform hovers. When I pay the check, she says, "Have a good day, Friend."

I go outside and sit on a bench to wait. It's cold, the fog coming down in waves. By the time Alice's old Jaguar pulls up, I'm frozen. I stand up, and as I'm checking to make sure I have everything, Alice walks over to the bench. She's wearing a serious suit, but she has changed out of heels into sneakers for the drive. Her black hair is damp in the fog. Her lips are dark red, and I wonder if she did this for me. I hope so.

She rises on her tiptoes to kiss me. Only then do I realize how desperately I've missed her. Then she steps back and looks me up and down.

"At least you're in one piece." She reaches up and touches my jaw gently. "What happened?"

"Not sure."

I wrap my arms around her.

"So why were you summoned?"

There's so much I want to tell her, but I'm scared. The more she knows, the more dangerous it will be for her. Also, let's face it, the truth is going to piss her off.

What I'd give to go back to the beginning—before the wedding, before Finnegan, before The Pact turned our lives upside down.

## 2

I'LL BE HONEST—THE WEDDING WAS MY IDEA. MAYBE NOT THE LOCA-
tion, the place, the food, the music, all the things Alice knew how to
do so well. The idea, though, that was mine. I'd known her for three
and a half years. I wanted her, and marriage was the best way to ensure
I didn't lose her.

Alice didn't have a                                    e. In her earlier
days, she was wild, im                              ly to a fleeting,
shining object. I wor                              would be gone.
The wedding, if I'm h                              anence.

I proposed on a b                              r had died, and
we were back in Alaba                            ive, and his unexpected death shook                            e spent the days
after the funeral clean                          a Birmingham
suburb. In the mornin                          tic, work space,
and garage. The house was filled with artifacts of her family life: her father's
military career, her dead brother's baseball exploits, her dead mother's recipe books, faded pictures of her grandparents. It was like an archaeological
treasure trove of a small, long-forgotten tribe from a lost civilization.

"I'm the last one," she said. Not in a pitiful way, just matter-of-fact. She'd lost her mother to cancer, her brother to suicide. She had survived, but not unscathed. Looking back, I can see that her position as the only living member of the family made her more loving and reckless than she might have been otherwise. Had she not been so alone in the world, I'm not sure she would have said yes.

I'd ordered her engagement ring weeks earlier, and it arrived via UPS moments after she learned of her father's death. I'm not sure why, but I slipped the box into my duffel bag as we were leaving for the airport.

Two weeks into the trip, we called a real estate agent and had him come out to appraise the house. We wandered through the rooms, the agent taking notes, scribbling frantically, like he was preparing for a test. At the end, we stood on the porch, waiting for his assessment.

"Are you sure you want to sell?" the agent asked.

"Yes," Alice said.

"It's just that—" He gestured toward us with his clipboard. "Why don't you stay? Get married. Have kids. Build a life. This town needs families. My children are so bored. My boy has to play soccer because we don't have enough kids to field a baseball team."

"Well," Alice said, looking out toward the street, "because."

That was it. "Because." The guy snapped back into real estate mode. He suggested a price, and Alice suggested a slightly lower one. "That's below market value for this neighborhood," he said, surprised.

"That's okay. I just want it over with," she replied.

He jotted a notation on his clipboard. "It will certainly make my job easier."

Within hours, a truck pulled up, guys got out, and the house was stripped of the worn furniture and aging appliances. All that remained were two lounge chairs beside the pool, which hadn't changed since the day it was dug and plastered in 1974.

The following morning, a different truck arrived with different men—stagers hired by the realtor. They loaded a whole new set of furniture into the house. They moved quickly and with confidence, putting large abstract paintings on the walls and small shining knickknacks on the shelves. When they were finished, the house was the same, only different: cleaner, sparser, devoid of the pesky items that give a home its soul.

The day after that, a parade of real estate agents led a pride of potential buyers through the rooms, all whispering, opening cabinets and closets, studying the sheet that provided the listing details. That afternoon, the agent called with four offers, and Alice accepted the highest. We packed our things, and I made reservations for a flight back to San Francisco.

In the evening, when the stars came out, Alice wandered outside to stare at the night sky and say goodbye to Alabama for good. It was a warm night, the scent of barbecues wafting up over the back fence. The outdoor lamps reflected brilliantly off of the pool, and the lounge chairs felt as comfortable as they must have been the first day her father dragged them out onto the patio, when his wife was beautiful and tan and his children were small and rambunctious. I sensed that this was as good as Alabama could get, and yet Alice seemed so sad, immune to the beauty that had snuck up on us without warning.

Later, I would tell our friends that the idea to seize that moment to propose came as an impulse. I wanted to make her feel better. I wanted to show her that there was a future. I wanted to bring her happiness on such a mournful day.

I walked out to the pool, knelt down, removed the ring from its box, and presented it to Alice in my sweaty palm. I didn't say a word. She looked at me, she looked at the ring, she smiled.

"Okay," she said.

3

OUR WEDDING WAS HELD IN A PASTURE ALONG THE BANKS OF the Russian River, a two-hour drive north of San Francisco. Months earlier, we'd gone out there to take a look at it. We drove right past it a couple of times, because it wasn't marked from the road. When we opened the gate and walked down the path toward the river, Alice hugged me and said, "I love it." At first, I thought she was joking. In places, the grass was five feet high.

The property was a huge, meandering dairy farm, with cows roaming the pasture. It was owned by the rhythm guitar player from Alice's first band. Yes, she had been in a band, and it's even possible you've heard their music, though we can talk about that later.

The day before the wedding, I drove right past the site again. This time, though, it was because it looked completely different. The guitar player, Jane, had spent weeks cutting, shaping, and resodding the pasture. It was amazing. It looked like a fairway from the world's most perfect golf course. The grass moved up over the hill, then sloped down to the river. Jane said that she and her wife had been looking for a project.

There was a large tent, a patio, a pool, and a modern pool house. A stage rose above the river shore, and a gazebo stood on a mound over-looking all of it. The cows still wandered around in their slow, meditative way.

Chairs were brought in, tables, equipment, speakers, and umbrellas. While Alice wasn't exactly keen on weddings, she loved parties. Although we hadn't had one in the years I'd known her, I heard stories. Big shin-digs in ballrooms, at beaches, in her past apartments; apparently it was a talent she possessed. So when it came to the arrangements, I stepped aside and let her do her thing. Months of planning, everything perfect, everything timed just right.

Two hundred people. It was supposed to be one hundred for me, one hundred for her, though in the end it was a bit lopsided. It was a funny guest list, like any wedding. My parents and grandmother, partners from my wife's firm, co-workers from the clinic where I used to work, former clients, friends from college, graduate school, Alice's old music friends, an off-kilter combination of others.

And Liam Finnegan and his wife.

They were the last to be invited, 201 and 202 on the guest list. Alice had met him three days before the wedding, at the law firm where she'd been working day and night for the past year. I know, it's weird, my wife is a lawyer. If you knew her, it would surprise you too. And we can also talk about that, but later. The important part here is Finnegan—Finnegan and his wife, Liam and Fiona, guests 201 and 202.

At the firm, my wife had been the junior associate on Finnegan's case. It was an intellectual property thing. Finnegan was a businessman now. Years earlier, however, he was a well-known front man for an Irish folk rock group. You've probably never heard his music, but maybe you've seen his name. It's been in all of those British music magazines—*Q, Uncut, Mojo.* Dozens of musicians claim him as a key influence.

For days after Alice got the assignment, we had Finnegan's discs on repeat in our house. The case was as straightforward as an intellectual property case can be. A young band had stolen a section of one of his songs and turned it into a huge hit. If you're like me and don't under-stand music on a technical level, you wouldn't see the similarities, but if you're a musician, my wife said, the theft was obvious.

The case resulted from a comment Finnegan had made a few years earlier. He told an interviewer that the band's hit sounded suspiciously like a song from his second album. He didn't plan to take it any further, but then the young band's manager sent Finnegan a letter demanding that he apologize for the comment and publicly declare the song had not been stolen. Things devolved from there, ultimately leading to my wife working a million hours on her first big case.

As I said, she was the junior associate, so when the judgment came back in Finnegan's favor, the partners took all the credit. A month later, the week before our wedding, Finnegan paid a visit to the firm. He had been awarded an insane amount of money, far more than he wanted, certainly more than he needed, so he wanted to thank everyone for their work. When he arrived, the partners led him to a conference room, where they regaled him with tales of their incredible strategy. At the end, he thanked them, but then asked if he could meet all the people who had really worked on the case. He cited a couple of the briefs and motions, surprising the partners with the level of attention he had paid to the finer details.

A brief he especially liked was one Alice had written. It was a funny, creative thing—insomuch as a legal brief can be either funny or creative. So the partners invited Alice into the conference room. At some point, someone mentioned that she was getting married that weekend. Finnegan remarked that he loved weddings. Alice, joking, asked, "Would you like to come to mine?" He surprised everyone by saying, "I'd be honored." Later, as he was leaving, he stopped by Alice's cubicle and she handed him an invitation.

Two days later, a messenger arrived at our apartment with a box. That week, a number of wedding gifts had been delivered, so it wasn't really a surprise. The return address said *The Finnegans*. I opened the envelope; inside was a folded white card with a picture of a cake on the front. Tasteful.

*To Alice and Jake, My supreme congratulations on the occasion of your impending nuptials. Respect marriage and it will provide you with much in return. Liam*

The gifts we'd received up until that moment had been fairly unsurprising. There was an equation of sorts that allowed me to predict the contents of each gift before it was opened. The total cost of the gift was usually a combination of the net income of the giver multiplied by the years that we had known the person, over pi. Or something like that. Grandma bought us six full place settings of china. My cousin bought us a toaster.

With Finnegan, though, I had no way to calculate. He was a successful businessman, he had just won a substantial judgment, and he had a back catalog of songs that probably didn't earn much money. The thing was, we hadn't known him for long. Okay, we didn't exactly know him at all.

Out of curiosity, I tore right into the package. It was a large, heavy box made of recycled wood, with a label burned into the top. At first, I thought it was a case of some tiny-production, crazy-elite Irish whiskey, which would have made sense. It's exactly what the gift equation would have predicted.

It made me a little nervous. Alice and I didn't own any hard alcohol. I should explain. Alice and I first met in a rehab facility north of Sonoma. I'd been practicing therapy for a few years by then, and I jumped at any chance to learn more. I'd been filling in for a friend, gaining work experience. On the second day, I led a therapy group that included Alice. She said she drank too much, and she needed to stop. Not forever, she said, just long enough to complete the changes necessary to stabilize her life. She said she'd never been a big drinker before but that a series of family tragedies had caused her to behave recklessly, and she wanted to get a handle on it. I was struck by her commitment and clarity.

Weeks later, back in the city, I decide to call her. I was running a group for schoolkids with similar issues, and I was hoping she might be willing to come and talk to them. She spoke about her own struggles in a way that cut to the heart of things, direct but engaging. I wanted to connect with the kids and I knew they would listen to her. It didn't hurt that Alice was a musician. With her beat-up biker jacket, chopped black hair, and stories of life on the road, she looked and sounded cool.

Short story: She agreed to talk to my group, it went well, I took her to lunch, we became friends, months passed, we started dating, we bought a place together, and then, as you know, I proposed.

So, anyway, when Finnegan's package arrived, I tensed up when I thought it was a bottle of some incredibly rare liquor. During the first few months I knew Alice, she never had a drink. But then sometime after that, she began to enjoy the occasional bottle of beer or a glass of wine with dinner. It isn't the traditional path for people with issues related to alcohol. Still, it seemed to work for Alice. Only beer and wine, though. Hard liquor, she always joked, "ends up with someone in jail." That was hard to picture, as Alice was more in control than anyone I knew.

I set the gift on the table. A substantial, elegant wood box.

The label on the front, though, seemed off.

THE PACT.

What kind of Irish whiskey is named The Pact?

I opened the box to find another wooden box inside, set in blue velvet. On each side, nestled into the fabric, was an extremely expensive-looking pen—silver, white gold, or maybe even platinum. I picked one up and was surprised by the heft, the construction. It was the sort of exquisite gift you bought for someone who had everything, which is why it was an odd gift for us. We both worked hard, and we were doing okay, but we didn't have everything, by any means. For Alice's law school graduation, I had, in fact, bought her a pen. It was a beautiful thing I'd purchased from a private dealer in Switzerland, after doing months of research into the surprisingly complex field of fine writing instruments. It was as if I'd opened a door expecting a small closet and had, instead, found an entire universe. I took great pains to pay for it in a roundabout way that hid the exorbitant cost. In the event that she ever lost it, I didn't want her to be weighed down by the true depth of the loss.

I picked up Finnegan's pen. Across the top of the wrapping paper, I scribbled a few circles, and then the phrase *Thank you, Liam Finnegan!* The ink flowed smoothly, the pen gliding across the slick paper.

Along the spine of the pen, something had been engraved.

The writing was so small I couldn't read it. I remembered a magnifying glass that had come with a board game Alice bought me for Christmas. I rummaged through the hall closet. Behind Risk, Monopoly, and

Boggle, I found the game, the magnifying glass still in its cellophane wrapper. I brought the pen into the light and held the glass up to it.

ALICE & JAKE, followed by the date of the wedding, and then simply DUNCANS MILLS, CALIFORNIA. I'll admit, I was a little disappointed. I expected more from one of the world's greatest living folksingers. Had the engraving contained the meaning of life, I wouldn't have been surprised.

I pulled the other pen out and placed it on the table. Then I lifted out the smaller box. It had the same reclaimed wood, the same fancy hardware, and the same logo branded across the front: THE PACT. It was surprisingly heavy.

I tried to open it, only to discover that it was locked. I placed the box back on the table and searched through the packaging, looking for a key. At the bottom, I found no key, just a handwritten note:

*Alice and Jake, Know this: The Pact will never leave you.*

I stared at the note. What could it mean?

Alice had to work late, tying up loose ends with cases and projects before the wedding and honeymoon. When she finally did arrive, a million things had come up, and so the gift from Finnegan was forgotten.

## 4

YOU CAN TELL HOW A WEDDING IS GOING TO GO FROM THE FIRST five minutes. If people show up a little late, moving slowly, you know it may be a grind. With our wedding, though, everyone arrived unusually early. My best man, Angelo Foti, and his wife, Tami, drove up from the city faster than expected. They stopped at a café in Guerneville to waste time. At the café, they noticed four other couples in wedding-type clothes. They introduced themselves, and apparently the party began then and there.

With the flow of friends and relatives, my nerves, and all the rest of it, it wasn't until the ceremony had already begun that I realized Finnegan had shown up. I was looking at Alice in her great dress, walking down the aisle by herself, en route to *me*, of all people, when I caught a glimpse over her shoulder of Finnegan, standing there in the back row. He wore an impeccable suit with a pink tie. The woman with him, maybe five years his junior, wore a green dress. I was surprised to see them smiling, clearly happy to be there. I guess I was expecting Finnegan and the wife to be all business, a late arrival and an early departure, attending the attorney's wedding—a social obligation, checking a box, nothing more. But it wasn't like that at all.

I didn't know this then, but I know it now. At a wedding, if you're paying attention, you can spot the happily married couples. Maybe it's a confirmation of the choice they made, maybe it's just a belief in the convention of marriage. There is a look, easy to spot, hard to define, and the Finnegans had it. Before I glanced back to Alice—beautiful in her sleeveless white dress with a retro pillbox hat—Finnegan caught my eye, smiled, and raised an imaginary glass.

The vows happened so quickly. The ring, the kiss. Within minutes of Alice walking down the aisle, we were husband and wife, and then just as suddenly the reception was in full swing. I was caught up in conversations with friends, relatives, co-workers, a few old high school buddies, all of whom eagerly retold their versions of my life, often in the wrong order but in a positive light. It wasn't until darkness had begun to fall that I saw Finnegan again. He was standing near the bandstand, watching Alice's musician friends work their way through an eclectic selection of songs. He stood behind his wife, his arms wrapped around her waist. She was wearing his suit jacket in the cool night air, that contented look still on their faces.

I had lost track of Alice, so I scanned the crowd to find her. Then I realized she was standing onstage. Since I'd known her, she had never performed; it was as if she'd left that part of her life completely behind. The lights were out, but in the darkness I could see her pointing to friends, calling them to the stage. Jane, their old drummer, a friend from the law firm with his bass, and others, a group of people I didn't know well, some of whom I'd never met, whose presence spoke of a whole life she'd had before me, an important part of her very essence that was somehow closed off to me. I was both sad and excited to see her in this light: sad because I couldn't help feeling left out and inessential, yet happy because—well, because she remained a mystery to me in the best possible way. Alice reached her hand toward Finnegan. The place began to glow with bluish light, and I realized that, as Finnegan approached the stage, people had quietly retrieved their cellphones and were recording.

My wife stood there for the longest time. The voices died down, as if in anticipation. Finally, she stepped to the microphone. "Friends," she said. "Thank you so much for being here." Then she pointed at me, and an organ note rose up behind her. Finnegan was in his element, playing the keyboard. It was a beautiful and elusive sound, the organ leading the other instruments slowly into the fray. Alice stood there, looking at me, swaying gently to the music. As the lights rose, Finnegan circled into a melody I immediately recognized. It was an old song, Led Zeppelin at their best, subtle and infectious, a beautiful wedding song, "All My Love." Alice's singing came in quiet and unsure, but then grew in confidence. I'm not sure how, but she and Finnegan seemed to be on the same wavelength.

As the music lurched forward, she stepped into a circle of light, closed her eyes, and repeated the beautiful chorus, such a plain statement, and yet for the first time I realized that, yes, she did love me. I glanced around the tent, and in the low light I could see our friends and relatives, all swaying to the melody.

Then the song took a slight turn, and Alice sang the critical line that I had long forgotten, a simple question, though one that washed the rest of the lyrics in a thin layer of ambiguity and doubt. For a moment, I felt off-balance. I put a hand on the top of a chair to steady myself and looked around, everything cast in the glow of the moon: the crowd, the pasture, cows dozing in the field, the river. To the side of the stage, I could see Finnegan's wife dancing in her green dress, her eyes closed, immersed in the music.

The party continued for hours. When dawn broke, a small group of us were left sitting around the pool, watching the sun come up over the river. Alice and I shared a lounge chair, the Finnegans sharing an adjacent one.

Eventually, the Finnegans collected their coats and shoes and moved to leave. "We'll see you out," Alice said. Walking them up the driveway, I felt as if I had known them for years. As they stepped into their Lamborghini—borrowed from a friend, Finnegan said, winking—I remembered the gift. "Oh," I said, "I forgot to thank you. We were supposed to talk about your intriguing gift."

"Of course," Finnegan said. "All in due time." His wife smiled. "Tomorrow we go back to Ireland, but I'll email after you return from your honeymoon."

And that was it. Two weeks in a mostly abandoned but once grand hotel on the Adriatic, a long flight home, and suddenly we were right back where we started—the same, only married. Was this the end, or just the beginning?

## 5

A FTER RETURNING FROM OUR HONEYMOON, WE WERE BOTH careful to avoid the letdown that could so easily have come following the brilliant party and weeks on a peaceful, sunny beach. The first night, back in our small house in San Francisco, ten blocks from the edge of the continent and the least sunny beach anywhere, I pulled out the china from my grandmother and prepared a four-course meal, setting the table with cloth napkins and candles. We'd already been living together for more than two years, and I wanted marriage to feel different.

I cooked a recipe that I'd found online for a roast and potatoes. It was terrible—a thick brown meaty disaster. To her credit, Alice cleaned her plate and declared it delicious. Despite her small size—she's just five foot five in her tallest heels—she can really dig into a plate of comfort food. I've always liked that about her. Fortunately, the yellow cake with chocolate frosting saved the meal. The following night, I tried another family dinner. I did better this time.

"Am I trying too hard?" I asked.

"Trying too hard to fatten me up, maybe," Alice said, swirling a drumstick in the mashed potatoes.

After that, we drifted back into our old habits. We'd order sausage pizza or takeout and eat in front of the television. It was sometime during our binge-watching of an entire season of *Life After Kindergarten* that Alice's cell pinged with an email.

Alice picked up the phone. "It's from Finnegan," she said.

"What did he say?"

She read aloud. *"Thank you so much for welcoming Fiona and me to celebrate your nuptials. There is nothing we love more than a beautiful wedding and a rousing party. We were honored to be part of your special day."*

"Nice."

*"Fiona says that you and Jake remind her of us from twenty years ago,"* she read. *"She insists you come stay with us next summer at our place in the North."*

"Wow," I said. "It sounds like they actually want to be friends."

*"Lastly, the gift,"* Alice continued reading. *"The Pact is something that Fiona and I received for our own wedding. It was left on our doorstep on a rainy Monday morning. It wasn't until two weeks later that we learned it was from my childhood guitar teacher, an old man from Belfast."*

"Regift?" I asked, perplexed.

"No," Alice replied, "I don't think so."

She looked down at the phone and continued. *"It turned out to be the best gift Fiona and I received, and frankly the only one I actually remember. Over the years, we've given The Pact to a few young couples. It is not for everyone, I should begin with that, but in the short time I've come to know you and Jake, I sense it may be right for you. So, may I ask you a few questions?"*

Alice quickly typed, *Yes.*

She stared at her phone.

*Ping.*

She read aloud again. *"Pardon my boldness, but would you like your marriage to last forever—yes or no? This only works if you are honest."*

Alice glanced at me, a little puzzled, hesitated for maybe a second too long, and then she typed, *Yes.*

*Ping.*

She was looking increasingly intrigued, as if Finnegan were leading her down a darkened street.

*"Do you believe that a long marriage will go through periods of happiness AND sadness, lightness AND darkness?"*

*Of course.*

*Ping.*

*"Are both of you willing to work to make your marriage last forever?"*

"That goes without saying," I said. Alice typed.

*Ping.*

*"Do either of you give up easily?"*

*Nope.*

*"Are both of you open to new things? And are you willing to accept help from friends if they have your success and happiness in mind?"*

Puzzling. Alice looked at me. "What do you think?"

"Yes, for me at least," I said.

"Okay, me too," she said, typing.

*Ping.*

*"Splendid. Are you available on Saturday morning?"*

She looked up. "Are we available?"

"Sure," I said.

*Yes,* she typed. *Are you in town?*

*"Sadly, I am in a studio outside Dublin. But my friend Vivian will visit your house to explain The Pact. If you are so inclined, I would be honored if you and Jake chose to join our very special group. Will ten a.m. work?"*

Alice fiddled with her phone calendar before answering, once again, *yes.*

*Ping.*

*"Brilliant. I'm certain you and Vivian will hit it off."*

After that, we waited, but no more emails came. Alice and I stared at the phone, waiting for it to ping again.

"Does any of this strike you as—complicated?" I asked finally.

Alice smiled. "How bad can it be?"

A LITTLE ABOUT ME. I WORK AS A THERAPIST AND COUNSELOR. Although I had loving parents and, from the outside, what appeared to be an idyllic childhood, growing up was sometimes difficult. In hindsight, I didn't choose my career so much as it chose me.

I arrived at UCLA as a biology major, though it didn't last long. At the beginning of my second year, I took a job as a peer counselor for the College of Letters and Science. I enjoyed the training, and after that, the work. I liked talking to people, listening to their problems, helping them find a solution. When I graduated, I didn't want my "career" in counseling to end, so I entered the graduate program in applied psychology at UC Santa Barbara. My postdoc internship brought me home to San Francisco, where I worked with at-risk teens.

Today I run a small counseling practice with two friends from that internship. When we started the group eighteen months ago in the remnants of an old vacuum repair shop in the Outer Richmond district, we worried we wouldn't be able to make ends meet. At one point, we even considered selling coffee and my secretly famous chocolate chip cookies as a side business to help pay the rent.

In the end, however, the practice did seem to be surviving without any desperate intervention. My two partners, Evelyn (thirty-eight, single, super-smart, an only child from Oregon) and Ian (British, forty-one, also single, gay, the eldest of three), are both engaging, likable, and generally happy people, and I think this happiness just somehow willed the business to survive.

We each handle our own areas. Evelyn deals primarily with addiction, Ian specializes in adult anger management and OCD, and I take the kids and young adults. Patients who fit clearly into one of those categories are assigned to the appropriate partner, while everything else is divided evenly. Recently, though, we decided to branch out, or at least Evelyn did. I returned from the honeymoon to discover that she had arranged for me to lead our expansion into marriage counseling.

"Because I have so much experience with marriage?"

"Exactly."

Evelyn, being the marketing genius, had already secured three new clients for me. When I protested, she showed me the emails in which she made it clear to the clients that I had a number of years of experience in counseling and precisely two weeks' personal experience with marriage.

I have a fear of being unprepared. So when Evelyn dropped the news, I immediately went into panic mode and started studying up. I researched the evolution of marriage and was surprised to discover that monogomous marriage was only established in Western societies about eight hundred years ago.

I also discovered that married people live longer than single people. I'd heard that factoid before, but I never examined the actual studies. They're quite convincing.

At the other end of the spectrum, Groucho Marx said, "Marriage is a wonderful institution, but who wants to live in an institution?"

I wrote down other quotes as well, gleaned from the Internet and a shelf of marriage books I purchased from the bookstore near my office.

*A successful marriage requires falling in love many times, always with the same person.*

*Don't smother each other, nothing grows in the shade.*

Things like that. Quotes may be an oversimplification, the last refuge of the dilettante, but I like having them on hand in counseling sessions. Occasionally, something will come up and I won't know what to say. A little Groucho Marx can break the ice, lead somewhere unexpected, or just give me a minute to collect my thoughts.

S ATURDAY MORNING, WE GOT UP EARLY TO PREPARE FOR VIVIAN'S arrival. At 9:45, Alice finished the vacuuming, and I took the cinnamon rolls out of the oven. Without discussion, we had both slightly overdressed. When I stepped out of the bedroom in a button-down shirt and khakis I hadn't worn in months, Alice laughed.

"If I need a flat-screen TV from Best Buy," she said, "you're my man."

Of course, we were just trying to present a slightly better version of ourselves and our tiny house with its sliver of a view of the Pacific Ocean. I'm not sure why we felt we needed to impress Vivian, but without ever acknowledging it out loud, we understood that we wanted to.

At 9:52, Alice finished changing clothes for the third time. She came into the living room and did a spin in her flowery blue dress. "Too much?"

"Perfect."

"What about the shoes?"

She was wearing serious pumps, the kind she only ever wore to work. "Too formal," I said.

"Right." She disappeared down the hallway and returned in a pair of red Fluevogs.

"Just right," I said.

I glanced out the front window, but there was no one there. I felt a little nervous, as if we were waiting to interview for a job that we hadn't even applied for. Still, we wanted it. Between the box and the pens and the cryptic emails, Finnegan had made it sound so appealing—and, I'll admit, so *exclusive*. At her heart, Alice is a true overachiever; anything she starts, she wants to complete. Anything she completes, she wants to win—whether it's good for her or not.

At 9:59, I looked out the window again. The fog was thick, and I could see no cars in either direction.

Then the sound of shoes on the stairs. Heels, serious heels. Alice looked down at her Fluevogs, then at me, and whispered, "Wrong choice!"

I walked self-consciously to the door and opened it. "Vivian," I said, more formally than I intended.

She was in a well-tailored but extraordinarily yellow dress. Tour de France yellow. She looked younger than I'd expected.

"You must be Jake," she said. "And you," she added, "must be Alice. You're even more ravishing than your picture."

Alice didn't blush; she's not a blusher. Instead, she tilted her head and gazed at Vivian, as if assessing her. Knowing Alice, she probably suspected Vivian had ulterior motives, but I could tell that Vivian was being sincere. Alice has that effect on people. Still, I knew Alice would have traded her high cheekbones, her big green eyes, her thick black hair—all of it—for a normal family, a living, loving family, a mother who hadn't poisoned her liver, a father who hadn't poisoned his lungs, and a brother who hadn't taken what people erroneously call "the easy way out."

Vivian herself was attractive in a way that comes from confidence, a good upbringing, and taste. She looked 80 percent business, 20 percent "Saturday-morning brunch with friends." She carried a fine leather satchel and wore a strand of gleaming pearls. As the light caught her face, it occurred to me that she was actually in her late forties. Her hair was shiny, her skin had a glow—I imagined it was the result of an organic diet, regular exercise, and everything else in moderation. I imagined her with a good position in tech, some stock options, and a yearly bonus that never disappointed.

In my practice, when I meet potential clients for the first time, I can usually gauge the depth of their problems from one good glance. Over the years, anxiety, stress, and insecurity reveal themselves on a person's face. Like a bend in a river, the stress or anxiety can wear on the face in tiny increments, until a slight pattern becomes noticeable to the naked eye.

In that instant, when the light broke through the fog, flooded into our living room, and literally shone upon Vivian's face, it occurred to me that this woman had no stress, no anxiety, no insecurities.

"Coffee?" I asked.

"Please."

Vivian sat in the big blue chair that cost half of Alice's first paycheck from the law firm. She opened her briefcase and removed a laptop and a tiny projector.

Reluctantly, I went to the kitchen. Thinking back, I realize I was nervous about leaving Alice alone with Vivian. When I returned with the coffee, they were talking about our honeymoon and the beauty of the Adriatic coast. Vivian asked about our hotel by name. How did she know where we had stayed?

I sat next to Alice and lifted three rolls from the tray onto three dessert plates.

"Thank you," Vivian said. "I love cinnamon rolls."

Vivian connected her projector to the laptop, then stood up. "Mind if I take this picture down?" But she was already removing the frame from its spot on the wall. It was a Martin Parr photograph Alice had given me for my last birthday, a picture I had always admired but had never been able to afford. From far off, the photo showed a solitary man on a stormy day, swimming laps in a shabby public pool beside a wild green sea in a run-down Scottish town. When I asked Alice where she had bought it, she had laughed. "Bought it? If only it had been that easy."

"So," Vivian said, turning. "How much has Liam told you?"

"Actually," Alice said, "he didn't tell us anything."

"Can we open the box?" Vivian asked. "You only need to bring the smaller one. We'll need the pens too."

I walked down the hallway into the back room, where we had stored the wedding gifts we hadn't gotten around to addressing. Miss Manners says you get exactly one year to write a thank-you note, but in the world of email and instant messages that seems like an eternity. Every time I saw the gifts, I felt guilty for all the cards we'd yet to send out.

I placed the box and the pens on the coffee table in front of Vivian. "Still locked," she said with a smile. "You passed the first test."

Alice nervously sipped her coffee. It wasn't until after the honeymoon that she'd seen the box. When she did, she tried and failed to pick the lock with a pair of tweezers.

Vivian reached down into her briefcase and pulled out a set of gold keys. She found the right key and inserted it in the lock but didn't turn it.

"I need verbal confirmation that you're ready to proceed," she said. She looked at Alice, waiting.

In hindsight, I realize we should have known, right then, that something was wrong. We should have sent Vivian away and refused to take Finnegan's calls. We should have ended it all, before it really began. But we were young and curious, and our marriage was still fresh. And Finnegan's gift was so unexpected, his messenger so eager, it would have seemed impolite to refuse.

Alice nodded. "We're ready."

VIVIAN SWITCHED ON THE PROJECTOR, AND A SLIDE DISPLAYED on the wall where my Martin Parr photo had been just minutes before.

THE PACT, it read.

Nothing more, nothing less. Courier font in big black letters against a blank background.

"So," Vivian said, wiping her fingers on a napkin left over from our wedding. It still came as something of a shock—a happy shock—to see our names printed on the napkin: *Alice & Jake*. "I need to ask you both some questions."

She pulled a black leather folio from her bag and opened it to reveal a yellow legal pad. The projector still shone the phrase THE PACT onto our wall. I tried not to look at those imposing words looming over us, over our new and fragile marriage.

"Neither of you has previously been married, correct?"

"Correct," we replied in unison.

"What is the length of your longest previous relationship?"

"Two years," Alice told her.

"Seven," I said.

"Years?" Vivian asked.

I nodded.

"Interesting." She wrote something on her notepad.

"How long did your parents' marriages last?"

"Nineteen years," Alice said.

"Forty-something," I said, feeling an unearned pride in my parents' matrimonial success. "It's still going."

"Excellent." Vivian nodded. "And, Alice, did your parents' marriage end in divorce?"

"No." The death of her father was too recent, and I could tell she didn't want to get into it. Alice is something of a closed book. As a therapist, not to mention her husband, I sometimes find it's not the easiest trait to accept.

Vivian leaned forward, resting her elbows on the yellow pad. "What do you think is the most common reason that couples in the Western world get divorced?"

"You first," Alice said, tapping me on the knee.

I didn't have to think too hard. "Infidelity."

Vivian and I looked at my wife. "Claustrophobia?" Alice offered.

Not the answer I was hoping for.

Vivian recorded our answers on the legal pad. "Do you think people should take responsibility for their actions?"

"Yes."

"Yes."

"Do you think marriage counseling can be helpful?"

"I sure hope so." I laughed.

She scribbled. I leaned over to see what she was writing, but her handwriting was too small. Snapping the folio shut, she named two famous actors who had recently split. Over the past month, the tawdry details of their divorce had been everywhere. "So," she asked, "which one of them, do you think, is responsible for the divorce?"

Alice was frowning, trying to figure out what Vivian wanted to hear. Like I said, Alice is an overachiever—she doesn't just want to pass the test, she needs a perfect score. "I imagine the responsibility lies with both of them," she replied. "While I don't think the things she did with Tyler Doyle were all that mature, her husband could've handled it differently. He shouldn't have posted those tweets, for one thing."

Vivian nodded, and Alice sat up a little straighter, clearly pleased. It occurred to me that this must have been the way she acted back in school, always the girl with her hand in the air, eager and prepared. Now it made her seem vulnerable, in a good way; there was something sweetly incongruous about my wife—with her big job and her multimillion-dollar settlements and her very adult wardrobe—trying so hard to get the answer right.

"As always, I completely agree with my wife."

"Good answer," Vivian said, winking. "Just a few more. What is your signature drink?"

"Chocolate milk," I said. "Hot chocolate when it's cold."

Alice thought for a second. "It used to be cranberry juice and vodka on the rocks. Now it's Calistoga berry. What's yours?"

Vivian seemed mildly surprised to have the tables turned. "Probably Green Spot, twelve year, neat." She flipped through her packet. "The biggie: Do you want your marriage to last forever?"

"Yes." I said it automatically. "Of course."

"Yes," Alice said. It seemed like she meant it, but then again, what if she was only saying it to pass the test?

"Finished," Vivian said, sliding her folio into her leather bag. "Shall we look at the slides?"

"THE PACT IS A GROUP OF LIKE-MINDED INDIVIDUALS INTENT ON achieving a similar goal," Vivian began. "Created in 1992 on a small island off Northern Ireland by Orla Scott, The Pact has increased exponentially in size and commitment since that day. While our rules and bylaws have changed, our membership has grown, and our members have spread far and wide, the mission and spirit of The Pact remain true to the concept that Orla conceived in the very beginning."

She edged forward in her chair, so that our knees were inches apart. Her computer still projected THE PACT on our wall.

"So it's a club?" Alice asked.

"Kind of, yes," Vivian said, "and also kind of no."

The first slide featured a tall, trim woman standing in front of a white cottage, with the ocean in the background. "Orla Scott was a barrister, a criminal prosecutor," Vivian narrated. "She was extremely driven—a careerist, in her words. She was married, no children. She wanted to be able to devote all of her time to her position, she wanted to rise within the Ministry of Justice, and she wanted nothing to hold her back. In her late thirties, all during the course of one year, Orla's parents died, her husband left her, and her position was made redundant."

Alice stared at the image on the wall. I imagined she felt a kind of kinship with Orla. She knew a thing or two about loss.

"Orla had prosecuted more than three thousand cases," Vivian continued. "The rumor is that she won all of them. She was a cog in the Thatcher machine, and in an instant Thatcher was out of power and Orla was out of a job.

"Orla retreated to Rathlin, the island where she had grown up. She rented a cottage, expecting to stay a week or two, figure things out, and plot her next move. In the days that followed, however, she found herself increasingly drawn to the pace of island life, the quiet existence she'd known as a child. She realized that the things she valued the most seemed flimsy. She went to the island to help herself work through the stress and anxiety of losing her job, only to find that the layoff wasn't as devastating as she'd imagined. What really threw her for a loop, it turned out, was the end of her marriage.

"Her husband was a man she had loved passionately in college. They married at a young age, then slowly drifted apart. When he asked her for a divorce, she was relieved—it was just one more complex set of problems she wouldn't have to think about. When she was brutally honest with herself, she realized she'd seen the marriage as a nuisance—something that made her feel guilty every time she had to work late.

"She had gotten into criminal prosecution out of an idealism and a desire to help victims. In the months following the divorce, however, she took a hard look at her career. She lived on adrenaline, moving quickly from one case to another, no time to examine things from a larger perspective. Over time, she became part of a changing political landscape for which she had no deep respect. The inertia of day-to-day events swept her along.

"When all of this became clear to her, she began analyzing the arc of her marriage. She made an effort to rekindle their relationship, but he had already moved on."

Vivian was talking faster now, enthralled with a story that she had probably told dozens of times.

"A year later, Orla was on her daily walk around the island when she met someone. Richard was an American tourist, traveling the islands of Northern Ireland alone, trying to connect with the distant roots of his family. Richard canceled his return flight, quit his job in the States, extended his room reservation at the only inn on the island, and eventually proposed marriage to Orla."

I could see that something was bothering Alice. "In this story," she said, "everyone gives up their jobs. Is that a requirement or something? Because Jake and I love our jobs."

"I assure you that The Pact has many members, like your sponsor, who are exceedingly successful in business," Vivian replied. "The Pact wants you to be you, only better."

I was pretty sure I'd heard that slogan in summer camp.

"Orla was hesitant about Richard's proposal," Vivian told us. "She had come to understand all of the things she'd done that had led to the dissolution of her marriage. She didn't want to repeat her mistakes. Orla believes that we are creatures of habit. Once in a groove, it's hard to change."

"But change *is* possible," I insisted. "My practice—my entire field— is predicated on that notion."

"Of course it is," Vivian said. "And Orla would agree with you. She decided that, if her second marriage was to succeed, she needed a clear strategy to make that happen. For days, she wandered the coastline, contemplating marriage: the things that make it fail and the things that help it thrive. In her cottage, she typed out her ideas on the same typewriter her mother, an aspiring novelist, had used decades before. Over a period of seventeen days, the typed pages stacked up beside the typewriter, the manual grew, and the system for a solid marriage was created. Make no mistake: It *is* a system—a highly effective, scientifically based system, the merits of which have been proven time and again. Because Orla believes that marriage should not be left up to chance. In the end, the ideas that Orla had during those walks make up the very foundation of The Pact."

"Did Orla and Richard ever get married?" I asked.

"Yes."

Alice leaned forward. "And are they still married?"

Vivian nodded vigorously. "Of course they are. We *all* are. The Pact works. It works for Orla, it works for me, and it will work for you. Simply put, The Pact is two things. It is an agreement you make with your spouse. And it is membership within a group"—she clicked to a new slide and gestured toward the projection of happy people on a green lawn—"a fellowship of like-minded individuals, to support and enforce that agreement. Is that more clear?"

"Not entirely," Alice said, smiling. "But I am intrigued."

Vivian clicked forward a few slides. Most of them featured photos of well-heeled people having a good time together on stately lawns and in well-appointed rooms. She paused on a photo of Orla standing on a balcony, addressing a rapt crowd, with the bright sun and a vast desert at her back.

"Orla was originally drawn to legal work," Vivian said. "She liked that the rules of law were hard and fast and, where they weren't, legal precedence lit the way. It was comforting to know that the answers were all there for her to find. Orla realized that marriage, like society, needed a set of laws.

"She believed that British society had run pretty smoothly for hundreds of years because of these laws. Everyone knew what was expected. While people might have wanted to cheat or steal or even, God forbid, commit murder, the vast majority of citizens did not break the laws, because they knew the consequences. After Orla's first marriage failed, it occurred to her that not only were the expectations for marriage unclear, so were the consequences."

"So," I said. "The Pact is an effort to bring the principles of British law to the institution of marriage?"

"It's more than an effort. It's really happening." Vivian turned off the projector. "I can't overstate the real value: The Pact brings community support, encouragement, and structure to the institution of marriage."

"You mentioned consequences," Alice said. "I'm not sure I understand."

"Look," Vivian said. "I was married once before. I was twenty-two, he was twenty-three. We met in high school and dated for an eternity. At first it was exciting, the two of us, together against the world, but then—I'm not sure when things changed—I started to feel so *alone*. We had problems, and there was no one I could turn to. He was cheating on me. I didn't know why; I worried that it was my fault, but I didn't know how to react. Divorce came so quickly, like it was the only door, and I just needed to get out."

Vivian had a single tear at the corner of her eye. She sat up straighter and flicked the tear away with her fingertip. "When I met Jeremy, I was gun-shy. Just like Orla had been. Jeremy proposed, and I said yes, but I kept putting things off. I was terrified of making the same mistakes. Marriage conjured up such negative thoughts."

"How did you end up in the organization?" Alice asked.

"I finally ran out of excuses. Jeremy was determined to set a date, so I let him, and everything moved forward rapidly. Two weeks before the wedding, I was away on business. I was sitting in the Virgin lounge in Glasgow, drinking Gordon's, maybe one too many. I remember sitting alone, crying. Sobbing, actually. Loud enough that people around me got up and moved. Embarrassing. And then an older gentleman, well dressed, nice looking, came over and sat down next to me. He was on his way to see his son at college in Palo Alto. We talked and talked. I told him all about the wedding, and it felt good to be unloading my fears on this stranger, someone who didn't have a stake in any of it. A volcano had erupted in Iceland, so our two-hour layover became eight hours. But the gentleman was so nice, so interesting, the delay turned out to be a pleasure. A few days later, a wedding present arrived in the mail. And here I am. Happily married for six years."

She reached for the wooden box, turned the gold key in the lock, and opened the lid. Inside was a set of documents typed in dark blue ink on parchment paper. She removed the documents and placed them on the table. Beneath the documents were two identical small books bound in gold leather.

Alice reached out and ran her fingers over the books, intrigued.

Vivian handed one gold book to each of us. I was startled to see they were embossed with our names, the date of our wedding, and, in large block letters, THE PACT.

"This is The Manual," Vivian told us. "You'll need to memorize it."

I opened the book and began flipping through it. The text was tiny.

Vivian's phone began to buzz. She pulled it out and, sliding her finger across the screen, said, "Page forty-three: When your spouse calls, always answer." When I gave her a quizzical look, she pointed at The Manual.

Vivian stepped out onto our front porch, shutting the door behind her. Alice lifted the book, eyes wide, and mouthed the word *sorry.* But she was smiling.

*Don't be,* I mouthed back.

She leaned over and kissed me.

As I've mentioned, I proposed to Alice because I wanted to keep her. Since we had returned from the honeymoon, I worried that she would experience a postwedding letdown. Things so quickly returned to exactly as they had been before the wedding, and I was nervous. Alice requires a certain level of excitement. She gets bored easily.

So far, I decided that marriage, in the physical sense, wasn't any different from living together. In the mental sense, however, marriage was a huge leap. I'm not sure how to explain it, but as soon as the minister spoke the words "I now pronounce you husband and wife," I *felt* married. While I hoped Alice felt the same way, I couldn't be certain. She did seem happier, but happiness sometimes fades.

For all of these reasons, I have to admit I liked this strange thing that Finnegan was dragging us into. Maybe it would bring more excitement to the new state of our relationship. Maybe it would make our bond feel different, stronger.

Vivian returned. "Time flies," she said. "I need to get going. Shall we sign?" She pushed the parchment documents toward us. The print was tiny, and at the bottom of the form were two sets of signature blocks. Vivian signed her name on the left, above the title "Host." Below that, Orla Scott had signed in blue ink. The word beneath her signature was "Founder." On the right side, Finnegan had signed above "Sponsor." My name had been typed in above the word "Husband." Vivian handed us the engraved pens that came with our wooden box.

"May we keep the contracts for a couple of days?" Alice asked.

Vivian frowned. "Of course, if you need to, but I'm going out of town this afternoon and I'd really like to get your paperwork started as soon as possible. I'd hate for you to miss the next party."

"Party?" Alice asked, perking up. Did I mention that Alice loves parties?

"It's going to be spectacular." Vivian gestured nonchalantly at the papers. "But I don't mean to rush you. Take as much time as you want."

"Okay," Alice said, turning to the first page. Perhaps she had become more of an attorney than a musician. I scanned the pages, trying to concentrate, to pierce the impenetrable veil of doublespeak and legalese. I watched Alice's face as she read; a couple of times she smiled, a couple of times she frowned. I couldn't begin to guess what she was thinking. Eventually she turned the final page, picked up her pen, and signed. When she registered the surprise on my face, she hugged me and said, "This will be good for us, Jake. Besides, do you think I'd miss the party?"

By now, Vivian had started packing away the projector. I knew I should probably read the fine print. But Alice wanted to do this. And I wanted to make Alice happy. I felt the weight of the pen in my fingers as I signed my name.

## 10

FOR ALL OF US, OF COURSE, THERE IS A GAP BETWEEN WHO WE ARE and who we think we are. While I like to think the gap for me is small, I'll acknowledge that it does exist. One indication? I think of myself as a fairly popular, likable person with an above-average number of friends. And yet I haven't been invited to many weddings. I'm not sure why. Some people, like Alice, for example, get invited to weddings all the time.

The upside is that I can remember every wedding I've ever been invited to, including the very first one.

I was thirteen, and one of my favorite aunts was getting married in San Francisco. The relationship had developed quickly, and suddenly there was a wedding date. It was a Saturday in July, the reception at the cavernous United Irish Cultural Center. The floor was sticky, the smell of cheap beer from long-forgotten weddings rising from every crevice. A mariachi band was setting up on the stage, and enchiladas and tortillas appeared from the kitchen. A full bar stretched along the entire back wall, Irish bartenders dashing among the bottles. The place was packed. A guy handed me a beer, and no one seemed to mind. In fact, I instinctively knew it would have been considered an insult if I had refused.

My aunt was the head of a labor union, serious stuff. Her husband-to-be was a labor leader of equal stature, though from another region. The place was so crowded, so festive. Even at my age, I sensed something important was going on. People flowed in through the doorways, loud and happy, checking their coats and bags and car keys, clearly planning to stay awhile. To say there was drinking and dancing and speeches and music and more drinking and dancing would sell the event short. It was the wildest, longest party I'd ever attended. I don't remember it ending, and I don't remember going home. To this day, the hazy memory stays with me, like a strange, noisy dream perched on a precipice, somehow, between childhood and adulthood.

I don't recall ever hearing that my aunt's marriage ended. Instead, it just seemed to fade away. One day my uncle was there, and one day he was not. Years passed. They both went on to success and notoriety in their respective careers. And then one morning, reading the *Los Angeles Times,* I saw that my former uncle had died.

Not long ago, I dreamed of the wedding—the music, the food, the drink, the crazy happiness in the packed, smelly room—and I wondered if it had really happened. It was my first real wedding, or at least the first wedding that taught me that marriage was supposed to be about happiness and joy.

# 11

IT'S LATE ON THE NIGHT OF VIVIAN'S VISIT AND WE'RE IN BED WHEN
Alice hands me my copy of The Manual. "Better study up. I don't
want you getting carted off to marriage jail."

"No fair. You went to law school. You have an advantage."

The Manual is divided into five parts: Our Mission, Rules of
Procedure, Laws of The Pact, Consequences, and Arbitration. The
longest part by far is Laws of The Pact. The parts are divided into
sections, the sections into units, the units into paragraphs, the paragraphs into sentences and bullet points, all of it in tiny print. It's a
real doorstopper, and I can tell just from glancing at it that I won't
do more than skim it. Alice, on the other hand, lives for details and
legalese.

"Uh-oh," she says, "I could be in trouble."

"What?"

"Unit 3.6, Jealousy and Suspicion." It's no secret that Alice has an
issue with jealousy. It's a complicated ball of insecurity that I've been
trying to unravel ever since we started dating.

"You could be looking at some hard time," I say.

"Not so fast, mister. What about this: Unit 3.12, Health and Fitness."

I try grabbing The Manual from her hands, but she pulls it back, laughing.

"That's enough reading for one night," I say. She drops The Manual onto the bedside table and presses her body against mine.

# 12

M Y OFFICE IS FILLED WITH BOOKS AND ARTICLES ON MARRIAGE. A Rutgers University study found that when a woman is content in her marriage, her husband is much happier; a man's level of satisfaction within the marriage, however, appears to have no bearing on his wife's happiness.

Short men stay married longer than tall men.

The best predictor of a marriage's success? Credit scores.

Babylonian law required that if a woman cheated on her husband, she should be pitched into a river.

When it comes to academics, a good study with a sound conclusion is usually the product of a large amount of data. The larger the data, the more the outliers fade and the real truth comes into focus. Sometimes, though, I find that too much data provides an overabundance of information, in which case the truth starts to slip out of reach. I can't say how it is with marriage. Certainly there is something to learn from the successes and failures of past marriages. Yet isn't every marriage unique?

Liza and John are my first clients. I study up on everything before they arrive in my office, because that's how I am, that's what I do. It's a rainy day, even more gloomy than usual in the Outer Richmond. He's a contractor, she works in marketing. They wed five years ago in an elaborate ceremony at a golf course in Millbrae.

I immediately like them. She wears a multicolored hat she knitted herself, which seems the opposite of vanity, and he reminds me of a good friend I had in high school, only smarter. Maybe this sort of counseling will be a nice counterbalance to my usual work with kids. I might like being around adults for a change, having adult conversations that don't turn to Nietzsche or Passenger or the scientifically proven benefits of pot. Don't get me wrong, I love kids. But what makes them so vulnerable—their sense of discovery mingled with despair, their naïve belief in the originality of their thoughts—can also make them repetitive. At times I've been tempted to put a sign on my door that says YES, I'VE READ FRANNY AND ZOOEY, AND NO, ANARCHY IS NOT A VIABLE FORM OF GOVERNMENT. So Liza and John are fertile new territory. I like the idea of helping people solve problems closer to my own. I could almost be friends with them, if the circumstances were different.

John works insane hours at his tech startup, developing an app that does something groundbreaking he can't quite explain. Liza is bored with her job advertising the wonders of a hospital that looks to her like a factory system for sick people. "I feel like a fraud," Liza confesses, adjusting her knitted hat. "I miss my friends. I want to move back to D.C.—"

"You miss one friend," John interrupts. "Let's just be clear on that." And then, looking at me, he repeats, "She misses *one* friend."

She ignores him. "I miss the excitement of life in the nation's capital."

"What excitement?" John scoffs. "Nobody in D.C. goes outside, even in the best weather. Nine out of ten restaurants are brewpubs. You can't get a decent salad. Don't tell me you want to go back to a life of onion rings and iceberg." I can see how maybe his negative energy would get on Liza's nerves.

She explains that six months ago she was contacted by a high school boyfriend who found her on Facebook. "He's in politics," she says. "He's *doing* something."

"I don't know what's worse," John says. "That my wife is having an affair, or that she's having an affair with some pompous policy hack."

"Liza," I say. "John believes you are having an affair. Would you describe your relationship with your former boyfriend as an affair?" Sometimes directness is good, but other times you need to come at the subject from the side. I'm not certain which type of situation we're in now.

Liza shoots him a dirty look and continues without answering my question. "We met for coffee while he was out here for work. And the next time, we went out to dinner." She mentions an outrageously expensive restaurant, describing the event with a sense of wonder and surprise at odds with the complete ordinariness of the situation. I want to tell her there is nothing original about leaving one's spouse for an old flame you hooked up with on Facebook. I want to tell her that she and the ex aren't reinventing the wheel, they're just riding a worn path that never leads anywhere good. But I don't. It's not my place. I have a hunch that John would be better off without her. A few months after Liza is gone, he'll find a nice coder girl and bike off into the sunset.

Liza mentions "mental and sexual compatibility," as if she's read some sort of manual. She uses the word *self-actualization*—which, though sound in principle, has become a catchphrase for "doing what's best for me, no matter whom I hurt." She's getting more irritating by the second, and John is getting more despondent. It doesn't take long to realize I'm just a short rest stop on their journey to divorce. Two Thursdays later, when John calls to cancel their appointments, I'm sad for him and disappointed in myself, but not surprised.

# 13

THREE DAYS AFTER VIVIAN'S VISIT, WE'RE INVITED TO THE ANNUAL party for Alice's law firm. Maybe *invited* isn't the right word: Attendance is mandatory for junior associates. It's at the Mark Hopkins Hotel atop Nob Hill. This is the first year that I'm on the guest list. It's a stodgy, conservative, traditional firm. Boyfriends and girlfriends are never welcome; spouses, on the other hand, are compelled to attend.

I break out my best Ted Baker suit, the one I wore to the wedding. I try to go a little holiday with a green plaid shirt and a red tie. Alice takes one look at me and frowns. She places a box from Nordstrom on the bed. "That one. I bought it yesterday." The shirt is blue, well made. "And that," she says. There's a tie box, also from Nordstrom. It's silk, a darker blue than the shirt, with subtle purple stripes. The collar chafes at my neck, and I struggle with the tie. I didn't learn how to properly tie a tie until I was thirty-one years old. I'm not sure if it is a fact that makes me feel proud or embarrassed.

I want Alice to come over and help me tie it, the way TV wives do, but of course, she's not that sort of wife. Not the kind who does the ironing and knows how to tie a man's tie, looking at you seductively in the mirror from behind with her arms wrapped around your neck. She's sexy, but not the domestic kind of sexy, which is okay. More than okay.

Alice is all decked out in a tailored black dress and a pair of black snakeskin pumps. Pearl earrings, a gold bracelet, no necklace or rings. I've seen pictures of her wearing bracelets stacked on bracelets, lots of earrings, necklaces hanging every which way. But these days, her rule of thumb for jewelry is straight-up Jackie O: Two pieces is ideal, three is pushing it, anything more begs to be edited. When did her wardrobe go from nineties rock steampunk to Junior Associate Chic? Still, she looks amazing.

We valet the car in the roundabout at Top of the Mark. We're a few minutes early—Alice hates being early—so we take a brisk walk around the block. She's not big on makeup but swears by a swipe of red lipstick combined with the healthy flush of exercise, and by the time we arrive at the party she's pink-cheeked and lovely. "You ready?" she asks, taking my hand, aware how much I hate this sort of thing.

"Just don't drag me into a conversation on torts."

"No promises. Remember, this is work."

We walk into the party, and a caterer greets us with champagne. "I don't suppose this is a good time to ask for a Bailey's on the rocks," I whisper to Alice.

She squeezes my hand. "There is never a good time for a man your age to ask for a Bailey's on the rocks."

Alice makes introductions, and I smile and nod and shake hands, going with the safe "Good to see you" instead of "Nice to meet you." A few people make the usual therapist jokes: "What would Freud say about this cocktail?" and "Can you just look at me and know my deepest darkest secrets?"

"As a matter of fact, I can," I reply somberly to a guy named Jason, as loud as he is arrogant, who manages to utter the words *Harvard Law School* three times within our first minute of conversation.

After a dozen or so similar encounters, I disengage from Alice—the shuttle separating from the mother ship—and head over to the dessert tables. They are substantial, featuring hundreds of delicate petits fours and miniature parfaits, mounds of truffles. I love dessert, but the real appeal of this corner of the room is the lack of people. I hate chitchat, small talk, getting to know people in that fake way that guarantees you'll know less about them at the end of the conversation than you did at the beginning.

The important clients arrive, and I watch from afar as the attorneys go to work. At this level, parties are less about the party and more about the business. Alice moves among the groups, and I can tell she's good. Clearly, she is well liked by the partners and her co-workers, and she has an appeal to the clients too. It's a formula, for sure; the firm wants to present a seamless team of older, experienced, evenhanded partners combined with energetic, ambitious young associates. Alice plays her role expertly, the clients smiling and happy as she glides through their conversations.

That said, as I watch Alice, the same half glass of champagne in her hand, something feels off. She's "at the top of her game," as her boss likes to say, but something about it makes me—well—sad. Sure, the money is good, and without it we wouldn't have been able to buy the house. Still, I think of Michael Jordan during those midcareer years, when he gave up basketball for a foray into professional baseball. I think of David Bowie and all that time spent acting—good movies, although in time they became nothing more than a hole in his musical back catalog.

A younger guy, Vadim, joins me at the dessert table. He seems less interested in meeting me, more interested in getting away from the game going on across the room. He's wearing a green shirt and red tie, apparently lacking a wife to goad him toward good taste. Nervously, he recites his résumé to me. He is the firm's investigator. When he tells me about his PhD in computer science and four years at Google Ventures, I understand why he was hired; still, I also understand why he will never entirely fit in at a place like this. The forced conversation leads us into some weird areas, including a lengthy account of his fear of spiders and of an ill-advised relationship with a Chinese national who was later indicted for corporate spying.

They say that Vadim is the future of Silicon Valley, that the Vadims of the Valley are procreating with the coder girls, producing a new generation of incredibly smart offspring whose offbeat social skills will not be considered a liability in the future but merely a different branch of evolution, necessary for ensuring the survival of the human race in a brave new world. While I believe the theory, as your basic arts and sciences kind of guy I sometimes find it hard to relate to guys like Vadim.

But then, after the résumé and the spiders and the long, involved story of spying, we finally do relate. Because what Vadim really wants to talk about is Alice. Apparently unaware that I'm her husband (although I'm not sure that would make a difference), he says, "I find Alice very appealing. Both in the physical sense and in the mental sense." Then he goes on to analyze his competition—"the husband, of course, but also Derek Snow." He points to a tall, good-looking man with curly hair and a yellow Lance Armstrong wristband standing a little too close to Alice, touching her on the shoulder. Watching Derek, I know that Vadim is correct: He isn't the only one at the firm who covets my wife. With her former fame and her musical talent, she's an anomaly at a firm filled with the usual crop of Ivy League grads.

"There was a betting pool about whether she would go through with the wedding to the therapist," Vadim says.

"Oh?"

"I did not partake, of course. Gambling on someone else's relationship is irrational. Too many incalculable factors."

"How many people placed bets?"

"Seven. Derek lost a thousand bucks."

I pick up a dessert labeled FLOURLESS ORGANIC FIG NEWTON WITH ORANGE ZEST and eat it in one bite. "In the interest of full disclosure," I confess, "I'm the therapist."

"You have deceived me!" Vadim exclaims. Then, apparently unoffended by my lie of omission, he turns and assesses me frankly. "Yes, you are a close-enough physical match," he decides, "when one considers that women often partner with men who are slightly less attractive, attractiveness being an amalgamation of height, fitness, and symmetry. You're of above-average height, you look like a runner, and your features are well aligned, if not perfect. The dimple on your chin makes up for the forehead."

I touch my forehead. What the fuck is wrong with my forehead?

"Alice doesn't seem to mind my forehead," I say.

"Statistically speaking, a chin dimple on a man atones for a number of minor flaws. True fact: Women with cheek dimples get extra points in the attractiveness department, but a woman gets docked points for a chin dimple, which is associated with masculinity. At any rate, if attractiveness were a tonal scale, the two of you would be close enough to produce harmony."

"Thanks. I guess."

"Of course, I have no way of knowing whether you are appropriately matched intellectually."

"Believe it or not, I'm brilliant. Anyway, thanks for not participating in the betting pool."

"You're welcome."

He asks about the wedding, the honeymoon, the hotel, the flights—always wanting more details. I have the feeling he's collecting data to plug into a program that will predict our chances of marital success, and thereby his chances of usurping me. I'm not sure why, but at some point I make a reference to The Pact. "Alice and I are solid," I say. "After all, we've got The Pact."

"Never heard of it."

"It's a club," I explain. "To help married people stay married."

He's already whipping his phone out and starting to type. "I can find this club online?"

Fortunately, before I share any real details about The Pact, Alice arrives to save me. "Hi, Alice," Vadim says nervously. "You look appealing this evening."

"Thanks, Vadim," she says, smiling sweetly. And then, to me, "I have to stay, but you've done your duty. I already summoned the car." I love her for this, and for the lingering kiss on the lips she gives me in front of Derek Snow and Vadim the Eager and her boss and everyone, the kiss that says without ambiguity, "I am taken."

# 14

THE FOLLOWING MORNING, MY PHONE RINGS WHILE I'M SITTING in the kitchen, eating breakfast. I don't recognize the number.

"Hi, Jake. It's Vivian. How is everything?"

"Good. You?"

"I only have a minute. At the bakery, getting a cake for Jeremy."

"Tell him I said happy birthday."

"It's not his birthday. I'm just getting him a cake because he likes cake."

"That's sweet of you."

"Right. You clearly haven't read The Manual."

"I started, but I didn't get very far. What does cake have to do with The Manual?"

"Read it and you'll see. But that's not why I called. Two quick things: One, you are invited to your first Pact party. Do you have a pen?"

I grab a pen and notepad from the counter. "Yep."

"December fourteenth at seven P.M.," Vivian says.

"I'm free, but Alice's schedule is complicated. I'll have to check and make sure."

"Not the correct answer." Vivian's tone changes without warning. "You are both free. Ready for the address?"

"Go ahead."

"Four Green Hill Court, Hillsborough. Repeat it back."

"Four Green Hill Court, Hillsborough. December fourteenth— seven P.M."

"Good. Two, don't mention The Pact."

"Of course not," I say, instantly replaying in my mind the conversation with Vadim at the party.

"Not to anyone," Vivian stresses. "Not your fault."

Not my fault? How could she know I'd mentioned it?

"Instructions about the secrecy of The Pact are included in The Manual, but perhaps I didn't emphasize enough the importance of reading it. All of it. Commit it to memory, Jake. Orla believes in clarity of communication and clarity of purpose, and I have failed you in terms of communication."

I imagine Vivian standing in the corner for her infraction: Lack of Clarity. It's ridiculous. How could she have known? Alice must have let it slip. "Vivian," I say. "You didn't fail—"

But she cuts me off. "See you on December fourteenth. Send Alice my love and support."

# 15

Alice has grown increasingly obsessed with work. Lately, around five in the morning, I'll reach toward the other side of the bed to find her missing. Minutes later, I'll hear the shower go on, but I usually fall back asleep. By the time I wander down the hallway around seven, she's gone. In the kitchen, I'll find dirty glasses and empty containers strewn about, crumpled yellow legal sheets. It's as if a raccoon with a law degree and a penchant for overpriced Icelandic yogurt breaks into our house each night, only to slip out in the early morning light. On rare occasions, I find other things—like her guitar on the couch, her MacBook opened to Pro Tools, lyrics scribbled on a notepad.

One morning, I find her copy of The Manual on the arm of the blue chair. I've been reading The Manual too—Vivian's orders—although usually during my downtime at work. Okay, maybe I've been skimming it. With each section, the writing becomes more specific and technical, culminating with the final section, in which the laws and regulations are laid out in numbered paragraphs and written with excruciating attention to detail.

My reaction to The Manual is equal parts fascination and repulsion.

In some ways, it reminds me of my undergrad biology classes. Like the sheep heart dissection on the first day of the semester, The Manual has taken something living—marriage, in this case—and torn it apart to the smallest cell, to see how it works.

Being more of a big-picture person, last in my statistics class, I find myself drawn to the more general sections. Part One is the shortest: Our Mission.

To paraphrase, The Pact was created for three reasons: first, to establish a clear set of definitions that can be used to understand and discuss the contract of marriage; second, to establish rules and regulations for the marriage participants to adhere to, designed to strengthen the marriage contract and ensure success (*"knowing the rules and regulations provides a clear, defined map and lights the path to happiness"*); and third, to establish a community of individuals who share a common goal and desire to help each other achieve their individual goal—a successful marriage—which in turn strengthens the group. From those principles, everything else is supposed to flow logically.

According to The Manual, The Pact has no agenda beyond that which is laid out in the mission statement. Nor does it have a political message. It does not discriminate based on ethnicity, national origin, gender, or sexual orientation.

Part One also outlines how new members are located, selected, and approved. New couples are chosen based upon their ability to bring something "unique, individual, and supportive to the community as a whole." Each Pact member with a minimum of five years is allowed to nominate one new couple for the approval process every two years. An Impartial Investigator is then appointed, who provides a thorough packet on the nominees. The Admittance Committee bases its decision to reject or approve the nomination upon the packet. The nominees cannot be informed of their nomination unless and until they are successfully approved for membership. Those couples rejected for entry never know of The Pact or their unsuccessful nomination.

Not surprisingly, from the look of her copy Alice is more drawn to the sections related to rules and regulations. She has left the book open to Rule 3.5, Gifts.

Every member is required to provide one gift to his or her spouse each calendar month. A gift is defined as a special, unexpected item or action that shows care of selection and/or execution. The gift is primarily intended to demonstrate the central, respected, and cherished role that the spouse inhabits in the member's life. The gift should also demonstrate a unique understanding of the spouse, his or her interests, and the current state of the spouse's desires. A gift need not be expensive or rare; its sole requirement is that it be meaningful.

Each regulation is accompanied by a corresponding notation under Penalties. For Gifts, 3.5b, the penalty is as follows:

Failure to provide a gift during a calendar month should be treated as a Class 3 Misdemeanor. Failure to provide gifts in two consecutive months should be treated as a Class 2 Misdemeanor. Failure to provide three or more gifts in a single calendar year should be treated as a Class 5 Felony.

That evening, home from work, Alice kicks off her shoes and stockings and skirt in the usual order, leaving a trail of clothes down the hallway, and changes into sweatpants before grabbing the book and retreating to the bedroom to read. She often reads after she gets home from work. It's her ritual, her downtime. Half an hour later, like clockwork, she comes into the kitchen, ready to cook dinner together. I wait for her to mention her reading material, but she never does. I think we're both hesitant to talk about The Pact, the weird experience with Vivian, the whole thing, simply because we're trying to wrap our minds around it. At first it would have been easy to dismiss the entire thing as strange, to mock it, but I think we've realized that wouldn't be entirely fair. The goal of The Pact—to create a good, strong marriage with the support of other, like-minded individuals—is both admirable and desirable.

The next morning, I wander into the kitchen to find Alice gone and, once again, the chaos of paper, an empty coffee cup, and a half-eaten bowl of Rice Chex, her usual scoop of Ovaltine still floating on top.

In the middle of the table, however, is a small package, gift-wrapped in paper emblazoned with dancing penguins. She has written my name in gold ink on a white card taped to the package. Inside, I find the world's coolest spatula. Orange on top, my favorite color, and yellow on the bottom. The label says MADE IN SUOMI, in English and again in Finnish. Not necessarily expensive, but perfect, and possibly quite difficult to find. I turn over the card. *You make the world's best chocolate chip cookies,* my wife has written. *And I love you.*

After opening the spatula, I immediately take a photo of myself, mostly clothed, holding it up, smiling. I email it to Alice with just three words, *Love you too.* When I make a batch of cookies using the spatula that night, neither of us mentions the connection to The Pact or its regulations.

Even though I'm still not entirely sure what we've gotten ourselves into, I'm happy that Alice is embracing The Pact. I understand that her acceptance of The Pact is proof that she is also embracing our marriage.

In the days that follow, I want to show her that I too am willing to accept The Pact and, more important, am equally committed to making our marriage work. So I dive more deeply into The Manual. Section 3.8 is entitled Travel.

While home is the sanctuary of a good marriage, travel is also essential. Travel allows a relationship the sun and space to grow in a more conducive environment. Travel allows partners to grow together through shared experiences. Travel allows spouses to reveal different sides of themselves outside of the context of everyday life. Travel can be rejuvenating for individuals, and shared travel can be rejuvenating for a marriage.

3.8a: Each member must plan one joint trip each quarter. Trip should be defined as travel away from home for a period of no less than thirty-six hours. Members should not be accompanied by individuals, friends, family, or other associates. While most travel should include only spouses, travel with other members of The Pact is acceptable and even encouraged. Travel need not be expensive, distant, or prolonged.

3.8b(1): Penalty: Failure of a member to plan at least one trip during a nine-month period should be considered a Class 2 Misdemeanor. Failure to plan at least one trip during a twelve-month period should be considered a Class 5 Felony.

I can't help chuckling at the language. A misdemeanor? The Pact seems to make it awfully easy to get in trouble. Nonetheless, I can see how honoring the travel rule would make for more excitement in the marriage, so I set about planning my first trip under the definitions of The Pact.

Four nights after receiving the spatula, while Alice is getting ready for bed, I sneak into the kitchen and place an envelope with her name on the table. The envelope contains the details of the trip I've planned—a weekend at Twain Harte in the Sierra Nevadas. The cabin I've rented doesn't have an address, just a name, the Mountain Ruby. Stapled to the rental agreement is a photo of the view from Mountain Ruby's front window: miles of blue lake stretching toward the snowy mountain peaks.

# 16

ALICE AND I ARE BOTH BUSY WITH WORK AND CHRISTMAS SHOP-
ping. December 14 comes sooner than expected.

Alice has been caught up in another new case; a reclusive writer hired her firm to file suit against a television studio, claiming that the studio stole three of his short stories for their new series. Because the man has a limited budget, Alice was made the lead on the account. She's been putting in a lot of extra hours, working late nights and early mornings; however the case turns out, it will have her name written all over it.

I leave work early and head over to the School of the Arts. A former patient, an eighteen-year-old I treated during his first two years of high school, invited me to a matinee production of *A Christmas Carol* in which my patient plays the lead. He's a sweet kid with some socialization issues. He put a lot of work into the production, and I've been excited to see it.

Alice and I haven't even discussed the Hillsborough party scheduled for tonight. When Vivian called, I immediately put it on our shared iCloud calendar, but then I forgot to follow up. Alice and I used to talk for hours, but since her work has ramped up, our opportunities for conversation have dwindled. My workday doesn't start until nine in the morning, and I have a hard time forcing myself to get up at five to see her off. Most nights, she comes home after eleven, holding takeout from a mediocre Chinese place around the corner. I'm embarrassed to admit we've gotten into the habit of eating our late-night dinner in front of the television.

We've been watching the show that forms the basis of Alice's case with the writer Jiri Kajanë. The stories in contention were part of his collection *Some Pleasant Daydream.* The television show is a series about a couple of male friends, one old, one young, who live in a small town in an un-named country. The show is called *Sloganeering,* which also happens to be the title of one of the stories in her client's book. It's a pay cable sort of thing, too quirky for network television but just weird enough to have amassed a surprisingly large and devoted audience over its five-season run. In the legal discovery process, Alice's firm received DVDs of the entire run of the show, so each night we watch an episode or two.

Maybe it sounds like we're in a rut, but it's not like that at all. We enjoy the show, and it's the perfect way to relax at the end of mentally taxing days. Besides, it feels soothingly domestic. If marriage begins as a wheelbarrow of wet cement, unformed and with endless possibilities for what shape it will eventually take, the nightly routine of takeout and *Sloganeering* is giving our marriage a chance to harden and set.

During the play's intermission, I text Alice to make sure she has seen the Hillsborough party on the calendar.

*Just noticed it,* she texts back. *What the hell?*

*We should go. Could be interesting. Can you make it?*

*Yes, but what does one wear to a cult meeting?*

*Robes?*

*Mine are at the cleaners.*

*Gotta go. Deposition in 5.*

*Let's leave by 6:15.*

*ok. XOXO.*

A journal article I read recently cited research indicating that couples who text each other throughout the day have much more active sex lives and report higher satisfaction with their spouses. I've taken the research to heart, and I never let a day go by without picking up my phone to send my wife a message, however small.

## 17

HILLSBOROUGH WAS FOUNDED IN THE 1890S BY RAILROAD AND banking barons who wanted to escape the riffraff invading San Francisco. The city consists of a maze of narrow, twisty roads, working their way through the canyons like origami. Hillsborough has few sidewalks, no businesses, just large houses set behind ivy-laden walls. If not for the vigilant and neighborly police force, which has a reputation for always being willing to show interlopers the way out of town, one could get lost in its maze for days, eventually running out of gas and being forced to survive on a diet of caviar scraps and organic truffled lamb shanks from the compost bins perched outside the imposing walls.

We get to the freeway exit at seven-fifteen. After arriving home late from work, Alice hastily tried on seven different outfits before we could get out the door. I'm twitchy and anxious as we take the exit, punching the GPS, which says NO SIGNAL AVAILABLE.

"Relax," Alice says. "What kind of party starts exactly on time?"

A 1971 Jaguar XKE flies past. The car is beautiful, British racing green, hardtop, rounded in back. My partner Ian has told me it's his dream car. I drive quickly, hoping to catch up. "Snap a picture for Ian,"

I tell Alice. But before she can find the camera icon on her phone, the Jaguar turns up a long driveway and disappears.

"Four Green Hill Court." Alice points to the mailbox where the Jaguar just turned in.

I slow to a crawl, pausing to look at her. "Are we sure we want to do this?"

The house at 4 Green Hill Court has a name: Villa Carina. The title is engraved on a stone plaque attached to the wrought-iron gate. Originally, Hillsborough consisted of nine estates—complete with guest homes and stables and servants' quarters—set amid hundreds of acres of gardens and trees. From the looks of it, this used to be the main entrance to one of those estates.

The long brick driveway is lined by manicured trees. Eventually, we come upon a broad area paved in stone, where a row of cars is dwarfed by a sprawling, four-story mansion. Alice counts fourteen cars, mostly Teslas. There's also an old Maserati, a restored 2CV, a blue Bentley, an orange Avanti, and the Jaguar.

"Look," Alice says, pointing reassuringly at a black Audi—perhaps Vivian's—and a dark gray Lexus sedan, "cars of the people, almost. And we thought we'd be out of place."

"Maybe we can still back out," I say, not entirely kidding.

"Forget it. This whole place is probably rigged with cameras. I'm sure we're already on video somewhere." I park at the far end, putting my Jeep Cherokee beside a Mini Countryman.

Alice opens the passenger mirror to check her lipstick and dab on some powder, while I check my tie in the rearview.

I step out of the car and go over to Alice's side to open her door. She unfolds herself from the car, stands, and takes my arm. Up ahead, lights shine down from the upper floors. Walking toward the door, past the cars, I catch a glimpse of the two of us reflected in the window of the Jaguar. Me in my Ted Baker suit and new tie, Alice in the deep red dress she purchased for our honeymoon. "Mature Sexy," she calls it. Her hair is pulled back in a serious but nice way.

"When did we grow up?" I whisper.

"We should have taken a picture," she says, "in case it's all downhill from here."

Whenever I feel old—which seems to be happening more and more often these days—Alice tells me to imagine taking a picture of myself, then to imagine myself twenty years in the future looking at that picture, thinking how young I looked, hoping that I had enjoyed or at least recognized my youth. That usually does the trick.

As we approach the house, I hear voices. When we round the hedge, there is Vivian at the bottom of the steps, waiting.

She never told me what to wear or what to bring, and it only occurs to me now that it was probably another test. I'm suddenly glad I went out of my way this afternoon to get a nice bottle of wine for the host. Vivian is wearing another bright dress, this one fuchsia. She has a drink in one hand, something clear on the rocks, and a bouquet of yellow tulips in her other hand.

"Friends," she says, embracing us without spilling a drop. She hands the tulips to Alice and takes a step back to look at her. "The yellow tulips are a tradition, though I can't say I know when or why it started. Come. I can't wait to introduce you both to the group."

As we climb the stone steps, Alice gives me a look as if to say, *Too late to turn back.*

The massive doors give way to a gigantic foyer. It isn't what I expected, though—no marble, no fussy French furniture, no painting of a long-dead railroad baron above a fireplace. Instead, it has natural wood floors, a brushed steel table topped with a concrete bowl of succulents, and lots of open space. Beyond the foyer is a huge room outfitted with floor-to-ceiling windows. The windows frame a group of people out on the patio.

"Everyone is excited to meet you," Vivian says, leading us through the living room. In the mirror above the fireplace, I catch a glimpse of Alice's face. It's difficult to read her expression. I like seeing her holding the yellow tulips, which make her look soft. Since taking the job at the law firm, she has developed sharper edges; the late nights and the intensity of the work have understandably made her a tad impatient.

An attractive woman in her fifties hurries toward a door to our left, carrying an empty tray. She seems frazzled, though underneath the nervous energy she has the bearing of a woman with wealth and influence.

"Ah," Vivian says, "perfect timing. Let me introduce our host, Kate. Kate, this is Alice and Jake."

"Of course it is," Kate says, nudging the door open with her shoulder to reveal an enormous kitchen. She sets the tray on the counter, then turns back to us. I reach out to shake her hand, but she pulls me in for a long hug. "Friend," she says, "welcome." Up close, she has the faint smell of almond paste. I notice a scar on the left side of her chin. Though she's covered it with makeup, you can tell it was a significant cut. I wonder how she got it. "My dear friend," she says, embracing Alice, "you're exactly as Vivian described."

She turns to Vivian. "Why don't you take them outside and introduce them to the group? I've got work to do. It's been a long time since I hosted a party for thirty-six without help."

"The rules require that no one other than members can be present during the quarterly party," Vivian explains as the kitchen door swings shut behind Kate. "No caterers, no servers, no chefs, no cleaners. For security, of course. Pay attention; your turn will come."

Alice raises her eyebrows at me, excited. I can tell she's already planning the party in her mind.

The backyard is massive. A bright blue rectangular pool, a fire pit, a lush lawn bordered by elms—it looks like a photograph for a luxury home-and-garden magazine. Tasteful tiki torches give the area a warm glow, and in the faint light I can see the guests scattered about in clusters.

Vivian hands us two glasses of champagne and leads us to the center of the patio. "Friends!" she calls out, clapping her hands twice. Everyone stops talking and turns to look. Though I'm not exactly shy, I don't enjoy a stage, and I feel my face turning red. "Friends, I am honored to introduce Alice and Jake."

A man in a blue sport coat and dark jeans takes a step forward. Suddenly noticing that most of the men are similarly dressed—more Silicon Valley entrepreneur, less Wall Street financier—I wish I hadn't worn the suit. He raises his glass. "To new friends," he says. "To new friends," the group choruses, and we all drink. After nods and smiles directed at Alice and me, the others return to their conversations and the man walks over to introduce himself.

"Roger," he says. "I'm so pleased to host your introduction at my home."

"Thank you for having us," Alice says.

Vivian takes me by the arm. "Let's leave these two to talk. There are people you need to meet."

It's a better crowd than I expected—relaxed, happy, no obvious arrogance or pretension. Two venture capitalists, a neurologist and her dentist wife, a former professional tennis player, several tech people, a local news anchor, a clothing designer, a couple in advertising, and Vivian's husband, Jeremy, a magazine publisher.

We approach the last group. As Vivian begins making introductions, I realize that one of the women is someone I used to know. JoAnne Webb—now JoAnne Charles, according to Vivian. We went to college together. More than that, we were in the same class, we lived in adjoining dorms our sophomore year, and we were both floor resident advisers. Each Tuesday for the entire year, I saw her at our weekly RA meeting in the Fireside Lounge.

While I haven't seen JoAnne in years, I've actually thought about her many times. It was JoAnne who influenced me to become a therapist. In the middle of our sophomore year, on a warm weeknight, I was eating dinner in the cafeteria when a kid from my floor came running up, looking pale and scared. "There's a jumper on Sproul," he whispered. "They need you." I ran out of the cafeteria, across the street, and up onto the roof of the neighboring dorm. Perched at the edge, I could see a kid I only vaguely recognized. His legs were dangling over the side, seven stories up. JoAnne Webb was the only other person there. I could hear her soft voice, talking slowly as she moved in closer. The kid seemed irritated, ready to jump at any moment. From the phone inside the stairwell, I contacted the campus police.

I stepped closer to where JoAnne had taken a seat next to the kid, her legs also dangling off of the roof. She made a subtle gesture with her hand, asking for time and privacy. As the kid's voice grew more agitated, JoAnne's became softer and quieter. The boy had a long list of things that were bothering him—grades, money, his parents, the usual, although it mainly sounded like a short, failed relationship was what led him to this moment on the edge. Two others had jumped from the very same roof earlier that semester; from the sound of the kid's voice, I sensed he would soon be number three.

For nearly two hours, JoAnne sat there with him as a crowd of students, campus police, and a fire truck gathered down below. Every time someone came onto the roof and approached them, JoAnne would raise her hand as if to say, "Give me time." At one point, she motioned me over. "Jake" she said, "I've got a sore throat, can you grab me a Dr Pepper from the vending machine?" And then she turned to the kid. "John," she said, "a Dr Pepper for you too?"

The kid seemed caught off guard. He paused, stared at her, and finally said, "Yeah, that sounds real good."

I can't explain why, but I instantly knew that in those ten seconds, in that simple offer of a Dr Pepper, JoAnne had somehow talked the boy out of killing himself. I was pretty good at my job, at working with people, but in that moment I realized I was years away from understanding people the way JoAnne understood that kid. A few months later, I switched my major to behavioral psychology. Ever since then, whenever I see a can of Dr Pepper in a vending machine, I always hear JoAnne say, "A Dr Pepper for you too?"

In college, JoAnne was plain, her long hair streaked with shades of gold and brown. Standing across from me now, lit by the torches, she looks different. Every hair on her head seems to be following the strict orders of some stern, dictatorial hairstylist from a fancy salon in Union Square. It isn't that her look is bad. It's just surprising. When did she learn about makeup?

"It's good to see you, Jake," JoAnne says.

"So you two know each other." There's a false cheerfulness in Vivian's voice. "How perfectly random. I'm surprised I wasn't told."

"We worked together in college," JoAnne explains. "A hundred years ago."

"Ah," Vivian says. "Outside the range of our current background policy."

Then JoAnne gives me a long hug, whispering in my ear, "Hello, old friend."

A man walks up—tan, wiry, average height, wearing a very expensive suit. "I'm Neil," he says, gripping my hand too tightly. "JoAnne's husband."

"I hope JoAnne doesn't mind me saying this," I say, "but I watched her save a boy's life one night."

Neil rocks back on his heels. He looks from me to JoAnne. I've seen that look before. He's appraising me, appraising his wife's reaction to me, deciding if I'm a threat. "She's a woman of many talents," he says.

"Oh," JoAnne protests quietly, "it wasn't like that at all."

Before we have time to talk, Vivian pulls me away. "We have more people to meet," she insists, guiding me over to where our host Kate is standing. Next to her, on the lawn, a plastic tarp is nailed down with stakes. Kate is toeing the tarp with her shoe, seemingly troubled by it.

"Do you need help?" I ask.

"No, no," she replies, "stupid mushrooms. Just when I had the yard looking so perfect, they popped up today. It's quite the blemish."

"Nonsense," Vivian says. "Everything looks marvelous."

Kate's still frowning. "I was about to pull them up and toss them into the compost this afternoon when Roger came running out of the house to stop me. Apparently, they're a rare, poisonous type. Could've killed me. Roger would know; he was a botanist before he went into banking. Anyway, we just threw a tarp over it. The guy's coming on Thursday."

"At our farm in Wisconsin when I was a child," Vivian says, "we had a nine-hundred-pound mushroom. It had grown underground to the size of a truck before we even realized it was there."

Vivian doesn't strike me as a farm girl from Wisconsin. That's the thing about Silicon Valley. Give anyone a couple of decades here, and the rough edges and distinguishing characteristics of their native states give way to a telltale Northern California glow. "Healthy with a side of stock options," Alice calls it.

Kate excuses herself to finish preparing the food, and Vivian ushers me into another group. Roger walks up with a bottle of wine and a fresh glass. "Thirsty?"

"Yes, please." I nod. He fills my glass halfway before the bottle runs out. "Hold on," he says, grabbing an identical bottle from the makeshift bar on the patio table. From his back pocket he pulls out an oval-shaped stainless-steel object, and with a flick of his wrist it is transformed from a strange piece of modern art into a plain corkscrew. "I've had this for nearly twenty years," he says. "Kate and I brought it home from our honeymoon in Hungary."

"Adventurous," Vivian remarks. "Jeremy and I just went to Hawaii."

"We were the only tourists around for miles," Roger says. "I'd taken a month off work, and we rented a car to drive around the country. We were living in New York City then, and Hungary was the least New York thing we could think of. Anyway, we were driving our Lancia outside the town of Eger when we threw a piston and the whole thing froze up. We pushed the car to the side of the road and started to walk. There was a light on in a small house. We knocked on the door. The owner invited us in. Long story short, we spent the next few days in his guesthouse. He had a side business making corkscrews, and he gave us this one as a parting gift.

"It's just a simple object," Roger says, "but I love it. It reminds me of the best time of my life." I've never heard a man talking so wistfully about his honeymoon. It makes me think that maybe this Pact thing is something special.

The night is a blur. The food is terrific, especially dessert, an impressively large stack of profiteroles; I'm not sure how Kate managed it all on her own. Unfortunately, I'm too nervous to really enjoy it. All night, I keep feeling as though I'm in the midst of one of those unorthodox Silicon Valley job interviews—endless odd questions disguised as small talk, though you know it's really a well-crafted conversation designed to elicit your very soul.

On the way home, Alice and I compare notes. I worry that I talked too little and probably bored everyone. Alice worries that she talked too much. She does that when she's nervous. It's a dangerous habit that has gotten her into trouble at social events. Winding down the driveway, along the circuitous roads and back onto the freeway, we're both buzzing with nervous energy. Alice is optimistic, even giddy.

"I'm looking forward to the next one," she says.

And at that moment, I decide not to tell her about my second encounter with JoAnne. It was later in the evening, when everyone had gathered by the fire pit. It seemed to be an organized sharing time, where couples related what gifts they'd given each other and what travel they'd done since the last quarterly party. Uncomfortable and a little bored, I slipped off to the bathroom. After washing my hands and taking a few minutes to gather my wits about me, enjoying the silence after a night of small talk, I opened the door to find JoAnne standing there. At first, I thought that she too had just come upstairs to use the restroom, but then I realized she had followed me.

"Hi," I said.

She glanced nervously down the hallway in both directions before whispering, "I'm sorry."

"For what?" I asked, surprised.

"You shouldn't be here. I didn't see your name on the list. The email must have gone out when we were on vacation. I would've stopped it, Jake. I could've saved you. Now it's too late. I'm sorry." She looked up at me with those earthy brown eyes I remembered so well. "Really, I'm so sorry."

"It's a nice group," I said, confused. "Certainly nothing to apologize for."

She put her hand on my shoulder and seemed about to say something, but then she just sighed. "You better get back to the others."

The day after the party, I arrive home from work to find a heavy box on our front porch. Inside, there's a case of Hungarian wine and a white card. *Welcome, Friends,* it reads in gold cursive letters. *Looking forward to seeing you again.*

## 18

ALTHOUGH WE WERE DEEP INTO THE CHRISTMAS SEASON, ALICE was still seriously busy at work. Impressed with the way she attacked the new intellectual property case, the partners had given her additional responsibilities.

I dove headlong into my own work. Through a contact at his church, Ian had started funneling more marriage counseling clients my way. Most were struggling with the usual things—the arrival of children, an affair, a downturn in financial fortunes.

It ran about seventy-thirty in terms of those who were headed for divorce, but I was determined to flip the ratio. It had gotten to the point where I could predict the couple's prospects of marital survival within the first ten minutes. Not to boast, but I'm good at reading people. It's a gift I have—a natural talent honed by years of practice. Sometimes, I could tell before we even got ourselves situated in my office. The couples who sat on the couch together were still trying to make it work, while those who went for the chairs had already—at least subconsciously—accepted an eventual divorce or separation. Of course, there were other telltale signs: the way they sat, feet turned toward or away from each other, arms open or folded, coats on or off. Each couple sent a hundred little signals about the direction their marriage was headed.

Winston and Bella—both Asian and in their thirties—were my favorite couple. He was in biopharmaceuticals, and she was an IT professional. They had a good sense of humor about their issues, and for the most part they were mature enough to rise above the petty back-and-forth that had begun to bother me with some of the others. That said, Bella's breakup with her previous boyfriend, Anders, had bled a little too far into the beginning of her relationship with Winston. This had all happened nearly ten years earlier, but it remained a regular obstacle to their progress. If it weren't for Winston's jealousy and insecurities, Bella insisted, she wouldn't have even thought of Anders at all during the intervening years. Unfortunately, Winston seemed unable to get over the details of their messy start.

That Thursday, while Bella was in the restroom, Winston asked me if I thought a relationship could overcome a rocky beginning. "Of course," I said.

But then Winston asked me, "Didn't you tell us during our first meeting that the seed of a relationship's end can always be found in its beginning?"

"True."

"My fear is that the seed was planted during our first month together, when she was still secretly seeing Anders, and now the tree has grown too large to eradicate."

"The fact that you're here means there's a strong chance of a positive outcome." I wanted it to be true, but I also knew that Winston, whether he realized it or not, was still nurturing that seed, watering it, allowing the tree to thrive despite his best intentions. I told him as much.

"But how do I get past it?" he pleaded. I could tell his heart was breaking. "She still sees Anders for lunch, you know. And she never tells me. I always find out secondhand, from some friend of a friend, and when I ask her about it she gets so defensive. How can I ever trust her, when she proves, every time she meets him in secret, that her past with him is so important it's worth risking our future?"

When Bella came back into the room, I decided to confront head-on the seed that had grown into a tree. "Bella," I said, "why do you think you still maintain a friendship with Anders?"

"Because I shouldn't have to give up my friends."

"Okay, I see where you're coming from. But knowing that this continued relationship is having a negative effect on your marriage, would you consider being more open with Winston about it? For example, could you tell Winston when you're going to have lunch with Anders? Maybe you could even invite him along."

"It's not that simple. If I told him, it would turn into a fight."

"When you keep it a secret, that too turns into a fight, doesn't it?"

"I guess."

"Often, if one spouse feels compelled to keep something from the other spouse, there is an underlying reason that goes beyond the deceived spouse's likely reaction. Can you think of an underlying reason?"

"There's just a lot of history," she conceded. "A lot of baggage. That's why I don't tell Winston."

I saw Winston's shoulders drop, I saw Bella's feet turn away from him, toward the wall, saw her arms cross over her chest—and I realized this was going to be more difficult than I had imagined.

19

"**D**ID VIVIAN CALL YOU?" ALICE ASKED OVER THE PHONE. IT WAS morning, the day before Christmas.

"No," I said, distracted. I was at work, going over a patient's folder, preparing for what promised to be a difficult session. The patient, Dylan, was a bright, often funny fourteen-year-old who'd been struggling with depression. His sadness, and my inability to cure it, weighed heavily on me.

"She wants to see me for lunch." Alice sounded agitated. "I told her I'm swamped, but she said it was important, and I didn't know how to say no, after she was so nice to us at the party and I never sent her a proper thank-you note."

I closed the folder, using my index finger to mark the page. "What do you think she wants?"

"I don't know. We have reservations for noon at Fog City."

"I was hoping you'd be home early."

"Doubtful. But I'll try."

When I got home at two, the house was cold, so I made a fire and started wrapping Alice's Christmas gifts. It was mostly books and albums she'd mentioned over the past few months, and a couple of shirts from her favorite store. Still, I wanted to make them look good. The main item was a silver necklace with a pendant crafted of a single, beautiful black pearl.

For Alice and me, as for many couples, Christmas plans are tricky. When I was growing up, my family always celebrated in a strange way. When my father came home from work on Christmas Eve, my parents would load us kids into the car, then my dad would disappear inside for a few minutes, claiming to have forgotten his wallet. By the time he came back, my mom would have the radio tuned to Christmas carols, and we'd all be singing along. Then my dad would climb behind the wheel and the search for pizza would begin, on a night when most of the pizza joints were closed. When we got back to our house, Santa would have come. The presents, never wrapped, would be scattered under the tree, and pandemonium would ensue.

Alice's childhood Christmases were more traditional. Early to bed on Christmas Eve, cookies left out for Santa, wrapped presents discovered under the tree on Christmas morning, followed by a long service at a Baptist church.

Our first Christmas together, we decided that it was only fair to split the holiday calendar. On odd years, we would celebrate my way, and on the even years we'd honor Alice's family traditions. But the nice thing about Alice was that she always conceded to me on the matter of Christmas Eve dinner; she loves pizza just as much as I do. This happened to be an even year, which was why I was wrapping everything.

I wandered around the house all afternoon, waiting for Alice. I cleaned and watched *A Christmas Story*. By seven o'clock, Alice still wasn't home.

Just as I was becoming a little annoyed that we'd probably missed our chance to get pizza, I heard the garage door open and her car pull in. I heard her shoes on the back stairs and, before I even saw her, I smelled pizza. She was holding a large pepperoni. She even had a few wrapped presents stacked on top of the pizza for me.

"Those look nice," I said, noticing the shiny plaid wrapping paper, the intricate green bows, the telltale gold SFMOMA sticker. I imagined that Alice had totally forgotten until this morning that it was Christmas Eve and probably stopped by the museum store on her way to lunch.

As Alice opened the pizza box and slid a slice onto my plate, I noticed that she was wearing a cuff bracelet that I hadn't seen before. It was modern, silver, some sort of hard molded plastic or maybe aluminum or fiberglass. It was two inches wide and very snug. I didn't see a clasp, or even how it was attached, or more important, how it might be detached. It was a cool piece of jewelry, but I was surprised that she would have bothered to shop for herself with everything she had going on.

"Nice bracelet," I said. "MOMA?"

"Nope," she said, folding her pizza in half lengthwise. "Gift."

"From whom?" My first thought was that guy at her firm's party, Derek Snow, the one with the curly hair.

"From our friend Vivian."

"Oh," I said, relieved, "that was nice of her."

"No, not really."

"What?"

She took a moment to eat her pizza. "Lunch was weird. Beyond weird. I'm not even supposed to talk about it—I don't want to get you into trouble."

That made me laugh. "Vivian is hardly the Gestapo. I'm sure I'll be fine. What did she say?"

Alice frowned, fidgeting with her new bracelet. "Apparently, at the party, I really did talk too much."

"What do you mean?"

"Vivian said that someone at the party had concerns about me. They were worried that I am not as focused on our marriage as I should be. They filed something with The Pact."

I stopped midchew. "Filed something? What does that mean?"

"A friend-of-the-court brief." Alice was twisting the bracelet. "Basically, somebody ratted me out—wrote some complaint and sent it in."

"In where?" I asked, incredulous.

"To 'headquarters,' whatever that means."

"What? Surely it's a joke."

Alice shook her head. "That's what I thought at first, that Vivian was just having a laugh at my expense. But it wasn't a joke. The Pact has a court that decides matters among members, even meting out fines and punishments."

"Punishments? For real? I assumed that part of The Manual was just symbolic."

"Apparently not. They use all of the jargon and methods of the regular court."

"But who would tattle on you?"

"I don't know. It's anonymous. Vivian pointed out that if I'd read the entire manual, I would understand. Everyone in the group is responsible to report anything of concern that might reflect negatively on another member and their marriage. She kept saying that the person filed it 'because they are our friends.' "

"But who do you think it was?"

"I don't know," she repeated. "I keep thinking of this one conversation I had. The guy with the French accent."

"Guy?"

"Yes, I can't recall his name."

"No, that *is* his name," I clarified. "Guy. His wife was Elodie. He's an attorney. International law. Elodie is a vice something at the French consulate."

"Exactly. He kept asking questions about my firm, my cases, the workload. I remember going on and on about all the hours I'd been working, and how I hadn't been sleeping. He gave me a disapproving look when I mentioned that we often don't sit down to eat dinner until super-late. It caught me off guard. He's a lawyer—how could he not work those hours sometimes?"

Alice was pale. I could tell she was exhausted from too little sleep and too much work. I put another slice of pizza on her plate and nudged it toward her. "This is weird, right?"

"The friend-of-the-court brief said that they liked both of us, that we both seemed committed to our marriage, but they were concerned that I spend too much of my energy and time on my work. According to Vivian, it's a common issue."

"I hope you told her it's nobody's business how much you work."

But from the look on Alice's face, I could tell she didn't say any such thing. "Vivian brought her copy of The Manual, and she'd bookmarked the page. Apparently, I might be headed toward a violation of Section 3.7.65, Primacy of Focus. The complaint wasn't that I had violated any of the rules, but the informant was concerned that if there was no intervention, I'd be likely to commit such a violation in the future."

"Informant? Jesus! I take back what I said about the Gestapo."

But then I realized that something else was bothering me—the calmness in Alice's expression, the resigned and nonchalant way she relayed all of this to me. "You don't seem angry," I said. "How can you not be angry?"

Alice touched the bracelet again. "To be honest, I guess I'm intrigued. All that stuff about The Manual, Jake, they take it *very* seriously. I need to reread it."

"So what's the penalty, then? A nice lunch with Vivian? I guess it could be worse."

Alice held up her arm, drawing my attention to the bracelet. "*This* is the penalty."

"I don't get it," I insisted.

"Vivian said that headquarters had decided I was a candidate for further observation."

Finally, it dawned on me what she was saying. I reached for Alice's hand, taking a closer look at the bracelet. It was warm and smooth to the touch. When I looked closely, I saw that the underside had a ring of tiny green lights embedded in the plastic, tracing a circle around Alice's wrist. On the front, where the face of a watch would be, was an arrangement of tiny holes in the shape of the letter *P*. "Does it hurt?" I asked.

"No." She seemed so calm, almost content. I realized that she hadn't mentioned work even once since she got home, except in the context of The Pact's concern that she was devoting too much time to it.

"How do you take it off?"

"I don't. Vivian said we would meet again in two weeks. Most likely it can come off then."

"What does it *do,* Alice?"

"Don't know. It *monitors* me somehow. Vivian said it's an opportunity for me to prove how focused I am on our marriage."

"GPS? Audio monitoring? Video? Christ! What do they mean, exactly, by monitoring?"

"Not video," Alice said. "She was clear about that. But GPS, yes, and maybe audio too. Vivian said she'd never worn one and that she wasn't certain what happens to it once it's removed. The instructions she received were simply to put the bracelet on me, explain why I was wearing it, and then remove and return it to headquarters after fourteen days."

I fiddled with the bracelet but couldn't figure out a way to get it off. "Don't bother," Alice said. "There's a key. Vivian has it."

"Call her," I said angrily. "Tonight. I don't care if it's Christmas Eve. Tell her it has to come off. This is absurd."

But then Alice surprised me. She rubbed her fingers lightly across the bracelet. "Do you think I'm too focused on work?"

"Everyone's focused on work. You wouldn't be a good lawyer if you weren't. Just like I wouldn't be a good therapist if I didn't focus on work." But even as I said it, I did a quick calculation in my mind of the hours I'd worked that week versus the hours Alice had worked. I thought about how many times I hadn't made it home for dinner since we'd been married—exactly zero times—and how many times Alice hadn't made it home for dinner: I'd lost count. I thought about her early mornings in the kitchen, going over cases and making calls to the East Coast while I was still in bed. I thought about how, during those increasingly rare moments when we were alone together, she was always glancing at her phone, always somewhere else. Whatever observations were made by the informant at the party, they weren't entirely wrong.

"I guess what I'm saying is, I want to try this," Alice said. "I want our marriage to work, and I want to try out The Pact, and if this is part of it I'm willing to go there." She gripped my hand tightly. "Are you?"

I looked into her eyes, searching for some sign that she was just performing for the bracelet. But there was no such indication. If there's one thing I know about my wife, it's that she's always up for something new, always keen for the next great experiment in health or science or social engineering. Having survived her dysfunctional family, she believes she can survive just about anything. She even applied to go to Mars, back when Elon Musk put out the call for layperson explorers to take the first manned spaceship. Thank God they didn't pick her, but the point is, she made her audition video, filled out the paperwork, and actually *applied to get her ass off Earth* and into space and quite possibly die in the process. That's just how she is. One thing I love about Alice is that she's so insanely open to new experiences. Risk doesn't scare her; it excites her. The Pact is weird, sure, but compared to a one-way ticket to Mars, how scary could it be?

That night, in the bedroom, on our large, high bed with its small but beautiful view of the Pacific Ocean, Alice and I made love. She moved with an intensity of passion and desire that, to be honest, I hadn't seen in a while, though neither of us said a word before or after. It was really amazing.

Later, after she'd fallen asleep, I lay awake, unable to shut off my brain. Was the performance for the bracelet or for me? Nonetheless, I felt grateful—for our marriage, for Alice, and even for this strange new thing we'd gotten ourselves involved in. This Pact seemed to be doing exactly what it was designed to do: bring us closer.

## 20

C HRISTMAS AND THE DAYS THAT FOLLOWED WERE ODDLY BLISSFUL. My partners and I had shut down the office for the week. It was something of an acknowledgment of the difficult but very successful year we had enjoyed.

We had expanded our visibility and improved our bottom line. In August, we completed the purchase of our building, a charming two-bedroom Victorian that had been turned into commercial space. Our practice had somehow managed to get over the hump and now seemed to be here to stay.

Five days after Christmas, however, my good luck streak came to an end. At five-thirty in the morning, I woke to find Alice standing beside the bed, holding my phone. She wore a towel knotted at her chest, a smaller towel wrapped turban-style around her head. She smelled like lemons and vanilla, this lotion she wore that she knew drove me crazy. I desperately wanted to pull her into bed with me, but the alarmed look on her face told me that wasn't going to happen. "It rang four times, so I answered," she said. "There's a problem."

As I reached for the phone, I ran through my client list in my mind, bracing for news.

"Jake?"

It was the mother of a girl from my Tuesday group—teenagers whose parents had recently divorced or were in the process of doing so. The woman was talking so fast that I didn't get her name or her kid's name. Her daughter had run away, she said. Without asking her name again, I quickly tried to figure out who it was. The previous week I had six teenagers in the group. Three girls, three boys. I immediately eliminated Emily, a sixteen-year-old who'd been coming to the meetings for a year and was about to quit, feeling that she'd finally come to terms with her parents' divorce. Mandy seemed unlikely too—she was looking forward to a ski week trip to Park City to help her father with his charity. That left Isobel, who was really shaken up about her parents' recent divorce. I worried that our week off for Christmas would affect her the most, after Dylan.

"Have you spoken with your husband?" I asked.

"Yes. She was supposed to take the Muni train to his place yesterday, but she never arrived," the woman said frantically. "We didn't realize it until this morning—my husband thought Isobel was with me. Have you heard from her?" Her voice was shaky with hope.

"I'm sorry, I haven't."

"We've left a hundred messages and texts."

"Would you mind if I call her?" I asked.

"Please do."

The mother gave me Isobel's cell number, as well as her email address, Twitter handle, and Snapchat name. I was impressed that she knew so much about her daughter's social media presence; most parents don't, even though social media is where a lot of kids face the most trouble. Isobel's mother told me they had already called the police but were informed that, at Isobel's age, she needed to be gone for twenty-four hours before they could open an investigation. Alice stood by the bed the whole time, in her flimsy towel and her turbaned head. When I hung up, she wanted to hear the story.

"Do you think she's in trouble?" Alice asked, pulling her serious blue suit out of the closet.

"Isobel has a head on her shoulders," I said. "She probably just spent the night with a friend. She's angry with her parents right now. She told me that she needed time away from their immature behavior."

Alice stepped into her skirt. "She said that?"

I nodded.

"Yikes. Did you tell the parents?"

"No. Patient-client confidentiality. But I told her not to do anything stupid. I said even if her parents have been acting like kids, they love her and have been pretty good parents, and they deserve to always know where she is."

Alice slipped a camisole over her head. "Doesn't really sound like you got through to her."

"Thanks."

"No offense," Alice said, pulling on her navy blue tights, shimmying them up under her skirt. "You should text instead of call."

I pulled up Isobel's number and texted, *Isobel, it's Jake Cassidy. There's a coffee shop just down from my office, at 38th and Balboa. Z Café. Can we meet today at noon? I'll buy you a hot chocolate. It will only be me, I promise. People are worried about you.*

I intentionally didn't use the word *parents*. Kids whose parents are going through a divorce feel all sorts of anger and guilt and love and pity toward their parents, tangled emotions that are difficult to unravel.

No response.

## 21

BEFORE NOON, I WALKED OVER TO Z CAFÉ. I GOT A TABLE IN THE corner. Because of the mediocre coffee and overpriced pastries, the place was always empty. I set up my laptop on the table, a newspaper laid out beside it. If Isobel did show up, I wanted to look relaxed, not threatening.

In my job, with adult clients, it's sometimes best to hit a problem directly and with force. But with kids, it's best to approach things from the side. Teenagers brace themselves for confrontation, always. Most of the kids I see have learned how to build quick and impenetrable walls.

At noon, I heard the door swing open. I looked up, hoping to see Isobel, but instead it was a hipster couple, decked out head to toe in expensive clothes made to look cheap, artfully torn to show their tattoos, both carrying the latest MacBook Air.

By twelve-thirty, I was beginning to worry. What if something had really happened to Isobel? What if she wasn't just taking some time off from her terribly immature, self-centered parents? I was about to give up, go to the office, and call her mother, when she slid into the seat across from me. Her brown hair was a tangled mess, her jeans were dirty, and she had dark circles under her eyes. "You didn't think I'd show up, did you?"

I'd already rehearsed my greeting, or part of it. "I actually kind of did. You strike me as someone who doesn't leave a friend hanging."

"True dat," Isobel agreed. Then, when I stood up, "Hey, where are you going?"

"I owe you a big hot chocolate. Whipped cream?"

"I think I need coffee."

While I was at the counter, I texted her mom. *Isobel's OK. I'm with her right now.*

*Thank God,* her mother texted back. *Where are you?*

*Near my office. Give us a few minutes. I don't want to scare her off.*

I waited for the frantic email demanding to know more, but to Isobel's mother's credit, she seemed to understand that, for the moment, delicacy was called for. *Thank you so much. I'll wait to hear from you.*

I went back to the table with the coffee.

"Thank you," Isobel said, dumping a sugar packet into her coffee. She looked like she hadn't slept.

"So," I said, folding the paper in front of us. "Some serious drama at home?"

"Yep."

"I told your mother that you're okay, and that you're with me."

Isobel blushed and refused to meet my eyes. I could tell she was wavering between anger and relief. "Okay. That's good, I guess."

"You want some food, a burrito, maybe? You know Chino's up the block? My treat."

"No, thanks. I'm good."

"Seriously." I shut my laptop and slid it into my messenger bag. "I feel bad for not feeding you. You're obviously starving." I stood and started walking to the door. Isobel followed.

I gave myself a silent high five for getting her out of the café, moving. Talking while walking is always more effective than the artificial constraints of sitting in a room, in a circle with a peer group. As we walked, Isobel seemed to loosen up. She's sixteen, but in some ways she seems younger. Unlike the other kids in the group, her parents' divorce surprised her. Usually, the kids see it coming for months. Many are actually kind of relieved when the parents finally break the news. Not Isobel. According to her, things were really great, their family was happy. She thought her parents had a good marriage, until the day her mother told her that she was moving out in order to be "true to herself."

"I know I'm not supposed to care that she moved out to be with a woman"—Isobel tossed her cup into a trash can—"but it really pisses me off. It's so unfair to my dad. And at least if she'd been with another man, there'd be, I don't know, maybe this slim possibility of them getting back together."

"If she'd moved out to be with another man," I asked gently, "would that be equally unfair?"

"I don't know," Isobel said, growing angry—not at me, I sensed, but at the world. At this wrench her mother had thrown into their previously happy life. "I mean, how could she not *know*? Why did she marry my dad in the first place? I have gay friends, and they're only in high school, but they already *know*. I don't understand how a person wakes up one day, forty-three years into her totally hetero life, and changes her mind."

"It was different for your mom's generation."

We walked a block in silence. Something was weighing on her, and finally she said it. "I can see how, for my dad, it really would have been better if she *had* known. I keep imagining this alternate life for him, where he gets to fulfill his dream of growing old with the same person. Can you believe he's been putting away a little money every single week since the day they were married for the beach house he planned to buy after they retired? My mom loves the beach, and the house was going to be his big gift to her, his grand gesture. For twenty years, he's nursed this stupid dream of surprising her with a beach house. But all along that dream has been false, and he never knew."

"Sad," I said.

Isobel glanced at me. "What I'm saying is this: My very existence is predicated on my father's eventual unhappiness. But I'd still choose my existence over his happiness. Does that make me a bad person?"

"It's a false choice. You're here because your parents got married and had you. Nothing you think or feel could change that. One thing I know for certain is that your parents love you very much. Neither of them, I guarantee it, would trade you in for a different life."

We passed by the Balboa Theatre, which was having a special showing of *The Matrix* trilogy, so we talked about that for a few minutes. As a project for her textiles class, Isobel said, she once designed a long black coat based on the one Neo wears. I was struck by the incongruity of Isobel; she seemed to have the knowledge and vocabulary and abilities of a person twice her age, but her understanding of human behavior, the real world, basic interactions, seemed to be somewhere slightly below her age range. I've seen this a lot lately. Kids are learning faster and faster about more and more, but their understanding of themselves and those around them seems to be developing even slower than when I was a kid. My colleagues often blame this on smartphones and videogames, but I'm not sure that's it.

"Here we are," I announced. "Chino's. Best burritos in the Richmond. What'll you have?"

"I'll order," she decided, and she stepped up to the counter and confidently ordered a burrito with carne asada, rice, no beans, and salsa verde—all in Spanish, like a true San Francisco kid. I ordered the same, plus chips and guacamole, and grabbed a couple of Fantas from the fridge.

"I looked up your wife on YouTube," Isobel said, twisting the top off her Fanta. "I watched like four entire concerts from ten years ago. She is so freaking *cool*."

"Yes," I said, "she is." I like to be reminded of this. I didn't know Alice ten years ago, when she was making her way up in the music world, playing shows most nights of the week, touring all over the West Coast. She wasn't huge, she wasn't famous in the traditional sense, but she did have a following, people who couldn't wait for her next album, who'd drop whatever was on their schedule to go see her band play at Bottom of the Hill or open up for someone bigger at the Fillmore. She even had groupies—guys, mostly—who'd follow her from show to show and make a point of talking to her afterward, so nervous in her presence that they'd start to sweat and stutter. She's told me she doesn't miss the groupies, who always scared her a little, but she misses some of the other stuff.

Mostly the music itself. These days, I worry that part of her is slowly getting buried under endless days and nights of legal work and corporate conversations.

"Her lyrics are brilliant," Isobel said. "Everything about her is brilliant. I was looking at her makeup, and all I was thinking was, why am I such a loser? Why can't I do my makeup like that?"

"A: You most definitely are not a loser. B: I'm sure you could if you wanted to."

Isobel was staring at me. "If I come over this weekend and make breakfast for you and your wife, do you think she'd teach me some of her makeup tricks?"

"Sure," I said, surprised.

The guy called our number and I grabbed our burritos. We took a seat by the window.

"I'm a really good cook," Isobel said, folding back the foil on her burrito. "I make some seriously great French toast."

I scooped up some guacamole with a chip. "Alice does love French toast."

Between bites of her burrito, she told me she'd spent the previous night on Ocean Beach with a surfer named Goofy and a bunch of people from Bakersfield. "It was freezing. I curled up with some smelly guy named DK. He was wearing stupid puka shells, but I was just so freaking cold."

"That doesn't sound like fun to me," I said. "And it doesn't sound particularly safe."

"It was fun at first, and then it wasn't. Everybody was stoned except me. But my phone was dead. My mom recently switched us to a new cell plan, we got new numbers. I haven't memorized them yet, so I couldn't even borrow someone's phone and call my parents. I even thought about walking to the Safeway, but that seemed really dangerous. A lot of creeps hang out around Ocean Beach at night. When I found a coffee shop this morning to plug in my phone, there were a bunch of messages, and I didn't know what to do."

I thought of Isobel huddled on the beach, unable to call anyone to pick her up, and my heart ached for her. I guess that's what I mean when I say kids seem a little younger these days. Back in my day, you memorized your phone number and your address before your first day of kindergarten.

"You know, you really need to go home," I said. "If not for you, then for your parents. Maybe they don't communicate as well as they should, but you know they love you. Maybe you don't want to hear this, but they're going through a tough time now too. You're certainly old enough to understand that parents are just regular adults, with regular adult problems that don't always revolve around their kids."

Isobel went to work on the tinfoil, meticulously folding it into smaller and smaller squares.

"I remember the first life lesson I learned," I ventured. For all their eye rolling and disdain, teenagers actually *depend* on adults having more life experience than they do, more wisdom. That's why it shatters their world when adults don't behave well, when they let their flaws and mistakes hang out like dirty laundry.

"Life lesson?"

"You know, something real, something that strikes a chord and sticks with you."

"Okay," she said, sounding interested.

"I won't waste your time with the specifics, but let's just say I was fifteen, things were bad for a few different reasons. I'd messed things up, and I just wanted to disappear. I was wandering around town, trying to figure out what to do, and I ran into my English teacher out at the Camera Obscura. It was so weird seeing him out of context. He was alone. He was in jeans and a T-shirt, not his usual coat-and-tie thing. He was clearly in a funk, nothing like the even, consistent teacher I'd come to know, or at least thought I knew.

"Anyway, when I texted you this morning, I was thinking of him. The day I ran into him, he must've been able to tell right off that I was in a bad way too. He asked if he could buy me a cup of hot chocolate."

"Sounds familiar," Isobel said, smiling.

"Long story short, I told him my troubles, and he didn't give me a lecture or anything. He didn't make me feel bad about the mistakes I'd made. He just looked at me and said, 'You know, sometimes you just have to walk back across that burning bridge.' That was it. When I saw him the following Monday, he didn't say anything about our conversation. He just asked, 'Did you make it across that burning bridge?' And when I said yes, he just gave me a nod and said, 'Me too.' That was it, but I remember it more than anything else I learned in high school."

As we walked back in the direction of my office, my cell rang. "That's my mother, isn't it?"

I nodded.

"Okay," she said, "make you a deal. If your wife promises to teach me makeup tricks this weekend, I'll go home."

"Deal," I agreed, "but you really have to give your parents a chance."

"I'll try."

I answered the phone. "Everything is good," I said. "We'll meet you outside my office."

As we stood waiting for Isobel's mom to drive up, I texted Alice. *Do you have a second?*

*Type fast.*

*Can you teach Isobel some of your secret makeup tricks from the old days?*

*Hells yeah.*

The blue Saab station wagon pulled up, and I opened the door for Isobel. "Saturday morning at nine," I said. I gave her the address and leaned into the open window to confirm with her mom, who grabbed Isobel in a long, tight hug. I was happy to see that Isobel hugged her back.

## 22

ALICE HADN'T MENTIONED THE BRACELET AT ALL THAT WEEK. Occasionally, though, I would notice her running her fingers over its smooth surface. Workdays, she always wore long sleeves, though that may have had more to do with the winter weather. When she got home—she'd started coming home much earlier than usual—she would quickly slip out of the long-sleeve blouse and into a T-shirt, or sometimes change right away into some sort of lacy nightgown, or a camisole with flimsy pajama bottoms.

I hate to say it, but she was far more attentive to me after her lunch with Vivian. If the purpose of the bracelet was to remind her to pay more attention to her marriage, then it was working. Of course, it was possible that its purpose was more nefarious. So I tried to watch what I said, to muffle my sounds when we were in bed together, to put the thought of surveillance out of my mind. Still, I made the most of our time together. I enjoyed cooking and eating together, I enjoyed all of our great sex, I enjoyed watching *Sloganeering* on the couch with our ice cream.

When Isobel got to our house on Saturday morning, the first thing she said to Alice was "I love love love your bracelet. Where did you get it?"

Alice glanced at me and smiled. "It was a gift from a friend."

As promised, Isobel had brought all the fixings for French toast and set about making us breakfast. Alice put on some music and stretched out on the couch to read the paper. She was wearing her old Buzzcocks T-shirt and some ripped-up jeans; she looked exactly like my old girl-friend Alice, not my lawyer wife Alice.

Later, as the three of us ate breakfast together, I felt as if I'd been zapped into a time machine. I had a sense of what it might be like to have a child of our own—but far in the future, after the diapers and the Mommy-and-me music time and the Daddy-and-me gymnastics, after the relief and heartbreak of kindergarten and the thrill of our kid's first trip to Disneyland, after a hundred visits to the doctor's office and a mil-lion hugs and kisses and a thousand temper tantrums and all the things that come between birth and the teenage years. It was nice. I could to-tally see Alice and me doing exactly this, one day, with a kid of our own. Although I understood that, with our own child, it would likely be more complicated. Isobel could be here with us, like this, because there was no history between us, no baggage. We hadn't disappointed her, and she hadn't worried us to death. Still: a family of three, together on a Saturday morning. I could see it.

After breakfast, Isobel and Alice retreated to the back room to do their makeup thing. Isobel had brought her laptop so she could pull up one of Alice's old videos. "*This* is the Alice I want to imitate," I heard her say.

"That one?" Alice said, laughing. "Are you *sure*? Back in 2003 I was going a little heavy on the eyeliner."

I left them alone, reading my book in the living room. Still, I could hear them laughing, and it made me happy, as if we were this perfect imperfect family. It seemed to be exactly what Isobel needed; it also may have been what Alice needed. Because of her own history, which she rarely discussed but which sometimes hung over her like a cloud, Alice had a fragile view of family. Seeing her with Isobel, I understood she'd make a great mom.

## 23

THE FOLLOWING THURSDAY, I WAS INVITED TO SPEAK AT A CONference at Stanford. On the way home, I stopped at Draeger's Market in San Mateo. I was in the frozen foods section, looking for my favorite vanilla bean ice cream, when JoAnne from the Pact party, JoAnne from college, JoAnne from my old life, turned the corner. She seemed surprised to see me. Her hair was combed down straight over her ears and shoulders, and she had a gold scarf wrapped around her neck.

"Hello, Friend," she said with a slightly evil smile. Then she looked over her shoulder, as if watching for someone.

"This is so weird," she said. "I wanted to call you after I saw you. I found your practice online. I must have picked up the phone a dozen times."

"Why didn't you?"

"It's complicated, Jake. I'm worried about you and Alice."

"Worried?"

She took a step closer. "Neil is here." She seemed nervous. "If I tell you something," she whispered, "can you promise me that you will absolutely keep it to yourself?"

"Of course."

To be honest, she seemed a little off. She used to be so normal, so calm. "No, really, don't even tell Alice."

I looked her in the eyes and said seriously, "I never saw you, we never talked."

She was holding a bag of coffee beans in one hand, a baguette wrapped in paper in the other. "I'm sorry to be paranoid, Jake, but you'll understand eventually."

"Understand what?"

"The Pact. It's not what it seems. Or worse, it *is* what it seems—"

"What?"

She looked over her shoulder again, and her scarf slipped an inch or two. And that's when I noticed the angry red mark on her neck. It was partially obscured by the scarf, but it looked painful, still fresh.

"JoAnne—are you okay?"

JoAnne pulled the scarf back into place. "Neil's very well connected inside The Pact. I've heard him on the phone, and I know they've been talking about Alice."

"Yes," I said, confused. "She has this bracelet—"

JoAnne cut me off. "It's *bad*. You can't have them focused on her, Jake. You need to turn their attention elsewhere. Alice needs to get out from under this. It only gets worse, I promise you. Be good. Read the damn manual. There are so many ways to trip up, and the punishments range from innocuous, if you're lucky, to severe." Her hand went to her neck, and she winced in pain. "Make them think everything is fine—no matter what. If that doesn't work, if they still seem to be watching her, have her blame you. That's very important, Jake. Spread the blame, the focus, across the both of you." JoAnne's cheeks were turning red. It was startling to see her in a panic, undone. I thought of the boy she'd talked down from the roof, the Dr Pepper, the way she'd sit in those weekly RA meetings, pen in hand, observing everyone. She'd always been so unflappable.

She glanced over her shoulder. "I have to go. Never saw you, never had this conversation." She turned to walk away, but then she looked back at me. "I like to shop at this Draeger's two or three times a week."

With that, she walked away, leaving me stunned and confused and, I'll admit, scared. Punishments? Severe? What the hell? Was JoAnne going insane? Surely, she must be. Or worse, was she a perfectly sane person trapped in a sadistic club? A club in which Alice and I were now members?

I milled about in the cookie aisle, still shaky, wasting time, not wanting to run into JoAnne and Neil at checkout. After a few minutes, I made my way toward the registers. I could see them heading toward the sliding glass doors—Neil in front, JoAnne walking behind. As the doors opened and Neil walked through, I saw JoAnne hesitate for a split second, then glance back into the store. Looking for me, I thought. What the fuck?

# 24

Up 101, across 380, north on 280, all the way home I tried to recall JoAnne's specific words. When I pulled into the driveway, I looked down to see that the entire pack of Stella D'oro cookies I'd just bought were gone, crumbs everywhere, though I couldn't recall eating even one.

Alice wasn't home yet, so I set about making dinner. Chicken over romaine lettuce, with bottled dressing. I didn't have the concentration to make anything more complex.

Alice showed up after seven, looking tired in her vintage Chanel suit. I gathered her in my arms and kissed her, held her tight. The bracelet felt smooth and warm as she laced her hands behind my neck. But now, after the conversation with JoAnne, it sent shivers up my spine.

"I'm glad you're home early," I said, maybe more for the bracelet than either of us.

She massaged the back of my neck with her fingers. "I'm glad to be home early."

I pulled her wrist toward my mouth and spoke into the bracelet, "Thank you for bringing home my absolute favorite ice cream, that was so thoughtful of you!"

Of course, I was the one who brought home the ice cream, but there was no way for them to know that, right?

She smiled. "Well," she said, speaking into the bracelet, "I did it because I love you. And because I'm happy I married you."

I wanted to tell her about the meeting with JoAnne. I considered picking up the pad of paper on the kitchen table and writing it all down, handing it over to Alice so we could silently discuss this thing together, figure out how to proceed. But JoAnne's warning raced through my mind: not a word to anyone, not even Alice. The more reasonable part of my brain told me that JoAnne was going through something, losing her grip. I'd seen it happen before—perfectly normal people, mentally stable, late onset cases of schizophrenia and paranoia. Unexpected reactions to certain drugs. Triggers that brought up some trauma from childhood and seemed to change someone's personality overnight. Middle-aged professionals who'd done too much acid in college and suddenly found that a weird, buried portal to insanity had opened up inside their brains. I wanted to believe that JoAnne's panic, her bizarre story of punishments, was caused by some personal demon she couldn't get out from under. I wished I had spent more time talking with her husband at the party, so I could get a sense of the kind of person he was. But the threat of action against Alice, the idea that Neil and others were discussing her supposed crimes and the appropriate punishments, gave me the creeps. How could I know what was real and what was a product of JoAnne's feverish imaginings?

As we were setting the table, Alice told me that she was meeting Vivian for lunch the next day. "It's been fourteen days," she reminded me. "Tomorrow the bracelet comes off."

Alice skipped her half hour of reading that night. A long dinner, no TV, a walk through the neighborhood, loving conversation, a slow, uncharacteristically loud encounter in the bedroom. Our performance of the happy couple was so complete that it would make other happy couples, like Mike and Carol Brady or Samantha and Darrin Stephens, seem like they were on the edge of a nasty divorce. The strange part was that we never acknowledged that our performance was for the bracelet or that it even *was* a performance, so that for me it became something else, something more genuine, as the night wore on. Yet when I woke up the next morning, my perfect wife of the night before was gone. There were her heels in the hallway, strewn haphazardly so I almost tripped over them, her mess of lotions and mascara and lipstick scattered on the bathroom counter, her empty yogurt container and coffee mug, smeared with lipstick, on the table. I half-expected a note—*Thanks for the amazing night, I love you more than words can express*—but there was nothing. When the clock struck five A.M., my devoted wife Alice had turned back into the laser-focused attorney she was. For her, I feared, last night's performance really had been for the bracelet.

As I was getting ready for work, I had a memory of the first time we spent the night together. It was in her apartment in the Haight. We'd stayed up late the night before, making dinner and watching a movie, and we fell into bed together at the end of the night but didn't make love. Alice wanted to take things slow, and that was fine with me. I loved lying next to her, holding her, listening to the sounds of the street down below. The next morning, Alice and I sat in bed, reading the paper. There was some music on—a great piano piece by Lesley Spencer. The sun was shining through the windows, and the apartment had a beautiful yellow glow. For some reason, the moment just felt right. And I knew the picture would remain with me for a long time.

I've always been surprised by the fact that our most indelible memories are often seemingly mundane things. I couldn't tell you my mother's age, or how many years she kept her nursing job after she had us kids, or what she did for my tenth birthday party. But I can tell you that one time on a hot Friday evening in summer in the 1970s, she took me to the Lucky grocery store in Millbrae, and as we walked through the door, she said that I could buy any food I wanted.

I can't remember the details of many of the significant markers of my life, the events that are supposed to carry so much meaning: First Communion, confirmation, college graduation, the first day of my first job. I can't even remember my first date. But I can, with incredible clarity, describe for you my mother on that summer night in Millbrae: the yellow dress she wore, the cork wedges with the flowered straps, the smell of Jergens lotion on her hands mingling with the clean, metallic smell of the freezer, the big silver shopping cart, the bright lights of the grocery store, the Flaky Flix and Chocodiles stacked in the seat at the front of the cart, the teenage clerk who told me I was a lucky kid, and the warm, happy feeling I had, my intense love for my mother at that moment. Memories, like joy, always seem to sneak up on me when I'm not seeking them out.

## 25

THAT NIGHT I GOT HOME AT FIVE. I WANTED TO HAVE DINNER waiting when Alice returned. I was nervous and strangely excited to hear the details of her lunch with Vivian. I wasn't sure if dinner should be something celebratory, or something restrained, so I made a simple paella, opened a bottle of wine, and set the table with candles.

At fifteen minutes after six, I heard the garage door open and Alice's car pull in. It was taking her so long to get upstairs, it made me nervous. I didn't want to show my anxiety, in case things with Vivian had taken a bad turn. Eventually I heard her on the back stairs, and then the door opened. She was carrying her computer bag, her coat, a file box—loaded down, as usual. I immediately looked down to her wrist, but it was covered by the sleeve of her trench coat.

"Yum," she said, noticing the pan on the stove. "Paella!"

"Yes," I said, "Michelin-starred nouvelle cuisine." I took the box from her and carried it into the living room. When I returned, her shoes and stockings and skirt were on the floor, her hair down. She was standing there in her blouse, trench coat, and underwear, looking like she could finally breathe. She'd developed a small imperfection on the inside of her left thigh, a vein that just months before had popped out a little. She'd shown me the vein on the day it appeared, upset beyond reason, I thought. "What the hell is this?" she'd demanded. "I'm in decline. Pretty soon I won't even be able to wear skirts."

"It's sweet," I'd assured her, getting down on my knees and kissing the vein, working my way up. It became a kind of code: Whenever she wanted that particular favor, she'd point to the vein and say, "Honey, I'm feeling really bad about this." The effect was that now, whenever I saw that small imperfection, it gave me a little erotic thrill.

"How did it go with Vivian?" I asked, kicking the shoes under the kitchen table so I wouldn't trip over them. I've often thought that any burglar who dared breach our front door would have a fatal accident with Alice's shoes long before he could steal anything.

And then she did a slow, sexy dance, taking off her trench coat, unbuttoning her silk blouse, baring her shoulders, and eventually removing the final sleeve to reveal that the bracelet was gone.

I took her hand in mine and gently kissed her wrist. It looked raw. "I've missed you," I said. I was so relieved, as if a physical weight had been lifted from my shoulders.

"So have I," she said, and then she danced around the kitchen in just her bra and underwear, her hands up in the air.

"Does this mean we passed the test?"

"Not exactly. Vivian said you can't always take the order to remove the bracelet as an indication that you've been cleared of subversive acts against marriage."

"Subversive acts? Are you kidding?"

"Sometimes," Alice said, "they continue their review after the bracelet has been removed."

In the dining room, I pulled out a chair for her and she sat, pale legs sprawled out in front of her. "Start at the beginning," I said.

"Well, I got to Fog City first so I could get us a table."

"Good move."

"Vivian had the tuna salad again, and I went with the burger. She didn't mention the bracelet until after we'd finished our entrees. Then she said, 'Good news, I've been given the key for your bracelet.' She asked for my wrist, I laid it on the table, and she pulled a metal box out of her bag. It had a bunch of tiny blue lights on the top. She opened it, and there was a key attached to the inside of the box by a wire. Vivian took my wrist and slid the key into the bracelet. Then she hit a button inside the box, and the bracelet just popped open. And she said, 'You're free.'"

"Weird." I brought the paella in from the kichen, then sat down with Alice at the table.

"Then Vivian put the bracelet and the key back in the box, closed it up, and put it in her bag. I was happy to see that thing gone. It wasn't all good, though. There were conditions for my release from the bracelet."

"No!" I said, thinking of my conversation at Draeger's. *Punishments*. I had the uncomfortable feeling that there was some truth in what JoAnne had said.

Alice took a bite of the paella and declared it delicious. "You know how, when she explained that whole thing about Orla and how The Pact is based on the British criminal justice system, we thought she meant it figuratively, not literally? As it turns out, we were wrong."

Alice explained the conditions of her release. It really was like the world of criminal courts. She had to sign some papers, pay a fifty-dollar fine, and agree to see an adviser once a week for the next four weeks. "Probation," she said.

"There's something I should probably tell you."

I described my encounter with JoAnne at Draeger's and how it had weighed on my mind the past couple of days.

"Why didn't you tell me before now?" she asked, sounding hurt.

"I don't know. The Pact is making me paranoid. I didn't want to say anything while you were wearing the bracelet. After everything JoAnne said, I didn't want to get you into trouble. And I didn't want to get JoAnne into trouble either. She seemed so nervous."

A cloud passed over Alice's face. I recognized it, and knew what she was going to say before the words were out of her mouth. "You said you worked together in college. But you didn't tell me whether you ever slept with her. Did you sleep with her, Jake?"

"No," I said emphatically. "And anyway, do we really have to go there? I'm trying to tell you something important."

"Go ahead," Alice said, but I could tell that the suspicion lingered.

"What I'm saying is, after your meeting today with Vivian, I have to reevaluate JoAnne's warning. We have to consider everything she said in a new light."

Alice pushed her plate away. "Now *I'm* getting paranoid."

It wasn't until we'd cleared the table and were washing the dishes that Alice told me the other piece of news from her day: The firm had announced the yearly bonuses. The amount Alice would receive was large enough that it almost cut her law school loans in half.

"That calls for champagne," I said. We got out the glasses and raised a toast to the bonus, as well as to our victory against, or perhaps within, The Pact. We toasted our happy life. Then we went to bed, and we made love in our private, quiet way.

Afterward, as we were falling asleep, Alice wrapped her arms around me and whispered, "Do you think the bracelet made me a better wife?"

"You are the perfect wife, no matter what. Does The Pact make me a better husband?"

"I guess we'll find out."

Looking back on that night, it strikes me that we were both a little scared, but not nearly as cautious as we should have been. The Pact had the mysterious draw of those things that both repulse and attract you at the same time. Like a sound in the garage in the middle of the night, or a romantic overture from someone you know you ought to stay away from, or a strange, shining light you follow deep into the woods, not knowing where it will lead, or what kind of danger awaits you there. We were both drawn to it, despite reason. It had a strong, inexplicable magnetic pull, which we were unable, or unwilling, to resist.

## 26

THERE'S A LOT OF DATA ABOUT WHAT PREDICTS A GOOD MAR-
riage. While statistics are open to interpretation, one of the
conclusions that researchers across the board agree on is this:
The higher your income, the more likely you are to get married. More
important, the higher your income, the more likely you are to *stay* married. On a side note, while you might expect that the amount a couple
spends on their wedding is directly proportionate to their chances of a
successful marriage, in fact, the opposite is true: Those who spend less
than five thousand dollars are far more likely to stay married than those
who spend more than fifty thousand.

When I shared this information with my partners, Evelyn speculated
that it had to do with expectations: Someone who's willing to blow fifty
grand on a wedding is someone who wants everything to be perfect, and
when marriage turns out to be less than perfect, the letdown is greater.
"It also shows a preference for short-term satisfaction and impressing
others over long-term stability," she said.

Ian agreed. "Let's say you put that extra forty-five grand toward a
house instead of a wedding. You've given yourself a leg up. You've made

an investment in your future. I don't mean to sound sexist, but I think women run the show when it comes to weddings. And a bride who needs a fifty-thousand-dollar wedding, with a hairdresser and a wedding planner and a five-course meal and all the rest, is probably high-maintenance."

I thought of our own low-key wedding, where the food was nothing to write home about, but everyone was drinking, everyone was having fun. Alice's dress looked amazing on her, though it was off the rack from a little vintage shop, because she refused to spend more than four hundred dollars on a dress she would only wear once. She bought her shoes half off at Macy's, because, she said, "how often am I going to wear white satin shoes?" My own suit was expensive, but that was because I wear my suits for years, and Alice had insisted that I invest in a good one.

Other interesting statistics: Those who date for more than a year or two before getting married are less likely to divorce. The older people are on the date of their wedding, the better their chances for success. And here's one that seems to defy intuition: Individuals who start dating their spouses when they are entangled in another relationship are *not* more likely to eventually divorce; in fact, the opposite is true. "Because they made an active choice," Evelyn speculated. "They had one thing, and they found something better, so maybe they're grateful to the spouse for showing up at just the right time, rescuing them from the wrong decision. Also, the spouse, in that case, feels chosen. The spouse knows that their husband or wife gave up someone else to be with them." I liked that logic and made a note to bring it up in my next meeting with Bella and Winston. "Bella chose *you*," I would tell him. I hoped it would help.

All the research I was doing made me feel pretty good about my own marriage. Given the price of our wedding, combined with the fact that Alice and I lived together before marriage and were both older when we wed—Alice thirty-four, me inching up on forty—plus her entanglement with her old bandmate when we met—statistics would say that Alice and I are pretty solid. In the end, though, every marriage is unique. Every marriage is its own universe, operating by its own intricate set of rules.

## 27

THE ONLY TIME WE REALLY TALKED ABOUT THE PACT OVER THE
next few weeks was on Thursdays, after Alice made her weekly
visit to her probation officer. Dave was a structural engineer
with an office in the Mission. He was in his midforties, Alice guessed,
moderately intelligent, mildly attractive. We had met him and his wife
at the Hillsborough party, Alice insisted, although I didn't remember
them. She was a little artsy, Alice said, although in a trust fund sort of
way. She had a separate studio in Marin and had participated in a couple
of local joint shows, but she didn't appear to have any need or desire to
sell her work.

On Thursdays, Alice would slip out of work early, take BART over
to Twenty-fourth and Mission, and then walk the long blocks to Dave's
office for their appointment. She always gave it plenty of time she didn't
have, so as not to be late. My conversation with JoAnne had made her
extra-vigilant. She usually arrived early to the block where Dave's modern office sat tucked beside a taqueria.

Alice's visits with Dave only lasted for half an hour. She didn't reveal
the specific details because Dave had told her that was "strictly against

the rules," though she did say the meetings usually consisted of the two of them sitting at his design table, drinking Philz coffee brought in by his secretary, talking about their weeks. Dave would pepper the conversation with a few direct questions about me and our marriage. He sometimes used lingo from The Manual, things one wouldn't ordinarily say in normal conversation, the result being that Alice was always acutely aware that she was in unknown territory. The conversations were pleasant, she insisted, but the questions were direct enough that she never felt entirely comfortable, nor did she feel relaxed enough to accidentally reveal any detail that might be used against us.

In the most recent meeting, Dave asked her about our travel. Having now become completely versed in the minutiae of The Manual, Alice relayed in great detail the weekend trip to Twain Harte that I'd planned and the four-day trip to Big Sur, which she'd planned for three months hence. We hadn't yet gone on either trip, but the fact that they were on our calendars should fulfill the travel requirement for this quarter and the next one. Alice used these conversations with Dave to check off as many boxes as she could, things that might get The Pact authorities looking elsewhere, as JoAnne had so emphatically said we must.

Dave talked about his recent trips as well, even writing down some hotel suggestions. While she knew he was likely reporting the details of their conversations back to someone, she felt that he was a nice guy who genuinely had our welfare in mind. He never came on to her in even the smallest way, which was a big plus in her book. After the first week, she didn't seem to mind the visits. As difficult as it was for her to slip away from work in the afternoon, she said it was a good way to clear her head. "Like therapy," she said. Although she'd never actually been to therapy, unless of course you counted those group circles in rehab the week we met.

Then, on her fourth and final week of conversations, she called me. I hit the Answer button, and all I heard was "Fuck! Fuck! Fuck!"

"Alice?"

"The fucking judge kept us late." She was breathless and running, and I could hear the street sounds around her. "I only have nine fucking minutes to get to Dave's. There's no way I'll make it. Uber or BART?"

"Um—"

"Uber or BART?"

"BART is your only chance. Blame it on me," I said, thinking of JoAnne's warning. "Tell him I made you late. Tell him—"

"No!" she yelled. "I'm not a rat."

"Listen to me," I said, but the phone had already gone dead. I called her back, but there was no answer.

# 28

I f I drove quickly, I could get to Draeger's at the exact time I last saw JoAnne. I was worried that Alice's tardiness was going to put her back on the radar, and I wanted to talk to JoAnne to find out what exactly that would mean.

I got there early, parked my car, grabbed a shopping cart, and started wandering the aisles. No sign of JoAnne. I held my phone, willing it to ring. Alice would surely call to say everything was fine. The whole thing was ridiculous. After all, showing up ten minutes late to a meeting in Northern California is like showing up ten minutes early for a meeting anywhere else.

I wandered for nearly half an hour, bought some cereal, Ovaltine, muscovado for my cookies, flowers for Alice. Eventually, I gave up, took my pricey bag of groceries, and left.

By the time I got back to the city, there was still no word from Alice. I drove home, but her car wasn't there, so I parked in the garage and walked to my office. I had several clients the next day, and I hadn't yet done any preparation. Email had stacked up in my in-box. Documents, journals, and internal billing items covered my desk.

Later, I got a text from Alice. *Went badly. Have to go back to work. Will be late. We'll talk when I get home.*

*OK. Text when you leave. I'll get Burma Superstar for dinner. Love, me.*

She texted back one word, *love*, followed by a sad-face emoji.

It wasn't until after ten o'clock that Alice and I finally sat down together at the kitchen table. Alice had kicked her shoes off at the door— her coat, suit, and pantyhose forming a trail to our bedroom and the dresser where she keeps her flannel pajamas. She wore the pajamas now, a ridiculous, oversize pair that I'd bought her one Christmas, covered with monkey faces. She had mascara smeared under her eyes, and a tiny pimple had emerged just to the left of the dimple on her left cheek— the exact same spot where she gets a pimple every time she's especially stressed out. It occurred to me that I knew this woman, really knew her, better than anyone else ever had, and probably better than I knew myself. Despite the walls she was so good at putting up, I specialized in my own course of study: the Observation of Alice. While there was much she could hide from me, there was much she could not. God, I loved her.

"So?"

Alice got up to grab a couple of beers from the fridge, then she relayed her meeting with Dave.

"I ran about a mile in my heels, and got there fourteen minutes late. If I hadn't just missed the first Daly City train, I almost could've made it. Anyway, I sprinted down Twenty-fourth Street, through the alley, up the stairs to his office. I was sweating through my blouse, and my shoes were pretty much destroyed." Her legs were crossed, and she swung the top one back and forth while she ate, as jittery as I'd seen her in a long time. "Dave could tell that I had raced over there. He got me a glass of water and led me into his office."

"That's good," I said. "So he understood."

"That's what I thought. I expected that when I apologized for being late, he'd say no problem. I thought he'd be impressed that I'd booked it all the way across town, even running a good part of the way. You know me, I never run anywhere. So I'm half-expecting Dave to give me a pat on the back and tell me how much he appreciates that I worked so hard to make our meeting. Instead, as soon as he closed his office door behind me, while I was still standing there catching my breath, he went and sat behind his big desk in his big chair and said, 'Alice, frankly, I'm kind of surprised that you're late. *Fourteen minutes.*'"

"Jerk," I muttered.

"I know, right? So I explain about being in Federal Court. I mention the case, the finicky clients, the difficult judge, and Dave doesn't say a word. He just sits there, turning a paperweight over and over in his hands, like the villain in a James Bond movie. No empathy at all. He just says, 'Alice.' He uses my name a lot, did I tell you that?"

"I hate it when people do that."

Alice took a bite of sesame beef and pushed the plate toward me to share. "He says, 'Alice, in our lives, we are forced to prioritize many different things each day, some large, some small, some short-term, some long-term.' I felt like a kid in the principal's office. He was so different from how he had been in our earlier meetings. It was like a switch had flipped from Friendly Dave to Bossy Dave. He goes on about how most of our priorities—family, work, eating, drinking water, exercise, leisure—are such ingrained habits that we don't even have to think to put them above the usual mundane things that life throws at us. The longer something remains a priority, he said, the more it becomes second nature, hardwired in our minds and actions."

Alice had finished her beer, and went to the cabinet for a glass. "Anyway, he says that one purpose of The Pact is to help people get their priorities straight."

"Vivian said the purpose was to strengthen our marriage. She never mentioned anything about priorities."

Alice filled her glass with water from the tap. "It's all about focus, Dave said. Each day, life tries to pull us in a thousand different directions. Sometimes, a shiny object catches our eye and we have to have it. It's when these things demand priority over marriage that we get into trouble." She sank back into her chair. "Dave said that work is especially insidious. He said that we spend so much time with our co-workers, we invest so much of our time and mental pursuits in our profession, that it's easy to forget that it shouldn't be our main priority."

"I wouldn't entirely argue with that." I thought of Alice's late nights before the bracelet and how the gears of my own mind sometimes churned all night long with concerns about my clients and their problems.

Alice mimicked Dave's deep voice. "'Don't get me wrong, Alice. Work is very important to all of us. Look around. You've seen the models in my conference room, you've seen the photos of past projects in the lobby.' Then he brags about how the structure he helped design for the Jenkinses' guest place out at Point Arena, Pin Sur Mer—"

"Jeez, name-drop much?" The Jenkinses owned a good percentage of the commercial buildings on the Peninsula, and Pin Sur Mer had been in the paper several times, not to mention *Architectural Digest*. I was growing increasingly irritated with Dave.

"I know. Anyway, he goes on about how he put a gazillion hours into it, how he spent three full months fighting with the architect."

"Pin Sur Mer," I said. "How pretentious."

Alice picked at her mango salad.

"He told me how he lost himself in the project, how his priorities got all fucked up. 'Maybe you don't want to hear this right now, Alice,' he said, 'but I'm glad I had The Pact to help me refocus and see what was important. It was very difficult, I won't lie, but I'm glad they were there for me, and I wish they'd done it earlier.' Then he listed off a bunch of awards Pin Sur Mer won, but—" Alice did the voice again: "'Not a single project, not a single detail, not a single bolt on any of these projects is as important as my wife or my family. Pin Sur Mer isn't there for me at the end of the day. Kerri is. Without her, I would be adrift.'"

"You're sure we met Kerri at the party?" I asked, still trying to picture her.

"Yes, remember? The sculptor slash painter slash writer in the Jimmy Choos. Personally, if I had to pick between Kerri and Pin Sur Mer, I might be tempted to take the house. Anyway, 'The Pact,' he tells me, 'is special. I know it's early for you, and maybe you're still trying to figure it out. But just let me tell you this: The Pact knows the fuck what it's talking about.'"

"Yikes."

"He said that twenty years from now, we'd be sitting next to each other at a quarterly dinner, laughing about this small misunderstanding."

"Twenty years? I don't think so."

"'You will thank me,' he said, 'and you and Jake will be happy that Finnegan brought The Pact into your lives. Right now, maybe not so much, but that's a hurdle we have to cross. Right now, it's my job to help get your priorities properly aligned, Alice. It's my job to help rid you of your wrong thinking.'"

I thought of a seminar on propaganda I'd taken back in college. "Didn't Mao use the phrase 'wrong thinking' during the Cultural Revolution?"

"Probably." Alice sighed. "The whole speech sounded very authoritarian. 'I like you, Alice,' Dave said, 'and Jake seems like a good guy. The work-home balance is tough. That's why we need to make a mind readjustment and get you refocused.'"

"A mind readjustment? What the hell did he mean by that?"

"I don't know. He told me that he had someone waiting in the conference room and our time was almost up. But he wanted me to know that, in the history of The Pact, not a single couple has ever gotten divorced. No trial separations, no living apart, none of it. 'The Pact may ask a great deal of you,' he said, 'but trust me, it provides a lot in return. Like marriage.'"

I took a big swig of my beer. "We have to get out of The Pact. Seriously."

Alice was picking at her salad, separating the mangoes from the cucumbers. "Jake . . . I don't think it's going to be that easy."

"What can they do, cart us off to marriage jail? There's no way they can force us to stay."

Alice bit her lip. Then she pushed the plates away and leaned forward to take my hands in hers. "That's the scary part. As I got up to leave, I said to him point-blank, 'I don't really like any of this. I feel like you're bullying me.'"

"Nice. How did he respond?"

"He just smiled and said, 'Alice, you need to make your peace with The Pact. I have made my peace with The Pact, Jake will make his.

It's necessary. You don't leave The Pact and The Pact doesn't leave you.' Then he leaned over, held my arm so firmly it almost hurt, and whispered in my ear, 'No one leaves *alive,* that is.' I pulled away from him; I was totally freaked out. And then he went back to being the jovial guy from the party. 'I'm joking about that last part,' he laughed. But Jake, honestly, it didn't sound like he was."

I imagined that bastard putting his hand on my wife, threatening her. "That's it. I'm paying him a visit tomorrow."

Alice shook her head. "No, that would only make things worse. The good news is, I don't have to see him again. He walked me out. And in front of his office, he told me this was our final meeting. 'Focus, Alice, focus,' he said. 'Get it right. Give my regards to my friend Jake.' Then he walked inside and left me standing there. It was so fucking creepy."

"We have to find a way out."

Alice gave me a quizzical look, like I had totally missed the point. "No shit, Jake. But what I'm telling you is this: I don't think there *is* a way out." She squeezed my hands tighter, and I suddenly saw something unfamiliar in her eyes, something I'd never seen there before. "Jake, I'm scared."

## 29

HERE'S THE THING: I DIDN'T TELL ALICE ABOUT MY DAILY TRIPS to Draeger's that week. I wasn't exactly hiding it from her, I just didn't want to increase her anxiety. When we were together, I acted casual, trying to convey the sense that I wasn't losing any sleep. When she mentioned The Pact, usually to say that she hadn't heard from Vivian or Dave that day, I tried not to look too worried. "Maybe we got all worked up for nothing," I'd say. I didn't really believe it, and I don't think Alice did either, but as the week wore on and nothing happened, our nerves seemed to calm.

Still, I finally understood how my patients felt, the teenagers who told me they'd been waiting for their parents to confront them with the news of their impending divorce. I went through each day fighting off anxiety, looking for JoAnne at Draeger's, waiting for bad news from The Pact. We figured that the most likely scenario would be a call from Vivian, an invitation—or a veiled order—to meet for lunch. Then she would hit us with something from out of the blue—some rule we'd violated, some order that had come down from above.

As the days went on with no call, I told myself that this fear of The

Pact was absurd. Why were we so afraid of a thing that had done nothing more than invite us to a great party and provide my wife with a temporary piece of jewelry and four weeks of free counseling that, except for the final week, was fairly wise and reasonable? Just as often, though, I'd succumb to paranoia. I would walk home from work, and as I turned the corner at Balboa onto our block, I would scan the street for anything unusual. One night, I saw a guy sitting in a black Chevy Suburban across the street from our house. Instead of going up our steps, I walked around the block and up the other side of the street, noting his license plate, trying to get a glance through the blacked-out windows. When a door of one of the houses opened and an elderly Chinese lady walked toward the Chevy and got in, I felt like an idiot.

After a few days had gone by with no word, Alice finally started to relax. But she didn't entirely go back to her old self. She still made it home for dinner every night, but she seemed distracted and wasn't in the mood for sex. The stress pimple beside her left dimple would vanish, then reappear. There were smudges under her eyes, and I knew that she was tossing and turning at night, getting up earlier and earlier to work on cases before she left for the office. "My hair is falling out," she said one morning, sounding more resigned than alarmed. "Nonsense," I said, but I could see evidence in the shower and the bathroom sink, tangled strands of it on her clothes. I went back to Draeger's, still with no luck. I started to have all kinds of weird thoughts. Why hadn't JoAnne shown up? I wondered. Was she in trouble? I didn't like the way The Pact was making me feel, and I didn't like the way it had turned into a black cloud over Alice.

On Tuesday, I called Vivian and asked if we could meet for coffee. She immediately suggested Java Beach in the Sunset district. "See you in half an hour," she said. I hadn't really expected her to pick up, nor had I expected her to suggest we meet so soon. More important, I hadn't really thought out exactly what I wanted to say.

Yes, I wanted out of The Pact, but how best to broach the topic? In my work over the years, I've found that people often react less to what you say than to how you say it. Everyone expects good and bad news—that is the contract of life, after all. The good and the bad are unavoidable, and at some point they strike us all. The news is the news. But the delivery of the news, the gestures, the words, the empathy and understanding—that's the gray area where the messenger has the power to make things a little easier or a lot more difficult.

On the drive over to Java Beach, I kept revising and editing the thing I had to say to Vivian. I wanted to get it right. I wanted to be clear but not confrontational, casual but considered. I wanted it to come out as part question—in order to deflect any anger she might feel—but mostly as a direct statement. Alice and I needed to leave The Pact, I would tell her. It was causing us stress and anxiety, and it was putting a strain on our marriage—the very institution that The Pact was designed to protect. It would be best for us and the wonderful people of The Pact to part ways, I would say. I would thank Vivian for her kindness and apologize for our change of heart. I would make the discussion short, but my meaning unmistakable. And then it would all be over. This weird fog of doom that had been shadowing Alice and me would disappear.

I found a parking spot a block and a half from Java Beach. As I walked toward the café, I could see that Vivian was already there, at a table on the patio. She had two cups in front of her. How had she gotten there so quickly? Her purple dress looked casual but expensive, her handbag simply expensive. She was wearing large sunglasses despite the fog, drinking her coffee, gazing off toward the ocean. She was exactly as Alice described her: perfectly ordinary at first glance but, upon closer inspection, not ordinary at all.

While others around her fidgeted incessantly, Vivian was relaxed, her face serene, not a cellphone or computer in sight. She was, it occurred to me, supremely at ease in her own skin.

"Friend," she said, standing. She pulled me in tight and held me for a second longer than I'd expected. She smelled nice, like the ocean breeze.

"Hot chocolate, right?" She motioned to the mug waiting in front of my seat and removed her sunglasses.

"Exactly." I took a sip, mentally rehearsing my speech.

"Jake. I'll save us a moment of awkwardness. I know why you're here. I understand."

"You do?"

She put her hand on mine. Her fingers were warm, her nails perfectly manicured. "The Pact can be frightening. It even scares me to this very day. But a little fear, when used for a noble purpose, can be a positive thing, an appropriate motivator."

"Actually," I said, slowly pulling my hand back, trying to regain control of the conversation, "about the fear tactics—" I regretted the words as soon as they were out of my mouth. Wrong tone. Too aggressive. I started again. "The reason I called is twofold. First, I want to thank you for your kindness." I tried to make it light. "Alice felt terrible that she never sent you a proper card."

"Oh, but she did!" Vivian exclaimed.

"What?"

"After our last lunch. Please tell her the yellow tulips were gorgeous."

Weird. Alice hadn't mentioned sending flowers.

"I will," I said, bracing to forge on.

Vivian reached across the table to put her hand back on mine. "Jake, Friend, please, I know why you're here. You and Alice want out."

I nodded, surprised at how easy this was turning out to be. "We love everyone we've met in the group. It's nothing personal. It just isn't right for us."

Vivian smiled, and I relaxed a bit. "Jake, I hear what you're saying. But sometimes, Friend, what we want and what is best for us are not exactly the same things."

"Ah, but sometimes they are."

"I'll be frank." Vivian let go of my hand, and the warmth in her eyes died. "I will not let you give up on The Pact. And The Pact, quite assuredly, is not going to give up on you. Not during good times, not during times of difficulty. Many of us have been in your position. Many of us have felt what you and Alice are feeling right now. Fear, anxiety, a lack of clarity about what the future might hold. And all of us have pushed through. All of us have—in the end—been the better for it." Vivian smiled, totally calm. I realized that she had been through this identical conversation with others in the past. "Jake—hear my words—you need to make your peace with The Pact. That is what is best for you, best for your marriage. The Pact is a river, strong and powerful if one resists but peaceful and serene if one is willing. If you move with it, it can transport you, Alice, and your marriage to a place of perfection, to a place of beauty."

I forced myself to remain calm. And as I do when therapy sessions suddenly get intense, I began to speak more quietly. "Vivian, Alice and I will be okay without this place of beauty. We need to find our own way. We *will* find our own way. The Pact is scaring Alice. It is scaring me. In all honesty, it sounds like a cult. The veiled threats, the fake contracts."

"Fake?" She raised her eyebrows in surprise. "I assure you, Jake, there is nothing fake about any of it."

I thought about that first day, when Alice and I had signed our names, imagining that it was all just a fun game with no real consequences. Those damn pens. The slide show. Orla and her cottage in Ireland.

"You're not the law, Vivian. You and Dave and Finnegan and the others. The Pact has no authority of any kind. You do understand that, don't you?"

Vivian sat motionless. "I'm sure you recall who invited you into The Pact," she told me. "Finnegan is the biggest client your wife's firm has, is he not? Truly a man of global stature, a man of influence. I believe he is worth a great deal to the firm, and it was his good word that prompted Alice's assignment to her big new case. Jake, as I'm sure you've seen by now, The Pact isn't just me and Orla and Finnegan. The Pact is a thousand Finnegans, all brilliant in their own way, all wielding their own unique brand of influence. Lawyers and doctors and engineers and judges, generals, movie stars, politicians—people whose names would make your head spin. Jake, your thinking is small, shortsighted. You need to take a moment, look carefully at the big picture, understand the road ahead."

I felt light-headed. I reached out for my hot chocolate, but somehow misjudged the distance. The mug crashed onto the concrete below, spattering brown spots all over Vivian's bag. People around us turned to stare. Vivian dabbed at her bag with a napkin, unfazed. I began picking up the shattered pieces.

A waitress came over. "Leave it. I'll get Anton to sweep it up." She had rings in her nose and her lip and tattoos on her arms and neck, and she gave off a faint whiff of wet dog, as if she lived with a lot of animals. I suddenly wanted to reach out and put my arms around her, as if she were some kind of life raft. I felt intensely jealous of her, jealous of the normal life she was living.

"I want the best for you," Vivian said coolly after the waitress walked away. "I am here to help you reach that destination."

"But you're not fucking helping us, Vivian."

"Trust me." Vivian was almost robotic in her persistence, her utter refusal to hear what I was saying. "Trust The Pact. What I'm saying is this, Jake: You need to step away from this small thinking, this *wrong* thinking, and see the big picture. You and Alice must accept the message that Dave communicated." Vivian put her large sunglasses on. "You must accept the strength The Pact can bring to your marriage, to your careers, to your lives. Like so many things—like earthquakes, tidal waves, tsunamis—The Pact will happen for you. It is unavoidable. The only question is how you will respond."

"You don't seem to have heard me. Alice and I are finished."

"No." Vivian stood, picking up her bag. "Go home. Go be with your lovely bride. You are my friend, Jake. Forever."

With that, she turned and left.

## 30

ALICE IS STRETCHED OUT ON THE COUCH, BOOKS AND LEGAL RE-search scattered around her. Her laptop is open on the table, but she's preoccupied with her guitar, playing that Jolie Holland song I love, a beautiful acoustic piece she sang at our wedding. Her guitar playing is so nice, her voice soft and gentle. The house seems to be soaking it up, straining in silence to hear. She looks up and smiles at me, then sings, "I'm still dressed up from the night before, silken hose and an old Parisian coat. And I feel like a queen at the bus stop on the street. Look what you've done to me."

My heart aches at the purity of her voice, at the sight of her sitting there. I hate that I failed her in my conversation with Vivian.

It has been a long time since Alice picked up one of her instruments. The song is so gentle, and in an instant it seems to strip away the layers from Alice, the invisible walls that are always there. How many times have I wondered about the Alice who rests beneath the veneer of her lawyer persona, the Alice underneath the conservative navy suits? Even as a child, Alice dreamed of being a musician. Her mother taught piano and guitar to the neighborhood children, and there was always music playing in their house. I can't imagine the childhood Alice dreaming of one day becoming a lawyer, but when I met her she was in her second year of law school. Although she was still recording songs, still playing shows, still updating her website, answering email, even producing occasional records for other musicians, I could tell she had already veered onto a different road. She started law school the year she turned thirty, "derailed by the passions of my youth," she said, and as a result she was one of the oldest members of her class. She felt she had a lot of catching up to do, a lot of lost time to make up for. But how could those years doing what she really wanted to do ever be considered lost time? They were the opposite of lost time, it seems to me.

"I wasn't happy," she told me once, a few months into our courtship. "Things had gotten out of control with the band. With"—she hesitated—"my relationships." I knew from articles I'd found online that difficulties in her relationship with the bass player, Eric Wilson, had caused problems for the band. The ugliness of their breakup made its way into the music, she said. The whole thing felt tainted. She decided it was time to grow up. That's why she started law school.

The melody is haunting, and it's nice to hear her voice echoing through the living room. When she finishes the song, she doesn't say hello or tell me about her day, she simply picks up the keyboard at the end of the couch and starts in on Leonard Cohen's "Dance Me to the End of Love." Throughout the song—a hymn to love and loss written when Cohen was well into middle age, at the height of his lyrical power—she is looking at me, flashing her wry smile.

I drop my bag onto the table, take off my coat, and curl up at the other end of the couch. Watching her—so clearly in her element—I can't help but think what she's given up. Did she do it for herself? Or did she do it for me? Eventually, she puts the keyboard aside and slides down to my end of the couch.

"You're so warm," I say. I can't bring myself to tell her about the conversation with Vivian. This moment is so perfect. I just want it to last. I just want to go back to the time before The Pact.

We sit in silence. And then she slides her hand into the pocket of her sweatshirt. She pulls out a crumpled piece of paper.

"What's this?"

It looks like a telegram. On the front, it has Alice's name but no address. "It was hand-delivered today," she says. It reads:

Dear Friend, You are hereby directed to appear this Friday at nine A.M. at the Half Moon Bay Airport. You will be met by our representative and provided further instructions at that time. It is not necessary to bring clothes or sundry items. Please do not bring any valuables, personal effects, or electronics. This is a directive, not a request. Failure to comply with a directive, as you are aware, is addressed at length in Section 8.9.12–14. We look forward to seeing you. Vty, a Friend.

Everything inside me sinks, dread welling up.

"I finally started to think that I'd been wrong about Dave. I almost decided it was all nothing, that I took what was really a pretty ordinary conversation and transformed it in my mind to something sinister."

"It's not nothing," I say. I tell her about the meeting with Vivian. Her eyes fill with tears.

"I'm so sorry, sweetheart." I pull her into my arms. "I should have never let us get involved with this."

"No, *I'm* sorry. I'm the one who invited Finnegan to our stupid wedding."

"You can't go to Half Moon Bay. What can they do?"

"A lot. If they push me out at the firm, if they . . ." I can see her mind fast-forwarding, panic setting in. "We have all those loans, there will be no glowing references, no new job, the mortgage . . . Vivian is right. Finnegan's influence reaches far and wide. And not just Finnegan, all the other Pact members we don't know."

A thought occurs to me. "How much does that matter? You looked so happy just now, playing your music. What would happen if you just took your bonus and left?"

"They haven't given the bonuses out yet. There's no check. We really need that money."

"We can do without it," I insist, although the truth is we're stretched thin with the new investments in my practice, with the mortgage on the Victorian, the mortgage on this house, just the expense of life in one of the most overpriced cities in the world.

"I don't want to be poor again; that's no way to live."

"Are you saying you should go to Half Moon Bay?"

"I think I have to. But there's a problem. This Friday I have a court appearance. We're set to argue my motion for summary judgment. I worked months on it. This is where we can win the entire thing. If we lose on Friday, it's all downhill—thousands of hours of work, pointless work, no chance of winning. I can't believe it. I wrote the damn motion, no one else can do it for me."

"The telegram mentions consequences. What are they?"

Alice gets up and pulls her copy of The Manual from the bookshelf. She turns to Section 8.9.12–14. *"Punishments are meted out according to the severity of the crime and calculated, similar to the CCCP, on a point system outlined below,"* she reads. *"Recidivism, as noted, is calculated at 2x. Cooperation and voluntary confessions are afforded appropriate concessions."*

"Well, that's helpful," I say.

"We could run away," Alice offers. "We could move to Budapest, change our names. Get jobs in that great market by the bridge, eat goulash, grow fat."

"I do love goulash." We're trying to keep it normal, but there is no levity in the air. It seems that we are truly and royally fucked. "There's always the police."

"And what, exactly, do we tell them? That a woman with a really nice handbag gave me a bracelet? That I'm worried I might lose my job? They'd laugh us out of the station."

"Dave threatened you," I remind her.

"Imagine telling this story to a cop. There's no way they would take us seriously. *'No one leaves The Pact'*? Come on. And if they talked to Dave, which obviously they wouldn't, he'd tell them it had been a joke. And then he'd offer them a tour of Pin Sur Mer."

It's quiet for a while as Alice and I struggle to come up with a solution. I feel as if we're two little rats trapped in a cage, both still convinced there must be some way out.

"Fucking Finnegan," she finally says. She picks up her keyboard and plays another song, a moody tune from her band's final album, the one she and the boyfriend wrote together while they were in the process of breaking up.

"Budapest isn't a bad idea," I say, when the song comes to an end.

Alice seems to be considering the proposal. I meant it as a joke, but maybe it doesn't have to be. It occurs to me that I'm good with whatever she decides. I love Alice. I want her to be happy. I don't want her to be afraid.

My heart sinks when she whispers, "They would find us, wouldn't they?"

## 31

ALTHOUGH I FOLLOW MY USUAL PATTERN TODAY—WAKING UP, walking to work, meeting patients—my brain isn't really in it. If Alice is supposed to report to the airport on Friday, we need to come up with a plan.

Last night, Alice wanted to clear her head, so we watched *Sloganeering*. It was a funny episode about the Minister of Slogans and his efforts to buy a smelly car from Italy. It was nice to curl up, think about something else. After turning off the TV, we went to bed and slept deeply. This morning, the usual mess of papers and printouts and legal books littered the kitchen table. The Manual sat on the arm of the big blue chair. Alice had placed a bookmark at the start of Section 9: Procedures, Directives, and Recommendations.

Between patients, I keep trying to come up with a way around this thing. While some people get increasingly paranoid when they ruminate too much on a problem, I usually go the other way. By three in the afternoon, I've almost convinced myself that the situation isn't as dire as it seemed yesterday. I'm thinking about this when Evelyn steps into my office and drops a white envelope on my desk. No stamp. Gold writing on the outside, just my name, no address. I stare at it, sweating.

"A bike messenger just dropped it off," she says.

Inside, there is a white card with a handwritten message, also in gold ink:

We appreciate the honor of your presence at the quarterly meeting of the Friends at 6 P.M. on March 10. The address is 980 Bear Gulch Road in Woodside. The security code for the gate is 665544. Do not under any circumstances share the address or the code with anyone.

There's no signature or return address.

## 32

On Thursday morning, I sit on the bed in my T-shirt and boxer briefs, watching Alice dress for work. "What are we going to do?" I ask.

"I'm going to go do my job," she answers. "You're going to do yours. Whatever the consequences are, we'll cross that bridge when we come to it. Vivian's threat was about Finnegan and the firm, but if I'm a no-show for the court appearance, I'll be on seriously thin ice at the firm anyway."

"And the part about the long reach of The Pact's influence?"

"I don't know." Alice says it firmly, without even a touch of the dread that I'm feeling. Is her confidence real, or is she faking it for my benefit? Still, just the fact that Alice is herself right now, ready to go into battle, makes me feel better. If the musician Alice is a delicate, mystical creature I wish I could see more of, the lawyer Alice is a tough, smart, entirely competent woman I'm glad to have on my side.

"I'll be thinking about you all day," I promise, watching her brush her hair. She puts on her subtle plum lipstick and her small gold hoop earrings.

"Right back at you." She kisses me, long but soft, carefully so as not to smear her lipstick.

For some complicated reason involving road construction and parking, she's catching a ride into work this morning with a colleague. A gray
Mercedes pulls up to the curb at six, and Alice is gone.

At a quarter to nine, I'm at work, brooding about our unsolvable
problem. All day, I'm in knots, going through the motions with patients,
waiting for the other shoe to drop, wondering what form it will take.
"What's gotten into you, Jake?" Evelyn wants to know. "You're not yourself. Are you coming down with something?"

"Not sure." I toy with the idea of telling her, but what good would it
do? I imagine her wavering between hilarity and disbelief. She wouldn't
immediately grasp the depth of The Pact and the threat it poses. I am
certain, though, her involvement would lead to more trouble for Alice
and me.

At two, my phone dings. It's a text from Alice, a perfectly ordinary
text. *I won't be home till midnight.*

*Let me give you a ride,* I text back. *I'll be out front around 11:30. Come
down when you're ready.* After yesterday, I want to hold Alice, see with my
own eyes that she's all right.

I arrive in front of her office early. The neighborhood is quiet, the
night chilly. I've brought two sandwiches, a bottle of cream soda for
Alice, and a couple of mini Bundt cakes. I leave the heater on, and I try
to read the new *Entertainment Weekly.* Even though the cover story is on
the viral growth of *Sloganeering,* I can't concentrate. I keep glancing up
at the lit windows of the law firm, looking for Alice's silhouette, wishing
she'd come down.

At midnight, the door opens. That guy from the party is with
Alice, the tall, curly-haired one—Derek Snow. I roll the window down
a crack, and I can hear him asking if she'd like to get a drink, but she
says, "No, thanks, my sweet husband came to pick me up." I'm absurdly
happy to see her. I lean over the passenger seat to open the door and she
slides into the car, turning around to drop her briefcase and purse into
the backseat. She gives me a lingering, passionate kiss, and I feel silly
for the sliver of concern that just passed through my mind. Clearly, the
guy is not her type; I am.

She sees the bag on the console. "Sandwiches!" she exclaims.

"Yep."

"You are the world's greatest husband."

I pull a U-turn on California Street as Alice tears into her dinner, recounting her day. Her team found some strong new evidence, and their chances with the summary judgment are looking good. It's not until we make the turn down Balboa that I bring up the subject we're clearly avoiding.

"What are your thoughts on tomorrow?"

"I called Dave," she answers. "It didn't go well. He insisted a directive is a directive. He said your stunt with Vivian didn't help. And then he repeated the same thing: We have to make peace with The Pact."

"What do you think will happen?" I ask, after a moment.

She's silent.

"I wish you hadn't even told Dave about your court date. We should just go with what JoAnne said: You need to blame it on me, spread it out."

"After your episode with Vivian," Alice warns as we pull into the garage, "I have a feeling you'll see your share of the blame."

## 33

O N FRIDAY, I WAKE AT DAWN. WITHOUT SAYING A WORD, I SNEAK into the kitchen and make breakfast. Bacon and waffles, orange juice and coffee. I want Alice to have energy, I want her to do well in court. More important, though, I want to show her how much I love her. Whatever the day holds, I need her to know that I'm on her side.

I put the breakfast on a tray and bring it to Alice. She's sitting on the blue chair in her pantyhose and underwear, focused on her work. She looks up and smiles. "I love you."

At six, she races out the door. I clean up, shower, and it's not until I'm on the phone with our receptionist, Huang, that I realize what I'm going to do. I tell him I'm feeling sick and may or may not make it in today. "Food poisoning," I lie. "Can you cancel my appointments?"

"Sure," he says, "but the Boltons won't be happy."

"True. I'm sorry. Want me to call them?"

"No, I'll handle it."

I leave a note in case I'm not here when Alice gets home. *Gone to the Half Moon Bay Airport. It's the least I can do. Love, J.* Then I add a postscript that seems melodramatic even as I'm writing it but expresses just what I feel: *Thank you for marrying me.*

On the drive down the coast, I make peace with my decision. The Half Moon Bay Airport is nothing more than one long runway lost among acres and acres of artichoke plants. In the dense fog, I can just make out a few covered Cessnas and the small building that houses the 3-Zero Cafe. I park in the nearly empty lot. Inside the restaurant, I take a table with a view of the runway. There is no security, no ticket counters, no baggage claim, just an unlocked glass door separating the runway from the café. A slender woman in an old-fashioned waitress uniform walks over.

"Coffee?"

"Hot chocolate, if you have it."

"Sure."

I scan the airport for anything out of the ordinary. There are only three cars in the parking lot: mine, an empty Ford Taurus, and a Chevy truck with a guy in the driver's seat. He looks like he's waiting for someone. I catch myself tapping on the table, an old nervous habit. The unknown has always scared me much more than any actual danger. Is someone planning to meet Alice here and give her more tough talk? Another bracelet, perhaps? Or are they coming to take her somewhere? Neither Vivian nor Dave ever mentioned plane trips. I should have paid more attention that day Vivian removed the Martin Parr photo and shined her PowerPoint on our living room wall.

A plane swoops in over the hills. I watch it make a big turn and come in for a landing in the swirling fog. The plane is a small, private affair, though larger and fancier than the Cessnas near the hangar. I check my watch—8:54. Six minutes to go. Is that the guy?

The plane glides up to the area near the fuel hose. A worker runs out, he and the pilot talk for a second, then the worker begins to fuel the plane. The pilot approaches the restaurant. I see him shiver and glance around the parking lot. Clearly, he's looking for something or someone. He steps inside and scans the room, hardly noticing me. He checks his cell, frowns, and heads to the restroom.

There are no other people in sight, and no more planes coming in for a landing—just me, the waitress, the worker, the man in his Chevy, and the pilot. It's nine on the dot. I put a five-dollar bill on the table and stand. The guy comes out of the restroom and scans the area again before walking out the front door to the parking lot. He's very tall, early forties, red hair, good looking, dressed in a denim shirt and khakis.

I step outside. "Good morning," I say.

"Hi there." He has a faint accent. I can't quite place it.

"Are you by any chance looking for Alice?"

He turns to face me, sizing me up. I extend my hand. "Jake." He looks at me skeptically, then shakes my hand.

"Kieran." The accent is Irish. Instantly, I think of Vivian's story of Orla and the island in Ireland. "Do you know Alice? She was supposed to be here." He seems a little irritated.

"I'm her husband."

"Great. Where's Alice?"

"She couldn't make it."

He smirks, like I must be putting him on. "But she will be here, right?"

"No. She's an attorney. She's stuck in court. It's a very important case."

"Well, this is a first." Kieran laughs. "That wife of yours has some moxie." He takes a stick of gum out of his pocket, unwraps it, and slides it between his teeth. "Maybe not a lot of brains, but definitely moxie."

"I've come in her place," I say.

He shakes his head. "You two are a trip."

I'm battling a whole tangle of feelings, trying not to let any of it show, certain that it does. "She couldn't come, and I didn't want you to be waiting here for her, so I've come in her place. As a courtesy."

"A courtesy? Seriously? I'm not sure how I'll explain this to Finnegan."

"Finnegan told you to come?"

Kieran narrows his eyes. He seems surprised at how dumb I am. Or how naïve.

"All of it is really my fault," I insist. It's true; I got Alice into this mess. Sure, Finnegan was her contact, and she alone invited him to our wedding. Still, the marriage was my idea. Alice would have been happy to continue living together, secure in our relationship, indefinitely. Like I said, I love her, but that's not why I married her.

"Well," Kieran says, "I appreciate you showing up, that was admirable, and even a little gutsy—but that's not how it works."

"She'd be here if she could."

He looks down at his watch, scans the email on his cell. The whole thing seems to have him confused. "Let me get this straight. She's really not coming?"

"No."

"Okay, nice to meet you, Jake. Good luck to that wife of yours. She'll need it." The pilot pivots and gets into his plane. Watching his small silver rig pull up through the fog, I have a sick feeling in my gut.

# 34

O N MY WAY BACK INTO THE CITY, I GET A CALL FROM HUANG. He tried to cancel my eleven o'clock with the Boltons, but the missus wanted none of it.

"Mrs. Bolton is scary," he says.

The Boltons, Jean and Bob, have been married for more than forty years. They were the first clients Evelyn signed up when she started the marriage counseling side. I later figured out why—the Boltons had already burned their way through every other therapist in the city.

I dread the hour I spend with them each week. They're a miserable pair, made more miserable by the fact of their union. The hour slips by at such a glacial pace, I suspect the clock on the wall is broken. The Boltons would have been divorced decades ago if not for the pushy pastor at their church who demands they attend counseling. Usually I give a client six months, then evaluate how things are going. If I feel we're not getting anywhere, I make a referral to another therapist. It's probably not a great business model, but I think it's best for the clients.

With the Boltons, somewhere around our third week I asked if they had ever considered divorce. Bob immediately responded, "Every single fucking day for the past forty fucking years."

It was the only time I've ever seen his wife smile.

"Okay," I tell Huang, "tell them I'll meet with them. The usual time. I'll be back in the office by ten-thirty."

"You're not sick anymore?"

"Define what you mean by sick."

The Boltons show up at eleven on the dot. I don't really hear anything they say—or rather, anything Jean says, as she's the one who does all the talking—but neither of them seems to notice that I'm out of it today. I'm pretty sure Bob is sleeping through most of it too, with his eyes open, like a horse. He actually seems to be snoring. At straight-up noon, I tell them our time is up. They lumber out of the office, Bob complaining about the fog. Last week, the weather was beautiful and he complained about the sun. Once they're gone, Huang wanders through the office spraying air freshener and opening windows. He's trying to get rid of the smell of Jean's terrible perfume.

At 1:47, I get a call from Alice. "We won!" she cries, ecstatic.

"That's fantastic! I'm so proud of you."

"I'm taking the team to lunch. Want to join us?"

"Enjoy this victory with your team. We'll celebrate tonight. Where are you eating?"

"They want to go to Fog City."

"I hope you don't run into Vivian."

"If I disappear, know that my car is parked near the corner of Battery and Embarcadero. It's all yours." The levity in her voice makes everything seem so normal, but in my heart I know that nothing is normal. I don't tell her about my visit to the Half Moon Bay Airport. I want to let her enjoy her victory before burdening her with the news.

After we hang up, I sit at my desk, halfheartedly checking email, trying to make sense of my interaction this morning with Kieran. What would have happened if Alice had been there? Would Kieran have put her on the plane and flown away? Where would they have gone? When would she have come back? Would she have fought with him, or accepted her fate and stepped onto the plane? I remember an eerie photo I saw years ago in *Life* magazine. It showed a group of men inside a fenced area in Saudi Arabia. The caption indicated that they all had been convicted of stealing, and they were waiting to have one of their hands chopped off. The most disturbing thing about the photo was that all of the men seemed so calm, sitting there passively, waiting for the inevitable horror.

I walk back to our house and drive down to the Peninsula. Destination: Draeger's. One of the clerks, a short, plump woman named Eliza, gives me a wave as I walk through the door. By now they must consider me a regular. "I love a man who does the shopping," Eliza says every time I go through her checkout lane.

In all of these trips, I still haven't succeeded in encountering JoAnne, and today is no different. I buy Alice flowers and a bottle of Veuve Clicquot to celebrate her victory. I buy myself some cookies.

Eventually I give up waiting for JoAnne and go to the register. "I love a man who does the shopping," Eliza says. Then, as she's scanning the cookies, she looks at me and says, "You need to get some protein in your basket, friend."

"What?" I stammer.

"Protein." She smiles. "You know, beef or pork or something that doesn't contain hydrogenated oils." I can't tell if it's a genuine smile, or a smile of warning. It's Eliza, I tell myself. Sweet, friendly Eliza. What she just said—that was *friend* with a lowercase *f,* not an uppercase *F.* "That stuff will kill you," she adds with a wink.

I grab the bag and rush out the door, scanning the parking lot for anything troubling. But how would I even know what's troubling? It's the usual mix of Teslas and Land Rovers, the occasional Prius hanging out by a BMW 3 series. Stop being paranoid, I scold myself. Or don't.

Alice arrives home a few minutes before six. I've thrown away the note I wrote to her this morning, telling her I was going to Half Moon Bay. I decide the news can wait until tomorrow. She's still wired from the victory, tipsy from the long, celebratory lunch. Her giddiness is infectious, and for the first time in months, I'm able to push away that clinging sense of unease—not obliterate it, but shove it to the side of my mind, for Alice's sake. I arrange cheese and crackers on a plate, and Alice pops the champagne. We move out to the tiny balcony off of our bedroom. The sun is about to set, and the fog is starting to move in, yet we can still see our sliver of the ocean. It's this tiny, perfect ocean view that inspired us to buy the house we couldn't afford. It isn't just the ocean that makes the view so special but the rows of squat 1950s houses, the funky backyards, the beautiful trees lining Fulton Street where our neighborhood meets Golden Gate Park.

We linger on the balcony, the champagne bottle empty. Alice replays the entire court appearance, even doing hilarious imitations of each of the opposing lawyers, as well as the crusty judge. Her performance is brilliant, and I almost feel like I'm there in the courtroom with her. She has put so much work into this case, and I'm insanely proud of her.

The disturbing encounter with the pilot, the toxic session with the Boltons, and the failed, paranoid trip to Draeger's fade. I realize that I am making a very conscious effort to be in the moment—to be mindful, as the popular terminology goes. This relaxed, private moment with Alice—celebrating her success, enjoying each other's company—is the very essence of marriage in its most perfect sense. I wish I could bottle it; I wish I could replicate it each day. I imagine holding this moment in my mind, storing it up for when I need it most. I want to urge Alice to do the same—but that's a contradiction, isn't it? If I were to tell her to hold this moment close and remember it, wouldn't I only be reminding her that this happiness is fleeting, that at any moment things could change for the worse?

And then Alice's cell rings, and I am snapped out of my reverie. Just as I'm about to say, "Don't answer," Alice clicks on her phone.

She smiles, and I breathe a sigh of relief. It's her client Jiri Kajanë, calling from his dacha along the Albanian coast. He's just heard the good news about their victory. Alice laughs and puts her hand over the phone to tell me that he has named a character after her in his sequel to *Sloganeering*. "I'm Alice the typist who solves the case of the missing page in the all-important U'Ren file. Kajanë says you can be the attendant at the Hotel Dajti bocce court. It's a small part, but important."

She winks at me. "Will Alice the typist and Jake the bocce attendant find love and happiness?" she asks Kajanë.

Long pause. Apparently, the answer is complicated. Then Alice turns to me. "True love is elusive, but they will try."

## 35

I STARTLE AWAKE IN THE MIDDLE OF THE NIGHT, CERTAIN THAT SOME-
one has been banging insistently on our front door. I wander around
the house, peering out all of the windows, checking the Dropcam,
seeing nothing. Late at night, our neighborhood is crazy quiet; the ocean
breeze and the thick fog deaden all sound. I shine the flashlight out
toward the yard. Nothing. Scanning the back fence, I see the red eyes of
four raccoons reflected eerily in the glow of the flashlight.

In the morning, Alice appears dead to the world, not having moved
an inch from the spot in the bed where she fell asleep. I put on coffee and
start to make bacon and waffles.

An hour later, Alice walks in. "Bacon!" She kisses me. Then she sees
that I've washed and folded all of her laundry. "Have I been asleep for
weeks? What day is it?"

"Eat your bacon," I say.

"I guess we were worried for no reason," she says over breakfast. "I
didn't show up at the airport, and nothing happened."

That's when I tell Alice about my encounter with the pilot. I held
off last night, not wanting to spoil her joy from the court victory. But

she has to know. I worry that Vivian or Dave is going to call—or worse, Finnegan—and I don't want her to be surprised. I tell her about the pilot's accent, his impatient demeanor; his incredulity that she wasn't there. I recount our brief conversation.

"He mentioned Finnegan by name?" She's frowning.

I nod.

She puts her hand on the back of my neck, twirling her fingers in my hair. "It's so sweet that you went in my place."

"We're in this together."

"Well, did it seem like he was there to tell me something? To deliver a package or something?"

"He wasn't holding a package."

"He was going to take me somewhere?"

"Yes."

Alice takes a soft breath. The worry line between her brows deepens. "Okay."

"Let's go for a walk," I say. I want to talk, but after the bracelet, after yesterday, I'm not even certain it's safe to talk in our own house.

She goes to our bedroom and returns in jeans and a sweater, her puffy coat. Outside, she scans the street. So do I. We turn left, our usual path down to Ocean Beach. Alice walks quickly and with purpose. Neither of us says anything. When we finally get onto the sand, she relaxes a bit. We walk side by side toward the waterline. "You know," she says, "I'm very happy that I married you, Jake. I wouldn't change it for anything. And this will sound strange, but I've been thinking about that moment when we were all in the conference room, after Finnegan's victory. The partners called me in. The room was packed, and all of a sudden I'm standing shoulder to shoulder with Finnegan himself. When Frankel mentions I'm getting married, Finnegan puts his arm around me so tenderly and says, 'I love weddings.' And I reply, 'Would you like to come to mine?'

"I didn't even know that I was going to invite him until the words were out of my mouth. I wasn't entirely serious. Everyone in the room laughed. When he said, 'I would be honored,' there was a weird hush. Everyone had been working their asses off to get his attention, to be noticed by the Amazing Finnegan, this legend who always seemed to hold himself apart, and it was as if they were all stunned at what had just transpired, by the generosity of his comment to me, although, of course, I'm sure no one thought he meant it. I didn't. Afterward, when he was leaving, he stepped inside my cubicle. The wedding invitations had just been delivered, and the box was sitting on top of my desk, and when Finnegan said, 'Where are the nuptials to take place, my dear?' I just pulled one off the top and handed it to him. It all seemed so natural. Like an extension of a joke neither of us was willing to admit was a joke. Or at least that's what I thought. It wasn't until after he left that I realized that it hadn't been a joke to him. And, Jake, here's the weird part: It was as if he knew it was going to happen, as if he *willed* it."

"He couldn't have."

"Are you sure?"

We're standing by the water's edge now. Alice takes off her shoes and tosses them behind us, into the sand, and I do the same. I take her hand, and we step into the surf together. The water is freezing.

"Here's the thing, Jake. Our wedding was such a magical day that I don't regret any of it. I don't regret meeting Finnegan, and believe it or not, I don't regret The Pact."

I'm struggling to process this, and I think I understand what she's saying. It's like when Isobel told me that her existence depended upon her father's unhappiness. Sometimes, two things cannot be separated. Once they're enmeshed, they just are. Turning back the clock wouldn't only unravel the bad but the good too.

"You've been so good to me, Jake, and I just want to be worthy."

"You're more than worthy."

A few yards away, a surfer is zipping up his wet suit, attaching his ankle strap. His dog stands beside him, panting. Alice and I watch as the surfer pats his dog on the head and wades out into the water. The dog follows him a little way, and then the surfer says, "Go back, Marianne," pointing to the shore. The dog obeys and swims back. Marianne, what a strange name for a dog.

"When I was a child," Alice says, "I was so independent and strong-willed, my mother used to say that she pitied the man I married one day. As I got older, she started saying that she didn't think I ever would marry. Once, she told me that even though she enjoyed being married to my father, that didn't necessarily mean marriage was for me. I needed to find my own way, she told me. I needed to create my own happiness. But I also remember reading between the lines, thinking that she meant I would disappoint anyone who married me. Until quite some time after you and I met—probably longer after we met than you might want to hear—I still knew in my heart I would never marry."

Her confession comes as a shock. The surfer is paddling out now, his strong arms stroking against the current. The dog is barking on the shore as the fog swallows her master.

"But, here's the funny part," Alice continues. "When you asked me, it seemed right. I wanted to marry you, but I was worried I would let you down."

"Alice, you haven't. You won't—"

"Let me finish," Alice says, tugging me deeper into the surf. The frigid water sloshes up my ankles, soaking my jeans. "When Vivian came that first day and gave us those papers to sign, I was *happy*. What she described sounded like a cult, or a secret society, or something that normally would have scared the shit out of me and made me run in the opposite direction. But I didn't want to run. Her whole speech about The Pact, the box, the papers, Orla—all of it made me think, 'This is a sign. This is meant to be. This is the tool that will help me succeed at marriage. It's exactly what I need.' As we got dragged deeper into The Pact, I still appreciated the gift. Even the bracelet, the afternoons with Dave, didn't bother me the way they would have bothered you. I found some sort of purpose in it. Those two weeks when I wore the bracelet were so mind-blowingly intense. I know it sounds odd, but I felt such a strong connection to you, deeper than anything I'd ever felt with anyone. That's why, despite everything, I can't truthfully say that I wish The Pact had never happened. What we're going through seems like a test we need to pass, Jake—not for The Pact, not for Vivian or Finnegan, but for *us*."

The surfer has completely disappeared now. Marianne has stopped barking and is whimpering pathetically. I think about something I read about toddlers, too young to process the idea that a person or thing that is not in front of them still exists. When a very young child's mother leaves the room, and the child cries, it's because he doesn't know that his mother will come back. All of his experience with her, all of the hundreds of times that she has left his side and returned, mean nothing to him at that moment. All he understands is that his mother is gone. He is quite literally hopeless, because he cannot fathom a future in which he is with his mother again.

A wave comes crashing up, soaking my calves and Alice's thighs, and we turn and run from the surf, laughing. I pull her close and feel her slender body beneath her big, puffy coat. I feel tears sting my eyes—tears of gratitude. In the past few minutes, Alice has revealed more to me about our relationship, about what it means to her, than she has in all the years I've known her. It occurs to me that right now, despite the threats hanging over us, the uncertainty, the dark chasm of the unknown looming before us, I am as happy as I have ever been.

"I guess what I'm saying, Jake, is that I'm happy I'm on this road with you."

"Me too. I love you so much."

Back home, at the bottom of our steps, Alice kisses me. Lost in the moment, I close my eyes for just long enough that I don't see the black Lexus SUV pull into our driveway. When I open my eyes, it is there. I put my mouth against her ear and whisper, "Please—just tell them it was all my fault."

## 36

S UBTRACTING SLEEP, THE AVERAGE MARRIED AMERICAN COUPLE spends barely four minutes a day alone together.

The word *bride* comes from the root of an old German word meaning "to cook."

More than half of all marriages end in divorce by the seventh year.

Three hundred couples get married in Las Vegas every day.

The average wedding costs the same as the average divorce: twenty thousand dollars.

The arrival of children decreases happiness in over 65 percent of marriages. Oddly enough, children also substantially reduce the likelihood of divorce.

One of the best predictors of a marriage's success in the modern day is whether the wife feels that the household chores are divided evenly.

Thousands of factoids about marriage are published yearly. Not surprisingly, many of them don't stand up to close inspection. The influence of religion and religious organizations on the various studies accounts for a large percentage of the incorrect information. Many of the widely accepted myths about marriage involve the deleterious effects of premarital cohabitation, marrying outside of one's religion, and premarital sex.

*A marriage is 57 percent more likely to fail if the spouses live together before the wedding,* I read on the website of a popular women's magazine. In a tiny footnote, the magazine cites a study conducted by the American Coalition for the Protection of Family Values. Scientific surveys, however, indicate that the cohabitation myth is patently false. Among the couples I've seen, those who lived together before marriage seem to be standing on far firmer ground.

One piece of data, though, is fairly consistent across the board, from study to study, regardless of the source: Most married couples report being happiest during their third year of marriage. Alice and I are only a few months into our marriage, and I can't imagine being any happier. On the flip side, I also can't imagine the idea of being *less* happy after our third year.

## 37

A MAN AND A WOMAN STEP OUT OF THE SUV. BOTH WEAR SUITS. The man is in his mid-to-late thirties, clean-cut, freckles, shorter than the woman. His suit strains at the chest and shoulders, as if he started lifting weights sometime after he went to the tailor. The woman stands beside the driver's-side door of the Lexus, hands behind her back. "Good morning, I'm Declan," the man says, approaching us at the bottom of the stairs. Like Kieran, he has an Irish accent. He reaches his hand out to me and I shake it.

"Jake," I say.

"This must be Alice."

"Yes," Alice says, squaring her shoulders.

"This is my friend Diane," he says. Diane nods. "Would you mind if we come inside?"

I can see the glimmer of defiance in Alice's smile. "Do we have a choice?"

Diane takes a large black duffel bag from the backseat of the Lexus. Declan follows Alice and me into the living room, while Diane waits in the foyer, black bag at her feet.

"Something to drink?" I ask.

"No thank you," Declan replies. "Perhaps we could sit for a minute?"

Alice, still in her puffy coat, sits in the blue chair. I stand beside it, my arm around her shoulders.

Declan pulls a folder from his messenger bag and lays some papers on the coffee table in front of Alice. "My understanding is that you received a directive to report to Half Moon Bay Airport. Is that correct?"

"Yes."

"She had to appear in Federal Court that morning," I add. "We expressed our wishes to leave The Pact, and when our request was refused, Alice explained that she wouldn't be able—"

"I'm sure she had her reasons," Declan interrupts, "but that's not really for me or Diane to determine."

He slides a sheet of paper in front of Alice. "I need you to sign this and date it at the bottom. Take a moment to read it, if you like. It states that you were aware of the directive to appear at the time and location stated."

"I can read," Alice says curtly. She scans the few paragraphs, and as she's about to sign I stop her hand. She looks up at me. "It's okay, Jake. Let me handle this. Really, that's all it says." She signs.

Declan slides a second sheet in front of her. "If I could also ask you to sign this form."

"What is this?"

"The form indicates your acknowledgment of my identity and the responsibility that Diane and I have to fulfill the requirements of the contract you signed on the date below, witnessed and notarized by Vivian Crandall."

"And what are those requirements?" I ask.

"It means that your wife needs to come with us this morning."

"I'll come too."

"No. Just Alice."

"Do I have time to get changed?" Alice asks.

"You're not actually going?" I protest.

She puts a hand on my arm. "Jake, it's okay. I want to follow this through. It's my choice." Then she looks at Declan. "I'm not signing that, though."

"You must," Declan says.

Alice shakes her head. "If you need me to sign that in order for me to go with you, then you'll have to leave without me."

Declan glances at Diane, who is listening intently but has yet to speak.

"It's procedure," Diane says.

"Well, call someone if you need to." Alice shrugs. "There's a limit to what I'll sign. I'm an attorney, remember?"

I think back to the original documents we signed, and despite what she said this morning on the beach, I wish with all my heart she'd been as cautious then as she is now.

"Fine." Diane's face is unreadable. "There's a list of procedures we need to follow. We'll go through them after you change."

"I would suggest," Declan adds, "you wear something comfortable and loose-fitting."

Alice gets up and goes back to the bedroom to change out of her damp beach clothes. I want to follow her, but I don't want to leave these two alone in my living room. There's no telling what they'd hide where.

"How long will she be gone?"

Declan shrugs. "I can't say for certain."

"Where are you taking her? Can I visit?"

"I'm afraid that won't be possible," Diane says.

"Can she at least call me?"

"Yes, of course." Declan smiles, as if to prove he is the most reasonable person in the world. "She'll get two phone calls per day."

"Seriously," I insist. "How long will she be gone? And what do you plan to *do* with her?"

Declan tugs at the shoulders of his tight suit jacket. I get the feeling I'm asking questions he shouldn't answer. "Look, I really don't know."

Diane takes a cellphone from her pocket. "I'll be outside." She steps out the front door and closes it behind her.

"Between us," Declan tells me, "if I had to guess, first time, newly married, new to the program, I'd say seventy-two hours max. Probably less. As for *what,* it's reeducation."

"Some sort of class, you mean?"

"Probably more a one-on-one situation."

I picture another counselor like Dave, albeit more intense.

"But I don't know," Declan adds, "and I can't say, and we didn't have this discussion."

I can hear Alice frantically going through drawers in our bedroom. "And what if she refuses to go?"

"Dude," Declan replies quietly, "don't even go there. Here's how it's going to work: Your wife is going to get dressed, she and I are going to go through the procedures, we're going to prepare her for travel, and then Alice, Diane, and I will get into the truck and leave. How that happens is up to your wife. She has a long ride ahead, and there's really no need to make it any more unpleasant than it has to be. Understand?"

"No. I don't understand." I hear the anger coursing through my words.

Declan frowns. "You both seem like friendly, practical people. I have a very small amount of flexibility here, so let me use it to make things as comfortable as they can be."

Diane, as if on cue, comes back inside, and Alice emerges from the bedroom. She's wearing a big sweater over leggings, and black sneakers. She's carrying her weekend travel bag, a plain canvas tote with her monogram on the front. I can see some socks and jeans sticking out of the top, along with her makeup bag. She seems oddly resolute, only a little bit nervous. "I can bring my phone and wallet?"

Declan nods. Diane walks over with a Ziploc bag, a label, and a Sharpie. She holds the open bag in front of Alice, who drops her phone and wallet into the bag. Diane seals the bag, affixes the label over the top, initials it. She hands it to Declan, who also initials.

"No jewelry," Diane says.

Alice removes the necklace I gave her for Christmas, the one with the black pearl pendant. She's worn it every day since I gave it to her. I hold on to her hand, unwilling to let go. I'm pretty sure I'm more nervous than she is. She leans in to kiss me and whispers, "It will be fine. Please don't worry." Then she looks at Declan, her eyes a challenge. "Shall we go?"

He gives her a slightly pained look. "I wish it were that easy."

Diane puts the duffel bag on the table. "I just need to conduct a quick search, to make sure you don't have anything on you."

"Seriously?" I ask.

"Ma'am, can I have you stand over here and put your hands against the wall?"

Alice gives me a wry smile, as if this is all some kind of game, nothing to be concerned about. "Yes, ma'am," she says to Diane lightly.

"Is this necessary?" I demand.

"Just part of the procedure." Declan refuses to meet my eyes. "We don't want anyone harming themselves on our watch."

As Diane pats Alice down, Declan turns to me. "To be honest, it's not always this calm. When people disregard a directive, sometimes it means they're not quite prepared to go with us. Understandably, the procedures were designed with that in mind."

Alice has her back to me, her hands against the wall. It seems incredibly surreal. Diane reaches into the duffel bag and removes chain restraints. She clicks each side around Alice's ankles. Alice doesn't move.

"Really." I step toward my wife. "This has gone too far."

Declan pushes me back. "This is why people never ignore the directives. It's an effective deterrent."

"Ma'am," Diane instructs, "can you turn around and extend your arms in front of you." Alice does as she is told. Diane pulls something made of canvas, buckles, and chains out of the bag. Alice seems to realize what it is before I do. Her face goes ashen.

Diane slides the straitjacket onto her outstretched arms.

"I won't let you do this!" I say, lunging toward Declan. Declan's forearm hits my throat, his left leg pivots, and I'm on the floor, Declan standing over me. I'm struggling to catch my breath, stunned; it all happened so quickly.

"Leave him alone!" Alice shouts, helpless.

"We'll do this the easy way, right?" Declan says to me.

I try to speak but can't, so I nod instead. Declan pulls me back to my feet. It is only then that I realize that he is at least forty pounds heavier than I am.

Diane looks at Declan. "Headgear?"

"Headgear?" Alice blurts out. The terror in her voice is heartbreaking.

"Can you promise me that there will be no yelling?" Declan asks her. "I want a quiet ride."

"Yes, yes, of course."

He considers that a moment, then nods.

As Diane pulls a strap through Alice's legs and begins to fasten it in the back, Alice asks, "Do we have to go out the front door? I don't want the neighbors to see me like this. Can we leave through the garage?"

Declan glances at Diane. "I don't see why not," he says.

I lead the three of them through the kitchen and down the back stairs. I press the opener, and the garage door creeps up. Declan unlocks the SUV and opens the back door. I keep telling myself this is a bad dream. This isn't really happening.

Diane nudges Alice past me. Alice hesitates, then she turns back to me. For a second, I fear she's going to try to run. "I love you," she says, kissing me. She looks into my eyes. "Don't call the police, Jake. Promise me."

I pull her into a tight hug, panicked. "Let's go," Declan commands. When I don't move, he seizes my forearm in his large hands. In an instant, I'm back on my knees, a sharp pain piercing through my shoulder.

Diane helps Alice work her way awkwardly into the backseat. When she is in place, Diane pulls the seatbelt down and snaps her in. I struggle to my feet. My heart is pounding. Declan hands me a card. There's a phone number on it, nothing more. "In case of emergency, contact this number." He locks eyes with mine. "Only in an emergency. Understood? Keep your cell with you, she'll call. It's not as bad as it looks."

Declan and Diane climb into the SUV and pull out of the driveway. I wave at the blacked-out back window, though it's unclear if Alice can see me.

## 38

THE HOUSE FEELS QUIET AND EMPTY. I DON'T KNOW WHAT TO do with myself. I watch television, pace the hallway, read the news, and pour a bowl of cereal that I'm too distraught to eat, all while watching my phone, willing it to ring. I want to call the police. Why did she make me promise not to? I try to imagine what she was thinking, and I think I understand: a big news story of a kidnapping, television cameras, all the sordid speculation about our private lives. That would crush her.

I stay up late. The phone doesn't ring. I wonder where Alice is, how far they have traveled. As the SUV drove up the street, I noticed that it had an out-of-state license plate. I couldn't make out the state name, only the colors and design. Online, I pull up pictures of the plates for all fifty states. I conclude the car was from Nevada.

By midnight, still no call. I bring the phone with me to the bedroom and lay it down beside my pillow. I check repeatedly to make sure the volume is turned up. I try to sleep but can't. Eventually, I pull my laptop out, power it up, and begin searching the Internet. I type in "The Pact," but all I find are references to a film and its sequel. I've done this search before, with similar results. Further down, there's a popular novel with the same title. I search "marriage cult" but find nothing. I search a whole bunch of different words combined with Nevada, nothing. I search Vivian Crandall and find her on LinkedIn, but her profile is set to private. If I log in to view it, she'll know I was there. There are a few references to Vivian on other websites, evidence of an okay career that hasn't gotten her too much attention—nothing that even hints of her membership in The Pact. I search for JoAnne and it's even stranger. There's a yearbook photo from junior year at UCLA on Classmates.com, but that's it. How does that happen? How can a person be nearly invisible online? I search the address for the house in Hillsborough from the last party, as well as the address in Woodside from the upcoming party. According to Zillow, both houses are worth millions. No shit.

Next, I read about Orla, going back to several pages Alice bookmarked after our first meeting with Vivian. There are hundreds of articles related to her work, a few dozen pictures. Apparently, she was a very respected barrister. There are articles from *The Guardian,* opinion pieces for and against her during her run for political office. Then nothing. I pull up Google Maps and zoom in on Rathlin, the Irish island Vivian mentioned. The map is grainy, low-resolution, Google's way of telling us that the island has no real significance. I scan the shoreline, looking for homes or villages; fog and clouds cover most of it. Wikipedia says the island receives more than three hundred days of rain annually.

I keep checking my email to see if Alice has tried to contact me. Nothing. How long do I wait to hear from her? And then what do I do? Calling the number Declan gave me "strictly for emergencies" seems like a bad idea. I keep remembering what Alice said: "I want to follow this through. It's my choice."

I leave text messages on Alice's phone, but my messaging app indicates that they remain unread. I imagine her phone in the plastic bag in a small box, in a large warehouse filled with hundreds of other small boxes, all of the boxes filled with phones, all of the phones ringing and pinging until the batteries die.

At a quarter to six the next morning, my phone bleats, and I wake up in a panic. But it's a wrong number.

I get up and shower. While I'm dressing, the phone rings again. It's an unknown number. Hands shaking, I hit Answer.

"Alice?" I say.

A recorded voice intones, *"You are receiving a phone call from an inmate at a correctional facility in the state of Nevada. To accept the charges please say 'I accept' at the tone."*

Inmate? The tone sounds. "I accept."

There is a beep, then another recording. *"The following telephone conversation may be monitored. All calls are limited to three minutes."*

Another beep. The call connects.

"Jake?"

"Alice? God, I'm so glad to hear your voice! Are you okay?"

"Everything's fine."

"Where are you?"

"Nevada."

"Yes, but where exactly?"

"Middle of nowhere. We drove 80, and then we took an exit in the desert, and we just kept driving on this dirt road until we arrived at this place. I tried to pay attention to the mile markers, but I lost track. It's way the fuck out in the middle of nowhere—no civilization except a gas station several miles from here. It's all concrete and barbed wire. Two huge fences. Declan said it's a prison The Pact bought from the state."

"Shit. Who *are* these people?"

"Really," she says, "I'm okay. Don't worry."

If she were in a panic, I'd hear it in her voice, I'm certain of it. But there is no panic. She sounds tired, impossibly distant. Not her usual supremely confident self, maybe, but not frightened either. Or if she is frightened, she's doing a superb job of hiding it.

"Don't freak out, Jake, but they've got me in a jail cell. It's a huge place, but there aren't that many people here, at least not that I've seen. There are forty cells in my section—I counted on my way in—but I think I'm the only one here. It's so quiet. The bed is tiny, but the mattress is decent. I must've slept for ten hours. This morning, I woke up when someone slid a metal tray through my door—chorizo and an omelet. Delicious. Really good coffee too, and cream."

There's a sharp beep and the recording about the call being monitored repeats itself.

"Have you met any other—" I search for the right word, and am startled by the word that comes to me. "Any other prisoners?"

"Sort of. They picked up someone else in Reno. He was in bad shape. I'm glad we were more accommodating; the headgear looked miserable. He sweated profusely the whole way here, but he couldn't say anything because they had him gagged."

"Ugh, that sounds sadistic!"

"But on the other hand, he did agree to come, right? They didn't drag him out of the house or anything. I watched him walk to the car."

Another recording warns that we have only one more minute.

"When can you leave?" I ask desperately.

"Hopefully soon. I have a meeting with my attorney in an hour. They assign everyone a public defender. It's crazy. I'm telling you, if you set aside the great food and the lack of people, this feels like a real prison. I'm even wearing prison garb. All red, with the word *prisoner* in big letters on the front and back. Nice material, though, really soft."

I try to picture Alice in prison gear. The image won't gel.

"Jake—can you do me a favor?"

"Anything." I want this call to last forever. I want to hold her in my arms again.

"Can you email Eric at work? I forgot I told him I'd stay late tomorrow night to take care of some paperwork. Just make something up. His email address is on my iPad."

"Done. Can you call me later?"

"I'll try."

Another beep.

"I love you."

"I—" Alice begins, but the line goes dead.

# 39

I CAN'T PUSH AWAY THE IMAGE OF ALICE, SITTING THERE IN HER TINY cell, wearing her comfortable red prison jumpsuit. I'm freaked out, of course. And scared. What's happening to her, and when will she be home? Is she really okay? But I'll admit, there's also this: Deep down, in some small corner of my psyche, I feel a spark of happiness. Complicated. Is it wrong that it pleases me to witness this incredible sacrifice she is making for me, for our marriage?

I plug the phone into the charger and search the house for her iPad. I can't find it anywhere. I search every room, her bags, her dresser drawers. Then I head down to the garage. Her car is an old blue Jaguar X-Type. She bought it with the advance she received from a record company for her first and only widely released record. Aside from her music equipment and some clothes crammed into the back of our bedroom closet, it's the only thing left from her old life. She once told me, only half-joking, that if I didn't behave myself, she would drive the Jaguar straight back to her old life.

The car is a mess of papers, files, and shoes, although I know that Alice considers it perfectly organized. She swears she has a system, that she can always find what she's looking for. She keeps an extra pair of sneakers in the backseat in case she wants to stop for a walk on the beach or in Golden Gate Park on her way home from work, but she also keeps a pair of black boots—because she wouldn't be caught dead walking the city streets in Nikes. In addition to those, she keeps a pair of black ballet flats, in case her feet have had it at work and she needs to change out of her heels into something less painful. There's also a shopping bag containing a pair of designer jeans, a black cashmere sweater, a white T-shirt, and an extra bra and underwear, "in case." And a ski vest, for the beach, plus a trench coat, for the city. On some level, of course, it makes sense to be prepared when you live in San Francisco; you can leave the house in short sleeves and need a coat ten minutes later, depending on the fog. But Alice takes it to the extreme. I can't help but smile at the tangle of shoes and clothes, so maddening yet so very Alice.

Inside the glove box, I find the iPad. It's dead, of course, like all of her electronic equipment. It's a pattern with her; she doesn't believe in charging her tech items. When she finds them dead, she claims that they must have defective batteries. If I could recover all the hours I've spent over the past few years searching for her phones and computers and chargers and mating them all up at the outlet in the kitchen, I would be a much younger man.

Upstairs, when the iPad comes to life, I open the email and do a search for Eric. I can't remember his last name. Eric is a younger associate, smallish and friendly. I often wonder how he has survived so long at Alice's firm. The place is a shark tank, where young associates are thrown in at feeding time. Eric and Alice have forged a fairly close working relationship, assisting each other on their various cases and tasks. "In an atmosphere of war, you have to have allies," she told me the night we first met Eric and his wife at a restaurant in Mill Valley. I liked them both, the only people from the firm I don't mind spending time with.

Still, I can't recall his last name. An aunt of mine came down with substantial memory loss at an early age, and every so often, when I've forgotten something simple, I ask myself whether I've reached the moment from which everything will go downhill.

The search reveals emails from only two Erics. Levine and Wilson.

I click on the first one—Wilson—and it immediately occurs to me why the name sounds familiar. Eric Wilson was the bass player and background singer from Ladder, the band Alice fronted before I knew her. Ladder had a short run, though not so uneventful as to go entirely unnoticed. Once, when I was reading one of the many British music magazines that arrive in the mail, I came across a reference to Ladder. A young guitar player from a Manchester dance band was being interviewed, and he cited the Ladder album as one of his early influences. When I mentioned it to Alice, she just made a joke and dismissed it, though later that week I found the issue turned to that page on our bedside table.

*Alice, when are you going to leave that loser and come back to me?*

The email is from the week before our wedding. I scroll to the bottom and see several friendly emails going back and forth, mostly about music and the old times. There are newer emails from Eric Wilson on the list, though not many. I resist the temptation to open them. It doesn't seem right. Besides, if I remember correctly, The Manual contains quite a few items related to snooping. I fetch my copy from the living room and find "email" in the glossary, then flip to 4.2.15.

Email snooping or spying is not to be tolerated. A strong relationship is built on trust, and spying diminishes trust. Email snooping, which is often the result of a moment of weakness or insecurity, is punishable by a Class 2 Felony offense. Repeat instances of snooping will be punished at the same level, yet with a four-point enhancement.

I flip back to the glossary and run my finger down the e column, looking for "enhancement." On the corresponding page, "enhancement" is described only as *an exponential application of the appropriate punishment for any offense. The exponentiality of the enhancement may be qualitative, quantitative, or both.*

Who writes this shit?

I click down to Eric Levine. I send him an email saying that Alice is suffering from food poisoning and won't be in tomorrow as planned. I put down the iPad, bring my computer back to the bedroom, and try to get some work done. I slog away for a few hours, then fall asleep. When I wake, the sun is setting and the phone is ringing. Where did the day go? I scramble to the kitchen and grab the phone off the charger.

"Hello?"

"Yay, I thought you weren't going to pick up," Alice says. Instantly, I struggle to assess her voice, her tone.

"Where are you?"

"Sitting in the hallway outside my attorney's office. I've been in and out of his office all day, with a break for lunch in a massive cafeteria. There were at least forty of us, but we weren't allowed to speak to each other. The view out the window is desert and cactus for miles and miles. I can see two huge fences. Floodlights. Visitors' parking but no cars. One prison bus. A yard, dirt track . . ."

"Can you see anyone?"

"No. There's a garden; there's even a whole thing for lifting weights out in the hot sun. It's like they just bought the prison and left it exactly as it was."

"What's the attorney like?"

"Asian. Nice shoes. Good sense of humor. I get the feeling he's like us. Maybe he did something wrong, and this is his sentence. Maybe he's here a day, a week, a month—it's hard to tell. I don't think he's allowed to talk about himself. No last name, just Victor. Most of the people here don't even use first names. They just address each other as 'Friend.'"

"Have they told you what happens next?"

"I appear before the judge tomorrow morning. Victor thinks he can settle it beforehand, if I want to. He says the first offense is always easy. Plus, he's friends with the prosecutor who's bringing the charges."

"What are you even charged with?"

"Lack of Focus. One count, Felony Six."

I groan. "What does that mean?"

"It means, according to The Pact, I was not as focused on our marriage as I needed to be. The indictment lists three overt acts, including showing up late to see Dave. But the main thing is that I skipped out on the directive to go to Half Moon Bay."

The absurdity of it hits me. "Lack of Focus? That's bullshit!"

"You can say that because you're not the one wearing a red prison jumpsuit."

"When can you come home?"

"I don't know. Victor is meeting with the prosecutor now. Jake," Alice says quickly, "I gotta go." The line goes dead.

I still have files to read before tomorrow, but I can't concentrate on my work, so I clean the house and do the laundry. I finish the household tasks that have been ignored for weeks: change lightbulbs, fix the dishwasher hose. While I'm pretty good at cleaning—thanks to a childhood with a mother and sister who were both compulsively neat—I've never had much talent for handyman stuff. Alice is the one who repairs broken doorknobs and assembles furniture, but lately she's been too busy. I read somewhere that men who do traditionally masculine tasks around the house have more sex with their wives than men who clean, but I haven't found that to be true in our case. When the house is clean, Alice can relax, and when Alice is relaxed, she's up for anything. I think about her in that bizarre getup she was wearing when they took her, and I'm ashamed to say it gives me a little erotic thrill, reminding me of an S-and-M joint we visited early in our relationship, a warehouse space in SoMa, where the music was loud, the lighting was low, and the upper floor featured a long corridor where the rooms all had a different theme, each one more severe than the one before it.

Finally, I hang the artwork Alice bought me for my Pact gift this month. It's a colorful lithograph, a big brown bear holding an outline of our state, above the words I LOVE YOU, CALIFORNIA!

The iPad in the middle of the room dings a few times, more email. I think about that email Alice had from Eric Wilson. I think about the ones I didn't open, and I feel drawn to read them, but I don't. Antsy, I walk down to the beach, cellphone in hand.

Ocean Beach is windy, freezing, and mostly deserted except for the usual homeless campouts and some teenagers messing around, trying to keep a bonfire going. For some reason I think of Loren Eiseley's brilliant piece "The Star Thrower." It's the story of an academic walking on a vast, long, abandoned beach. Way up in the distance, he sees a small, blurry figure, constantly repeating the same motion. When he gets closer, he realizes it is actually a boy. The boy is surrounded for miles on all sides by millions of scattered, dying starfish that have washed ashore with the tide.

The boy is picking the starfish up and throwing them back into the water. The academic approaches and asks, "What are you doing?" And the boy tells him that the tide is going out and the starfish will die. Confused, the academic says, "But there are so many, millions even, how can it matter?" The boy leans down, picks one up, and throws it far out into the ocean. He smiles and says, "It matters for that one."

I wander up past the Cliff House and stop at the Lands End Lookout Café. It's open late tonight for a neighborhood fundraiser. I buy hot chocolate and roam through the gift shop, drawn to the books with old pictures of San Francisco. I find one with a history of our neighborhood, the eerie cover showing a lone Edwardian house lost among miles of sand dunes. An empty road cuts straight through it, a streetcar waits at the end. I buy the book and have it gift-wrapped. I want to have something nice for Alice when she returns.

Back home, I sit down again with my laptop, still trying to muddle through the write-ups from the previous week's sessions. I hear the iPad email ping three or four more times. I think about the email from Eric Wilson, and I try to remember what he looks like. I do a Google image search. The first thing that comes up is a picture of him and my wife standing in front of the Fillmore, the marquee above them announcing, THE WATERBOYS AND LADDER, DOORS OPEN AT 9. The picture must be from ten years ago. Eric Wilson looks good, but then I may have looked good ten years ago too. If I hadn't seen hundreds of other photos of Alice, I may not have recognized her in this photograph. A blue mohawk, serious black eyeliner, Doc Martens, a Germs T-shirt. She looks cool. Wilson does too: sunglasses, scruffy beard, holding his bass. I can't even remember the last time I went a week without shaving.

The iPad pings again. Even as I reach for it, I know I shouldn't, yet I can't stop myself. The sound of the email ping is like the telltale heart, shaking me at the very core. I punch in the password, 3399, the address of Alice's first home: 3399 Sunshine Drive.

The email pings are not from her ex. Of course they aren't. No, there's a legal newsletter, a solicitation from her alumni association, a mailer from Josh Rouse, and a response from Eric Levine at work. *Hope you recover from the food poisoning soon,* he writes, *and stop eating in the Tenderloin.*

It's then that I should stop reading, put the iPad down, and return to my work. I don't. Scrolling down the list of endless emails, I find seventeen from Eric Wilson. Three of them contain audio files—new songs he has written, plus a cover of the great Tom Waits song "Alice." I love the song, and Wilson's version isn't bad. It gives me chills, but not in a good way.

I race through the other emails. It's mostly group emails, something about a band they all once knew. Eric wants to see her, but she doesn't seem interested. It's hard to tell. I feel bad for having opened the emails; I feel especially bad for having listened to the song. Why did I do it? Nothing good comes from such things. Nothing good comes from insecurity and anxiety. I have a frightful thought, and I quickly look over my shoulder. For some bizarre reason, I expect to see Vivian standing there, watching, disapproving. I turn off the iPad.

I sleep fitfully. The next morning, I wake up more tired than I was when I went to bed. I call Huang at the office and ask him to cancel the day's appointments. I know I'd be no help to anyone today. After showering, I decide to make cookies. Chocolate chip, Alice's favorite. I'm thinking that she might need something like that when she gets home.

As the first batch of cookies go in, my phone rings. Unidentified number.

"Alice?"

"Hey." As soon as I hear her voice, I feel guilty again. I shouldn't have gone through her email. She's so far away, making this strange sacrifice for our marriage. And here I am, violating Section 4.2.15 of The Manual.

"What happened in court this morning?"

"I pled guilty. My attorney was able to get it down from Felony Six to Misdemeanor One."

My head is pounding. "What's the punishment for a misdemeanor?"

I think of the "enhancement" section of The Manual, how it leaves everything open to interpretation.

"Two-hundred-fifty-dollar fine. Eight more weeks of probation with Dave."

I relax. Sure, it's weird to be fined for lack of focus. Still, it occurs to me that I expected worse. "That's manageable, right?"

"After it was all decided, the judge gave me this long lecture on the importance of marriage, the importance of setting goals and seeing them through. He talked about honesty, directness, trustworthiness. Everything he said was reasonable, there wasn't really anything I could disagree with, but it seemed so ominous coming from the bench."

"I'm so sorry," I say. Alice is clearly shaken, and I feel bad. I want desperately to be with her.

"In the end he told me to go back to my husband."

"Well, that's a sentence I can agree with."

"He said that I seemed like a nice person, and he doesn't want to see me here again. It was like in real court, when they admonish minor criminals for first-time drug offenses and petty theft—only I was the one being admonished. I mean, standing where I was standing, for the first time in my life, I finally understood how some of my clients must have felt back when I was working for Legal Aid."

"And that was it?"

"Yes and no. The judge ordered that I be outfitted with a focus mechanism."

"What the hell is that?"

"I don't know yet." Alice sounds scared, and my heart aches for her. "Look, Jake, I have to go. But Victor promised me I'll be released this afternoon. He said you should pick me up at the Half Moon Bay Airport at nine P.M."

"Thank God," I breathe. "I can't wait to see you—"

"I have to go," she interrupts, and then, quickly, "I do love you."

## 40

I DRIVE SOUTH THROUGH DALY CITY, THEN DOWN INTO THE BLEAK-
ness of Pacifica, up the hill and through the beautiful new tunnel.
When I emerge on the other side, into a terrain of mountain cliffs,
winding turns, and beaches glowing in the moonlight, it feels like a different world. And I think what I think every time I exit the tunnel: Why
don't we live here? The peacefulness is undeniable, the views impressive,
the real estate less expensive than San Francisco. The smells of the artichoke and pumpkin farms mix gently with the salt air of the Pacific.

Minutes later, I pull into the parking lot of the Half Moon Bay Airport, expecting to spend some time in the café while I wait for Alice's
flight to arrive. I'm disappointed to find everything dark, the café closed,
no lights on anywhere.

I park by the fence near the end of the runway. I'm half an hour
early. I didn't want Alice to land in Half Moon Bay and be stuck here
alone, in the dark, waiting for me. I turn the lights off and the radio on
and recline my seat. I roll my window down to let in the breeze and to
listen for Alice's plane. There's no air traffic control here, no lights on the
runway, and I wonder how the pilots find this narrow strip of asphalt

by the sea. Small airplanes scare me, just the random precariousness of
it all, tumbling suddenly out of the sky. Every week, it seems, there's a
new report of a dead sports star or musician or politician or the CEO
of some tech company, some guy who decided to take his family on
vacation in his private plane. It seems crazy to me, trusting one's life to
flimsy aerodynamics.

KMOO is on the radio. It's that great show *Anything Is Possible*.
The host, Tom, is just wrapping up an interview with the creator of *Sloganeering*. The showrunner is outlining the direction for the new season.
He brushes off their loss in court to Alice's client as a small misunderstanding, no mention of the judicial nastiness. "Wonderful book," he
says. "We're working with the writer, and in the end I think this will actually make the show better." The show concludes, the news starts, and
I flip the radio off. I think I can hear the ocean in the distance, though
maybe it's the wind blowing through the artichoke fields.

I read for a while, one of Alice's music magazines. The feature story
is a long article on Noel and Liam Gallagher. Then I put the magazine
down and sit in the dark. I obsessively check the clock on the dashboard:
8:43. 8:48. 8:56. I start to think they're not going to arrive. No lights on
at the airport except for a dim glow in a room at the back of the café. Did
I get it wrong? Did they change their minds and decide not to release
Alice? Did something happen?

It's 8:58. Maybe the plane never took off. Maybe she's not coming
home yet. Or worse, maybe there was bad weather in the mountains.

And then, the clock hits 9:00 and the world comes to life. Brilliant
yellow lights spark on both sides of the runway. I hear the faint hum of
an engine. I look up, but I can't see anything. Then in the distance, coming in over the trees, is the outline of a small plane. The aircraft flies low
and slow, touching down smoothly. It glides to a stop at the end of the
runway, not more than fifty yards from where I'm parked. The engine
goes silent, leaving the night still again. I flash the headlights to signal
that I am here. The plane sits motionless.

Where's Alice? I flash the lights again and step out of the car. And
then a door on the plane pops open and the staircase descends, opening
onto a rectangle of light. I recognize Alice's ankle as it emerges from the

plane and hits the first stair. My heart surges. Her legs and waist appear, her chest and face, and then she is standing on the runway. She's wearing the same clothes she was wearing when Declan put her into the SUV days ago. She's walking carefully, oddly upright. Something's wrong, I think. Is she in pain? What have they done to her? Behind her, the staircase folds into the plane. As Alice walks through the fence, under the lamppost, toward the car, I see the reason for her strange posture. There is something around her neck.

She turns her body and waves to the pilot, who flicks on his runway lights and revs his engine. As we meet, she puts her arms around me, shivering. I pull her in close as the plane lifts into the sky. My hands touch the soft mass of her hair and, beneath it, something rigid. The pilot flashes his lights one last time as he soars over the trees and out toward the ocean.

Alice holds me close, and I can feel the stress and tension passing out of her body, but she is standing so straight, so stiff. As I lean back to look at her, I see tears on her cheeks, though she is smiling. "So," she says, as she steps back to model the large collar around her neck. "Here it is, the Focus Mechanism."

The collar circles her neck, extending all the way up to her jawline, where it cups her chin, holding it firmly in place. Like the bracelet she wore on her wrist, it has a smooth, hard gray surface. A narrow ridge of black foam lines the top of the collar where it meets her chin and jawbone. The collar disappears into her shirt, extending just below her shoulders and halfway up the back of her head. She is staring at me, her eyes full of tenderness.

"Are you okay?" I ask.

"Yes. Just between you and me, ever since they put this monstrosity around my neck, I've thought of one thing, and one thing only. *You*." Then she steps back and models her new look one more time. She asks brightly, "How do I look?"

"More beautiful than ever," I say, and mean it.

"Please take me home."

## 41

ARLY THE NEXT MORNING, I SMELL COFFEE, SO I HEAD DOWN THE hallway. I expect to find my wife in her usual spot, typing on her laptop, frantically catching up on work. But she's not there. I pour myself some coffee, then wander back toward the bathroom. No Alice.

Then I see a strip of golden light emanating from the guest bedroom. I push the door open and see Alice standing in front of the full-length mirror, naked. Alice's chin is held up firmly, her eyes focused on her reflection. Her neck remains motionless, locked in place, but her eyes shift to meet mine in the mirror. Her gaze is so direct, I feel unsettled. There is something undeniably pure—sculptural, even—about the collar around her throat. It molds perfectly to the bends and curves of Alice's body, seamless where it hovers a few centimeters beyond her shoulders and chest. Instead of hiding or restricting her, it seems to be framing her beauty. Here in the faint golden light, I think I understand the purpose not only of the collar's design but of The Pact itself: My wife stands before me, more present in the moment than I have ever seen her, completely undistracted, astonishingly resolute in her focus and direction.

I don't know what to say. I stand between her and the mirror. Instinctively, I put my hands on the collar, moving my fingertips along the surface, then along the soft foam cupping her chin. Alice's eyes remain trained on me. The tears from last night are gone, replaced by something else. A look of fascination? I hear Vivian's voice in my head: "You need to make your peace with The Pact."

"Somehow," I say, "it makes you more mysterious."

She steps forward to kiss me, but because she can't lift her neck I have to bend at the knees to meet her mouth with my own.

I go to the corner and sit down in the chair by the window. She doesn't move away from the mirror, and she doesn't attempt to hide her nakedness from me. I don't know that Alice has made her peace, but she does seem to be in another place. As we drove home last night, she seemed energized, although maybe she was just happy to be reunited. When I asked her to give me all the details of the trip, to leave nothing out, she simply said, "I survived." Later, she told me she was proud of herself for pushing through it.

"The only thing that truly scares me," she said, "the only thing that gets under my skin, is the unknown. The unknown terrifies me. Going into this, it was all completely unknown. I have this strange feeling of accomplishment, like I went into something utterly unpredictable and came out on the other end."

"I'm proud of you too," I said. "I feel like you did this for us. That means so much to me."

"I did do it for us."

After dinner, she just wanted to watch an episode of *Sloganeering,* eat ice cream, and retreat to the bedroom. I propped three pillows under her head to make her more comfortable. I thought she would be asleep in a matter of seconds, but she wasn't. She pulled me close, holding on to me with a drowning grip. When I asked what she was thinking, she responded, "Nothing." Which is what she always says when I ask what she's thinking. Sometimes, I believe her. Other times, though, I know the wheels of her mind are spinning, and that's the feeling I had at that moment: me on the outside, looking in.

Eventually, we had sex. I don't know that I'd like to describe it here, though I will say it was unexpected, somewhat unusual. Alice seemed determined and, more than that—possessed. I wanted so badly to know what had happened to her in the desert. Instead I gave in to her passion, her persistence, to this uncanny iteration of Alice. My Alice, only different.

## 42

ALICE TAKES THE DAY OFF FROM WORK. EVEN THOUGH IT'S VALentine's Day, I'm more than a little surprised. I guess it makes sense. Her priorities have shifted. The Pact is working.

Of course, there are the practical concerns: She can't find a suit or even a blouse that will fit around the collar, and besides, she hasn't figured out how to explain it. She emails her paralegal, says the food poisoning has taken a turn for the worse, and that she'll be out of the office for a day or two or three. When I call in to cancel my appointments for the second day in a row, Huang puts Evelyn on the line.

"Everything okay?" Evelyn wants to know.

"It's fine," I say. "Family emergency." Evelyn doesn't pry.

At first Alice seems a little antsy, like she doesn't know what to do with herself, but by ten she seems happy to be free from work, a whole day spread out in front of us.

We take a walk down the beach. Alice wears her baggy coat and wraps a wool scarf around the collar. I bring the camera. When I go to snap a quick picture of her, she yells at me. "I don't want a picture of me in this thing!"

"Come on."

"Never!"

"Just one?" Alice pulls off the scarf and coat, revealing the collar. She looks straight at me and sticks out her tongue.

On the way home, she doesn't even bother with the scarf or coat. I think she's surprised when the people walking by don't seem to notice or care. We stop by Safeway, and our cashier looks up as she finishes bagging our groceries. "Ouch," she says. "Car accident?"

"Yes," Alice says.

And that's it. For the next thirty days, whenever someone comments on it, Alice simply says those two words: "Car accident." That's what she tells them at work, that's what she tells our friends, that's what she tells Ian and Evelyn and Huang when she comes by the office to fetch me for lunch—something she never made time for before. Sometimes, she'll also add the sound of smashing cars and make a dramatic gesture with her hands. No one ever asks any follow-up questions. Except Huang. "Was it a Toyota Corolla or a Honda minivan?" he asked. "My money's on the Corolla—worst drivers ever."

I'll be honest. Every time I glimpse the collar, or just glimpse my wife—sitting or standing upright, chin straight ahead—it makes me sense how committed she really is. Each night, I help her wash beneath the collar, running a warm, soapy washcloth over her skin, threading it between the fiberglass stays. As I watch her, as I cook for her, as I make love to her, as we hold hands in front of the television, what I never say to my wife, what I never confess, is this: Our marriage was my idea, my way of keeping her, yet here we are, just a few months into it, and she has already sacrificed so much more than I have.

# 43

I

T'S ESTIMATED THAT MORE THAN 10 PERCENT OF MARRIED COUPLES got engaged on Valentine's Day. I've taken to asking my clients about the whys and whens of their engagements; interestingly, I've read that couples who got engaged on Valentine's Day have weaker marriages with far less resolve. All I can figure is that a marriage with an impetuous, overly romanticized beginning is likely to end with less resistance.

If engagements occur in February, then divorces, more often than not, occur during the month of January. Studies show that January divorces are slightly more prevalent in the cold-weather states, although January isn't a great month for marriage in places like L.A. and Phoenix either. If I had to guess, I'd say the holiday effect has something to do with it—expectations not met, or maybe the pressure of spending too much time together under the prying eyes of disapproving family members. If close relatives are divorced, it puts even more pressure on a couple. Divorce within a family, in fact, is a strong predictor of other divorces in the same immediate family. When Al and Tipper Gore divorced after forty years of marriage, a year after their daughter Kristin's divorce, the dominoes started to fall. Within the year, another one of their three daughters had also divorced, and by the end of the following year the final shoe dropped; the third daughter was divorced as well. There is some indication that, when people close to us end their marriages, divorce suddenly becomes a viable option.

If divorce begets divorce, it stands to reason that belonging to a private club in which divorce is not only frowned upon but actively discouraged with a strict set of rules and regulations may make divorce far less likely. What I mean to say is: For all its questionable tactics, its weird manual and legal jargon, its secrecy, The Pact may really be onto something.

# 44

On March 10, Alice comes home early to prepare for The Pact party in Woodside. Our host, a guy named Gene, mentioned his love for pinot noir when I met him at the last party, so I stopped at a wine store to pick up a fancy bottle from a Russian River vintner. The production was small, the bottles were hard to get, and the cost was substantial. Alice and I decided the investment was appropriate and necessary.

Ever since Alice returned home from the desert, we haven't discussed our earlier intentions to free ourselves of The Pact. Her time there was so intense, and our relationship since then has felt on such solid ground, that all of the things we hated about The Pact seem, somehow, less onerous. Even the memory of Declan and Diane taking her away has been cast in a new light. It was necessary, Declan said as Diane fastened the cuffs around Alice's ankles, and though I don't believe that's true, I do see how the experience changed her, how it changed us. How it has made us, if possible, *more married.* I can't deny that we are closer now. I can't deny that we are even more in love. If we haven't made our peace with The Pact, we have, at least for the moment, ceased to resist it.

When I finally get home, Alice is already dressed and ready to go. After almost thirty days in the collar, after nearly thirty days of Alice clad in turtlenecks, scarves, blouses with high bows, and baggy trench coats, it's a shock to see her in a tiny gray strapless dress, tall sparkly shoes, and stockings. The collar almost appears to be a part of the dress. She has arranged her hair to work with it, teased up and out. Her hair and her long dark blue nails are Alice circa 2008, her dress is Alice circa now, and the collar is something else altogether.

"So?" she asks, doing an awkward turn.

"Gorgeous."

"Really?"

"Really."

Still, I can't figure out what statement she's making. Is she thumbing her nose at the people of The Pact? Is this her way of telling them that they can't shame her, can't imprison her? Or is the opposite true? Is she showing them that she has accepted their punishment and she is stronger for it? Then again, maybe I'm overanalyzing things. Maybe Alice is just relieved to be going somewhere she doesn't have to hide, doesn't have to answer questions.

I throw on my gray Ted Baker jacket, the one I didn't wear to the first party. I skip the dress tie and opt for dark jeans and the funkier shoes. As I slip the shoes on, it occurs to me that Alice and I are becoming more comfortable in our role in The Pact. Humans, like all animals, have an incredible ability to adapt. Survival requires it.

The traffic is light, so we reach the Woodside Road exit with plenty of time to spare. In town, I ask if Alice wants to grab a drink at the bar in the Village Pub. She thinks for a second, then shakes her head. She doesn't want to be late.

"I could use a drink, though," she says. So I stop at Roberts Market for a six-pack of Peroni. I drive to Huddart Park, pull the car under a sprawling elm tree, and pop a beer for each of us. I can use one too. Eventually I stopped going to Draeger's to look for JoAnne. I worry that she'll be at the party tonight, and I worry that she won't. Alice clinks our bottles together and says, "Bottoms up!" She has trouble bending her head to guzzle it down, but guzzle she does, with only a few drops trickling down her neck and into the top of the collar.

Maybe we are a little nervous, after all. I know the look in her eyes as she swigs the last sip; she's fortifying herself. I check the rearview mirror, half-expecting the police to show up soon.

"Do we have time for another?"

"Maybe." I pull two more out of the bag.

Alice snatches the bottle out of my hand and sucks it down. "Light-weight," she says. "Don't let me have even one more drink tonight. I can't afford to say something I'll regret."

Alice sometimes has trouble controlling herself at parties. Her residual middle school nerves make it hard for her to initiate conversation, and when she does start talking, she doesn't always know when to stop. At the opening party for my new office, she mistook the head caterer for Ian's partner. Of course, at parties like that, one beer too many and a few wrong words only lead to embarrassment and maybe an awkward apology down the road. Tonight, one wrong sentence and she might find herself in a black SUV speeding into the desert.

"Ready?"

"No," Alice says, taking a deep breath.

We turn onto Bear Gulch Road and pull up to a keypad in front of a large, intimidating gate. 665544, just like the card said. The gate rumbles to life.

"It's not too late," I say. "We can turn and run, maybe head for Greece."

"No," Alice says. "Greece has extradition. It would have to be Venezuela or North Korea."

We work our way up the mountain road, past estates and pastures. Around every turn, if you look carefully, you can see a grand house hiding in the woods. Woodside is just Hillsborough with horses. The road goes on and on. Alice doesn't say a word, even as I identify the address and turn up the long driveway. While this place is not quite on the level of the mansion in Hillsborough, it is impressive. Gene, our host, is an architect, and it shows. Globe lights line a path up to the main structure, a tall, wide sculpture of a house. When they invented the phrase *real estate porn,* this is what they had in mind.

I pull into a spot at the end and kill the engine. Alice sits there for a moment, her eyes closed. "I might need another beer."

"No," I say.

She frowns.

"You'll thank me later."

"Bastard."

We exit the car and stand for a minute, both awed by the beauty of the house and the maze of a path leading up to it. We stand at the edge of the path for a full minute, holding hands, not speaking. It's very possible that we are on the wrong path; unfortunately, turning around is not an option.

## 45

IN HINDSIGHT, I SUPPOSE IT WAS FAST: ALICE AND I HAD ONLY KNOWN each other for a little over a year when we decided to purchase a house together. Buying property in San Francisco, of course, is insanely difficult. Alice and I spent less than twenty minutes in the house before we offered a million and change, with 20 percent down, no contingencies. That was a couple of years ago, when houses were still "attainable."

Months after moving in, I noticed a power line going up and under one of the walls in the garage. It puzzled me, so I pulled back on all of the plywood, one piece at a time. At first I was just expecting to find the innards of the wall, electrical stuff, whatever. But there, behind the plywood, was a tiny room, complete with a chair in the middle and a built-in desk. On the desk there was a packet of photos. They appeared to have all been taken on a family vacation to Seattle in the 1980s. How could we not have known about the secret room when we first moved in?

I think of Alice that way sometimes. I keep searching for the small, hidden mystery. Usually, Alice is exactly who I think she is, but every now and then, when I'm really paying attention, I find that hidden room.

She doesn't talk about her family, so I was surprised recently when she commented about a trip her father had taken. The television was on, an old episode of *Globe Trekker,* and the hosts were working their way through the Netherlands. "Amsterdam's a great city," she said, "but I can never get out of my own head when I'm there."

"Why?"

She told me about how, soon after her mother died, her brother joined the Army. I don't know much about the brother, beyond the fact that in his teens he suffered depression and became an addict, demons that plagued him until his suicide in his early twenties. Alice told me that no one had expected him to enlist, and that it seemed absurd that the Army would let him in, with his documented history of depression. Alice's father went to see the recruiter and tried to talk him out of it, explaining all the reasons why it was a terrible idea. But the recruiter had quotas, and once he had gotten the signature, it was clear that he wasn't letting go of the stat.

Alice's brother shocked the whole family by making it through basic training. They were proud of him but worried when he was shipped off to Germany. "I told my father maybe it was a good thing," Alice said. "Maybe it would straighten him out. And my father just gave me a look like I was an idiot. 'There is no magic cure for things,' he said." Ten weeks later, when the family got the call that Alice's brother had gone AWOL, no one was really surprised.

"So close on the heels of my mother's death," Alice said, "Brian's disappearance struck my dad and me like a ton of bricks. When I woke up the next morning, my father was gone too. He left me some cash, a fully stocked kitchen, the keys to the car, and a note saying that he'd gone to find Brian. The world seemed enormous to me then, and so the idea that my father was just going to wander around, expecting to find Brian, seemed crazy."

Alice's father called her that night. And every night for the next three weeks. When she asked where he was, he would simply say that he was finding Brian. Then one night he didn't call. "I cried," Alice told me. "I'd never cried like that before, and I've never cried like that since. I'd lost my mother and my brother, and now I thought I'd lost my father too. You have to understand, I was seventeen. I felt so alone."

The next day, she didn't go to school. She stayed home, miserable on the couch, watching TV, not sure what to do or whom to call. She made macaroni and cheese for dinner and was eating in the kitchen, over the stove, when she heard a taxi pull up. She raced to the window.

"It was crazy," Alice told me. "I see my father get out one side, my brother get out the other. They come in, and we all sit down and eat the mac and cheese."

Alice said that she always assumed that Brian had gone back to the Army and her father had gotten him discharged. It wasn't until years later that she learned the amazing truth. Her father had spent those three weeks wandering around Amsterdam, hundreds of miles from where Brian had last been seen—going to cafés, hostels, train stations, wandering around at night looking for him. Her brother and father had always had an intense connection, like her father could almost read Brian's mind, Alice said. Although Brian had never been to Amsterdam, somehow their father just knew that he would be there, knew exactly where to look.

When Alice told me the story, it felt like that mystery room in our garage. It resonated and made me see Alice in a new light. Brian was obsessive, driven in all the wrong ways, the world outside fading as he pursued something only he could see. Alice's father, unwilling to accept that his son was gone, was equally obsessive, undeterred in his unlikely search. The genetic foundation of Brian's illness certainly began somewhere. It was the full spectrum of obsessive behavior, both the best and the worst of it, all in one family. Seen in that light, Alice's obsessive need to succeed at any pursuit, to follow a plan through to the very end, no matter where it might lead, somehow makes sense.

# 46

I TAKE ALICE'S ARM IN MINE AND WE WALK UP THE LIT PATH. The trail winds through a grove of fragrant trees that end at the entrance to the majestic home. Glass, wood, steel beams, polished concrete, indoor-outdoor living, a pool, and an unexpected view out across Silicon Valley.

"Nice house," Alice says, deadpan.

Gene steps out through the massive, heavy front door. "Friends."

I hand him the bottle, and he says, "You shouldn't have." Then he glances down at the label. "Oh, you really shouldn't have! But I'm glad you did."

Turning toward my wife, he says, "Alice, Friend, you truly sparkle." Gene is old enough to get away with saying something like that, and he's apparently familiar enough with The Pact not to be surprised by the Focus Collar.

"Thank you, Gene. I love your house."

From across the patio, Vivian appears. "Well, if it isn't my favorite couple!" She gives Alice a big hug. Like Gene, she doesn't acknowledge the collar. Then Vivian turns to kiss me on both cheeks, as though our conversation at Java Beach never happened, as though I never told her we wanted out of The Pact. "Friend," she whispers in my ear, "I am so happy to see you." Perhaps I'm wrong, but I suspect this is her way of telling me that the unpleasant business is now behind us, my sins washed away.

Gene leads us through the house, stopping for a moment at the bar, where two glasses of champagne are waiting. A dozen bottles of Cristal are lined up behind the bar. He holds his glass up to ours, toasting, "To Friends."

"To Friends," Alice repeats.

Gene notices me looking at the painting above the concrete fireplace. In college, my roommate had a poster of this painting over his desk, something he purchased when he wanted to be "more adultlike."

I'm mesmerized once again by the three stripes, the brilliant colors, complementing and contrasting one another, all evoking a specific feeling, both together and separate. Somehow I am transported back to that dorm room, only now I really am more adultlike.

Alice turns her gaze upward. "That is *not* a freaking Rothko!"

Gene's wife, Olivia, joins us. She's wearing an apron over her dress, though she carries herself so gracefully I doubt she's ever spilled anything on her clothes. Like Vivian, she has an air of almost eerie calm about her.

Olivia slides her arm around my waist and shepherds me closer to the painting. "Rothko recommended that the painting be viewed from eighteen inches. He believed his works needed companionship." She leaves her arm around my waist long enough that I begin to feel uncomfortable, unsure what to do with my arms. So I cross them and stand as still as possible. "This painting is a pain in the ass," she remarks.

"Why?"

"It was a gift from Gene for our tenth anniversary. But the accountant made us have it appraised, and now all I do is worry about it." Olivia tugs at my hand. "Come, let's join the others outside. They're all waiting to see you."

At regular parties, people tend to show up fashionably late. Not here. It's six-ten, and it appears that all of the guests have arrived, parked, and begun drinking champagne and enjoying the hors d'oeuvres. Unlike at the first party, the food isn't fancy. Apparently, not everyone can pull off a canapé in their sleep. I'm relieved to see the simple platters of cheese and fruit, along with basic crudités and some shrimp wrapped in bacon. When it comes our turn, Alice and I might actually be able to pull off this kind of spread.

Everyone greets us with smiles and hugs, addressing us as "Friend." It gives me the creeps, but in a warm kind of way, if that's possible. They all seem to remember everything about us, and I try to recall the last time anyone at Alice's firm remembered anything about me. These people pay attention. Maybe too much attention, but still there's something flattering about it. Men I only vaguely recognize walk up and pick up exactly where we left off in our conversation three months ago.

A guy named Harlan is asking me about my therapy practice, his wife quizzing Alice about law, when I notice JoAnne talking to a couple by the pool. I try to catch her eye but fail. Just then, Neil appears at my side. "JoAnne looks lovely tonight, doesn't she?" he says, so quietly that only I can hear.

"Certainly," I say. But the way he squeezes my shoulder—too hard, not exactly friendly—makes me think it was the wrong answer.

He glances at Alice, his eyes lingering on the collar. "I must say, Friend, you look stunning."

She touches the collar. "I can't take credit for the accessory."

I'm biting into a brownie, trying to think of something to say to Neil, when our host from last time appears. "You might want to hold off on that," Kate teases. I stop midbite, uncertain. "Hello, Friend," she says. "Nice to see you again!"

"Hello, Friend," I echo. Alice glances at me, startled.

Kate leans in and gives me a kiss on the lips. I taste her earthy lipstick and smell the vanilla in her fragrance. There is nothing sensual about the kiss, but it does tell me that we are far closer friends than I realized. It seems to be this way with all of the members.

"Are you two ready for your weigh-in?"

Alice and I stare at her blankly.

Kate laughs. "Clearly you haven't read all of the attachments and appendices."

"I don't recall any attachments."

"Each year the Guiding Committee puts out updates and new regulations," Kate explains. "Your manual should have contained them. They would have been loose papers in the back of the book."

"I'm sure there were no loose papers." Alice is frowning.

"Really?" Neil says, surprised. "I'll have to talk with Vivian."

I'm secretly pleased. Apparently, Vivian has screwed up. I wonder what the punishment will be.

"Oh well," Kate says. "Oversights are unusual, but they do occur. The new regulations came out right before you two joined, which might explain it. For our group, first-quarter meeting is the annual weigh-in. We do the fit test during the third quarter. Better to split them up, I think."

Kate turns to Alice. Unlike the others, she acknowledges the Focus Collar. "Ah, I trust you've found this enlightening," she says, running her finger over the smooth gray finish. She confides, "Just between us, Friend, I had one too, years ago. This new model is certainly an improvement. These days, they use a three-D printer, I hear, so each one fits perfectly. It's expensive, of course, but as you probably know, the investment team had a spectacular year."

"Investment team?" Alice asks.

"Of course!" Kate says. "Those three members from the London School of Economics and our friends from Sand Hill Road have certainly changed things for all of us. There's funding for pretty much anything The Pact deems necessary. My collar was so heavy, even a few rough edges. No foam." Her fingers flutter to the scar on her chin.

Then she shakes her head, as if coming out of a trance. "So, should we head to the bedroom and get this done? You two are my last." She takes us arm in arm and marches us toward the house. Alice awkwardly turns her body sideways to shoot me a quick glance. She doesn't seem the least bit afraid, just amused.

Kate leads us into a palatial bedroom with floor-to-ceiling windows. On the wall, there's a large canvas print signed by Matt Groening. It's a drawing of Gene, in the style of *The Simpsons*. The character is dressed exactly the way Gene is dressed tonight. He is also holding a champagne glass. Underneath, there's sloppy writing: *Gene, the house is marvelous. Thank you.*

"The bathroom is through there," Kate says, pointing. "Strip as far as you like. Don't be modest; I went the full monty myself. Every ounce counts. The requirement is that you must always remain within five percent of your weight on the day of your wedding."

"What if I was fat on the day of my wedding? I wouldn't be allowed to lose more than five percent of my body weight?" I wasn't, but it's a fair question.

"Oh, that never happens," she says, smiling. "All of our members, as you know, are vetted thoroughly before being invited into the fold. Anyway, the penalty for the first violation is a Misdemeanor Six. After that, things get a little sticky. You two really need to do your homework."

"I couldn't agree more," I say jovially, trying to play along.

"Who's my first victim?" Kate asks.

"That would be me." Alice moves toward the bathroom. "I need every last ounce I can shed. The collar puts me at a disadvantage."

"Don't you worry about that," Kate says. "It's three pounds, two ounces, we have it in your records. The weight of the collar is subtracted."

While we wait for Alice to return, Kate fiddles with a sleek scale on the floor, then opens a laptop on the dresser. I watch her access a website featuring a blinking blue *P* and a log-in bar. She types quickly, and in an instant a spreadsheet appears on the screen. On the left of the spreadsheet is a row of photographs—Alice and me among them. Next to the photos is a series of numbers. I move toward the dresser to get a better look, but Kate snaps the laptop closed.

When the bathroom door opens, Alice is standing there in just the collar, her bra, and underwear. She steps onto the scale. Kate reads the number and punches it into the laptop. "Your turn," she says to me. I follow Alice into the bathroom.

When the door is closed, I whisper, "This is so freaking *weird*."

"If I'd known, I would've skipped those beers beforehand. I was in here trying to pee as much as I could."

"Good idea," I say, standing in front of the toilet with the heated Japanese seat. "Should I fully strip down? And how the hell do they know what I weighed on our wedding day?"

Alice puts her clothes back on as I take off my shoes, pants, and belt.

I leave the underwear, shirt, and socks on. "Honey," Alice says, "you might want to lose the rest of it if you think it's going to be close."

I think for a second, then strip off my shirt and socks. "The boxer briefs stay," I insist. Laughing, Alice opens the door, and Kate looks up from her computer and winks at Alice as if they're in on some private joke.

I step on the scale and suck in my stomach, not that it will make a difference, but still. Kate reads the number aloud and punches it into the computer. While I'm getting dressed in the bathroom, I can hear Alice and Kate talking in the bedroom. Alice asks how we did.

"Oh, that's not in my duties; I just punch in the numbers."

"How did you become responsible for the weigh-in?"

"It was like any other directive. One day I received a package by messenger. It contained instructions, some access codes, the glass scale, and this laptop. As far as Pact jobs go, it's not a bad one."

"Does everyone have a job? I haven't heard anything about that."

"Yes. Soon, you and Jake will be assigned duties according to your abilities and skill sets, as determined by the Work Committee."

Alice raises her eyebrows, surprised. "What about my actual job?"

"I'm certain you'll find your duties in The Pact are an actual job. I assure you, the Work Committee never gives a member more than he or she can handle."

I step out of the bathroom. "And what if someone refuses?" I ask.

Kate gives me a slightly disapproving look. "Friend" is all she says.

We head back to the party. The dinner is a salad and a small slice of tuna on a bed of rice. Bland but serviceable. I'll try to talk Alice into stopping for a burger on the way home. After everyone has helped clear the plates away, Gene and Olivia appear from the kitchen carrying a three-tiered birthday cake, lit with dozens of candles. All of the members who have had birthdays this month stand up as we sing "Happy Birthday."

JoAnne approaches the cake; apparently she recently turned thirty-nine. I haven't talked to her all night. For some reason, whenever I look for her, she is on the far side of the party. The assigned dinner seating had me between Beth, a scientist, and Steve, her news anchor husband.

JoAnne was on the other side of the table at the far end. Now, as she walks past, she doesn't even acknowledge me. I suddenly realize that she's the only one who hasn't greeted me with an overly generous hug and the words "Hello, Friend."

JoAnne is wearing a conservative blue dress. She looks thin and pale. On the back of her calves, I notice marks, maybe bruises.

Later, Alice and I are talking to a couple, Chuck and Eve, on the patio, when I see JoAnne heading inside the house. Her husband, Neil, is standing with Dave, Alice's counselor, at the far end of the yard, where a big screen has been set up to broadcast tonight's Warriors game. They're leaning against a wide, low concrete wall, about four feet high, that seems more sculptural than functional. I slip away from the conversation and follow JoAnne inside. I don't think she's seen me, but as I round the corner to the bathroom she's standing there waiting for me.

"You can't do this, Jake."

"What?"

"You have to stop going to Draeger's."

"What?" I'm confused and embarrassed. Has she seen me and said nothing? "I have so many questions—"

"Look, I shouldn't have said those things. My mistake. Just forget it. Pretend it didn't happen."

"I can't. Can we just talk?"

"No."

"Please."

"Not here. Not now."

"When?"

She hesitates. "Hillsdale food court, across from Panda Express, next Friday, eleven A.M. Make sure you're not followed. Seriously, Jake. Don't fuck it up." She walks away without looking back.

Outside, Neil is still watching the basketball game. Dave has wandered off, and Neil is alone, sitting on the concrete wall, his legs dangling over the side. Something about him strikes me as familiar, but I can't put a finger on it. Alice is still talking to Chuck and Eve. Chuck is telling the story of how they came to have Gene design them a vacation house. Chuck has a slight accent, maybe Australian. "It was a while back, before we were established. He offered to do it, so we scrambled to find the funds to buy a piece of property. My friend Wiggins told me about a lot adjacent to his spread in Hopland. It was cheap, so we snagged it. The whole thing is glass and concrete, views everywhere. Gene is a magician."

"You guys have to see it," Eve says. "Want to join us for a weekend?"

I'm fishing through my mind for the appropriate excuse to decline the invitation when I hear Alice say, "Sure, that sounds fun."

Before I can protest, Chuck is already on to picking a date. "We're family," he says, "so this will count for one of you toward your trips for the year."

Alice blurts out, "Dibs."

"We have a pool," Eve adds, "so bring your suits."

Just before midnight, the party clears out. In an instant, it goes from thirty people standing around talking and drinking to a nearly empty patio, with just me, Alice, Gene, Olivia, and one other couple. Alice obviously doesn't want to leave. I'm very surprised. While she has always been more social than me, and while we haven't really gotten out much lately other than our required date nights, I figured we were on the same page with The Pact. My simple logic was that if it didn't look like there was any way out, and it didn't, the best thing to do was to minimize the amount of time we spent with the members. The less we see them, the less they see us, the less likely we are to get into trouble. More time together means more risk. Has Alice forgotten this?

We say our goodbyes, and Gene sees us to the door. All the way down the long path to where we're parked, neither of us says a word. I open the car door and wait as Alice maneuvers herself, collar and all, into the passenger side. Once in the car, I relax. We have, as far as I can tell, survived our first quarter in The Pact.

"That was fun," Alice says, no trace of sarcasm in her voice.

As I pull out, I notice Gene and Neil standing at the top of the driveway, watching us.

## 47

On Tuesday, Vivian calls Alice and asks her to meet for lunch at Sam's, an old-time Italian restaurant in the Financial District. All day, I'm nervous, wondering what they'll talk about, what bizarre new punishment or directive Vivian will pass down from on high. Or maybe we performed well at the party, and today will bring good news. Does The Pact ever deliver good news? Could this be the end of the collar?

I get home from work at five-fifteen and sit at the window, reading, watching for Alice. At six-fifteen, her car pulls into the driveway. The garage door opens, then I hear her steps on the side stairs. I'm in the kitchen waiting when she opens the door, and the first thing I notice is her posture: more relaxed, more easy, more *Alice*. The scarf she wore this morning is gone. Her blouse is open at the neck. She does a little spin for me and grins.

"It's gone," I say, taking her in my arms. "How does it feel to be free?"

"Great. But strange. I guess I wasn't using my neck muscles, and now I'm paying the price. I think I need to lie down."

We go back to the bedroom, and Alice lies on top of the sheets. I fix up her pillow so she's comfortable and sit on the bed beside her.

"Tell me everything."

"Vivian was already there when I arrived," Alice says. "She was sitting in one of the enclosed booths. I went in, and the waiter closed the curtain to give us privacy. There was no small talk. She didn't even mention the party. She told me she'd received the directive to remove the collar. The removal directive was set for one o'clock, though, so I had to wear it during lunch." She sits up to readjust the pillow. "I asked Vivian if I could keep it."

"Why on earth?"

Alice shrugs and lies back down again. "It's hard to explain, but I wanted it as a souvenir, I guess. Vivian just said it was against protocol."

The next morning, after Alice has left for work, I'm in the kitchen making coffee when there's a knock at the door. It's a bike messenger, a kid of about twenty, carrying a large envelope marked with the telltale *P* in the upper left-hand corner. He's out of breath, so I offer him a glass of water and invite him inside. He follows me into the kitchen, filling the room with his nervous energy, answering questions I haven't asked. "I'm Jerry," he says. "I moved to San Francisco from Elko, Nevada, three years ago, chasing a job at a start-up. The start-up folded a few weeks after I arrived, and I landed this gig."

I hand him a glass of water. He downs it in one long gulp. "You guys live way the fuck out here. I've got to get a new job. If these Wednesday packages didn't pay so much, I would've a long time ago."

"You deliver others like this?"

"Yep. They've got me on retainer—Wednesdays only. Sometimes I'll have two or three, other days I have none."

"Where do you pick them up?"

"This tiny office on Pier Twenty-three, always the same guy. He tells me I'm their only messenger, I'm the only one they trust. The application process was a bitch. Background check, fingerprints, the works. Although I didn't apply, exactly. They called me with some story about how they'd gotten my name from my former employer, although my former employer was already in Costa Rica by then, spending the VC's money. Anyway, as soon as I'd passed their test, they sent me out on my first delivery. It's been every Wednesday since then, just about."

"Always in San Francisco?"

"Nah, I cover the East Bay, the Peninsula all the way down to San Jose, and Marin. I bike it when I'm in the city, but otherwise I have to drive. I don't know who they are, but I know they have deep pockets, 'cause I make more money on Wednesday deliveries than I do during the entire rest of the week. Yikes, I'm pretty sure I wasn't supposed to tell you any of that. We're good, though, right?"

"Yes, we're good."

He sets his glass on the counter and checks his wristband—an activity tracker. "Gotta go. I've got one last one in San Mateo." As he's putting on his helmet, he asks, too casually, "Do *you* know who they are?"

If this is a test—and isn't everything with The Pact?—there's only one correct answer: "Not a clue."

Before I can ask him any more questions, he's out the door, back on his bike.

The envelope has Alice's name on the front, so I text her: *You just got a package from The Pact.*

She replies with one word: *Shit.*

I shower and get dressed for work. I stare at the unopened envelope, the large *P* printed in gold ink, Alice's name in an elegant script. I pick it up and hold it to the light, but I can't see anything. I place it back on the table and walk to work, vowing not to think about it. Of course I think about it all day.

When I get home that evening, Alice is sitting at the table, looking at the package. "I guess we have to open it," she says.

"Guess so."

She breaks the seal and carefully pulls out the document. It's just one page, divided into four sections. She reads each one aloud. Under the heading Rules is a paragraph about the yearly weigh-in. The footnote says that the paragraph is *"excerpted from the most recent amendment appendix."* That would be the amendment appendix Vivian failed to include in our manuals.

The second section is *"Infraction: You have exceeded the allowed weight gain by three pounds, six ounces."*

"It was the beers," Alice groans. "The ones I drank right before the weigh-in. Also, it was a couple of days before my period. Women should be allowed a higher fluctuation than men. You'd think Orla would take that into consideration."

The third section, Mitigating Circumstances, states, *"It has come to our attention that your Handler may have omitted this appendix from your manual. This issue will be addressed separately."*

Alice looks up and grins. "Looks like Vivian may get a taste of her own medicine."

"What else does it say?"

She reads on: *"While the Rule must still be applied, due to the failure of the Handler to provide proper documentation, in addition to this being your first weight-related offense, you will be offered a Diversion Program."*

Then she falls silent, her eyes scanning the page.

When she puts the paper down, she's close to tears.

"What the hell have they thought up this time?" I ask, worried. She's very pale.

"No, it's not the punishment. It's—oh, Jake. I feel like this whole thing is a test, and I've failed."

"Sweetheart." I take her hand. "None of these rules are *real*. You realize that, don't you?"

"I know," she says, pulling her hand away. "But still, you have to admit that if I were to follow all of the rules, I'd be a better wife."

I shake my head. "That's not true. You're perfect, exactly as you are."

I pick up the document and read the fourth section, Punishment.

You have been assigned a daily workout regimen. You must report to the corner of Taraval and the Great Highway every morning at five, including weekends. Your trainer will be there waiting for you.

# 48

I WAKE ABRUPTLY FROM A DEEP SLEEP. I WAS IN THE MIDDLE OF A nightmare, though I can't recall the details. Alice is asleep. I pause for a moment to watch her. Her hair is a mess. In her Sex Pistols T-shirt and flannel pajama bottoms, she looks like the woman I first met.

The details of the dream come to me: the desperate kicking, the endless ocean stretching on for miles. A water dream. I've had them off and on for years, and I do what I always do when I awake from one of these dreams: wander down the hallway to the bathroom. Then I peer into the kitchen to check the time: 4:43 in the morning. Crap.

"Alice!" I yell. "It's four forty-three!"

I hear her flop out of bed in a panic, two thuds as her feet hit the floor. "Holy shit! What happened to the alarm?"

"I'll give you a ride. Get your workout clothes on. *Fast.*"

Panicked, I race around looking for the keys and my wallet. I throw on pants, hurry down to the garage, get the car started, pull out of the garage. Alice comes running out of the house, holding her shoes and sweatshirt. She jumps into the car and I take off down Thirty-eighth, then left at the Great Highway. I pull up onto the side of the road, right at the Taraval intersection. There's a guy standing there. He's thirty-five maybe, impeccable shape, stylish workout gear in Euro colors—army green and pale orange. Alice jumps out. I roll down the window to wish her luck, but she's not even looking back.

"Four fifty-nine," the guy says, looking at his watch. "Nice timing. I was starting to think you weren't going to make it."

"No way," she says. "I'm here." Within seconds of their introduction, he has her doing high kicks. I turn the car around and head home. Feeling too wired to go back to sleep, I sit down with my laptop.

At 6:17, Alice walks through the door, sweaty and exhausted. I offer to make her a smoothie. "No time," she insists, "I've got to get to work."

"How was it?"

"Sorry, I'm late; we'll talk about it tonight."

But that night we're both beat. We eat takeout in front of the TV, watching *Sloganeering*. I mute the TV when a pharmaceutical commercial comes on, a forgettable florist smilingly greeting her forgettable husband. "How was the trainer?" I ask.

"His name's Ron. Lives in the Castro. Nice guy, very gung ho. Lots of jump squats." She reaches down to massage her calves. *Sloganeering* comes back on, and she nudges me to turn up the volume.

The next morning, the alarm goes off at four-thirty. I roll over to wake Alice, but she's already up. I find her sitting on the couch, dressed in workout gear. She offers me a smile, but from the puffiness of her eyes and the look on her face I think she may have been crying. I fix her a quick cup of coffee. "Want a ride?"

"Yes."

We walk down to the car in silence. On the six-minute ride to the beach, Alice falls asleep. I wake her when we get there. I see Ron jogging down Taraval toward us. It's possible that he has run all the way here from the Castro.

The following morning, my alarm once again goes off at four-thirty. I sit up just in time to hear Alice pulling out of the garage.

The next morning, when the alarm wakes me, Alice is already gone.

## 49

MY NEW CLIENTS, A COUPLE FROM COLE VALLEY, SMILE AS THEY walk through the door and sit side by side on the small sofa. Neither even seems to consider the big, comfy chair. Their marriage will survive; I know this already. Nonetheless, we'll talk. We'll probably meet three more times before they come to the same conclusion.

During our last meeting, I asked them to think about a good memory they have together. In response, the wife has brought pictures from their wedding. "You have to see the bridesmaids' dresses," Janice says. "I'm surprised my bridesmaids still talk to me." I laugh when I see the photographs of Janice in a simple white dress, flanked on both sides by girls covered in green taffeta, and lots of it.

"Did you know that bridesmaids' dresses were traditionally white?" I say.

"How could anyone tell the bridesmaids from the bride?" Ethan asks.

"They couldn't. It's the whole reason the concept of the bridesmaid came about. In tribal times, the bridesmaids, clad in white bridal dresses, served as decoys. If the wedding was raided by a neighboring tribe, the hope was that the invaders would be confused and would accidentally kidnap a bridesmaid instead of the bride."

It's an easy session. They clearly like each other but have begun to drift apart. We talk about some strategies they can implement to spend more time together and liven up their conversations. It's not rocket science, just the usual fixes, which actually work pretty well. I nearly laugh when I catch myself suggesting that they should make it a goal to get away on one trip every quarter.

Occasionally, a couple will show up for counseling and I won't be entirely sure why they're here. Janice and Ethan are like that. I feel a little guilty for accepting their money, because they don't need me at all. Still, I'm encouraged by their commitment to making it work. I find myself envying the natural ebb and flow of their marriage, existing in peace far from The Pact.

After Janice and Ethan leave, I place my phone in a sealed envelope and go over to Huang's desk. "Why don't you take a long lunch?" I suggest.

"How long?"

"Maybe go to that place you like in Dogpatch. My treat." I hand him a couple of twenties and set the envelope on his desk. "And, while you're at it, would you mind keeping this with you? Just put it in your pocket and forget about it."

Huang stares at the envelope. "You mind telling me what's in that?"

"Long story."

"It's not going to explode or anything, right?"

"Definitely not."

He feels the envelope and frowns. "If I had to guess, I'd say you stuck your cellphone in here."

"You'd be doing me a big favor," I say. "Just hold on to it, and when you get back from lunch you can leave it on my desk. And if you don't mind, don't mention it to Ian and Evelyn."

"Mention what?"

"Thanks. I owe you."

I walk home, get my car, drive downtown, and park in a lot on

Fourth Street. I walk over to the Caltrain station and buy a round-trip ticket to the Hillsdale station in San Mateo.

I haven't told Alice that I set up this meeting with JoAnne. I thought about telling her this morning, but then I ended up leaving before she got back from her workout. Anyway, I didn't want to bother her with it. She's got the workouts with Ron every morning and has resumed seeing Dave once a week in the afternoon as part of her probation; and her job just keeps getting more demanding. Alice is overwhelmed, and I don't want to add this business with JoAnne on top of everything else. And okay, if I'm honest, I have to admit maybe I don't really want to tell her. I know she'd have all kinds of questions about JoAnne, and I don't necessarily want to answer them. She wouldn't like the idea of me meeting another woman for lunch, a woman who isn't a colleague. Of course, lies of omission are against the rules of The Pact. But as I'm walking from my car to the station, I convince myself that this obfuscation is a noble act. If anyone were to discover my lie of omission, it would be on me, and I'd be saving Alice from committing yet another felony, one that The Pact claims to take very seriously: jealousy.

One way to look at it is this: I'm trading Alice's future crime for my present one. Turn their attention away from Alice, JoAnne urged at Draeger's that day.

I walk the entire length of the train but don't see anything out of the ordinary. These days, the trains are packed at all hours with tech workers commuting between San Francisco and Silicon Valley. They're mostly young, mostly thin, mostly entitled—white and Asian newcomers who, as a group, have driven rental prices through the roof and have shown little appreciation for what is unique and cool about San Francisco. They don't seem to care about the great bookstores, the iconic record stores, the grand old theaters. Maybe it's unfair to lump them all together, but they seem to care about only one thing: money. They have an air of dull inexperience, as if they've never traveled or read books for pleasure or gone to bed with some girl they met in a Laundromat. And right at this moment, they're taking up the handicap seats, laptops spread across their knees.

At the Hillsdale station, I get off with about twenty other people—

locals, mostly, because the techies don't stop here, at least not yet. I linger in the station until everyone else has moved on. There's one woman in a tailored black suit who keeps hanging around, looking out of place, and I've pretty much decided she's spying on me, but then a Mercedes pulls up, a younger man inside. She tugs at her skirt in a way that suggests she's wearing garters under the business suit, walks to his car, and climbs in. They drive away.

I walk across El Camino and up toward the mall, feeling slightly foolish, like a kid playing spy games. I tell myself none of this is necessary, but then I think about the bracelet, the collar, Alice's harrowing trip to the desert, and I realize once again that it *is* necessary.

I stop into Trader Joe's, killing time, watching for anyone suspicious, and end up walking out with only a bottle of water and three chocolate bars. Of course, now every time I eat sweets I instinctively think of the next weigh-in. Is this the ounce of fat that might put me over the limit? Is this the calorie that might land me in the desert? I hate The Pact for that.

I wander into Barnes & Noble and pick up the new issue of *Q* for Alice. Paul Heaton and Briana Corrigan are on the cover—she'll be happy. I cross the street and enter the mall. I still have thirty minutes to kill, so I wander around the shops. I've been having an inexplicable longing for a comfortable plaid flannel shirt—Freud would probably say it comes from a nostalgia for youth—so I do a speedy walk-through of all of the usual mall places. I find something on the sale rack at Lucky Jeans and walk out with a bag, now looking like everyone else in the mall, only older.

Over at the food court, I'm still seven minutes early. I hang out at the far end, just watching the people come and go.

I see JoAnne enter the food court through the side door that leads out to the parking lot. Her furtive glances, like a deer in a wide-open field, make me nervous. Do I really want to go through with this? I stand back, watching her. She sits across from Panda Express, at a table by the window. I wish she'd chosen a more discreet spot. She pulls a phone out of her purse and begins to fidget. I wish she hadn't brought her phone. The words she whispered to me at the party echo in my head: *Don't fuck it up.* Until now it hadn't occurred to me that she might be the one to fuck it up.

I continue watching her, scanning the space to see if she was followed. She makes a call that only lasts a few seconds. Unlike me, she seems oblivious to the crowd in the food court. She pulls something out of her purse—a granola bar—unwraps it, and eats it with tiny bites, head down. Occasionally, she looks up abruptly, but never in my direction. She's paranoid, it seems, but not thorough. She acts a little manic, a little edgy—nothing like the JoAnne I knew in college. That JoAnne was remarkable for her incredible calmness. Even in the most difficult situations, she seemed uncannily mellow. She was never beautiful or even striking, but it was this placid confidence, this utter lack of insecurity, that made her stand out in a crowd.

The woman across the food court from me now is unrecognizable. Although I would never say this to my clients, deep down I've come to believe that most people don't change. Maybe they are able to accentuate some parts of their personality over others; there's no doubt that good nurturing in childhood can guide one's natural inclinations in a positive direction. I've spent a great deal of my professional life searching for useful tools to help people direct their personalities in a positive way. However, for the most part, I believe that we all have to work from the hand of cards we are dealt early on. When I see people who have undergone extreme personality shifts, I'm always curious to know the root cause. What is the button, the push point, the inciting action that overrides someone's nature? What makes people appear, to those who know them well, so different?

As I said, over time stress, anxiety, and psychological difficulties always show in a person's face. I've seen signs of trouble in JoAnne: the pronounced vein snaking from her left brow into her hairline, the downward tug at the corners of her mouth, lines near the eyes. Something tells me she needs help, but I'm not the one to offer it. Something tells me to walk away, but I can't.

Because here's the thing: I still want to hear what she has to say. I want insight into The Pact. I refuse to give up hope that there is some way out for Alice and me. Maybe JoAnne's anxiety, the changes in her face and body, her voice, are a perfectly logical response to The Pact. If so, I don't want to see that happen to Alice.

At Hot Dog on a Stick, I order two hot dogs and two green lemonades. I walk to JoAnne's table and set the tray of food down in front of her.

She looks up from her phone, and the vein in her forehead throbs. "Jake," she says. Just "Jake," not "Friend." There's a weary softness in her voice. I see beyond the exhaustion in her eyes to something else—warmth—and it relaxes me.

"Hot dog on a stick?"

"You shouldn't have," she says, but she grabs one and takes a big bite. Then she stabs the straw through the hole of the plastic lid and takes a long drink.

"I was thinking you might not show up," she says.

"Have I ever not shown up?"

"If you knew what was good for you, you wouldn't have. But I'm glad you're here."

She puts her hands on the table, pointing in my direction. I'm tempted to glance under the table and look at her feet. It's the direction the feet are pointing—not the hands—that indicates a person's true interest. She has long, shiny pink nails. I remember her short unpolished nails from college. "What have we gotten ourselves into, Jake?"

"I was hoping you could tell me."

"When I saw you at Villa Carina, I wanted to whisper in your ear, 'Run, don't come back,' but I knew it was already too late. At the same time, and I apologize for saying this, I was happy to see you—for my own selfish reasons. I've felt so alone."

"You said I shouldn't be here—but why?"

JoAnne plays with her phone. I sense she's deciding what to tell me. I can almost see her editing the sentences in her head.

"The Pact doesn't trust me, Jake. If they saw us together it would be bad. Bad for me, bad for you."

"Bad how?"

"I heard Alice was at Fernley."

"You mean the place in the desert?"

"I've been there." She shudders. "The first time wasn't so terrible—confusing, embarrassing, but manageable."

"And then?"

"And then it gets worse."

Her evasiveness is frustrating. "How much worse?"

She sits up straighter. I can see her editing in her head again. "Just do everything you can to keep Alice from going back."

"Jesus, JoAnne, how did you get sucked into this?" But even as I ask the question, I imagine someone else—Huang, maybe, or Ian, or Evelyn—innocently asking me the exact same question.

"The real story?" JoAnne's voice is sharp, and the anger seems directed at herself. "It started with a stupid car accident. I was in a hurry to get back to work. It had just started to rain, the road was slick. A Porsche cut over into my lane, clipped the bumper of my car, and I started to fishtail. I woke up in the hospital. When I came to, I'd been having such an intensely vivid dream—not vivid in a colorful, acid trip sort of way, but rather in an *idea* sort of way. You know how sometimes something happens and all of a sudden you see everything in your life from a different viewpoint? And the solutions, or at least the direction forward, seem so clear? Anyway, I suddenly realized what a joke the past few years of my life had been. All that schooling, the dissertation I couldn't finish, my stupid condo—it all seemed wrong. Like I'd wasted all that time . . ."

"Were you hurt in the accident?"

"Concussion, stitches, broken rib, broken pelvis—something with the steering wheel. I was very lucky. Did you know that there are only two bones in the human body that, when broken, can lead to death? The pelvis is one of them."

"Really? What's the other?"

"The femur. Anyway, I was trying to recall the vivid dream when this doctor walked up. He introduced himself as Dr. Neil Charles. Then he started asking me all of these questions, really personal questions. You know, stuff to gauge the concussion and whether I was in shock. Everything was still pretty hazy at this point, with all the medication. He started filling out forms, asking me about my medical history, do I smoke, do I drink, am I allergic to anything, how much do I exercise, am I sexually active. Then a nurse carefully removed my gown. She stood by my bed, holding my hand, while Neil examined my whole body for bruises, scrapes, cuts from the crash. I had this incredible sense, as he touched me with these big, warm hands, that he was also analyzing all of the big and small scars of my life. He touched nearly every part of me. I was all wired up with IVs and who knows what, and I felt as if I couldn't move, couldn't escape—but I kind of liked it. I felt safe. I won't bore you with the rest, Jake. Let's just say we got married, Carmel-by-the-Sea, big crowd, string quartet. I did a one-eighty; my entire life changed."

"Sounds wonderful."

"No. Not so wonderful, Jake. It turns out that my super-vivid dream was nothing more than a false epiphany. In hindsight, I can see that I was already on the right path. I had made the right decisions, the right sacrifices. I was working toward my PhD in psychiatry. It was taking longer than I planned, and I was going into debt on the condo, but I should've stuck with it. It was Neil's idea that I was 'too smart' to be a psychiatrist."

I grin. "Thanks, says the lowly therapist."

"Neil doesn't have a clue. He's the one who convinced me to get an MBA and take the job at Schwab, but I didn't realize until later that it was because he had a really strong bias against psychiatry. Long story short—a few months after we met, I dropped out of my PhD program and started business school."

"What a waste. You were so good at what you did."

"It would have been nice if you'd been around back then to tell me so," she says. I sneak a glance under the table. Both of her feet are pointed straight at me. "You remember I wanted kids, right?"

"You used to say you wanted a whole brood."

"Well, it's not going to happen."

"I'm sorry," I say, not sure what she's getting at.

"Me too. Here's the thing, Jake. I've *been* pregnant. I can have kids. I probably still could, if I weren't trapped with Neil. But Neil never wanted to talk about it, and then when we got careless and I got pregnant, he said it wouldn't be a good fit for our life in The Pact."

It occurs to me, for the first time, that no one at either of The Pact parties ever mentioned kids.

"Are you telling me that none of the members have children?"

"A few do. Most don't."

"Is it against the rules or something?"

"Not exactly. Orla has said, however, that children can be an impediment to marriage."

"But wouldn't children ensure more future Pact members?"

"Doesn't work that way. Just because you grew up in The Pact doesn't mean you automatically receive a nomination. Anyway, it's about the marriage, not about kids. You *must* love your husband—with the kids you're supposedly free to choose."

"Have you ever tried to quit?" I ask bluntly.

She laughs bitterly. "What do you think? I got my courage up after the abortion and went to see a divorce lawyer. Neil reported me to The Pact. They called me in, showed me a long list of my failures. If I went through with divorce, they threatened, I'd lose the house, my job, my reputation. They said it would be easy to make me disappear. The crazy thing is, Neil didn't even want to join The Pact. He's not a joiner. By the time we received the package from an old flatmate of Neil's, I was already regretting my decision to get married. The Pact seemed like a lifeline. Long story short, I talked Neil into giving it a try. We did, and for whatever reason, everything went sideways for me. Neil, on the other hand, the golden child, was loved by all. It wasn't even surprising when he got the call from Orla, when they asked him to chair the North American Regional Board."

"Regional Board?"

She swirls her half-eaten hot dog on a stick in a pool of ketchup, and I can't help noticing that, despite the fancy nails, the cuticles around her thumbs are torn and bleeding. "There are three regional boards, each composed of seven people. All three boards report back to a small group in Ireland. Every three months, they meet."

"Where?"

"It changes—Ireland at least once a year, sometimes Hong Kong, occasionally out at Fernley."

"And what do they talk about?"

"Everything," she says grimly. Then, leaning close, "*Everyone.* Do you understand what I'm saying?"

I think of the bracelet, the collar. The way Vivian and Dave always seem to know so much more than we tell them.

"They make new rules," she says. "They draft the yearly appendices, review the judges' decisions, hear appeals. They manage the finances and the investments. They review the files of problematic members."

"But *why*?"

"According to Neil, the purpose of the boards is to ensure everyone's marriage succeeds. No matter what."

"And what if a marriage fails?"

"That's just it—they *don't*."

"Some must," I insist.

She shakes her head wearily. "You know how they told you that no one in The Pact has ever gotten divorced?" She's in my face now, whispering. I can smell the ketchup on her breath. "Well, that's true, Jake. But what they don't tell you is that not all The Pact marriages last."

"I don't understand."

"Fernley crap is bad, really bad, but I can take that, as long as I get myself in the right mindset. I even like the rules—I like the mandatory dates, the gifts."

"But?"

She seems overwhelmed by an impossible sadness, a cloud of hopelessness. "I have no facts, and even if I did I shouldn't say anything. But one time, when a board meeting was being held in San Francisco, we had dinner with Orla. Just her, Neil, and me. I'd never met her before. Neil insisted on picking out my outfit. He made me promise not to ask any personal questions. Over the years, The Pact had sure asked me a lot of personal questions—in the forms I'd filled out, the counselors I'd had to see, the recorded interviews at Fernley. Integrity Checks, they called them."

"They *recorded* you?"

JoAnne nods. "When I told Neil I was worried Orla might have heard the recordings of my Integrity Checks, he didn't deny it. He told me to be on my best behavior. Let Orla lead the conversation."

"So, what's she like?"

"Charismatic, but also strangely removed. One minute she'd be so interested in me, and the next minute she just looked right through me—it gave me shivers."

The more JoAnne talks, the more she seems to lose the thread. In the stuff I found about Orla online, she didn't seem like the person JoAnne is describing. In photographs, she looked friendly, intelligent, and nonthreatening, like a great-aunt or the high school English teacher you always remember fondly. "You said that not all Pact marriages last. What did you mean?"

"The Pact has no divorces, but it also has more widows and widowers than you would expect."

"What?" My throat goes dry.

"It's just that—" She glances around nervously. Sweat appears on her forehead, and suddenly she starts to backtrack. "It's probably nothing," she evades, toying with her cellphone. "Maybe I'm thinking too much, like Neil says. Maybe my time at Fernley got me turned around. I don't always think straight, you know."

"The JoAnne I remember always thought straight."

"That's nice of you to say, but then you always put women on a pedestal."

"I do?" I ask, temporarily sidetracked by this odd accusation.

"Girlfriends, friends, colleagues. I don't mean to sound rude, but you probably think that wife of yours hung the moon."

There's something in her tone, something I don't like. Anyway, I don't think that's accurate. I admire Alice, because there is much to admire in her. I love her, because she is easy to love. I think she's beautiful because—well, because she is.

"JoAnne," I say, trying to reel her back. "Tell me about the widows."

"There's probably a lot of reasons." Her words spill out in a rush. "Pact members travel more, do more, than most people." Her gaze skitters around the room. "We probably all lead riskier lives. I mean, if we didn't, we wouldn't have joined The Pact, right? The Pact attracts a certain kind of person?"

I think of Alice being forced into a straitjacket and carried off to Fernley with strangers in a black SUV. I think of the pilot in his flimsy Cessna. "There could be a hundred different reasons," JoAnne says, as if trying to convince herself.

"Reasons for what? What risks?"

"Freak accidents. Drownings. Food poisoning. Maybe it's a coincidence, but an unusual number of Pact members seem to die at a young age. And as soon as someone loses a spouse, there's almost always a new relationship, fostered by The Pact, that leads pretty quickly to marriage."

"Who?" I'm desperate to know if there are real facts and names behind what she's saying.

"You know Dave and his wife, Kerri?"

"Of course. Alice has been meeting with Dave once a week."

"I know."

"How?" I ask, but she just waves her hand in the air as if this is an irrelevant detail.

"Dave and Kerri were both married before," she says.

"You're saying their spouses died?"

"Yes. Years ago, around the time that Neil and I joined The Pact."

"They seem so young."

"They are. They actually met through The Pact. Maybe it was just a coincidence, their spouses dying within three months of each other. Kerri's husband, Tony, had a boating accident on Lake Tahoe." She shudders. "Dave's wife, Mary, fell off a ladder at her house while cleaning the second-floor windows and hit her head on the stone pavers of their driveway."

"It's horrible," I say, "but these things happen."

"Mary didn't die right away. She was in a coma. Dave decided two months in to take her off life support." That vein in JoAnne's forehead, throbbing.

"Do you have proof?"

"Look, both Dave's wife and Kerri's husband had made multiple visits to Fernley. Both of them had 'wrong thinking,' Neil told me. According to rumors, their crimes ranged from obfuscation to misrepresentation of Pact doctrine to adultery. I went to Dave and Kerri's wedding—it took place so soon after the deaths of their spouses. At the time, I was happy for both of them. They'd both been through so much. I thought they deserved something good in their lives. Neil and I were new, and I was still pretty gung ho. I didn't think twice about the timing and the coincidence. But I do remember one strange thing about the wedding."

"What's that?"

"Well, normally you'd think that this happy occasion would be tinged with sadness, right, because of all they'd lost? And you'd think that the spouses' names would come up in the toast, or in conversation, that somebody would fondly mention the dead wife and the dead husband. After all, everyone at the wedding knew both of the former spouses. But it was as if Mary and Tony had been entirely forgotten. No—not forgotten—*erased*."

"But what you're accusing The Pact of goes way beyond threats and slander. You're talking about murder."

JoAnne looks away. "Right before I saw you at the Villa Carina party, something else happened," she says softly. "A couple joined just a few months before you and Alice. Eli and Elaine, hipsters from Marin. Nine days before the Villa Carina party, their car was found out near Stinson Beach. I tried to press the issue with Neil, but he refused to talk about it. I scoured the newspapers and couldn't find anything. They vanished. Jake, when Eli and Elaine joined, Neil made some comments. It was strange—people in The Pact just didn't like them. I don't know why. They seemed nice. Elaine was a little overly affectionate with the husbands, maybe, but nothing serious. They dressed a little different, and they were into Transcendental Meditation, but so what? Anyway, when they disappeared, I started thinking about Dave's and Kerri's spouses, and all the inter-organization weddings that have happened over the years. I've even heard of cases in which The Pact deems a *nonmember* to be a threat and takes steps against that individual in order to prevent damage to the marriage."

JoAnne leans back in her seat and sips the green lemonade. She's staring at me, but I have absolutely no idea what she's thinking. A mother and her two kids are next to us, eating Panda Express. The kids are giggling over their fortune cookies. I look at JoAnne's phone. It has been on the table between us this whole time.

JoAnne sets her cup down. One by one, she touches the tip of each nail underneath the nail on her thumb. Then she repeats. It's subtle but a little manic. "They just disappear without a trace, Jake."

Whenever I meet with new patients, the first thing I do is try to figure out their normal states. We all live within a range of emotions; we all go up and down. With teenagers, the range can swing wildly. I always want to know where each person's "normal" lies, because it allows me to more quickly recognize when someone is especially up or, more important, especially down. With JoAnne, I'm still trying to find her *normal*. She's clearly riddled with anxiety. I want to know how to interpret this fear, I want to understand the context for the stories she's telling me. Are they the product of an unbalanced mind? Should I trust her perception? Looking down at her phone, I'm worried. What if Neil finds out we've met?

JoAnne is rubbing her nails slowly along her palm.

"You used to wear them short." I reach over and touch one of the long, slick nails.

"Neil wants them this way, so I do it." She holds them up in front of me, in a faux-glamorous sort of way. I notice that her ring fingers are longer than her index fingers. There's actually a correlation between finger length and the likelihood of infidelity. According to a fairly convincing study, when the ring finger is longer than the index finger, the person is more likely to be unfaithful. The explanation has to do with testosterone levels. After reading the research, I found myself staring at Alice's hands, inordinately relieved to discover that her ring fingers are shorter than her index fingers.

"Should I be worried for our safety?" I ask.

JoAnne thinks for a moment. "Yes. They don't know what to make of you. You make them nervous. Alice is different. They either really like her, or they really don't. Either way is probably bad for you."

"So what should I do?"

"Be careful, Jake. Fit in. Be less interesting. Be less argumentative. Don't give them reason to think about you; give them even less reason to talk about you. Don't write anything you can say, don't say anything you can whisper, don't whisper anything you can nod. Don't wind up at Fernley. Don't *ever* wind up at Fernley."

JoAnne reaches for her purse. "I need to go."

"Wait," I say. "I have more questions—"

"We've already stayed too long, Jake. This wasn't smart. Let's not leave together. Stay here for a few minutes, then go out a separate entrance."

I point to her phone, which still sits on the table between us. "That thing makes me nervous."

JoAnne looks down at the phone. "Yes, but turning it off or leaving it at home might be more problematic."

"Can we meet again?"

"It seems like a bad idea."

"Not meeting seems like a worse idea. Last Friday of the month?"

"I'll try."

"Leave your phone at home next time."

JoAnne picks up the phone and turns away from me without saying goodbye. I watch her walk all the way across the food court. She's wearing tall shoes. The shoes don't seem like the JoAnne I once knew, and it occurs to me that maybe they're Neil's idea too. Marriage is a compromise; so says section two of The Manual.

I sit at the table for another ten minutes, running through the conversation in my mind. I don't know what to make of it. When I came to meet JoAnne, I'd been secretly hoping that one of two things would happen; either we were going to commiserate about all of The Pact's weird rules and punishments, or I was going to discover that she fell somewhere on the spectrum for paranoia. And maybe she is paranoid. Maybe I am too. But paranoia must be considered in context. Fear of a group is only paranoia if the group is *not* out to get you.

I walk back through the mall. I need to get Alice a gift for this month. In Macy's, I select a scarf. I like her in scarves, even though she never wore them before we met. I decide that the bright blues will go well with her complexion. On the train back to the city, I pull the scarf from the bag and run my hands over the silk, suddenly ashamed. The first time I gave Alice a scarf, she said she loved it. But she wore it only when I asked her to. With the second scarf, it was the same, as well as the third. What if I'm no better than Neil, dolling my wife up according to my own tastes, my own inclinations? I shove the gift back into the bag and leave the bag on the train. What compromises has Alice made, already, for this marriage? What unfair things do I demand of her, and she of me?

## 50

THE FOLLOWING WEEK, ALICE AND I CELEBRATE MY FORTIETH birthday with a low-key dinner at my favorite neighborhood restaurant, The Richmond. She gives me a beautiful watch that must have cost a whole paycheck, with the inscription TO JAKE—WITH ALL MY LOVE. ALICE—on the back. The week after that, I end up working late, writing session reports, editing an academic paper an old colleague talked me into co-authoring. On the way home, I stop to get a couple of burritos for dinner. As I walk up the steps to our house, I feel the vibration of music coming from our garage.

When Alice and I moved into the house, she had recently finished law school. The gilt had rubbed off of the idea of a life in law, and she was a little depressed, slogging through a clerkship for a local judge. She often worried that the whole idea had been a mistake. She missed her music, her freedom, her creativity, and maybe, I suspected, she missed her old life. If she hadn't already committed to a law career by taking on so many outrageous loans, I think she might have quit.

During one of her low periods, while she was upstairs studying through an entire Sunday, I worked downstairs in the garage to build a special music area for her. It seemed important to give her that outlet, a small door into her old life. I sectioned off one large corner in the back, put some mattresses against the walls, and layered shag rugs on the floor. I gathered up the many musical instruments, stands, amps, and microphones that had been hiding in boxes, some stored away in the tiny secret room. At dusk, taking a break, Alice came down to see what all the racket was. When she saw the cozy little studio, she was so happy she actually cried. She gave me a hug, and then she played for me.

Since then, I've heard her down there a bunch of times. Usually I respect her privacy. I just let her play her music, and wait for her to come upstairs. I like that she has such an outlet, and I like that she always comes back upstairs to me.

Tonight, as I walk into the house, I notice that the music coming from the garage is different. At first, I assume she has the stereo on, but then it occurs to me that it is indeed live music, but she isn't the only one playing. I change and put the burritos on plates, expecting the music to stop, expecting her and the guests to come upstairs—I wish I'd bought more burritos—but it doesn't happen. Eventually, I open the kitchen door to get a better listen. It sounds like there are three or four people down there. I take a few steps down toward the garage, not enough to be seen, just enough to hear the music better.

The next few songs are from Ladder's first album. I recognize the male voice blending with Alice's. I'll be honest: Over the past couple of months, it's possible that I may have done some more Internet surfing related to Eric Wilson. It's also possible that I noticed he and his new band were playing the Great American Music Hall this week.

A few songs in, the noise gives way to acoustic guitars, organ, and the Grateful Dead's "Box of Rain." I sit on the stairs, listening to the guitars build. Alice's voice works its way through the cacophony, always finding the melody and the groove. It makes me shiver. The way Eric's rich baritone voice intertwines with Alice's voice is seductive and disturbing.

I love music, but I can't carry a tune in a bucket, as my mother used to say. Hearing them, I feel like an outsider, a foreigner eavesdropping on a private conversation between the locals. Still, I want to hear the entire song. I don't want to tug Alice away from this thing she is so clearly enjoying. Their voices work superbly together, hers circling around his, then coming together at the right moment, hitting the perfect harmony. I'm not sure why, but sitting here in the dark, on the stairs, as the song finds its way to the final reveal, tears well up in my eyes.

I've thought far more about marriage in recent months than I ever did before. What is the marriage contract? The general assumption we have about marriage is that it involves two people building a life together. But what I wonder is this: Does it require each person to give up the life they built before? Must we shed our former selves? Do we have to give up that which was once important to us as a sacrifice to the gods of marriage?

For me, the transition into marriage with Alice was nearly seamless. The house, the wedding, our life together, flowed naturally from the life I'd been living before. My education, my job, and the practice I was building would, I knew, provide a fertile support system for this new life. For Alice, I imagine it was different. In the space of a few years, she went from being an independent artist, a single woman who reveled in her freedom, to being an attorney weighed down by responsibility, constrained by a newly inherited set of limitations. Although I often encouraged Alice to hold on to the person she used to be, when I'm honest with myself, I'm not sure I pushed as hard as I could have. Sure, I supported her in the small ways, like creating the garage studio. But when it came to the larger things—like encouraging her to do cameos when musicians asked her to join them in the studio, I never said no, but maybe I sent the wrong signals. "Isn't that the weekend we're going to the Russian River?" Or "Aren't we having dinner with Ian that night?" I would say.

I resolve to walk down the stairs. I move quietly, so as not to distract them. At the bottom, I realize the cavernous garage is pitch-black except for the corner where they're playing. Alice has her back to me, facing the others, and the drummer and keyboard player seem lost in the music. Eric, though, is facing me, and he sees me. He doesn't acknowledge me and instead mumbles something to the others. Immediately, the four of them launch into "Police Station," a Red Hot Chili Peppers song about an on-again, off-again relationship between the narrator and the woman he loves. Eric's bass line sets the windows rattling.

Alice leans toward him, sharing a microphone, their faces so close they could kiss. She's still wearing her navy suit and pantyhose, though her shoes are gone and she is jumping up and down, her sweat-soaked hair bouncing. I realize that Eric chose the song as much for me as for Alice.

The verses end, but the music goes on. Eric is no longer looking at me. He is gazing at Alice and, as I quietly move to a better angle, I see that she is gazing at him. She is watching his hands, following the notes. The drummer's eyes are closed, and the keyboardist gives me a slight nod. Every time the song is about to end, Eric leads it into another refrain. And though I can see exactly what he's doing, trying to provoke me, I don't want to be the kind of guy who can't handle it. I don't want to be the jealous husband. Alice has told me that one of the things she loves about me is my confidence. It's important to me to be the man Alice believes I am.

Eventually, the song ends. Alice looks up, surprised to see me, sets down her guitar, beckons me over, and gives me a kiss. I can feel her sweat on my skin. "Fellows, this is Jake," she announces happily. "Jake, this is Eric, Ryan, and Dario." Ryan and Dario nod and quickly set about packing their things.

"So this is the guy," Eric says, looking at Alice, not at me. His hand grips mine painfully. I grip back just as hard. Okay, maybe harder.

He pulls his hand away and turns to hug Alice. "Join us tonight at the show," he says, not a question, exactly, but a command, and I see how it might have been with them, when she was much younger. How he was the one to make the decisions.

But my Alice isn't that Alice. "Not tonight. I have a hot date with this guy," she says, putting her arms around me.

"Ouch," Eric says.

"News flash," Ryan says good-naturedly. "Alice is married."

## 51

THE FOLLOWING DAY IS ALICE'S LAST DAY WITH RON—watching the sunrise, doing squats and push-ups, running up and down the sand dunes at Ocean Beach. She's up and out of the house before I even realize she has left our warm bed. Surprisingly, she has come to enjoy her time with Ron. She likes the stories of his past boyfriends, she likes following the soap opera of his chaotic life, which seems to be equal parts hardcore sports and hardcore partying. Mostly, though, she likes that he is not, apparently, a part of The Pact. He was hired by Vivian to train Alice, and it is Vivian who pays him weekly—in person, with cash.

Alice has lost seven pounds and developed serious new muscles. Her stomach is hard, her arms defined, her legs lean. Her clothes don't fit properly anymore, skirts sagging where they used to hug her curves, and one afternoon she asks me to help her carry all her suits out to the car. She's bringing them to the tailor to be taken in. To me, she seems unnecessarily bony, and her face has lost its softness, reverting to harder edges I never knew were there. For that, I blame The Pact. Still, she seems happy.

She also seems to have worked through her annoyance with Dave; she appears to actually like him now. She has to meet him two more times, and then she's finished with probation, fully rehabilitated. I think of JoAnne's crazy stories—the couples who never divorced but ended up married to a better partner. What if Alice is becoming a better person, while I'm just staying the same? What if this is all part of a plan to transform Alice, while leaving me behind? I shake off the thought that someone on high has already decided to make Alice a widow.

## 52

THE MONTH HAS PASSED QUICKLY. ON THE AGREED-UPON DATE, I find myself back at the Fourth Street station, waiting for the train to take me down the Peninsula to the Hillsdale mall. I've done research—hours and hours of research—but I can't find any reference to Eli and Elaine, the disappeared couple JoAnne mentioned the last time I saw her. A couple vanishes, leaving only an empty car, yet there are no blog posts, no news articles, no conspiracy theories, no Facebook page devoted to finding them. How is that possible? But then I'm often surprised by which news stories make it big and which ones fail to linger. Still, I begin to wonder if it was all a figment of JoAnne's imagination.

I never told Alice I'd gone to see JoAnne, and I haven't told her about this meeting either. I was worried that she might want to come with me, which would get her into trouble if JoAnne lost her grip and started to blab to Neil.

I'll admit, it does feel weird—almost illicit—going to meet her again. Nonetheless, I want to get more details about Eli and Elaine, and I want to see if she will reveal anything else about Neil or The Pact. Last time, I was certain there were things she wasn't telling me. I got the feeling that maybe she just wanted to get a better sense of me, to renew our old friendship before she got down to the real details.

I don't leave my phone with Huang. I take Uber to a coffee shop near the ball park. While waiting for my hot chocolate, I remove the battery from my phone. Then I head over to the Caltrain station and take the first train south to Hillsdale. I buy the office some chips and candy bars at Trader Joe's, so I'll have a bag to carry around the mall. I walk through Trader Joe's and Barnes & Noble, alert to my surroundings. As far as I can tell, I'm alone. I wander through a few more stores, just to make sure.

Ten minutes before the hour, I set up in the corner at the far end of the food court, about a hundred yards from where JoAnne and I last sat. I watch the doors, waiting for her to walk in. I buy a couple of corn dogs and another green lemonade.

I wait. Ten minutes, nineteen minutes, thirty-three. I keep checking the time, watching all the entry points, getting more nervous by the minute. At some point I look down and realize that I've eaten both corn dogs, though I don't even remember putting them in my mouth. The lemonade is gone too.

JoAnne doesn't show. Shit. What can it mean?

At twelve forty-five, I stand, clear my table, and retrace my steps, up the escalator, back into the mall. What do I do now? I didn't plan for a no-show. For some reason, I'd convinced myself that JoAnne was as eager to talk to me as I was to talk to her.

I walk around Nordstrom, through Uniqlo, and out the back of the mall. I'm confused. Anxious. Worried for JoAnne, worried for myself, and—okay—maybe disappointed. Maybe there was something more to this meeting than wanting to learn about The Pact. I realize guiltily that some part of me just really wanted to see JoAnne. If Alice was someone else in another life, so was I. Not to the same extreme, and for me it was so long ago. By the time I met Alice, I was fully the adult version of myself. But before that, there was college me—not exactly confident, but blindly hopeful, naïvely idealistic—and JoAnne was there during those years. JoAnne knew that version of me.

I try not to let paranoia set in. I decide to head back, give the food court one last chance. I stand at the top of the escalator that leads down into the food court. I can see almost every table from here. Nothing. As I'm about to step onto the escalator, I notice a large guy in a black turtleneck standing in front of the tempura place. He isn't with anyone, and he isn't eating anything. I've been watching him for a couple of minutes when he pulls out his phone and makes a call. I've never seen him before, but something seems off. He's not Declan, the guy who came to take Alice to Fernley, but he's certainly a reasonable facsimile. I quickly retreat into the mall. Then I escape through the Gap and out a side door.

A black Cadillac Escalade is idling by the curb. There's a woman sitting at the wheel, but I can't make out her face through the tinted windows. Is it JoAnne? Five parking spaces down from the SUV, I see an empty Bentley. Blue, very nice, just like Neil's. With the rise of Silicon Valley, all of the recent IPOs, the vesting of Facebook and Google, there's a lot of money on the Peninsula these days, so a Bentley isn't really that surprising. Although what would a guy with a two-hundred-thousand-dollar car want to buy at the mall?

There are a million reasons JoAnne might have missed our meeting today, and I run through each of them on my long journey back to the office.

## 53

"How did your meeting go yesterday?" I ask Alice. It's the end of March, and I'm looking forward to the start of a new month. Spring always makes me feel optimistic, and I tell myself this year should be no different.

"Okay," she says, kicking off her heels in the entryway. "Dave took me for an early dinner at a Mexican place by his office. He can be a jerk, but in the end I think he means well."

"That's awfully forgiving of you, after the way he behaved."

She heads into the kitchen and returns with a bottle of orange Calistoga. "I asked him about all that, actually." I take down two glasses, and Alice pours. "He said he almost lost his first wife due to working too much—he didn't want to see me go through the same thing."

"So," I say, unable to hide my sarcasm, "he was doing it for me?"

"Yes. We are happy now, aren't we?"

"Of course." I take some cheese out of the fridge and melt butter in a skillet. I put the cheese between slices of sourdough bread. "You're almost all done with Dave, then."

"Actually, he hired me for a suit he's filing against a builder. It's small, but it won't hurt with the partners."

"Are you sure that's a good idea? How do you know he's not just hiring you so that he can continue to pry into our lives?" The butter sizzles and I slide the sandwich into the pan.

"It's not like that," she says, staring into her glass. Yet I don't trust Dave.

"I got you something," she says. She goes into the entryway and returns with a wrapped gift. I can tell without opening it that it's a book.

"You didn't need to do that. You just gave me a birthday present."

Alice gives me an appraising look. "You still haven't finished The Manual, have you?"

I flip the sandwiches with a spatula. "It's so long."

"*Gifts related to special occasions, to include birthdays, Christmas, and other holidays such as Valentine's Day, should not be counted as satisfaction of the monthly gift requirement,*" she recites.

As I tear off the wrapping paper, I realize I'm in trouble. I don't have anything for Alice. Shit, I should have kept the scarf. Inside the box, I discover a copy of a Richard Brautigan book, *Willard and His Bowling Trophies*. For years, I've been collecting first editions of the novel, Brautigan's best. As they've become increasingly hard to find, the joke has grown that I might soon own every copy. Alice has snapped up several copies online, but she takes particular pride in the ones that require actual legwork. Whenever she travels outside of the Bay Area, she checks used bookstores to see if she can find another copy.

It's a nice specimen, even signed on the title page with an inscription to a girl named Delilah. Brautigan was popular with the hippie girls.

"Perfect," I say. I go into the living room and put it on the bookshelf beside the other copies. Back in the kitchen, I find Alice plating the sandwiches with some raspberries and spoonfuls of crème fraîche. She carries the plates into the dining room and beckons me to sit.

"I thought this was the thirtieth," I say.

"Thirty-first." She checks her watch. "It's seven twenty-nine. You can still pick something up if you hurry—try Park Life, maybe."

"Good idea." I eat a few bites of the sandwich and leave the raspberries. Of course, it's not Alice I'm worried about; it's The Pact. But how will they know if she doesn't tell them?

It takes me sixteen minutes to get to Park Life, but of course there's no parking. I circle the block twice before maneuvering the Jeep into an illegal spot. When I get to the door, it's already closed. Shit. I run three blocks to the bookstore. It's not very creative, since she already gave me a book, but she does love to read. The bookstore is closed too. There's nothing else around here but bars, Chinese grocers, and restaurants. I'm screwed.

When I get home, I apologize profusely. "I actually bought you something, but I left it on the train."

She looks at me intently. "When were you on the train?"

"Just for some meeting in Palo Alto."

"What meeting?"

"Work stuff. Don't make me bore you with it. Anyway, sorry about the gift."

"It's no biggie," Alice says, but I can tell she's disappointed. And she still seems to be mulling over my story about the train. "Let's just hope they don't find out."

"I'll get you something tomorrow," I promise.

The next day, I drive back to Park Life as soon as it opens. Thinking ahead, I buy three gifts—a bracelet with a gold pendant shaped like California, a coffee-table book about street photography, and a T-shirt that says I LEFT MY HEART IN OSLO. I have them all nicely wrapped. When I get home, I hide two of the gifts in my closet. Of course, there's probably some rule against stocking up on presents. That night, when she gets home from work, I hand her the most expensive of the three—the bracelet.

"Good work!" she says.

I know there's no way The Pact can discover my gift tardiness, yet it doesn't stop me from worrying about it.

## 54

THE NEXT WEEKEND, WE'RE SCHEDULED TO JOIN CHUCK AND EVE at their vacation house in Hopland. I beg Alice to make an excuse, but she refuses. She has claimed credit for this weekend trip as her quarterly requirement, and she doesn't want to sacrifice it.

"Can't we just tell them I had something come up at work?" I find time with Pact members to be extremely stressful. I'm worried that I might do something that will get me into trouble. I'm even more worried for Alice.

"You need to make your peace with The Pact," she tells me. It's something we've been saying to each other since we heard it repeated by Dave and Vivian. It's a joke between us, a black humor reminder of this weird, crazy rabbit hole we've tumbled into. Oddly, though, this time Alice doesn't seem to be entirely joking. "Besides, I need some sun, and it's supposed to be eighty in Hopland."

An hour later, we're in the car, headed across the Golden Gate Bridge. A double double at In-N-Out in Mill Valley improves my mood. Past San Rafael, as the darkness starts to come on, I ask Alice about her session with Dave today. It was her last, finally, and I'm relieved she's finished.

"I think it might not be all bad to have a sounding board," she says. "It lets me get out of my own head. I used to wonder about your patients, about why they would pay so much to come see you. Now I understand."

"What did you talk about?"

Alice pushes her seat back and props her bare feet up on the dashboard. "Today we talked a lot about you. Dave asked about your practice, how it's going, whether you have new clients—those sorts of things. He had an odd question, though. He wanted to know if you'd thought about opening an office down the Peninsula. He said there's a good market for your sort of thing in San Mateo. He said to tell you to consider checking out the area around the Hillsdale mall."

"What?" I blurt, alarmed.

"It seemed important to him—not sure why."

I know why, of course, but if I tell Alice that The Pact has been spying on me at the Hillsdale mall, I'll have to tell her why I was there. Shit.

The weekend turns out to be more fun than I expected, although I can never entirely relax, thanks to Dave's reference to Hillsdale. I assumed there'd be a lot of talk about The Pact, in a gung ho Amway sort of way, but there's none of that. There is a third couple, one we didn't know were coming. Mick and Sarah are our age, from North Carolina, and when Chuck introduces us he jokes that they are our Southern doppelgängers. They have a good sense of humor, they watch the same television shows, and Mick, like me, hates olives and bell peppers. Sarah, like Alice, has brought four pairs of shoes. If I'm honest, though, from a purely aesthetic point of view, maybe the husband is slightly better looking than I am, the wife slightly less attractive than Alice. Sarah works in sales for a solar company; Mick is a musician—a keyboardist for a band you might have heard of. I find myself watching Alice, wondering: Would she be happier if she were married to a guy like Mick?

Still, the weather is perfect, Alice is relaxed, and Chuck and Eve are generous, attentive hosts. On the second morning, The Pact has yet to come up. Chuck has gone for a run, Mick and Sarah are visiting a winery, and Alice is on her laptop in our room, working on a brief. I find myself alone on the patio with Eve.

"By the way," I say, trying to sound nonchalant, "do you remember a guy from The Pact named Eli?"

"No," she says sharply. Then she gets up and heads into the house.

I sit alone on the patio, staring at the grapevines on a nearby hill wilting in the drought, thinking of a Soviet story I read in college. The piece was about a waiter who lived on one side of a duplex. The other side was inhabited by a grumpy elderly man. As the story goes, the police show up at the waiter's apartment over and over, asking if he has been spying on his neighbor. He says no, and they go away only to come back the next day with the same complaint. It goes on for weeks, the police continually harassing him for spying on his neighbor. The weird part is that he'd never thought much about the neighbor until the police showed up.

After being accused of spying ten or fifteen times, the waiter starts to wonder: What could the old man be doing that made him so paranoid? What was he hiding? The waiter gets so curious, he climbs through the attic and looks down on his neighbor's apartment. The roof caves in, the police show up, and things go downhill from there.

## 55

TWO DAYS AFTER WE RETURN FROM HOPLAND, I HAVE THE GROUP meeting for teens of divorced parents. Conrad and Isobel arrive a few minutes early, and everyone else arrives a few minutes late. While waiting for the session to begin, I arrange cookies, cheese, and soft drinks on a foldout table. Conrad and Isobel, who attend the same pricey private school, sit in the foldout chairs talking about their senior theses. Conrad, who drives a brand-new Land Rover and lives in a mansion in Pacific Heights, is doing his on the need for socialism in America, without a trace of irony. Isobel is doing hers on cults.

"How do you know what's a cult and what's not?" Conrad asks.

She flips through her big orange binder and settles on a page filled with tiny handwriting. "That's the key question. I'm still sorting it out, but my impression is that a cult has to have some or all of the following things." She reads from a list: *"A) A taboo against sharing the group's secrets with outsiders. B) Some sort of penalty for leaving the group. C) A set of goals or beliefs that are outside of the mainstream. D) A single charismatic leader. E) An insistence on having members donate their work, personal property, and money to the group without compensation."*

"I think B and D are the most interesting," she says.

"Is the Catholic church a cult?" I ask. "You've got the charismatic leader—the Pope—and you can be excommunicated if you don't follow the rules."

She frowns, thinking. "I don't think so. If something is around for long enough, or becomes super-popular, I'm not sure it can be classified as a cult. Also, a cult is desperate to keep people in the fold, and the Catholic church seems like it would rather lose members than have members who overtly disagree with its teachings. Also, the church's views are mostly noble—charity and good deeds—and aren't outside the mainstream."

Conrad gets up to check out the snack table. "What about the Mormons?"

"No, I think they're legit. They have some odd rituals, but the same can be said of every major world religion."

When he comes back to the circle with his paper plate and two Cokes, Conrad sits one seat closer to Isobel. "Legitimacy is relative, isn't it?" he says, handing one of the cans to Isobel.

She reaches over and takes a cookie from Conrad's plate, and I can tell it makes him happy. Isobel could do worse than Conrad; despite the mild case of affluenza—not his fault, really—he's a good kid.

"What was it like to grow up in San Francisco during the era of the People's Temple?" Conrad asks me. I can tell he's trying to impress Isobel.

"Just how old do you think I am?" I ask, curious.

He shrugs. "Fifty?"

"Not quite," I say, smiling. "I was just a baby when Jim Jones lured his followers to Guyana. When I was growing up, though, I sometimes heard my parents talking about a family they knew who had died at Jonestown." I think of photos I saw a few months ago on the anniversary of the massacre. I was amazed to see that the jungle had grown over the entire encampment, leaving almost no clue that Jones and his followers had ever been there.

"The good news is that cults aren't nearly as popular now as they were back in the day," Isobel says. "My thesis is that the Internet and increased public information have drastically reduced the appeal of cults.

The ones that do exist work really hard to cut their members off from information."

As the other kids trickle in—Emily, Marcus, Mandy, and Theo—I mull over the conversation. By Isobel's definition, The Pact doesn't qualify as a cult. While Orla may be a powerful figure, the goal of the group isn't outside of the mainstream. In fact, The Pact's goal is the very definition of the mainstream. Also, The Pact doesn't ask for financial support, to my knowledge. The opposite is actually true, when you consider the nice parties, personal trainers, and access to relaxing weekend getaways. Of course, it does check a couple of key boxes: You're not allowed to discuss it with anyone on the outside, and, once you're in, there's no easy way out.

At the heart of it, though, the mission of The Pact and my primary goal in life happen to be identical: a successful, happy marriage to the woman I love. In my heart, I know that The Pact is bad—very bad—and yet there's no denying that its aim is to provide me with the one thing I want most.

Conrad pulls a book out of his backpack and shows me the cover. "Our right-wing lit teacher wants us to read *The Fountainhead*—not going to do it."

"You should give it a chance," I suggest.

Isobel scowls at the book in disgust. "Why should we read that scary fascist propaganda?"

"It is scary, but not for the reason you think. The scary part is that you might find yourself agreeing with some of it."

"If you say so," Conrad says. But the eye roll he gives Isobel is a clear signal that they're in this together. When did I become the face of authoritarianism?

## 56

EVERY TIME I HEAR A BIKE COMING DOWN THE STREET, I FIND MY-self tensing up, thinking of all the things I've done wrong. Usually, as I hold my breath, I hear the wheels, the chain, the gears, flying past the house and down toward Cabrillo. Today, however—Wednesday—the bike stops at our house. I hear the telltale *click* of bike shoes pattering up our front steps.

It's the same messenger as last time. "Dude," he says, "you guys are getting my legs in shape."

"Sorry. Want something to drink?"

"Sure." And then he's in the house. He places the envelope facedown on the console in the entryway, so I can't see whose name is on the front.

In the kitchen, I pour him a glass of chocolate milk. I pull out a bag of cookies and he sits down at the table. To be polite, I sit down too, but all I really want to do is go over and check the name on the envelope.

He launches into a long story about how his girlfriend just moved out here from Nevada to be with him. I don't have the heart to tell him it probably isn't going to work out. There is a whole range of telltale signs, and I've been subconsciously checking the boxes as he talks. Because of the outrageous rental prices, she moved in with him. He admits it's too fast, that he wasn't yet ready for that step, but she'd given him an ultimatum. If she didn't move to San Francisco, she told him, the relationship was over. I can already tell that the premature cohabitation, combined with the fact that he feels pushed into it and that she's the kind of person who feels comfortable giving ultimatums, can't lead anywhere good.

As soon as he's out the door, I pick up the envelope. I flip it over and my gut hurts. It's for me. And then I'm ashamed, because I should be *happy* it's for me. I remember what JoAnne said: Spread the blame, don't let them get too focused on Alice. The only thing I can figure is that they know I forgot Alice's present. Of course, I think, shuddering, it could be worse. It could involve my trip to the Hillsdale mall.

I dial Alice's number. I'm surprised when she picks up on the second ring, but then I recall The Manual: *Always answer when your spouse calls.* Today, they're doing the deposition of an infamous tech executive who assaulted an intern last year. Apparently, in a room full of people, the executive started screaming at the intern for not being fast enough with the PowerPoint. The exec pushed the intern out of the way, and the poor girl fell and hit her head on the table. Blood everywhere.

There's noise in the background. "We just took a five-minute break from the shitshow," Alice says. "Be quick."

"The bike messenger came by."

Long pause. "Fuck. I hate Wednesday."

"It's for me."

"That's weird." Is it just me, or does she not sound as surprised as she should?

"I haven't read it yet. I wanted to wait until I had you on the phone." I tear open the envelope. Inside, there's a single sheet of paper. In the background, I can hear Alice's associate telling her something.

"Read it." Alice sounds impatient.

*"Dear Jake,"* I read aloud. *"Periodically, Friends are invited to travel to participate in inquiries both broad and specific. An inquiry is an opportunity for the board to obtain and evaluate information related to a subject of relevance to one or more members of the organization. While your attendance is optional—this is an invitation, not a directive—you are strongly*

*encouraged to attend and assist the Reeducation Committee in this matter.*
*The goals of each individual Pact member are the goals of all members."*

"It's a subpoena," Alice says, her voice tense.

I read the fine print at the bottom of the page. "They want me at the Half Moon Bay Airport tonight at nine."

"Are you going?"

"Do I have a choice?"

There's another commotion in the background. I'm waiting for Alice to talk me out of this, to tell me it's a very bad idea, but instead she says, "No, not really."

I toss the letter onto the table and walk back to my office. I wish I hadn't come home for lunch.

A session in the afternoon with my preteen trouble-diversion group keeps my mind off of the matter for a few minutes, at least. Preteens are always the most difficult to assess, so I have to focus intensely on every comment and every nonverbal cue. Adults' motivations are generally easier to discern; with kids, it can be difficult to pinpoint motives they usually don't consciously recognize themselves.

Afterward, I'm exhausted, so I go for a walk in the neighborhood. I buy the last lemon chocolate chip scone at Nibs. By the time I get back to the office, I already know that I'm going to the airport tonight. With The Pact, the best policy is to always do the thing that will attract the least amount of attention. There's no question that I love Alice, but if The Pact were to comb through my actions or nonactions as a husband, I'm certain they could paint me as a one-man crime wave. Evelyn frowns when I tell her I won't be in tomorrow. I feel terrible canceling on clients again, but what choice do I have?

At home, I pack an overnight bag with toiletries and a change of clothing, something nice but not too formal. When Alice gets home at 7:03, I'm sitting in the blue chair, the packed bag at my feet.

"You're going," she says.

"Every bit of logic tells me not to answer their beck and call. On the other hand, I don't want to deal with the consequences of not showing up."

Alice stands in front of me, biting a nail. I want some acknowledgment that she's proud of me, or at least grateful, for the sacrifice I'm about to make, but instead she seems irritated. Not with The Pact, but with me. "You must have done something," she says.

"The gift was late," I say. Then I throw a bomb into the whole situation: "How do you think they knew?"

"Jesus, Jake. You think I ratted you out? It's clearly something else." She gives me an accusing look, as if she's waiting for me to confess to some grand crime, but I just smile and say, "I'm clean."

She hasn't even taken off her coat or shoes. No hug or kiss. "I'll give you a ride."

"You want to change first?"

"No," she says, glancing at her watch. "We better go." I have the strange feeling that she just wants to get rid of me.

Traffic is light on Highway 1, so we have time to stop for a burrito in Moss Beach. "Please tell me you had a bad day at work," I say, setting guacamole and two beers on the table between us. "I can't stand it if all this coldness is about me."

She scoops up guacamole with a chip and chews it slowly before answering. "The freaking deposition was hell. The executive called me petulant. I hate that bitch. Let me see the letter."

I pull the letter out of my bag. While she's reading it, I go over to the counter and grab our burritos. When I get back, she's wiping up the last of the guacamole with the last chip. It's a small thing, but it's unlike her. She knows how much I love guacamole.

She folds the letter into thirds and slides it back across the table. "How bad could it be? They didn't send some big guy in an SUV to frisk you and drag you out to the desert."

"Jesus, Alice, you almost sound disappointed."

"Like you said, you haven't done anything. Right?"

"Right."

"After all, if you'd done something, I would know." She takes a long swig of her beer. Then she looks me in the eye, smiles, and says the next part in this funny James Earl Jones voice that we've each been using whenever quoting The Manual: *"The rules of The Pact come down to one essential rule: no secrets, tell your spouse everything."*

"You've told me everything, right?" she asks.

"Of course."

"Then you'll be fine, Jake. Let's get out of here."

At the Half Moon Bay Airport, all of the lights are off. Alice and I sit in the car in the dark and talk as we wait. Gone is the edge in her voice, the accusation. It's as if my Alice has come back to me, and I'm grateful. I start to wonder if I misconstrued everything she's said for the past few hours. At 8:56, a light in the office building comes on and then the landing strip flashes and ignites the night sky. I roll the window down a crack, and I can hear the sound of a plane turning over the water and angling toward the runway. Across the parking lot, the light comes on inside a car. It's a Mazda hatchback.

"Isn't that Chuck and Eve's car?" Alice says.

"Shit. Who do you think is more likely to be in trouble?"

"Chuck, for sure."

The plane lands and taxis down the runway just outside the gate. We watch as Chuck and Eve get out of the car. They stand and give each other an awkward hug, then Eve gets into the driver's seat. We get out of our car. I kiss Alice, and she holds on tight to me for a minute before letting go.

Chuck and I reach the gate at the same time. I'm carrying my bag; he's carrying nothing. "Friend," he says, motioning me through the gate.

"Friend," I reply. The word sticks in my throat.

As we approach the plane, a stairway descends. "Mates," the pilot says with an Australian accent. I climb the steps and take the first seat behind the cockpit. Chuck goes one row behind me. The plane is remarkably nice—a row of leather seats on each side, a beverage bar in the back, magazines and newspapers in the seat pockets.

"Could be a bumpy one," the pilot warns as he pulls the stairs up and closes the hatch. "Want a Coke? Water?"

We both decline, Chuck with a silent wave of the hand.

Chuck grabs a *New York Times* and begins reading, so I take it as permission to close my eyes and nod off. I'm glad I had that beer. Otherwise, I wouldn't be able to sleep. I wake up an hour later at the hum of the landing gear. The plane touches down on a bumpy runway.

"Well rested?" Chuck asks me. His mood seems to have improved. "Is this what I think it is?"

"The one and only Fernley. Good thing you slept. You're going to need your strength."

Shit.

## 57

WE TAXI DOWN THE RUNWAY AND PULL UP ALONGSIDE AN electric fence. After a couple of minutes, the door of the airplane opens and the stairs flip down. "And so it begins," Chuck says.

On the tarmac, a man and woman approach us, both dressed in a navy shirt and navy pants. The man motions Chuck to step to one side. He asks him to stand on a yellow line and put his hands up. He runs a metal-detector wand over him and conducts a surprisingly thorough search. Chuck stands there, expressionless; I can tell this is not his first visit to Fernley. When the search is complete, the guy pulls out handcuffs and leg restraints, all attached to a wide leather belt that he snaps around Chuck's waist. I brace myself, waiting for the same thing to happen to me, but it doesn't. "Ready!" the guard yells. I hear a loud buzz. The gate slides open. Chuck walks through, as if he knows the drill; the guy follows about six paces behind. The woman and I just stand there watching. I sense there is some sort of protocol, but I don't have a clue what it is.

Chuck walks up the long yellow line that stretches from the landing strip to a massive concrete building. The guard towers, double fences, barbed wire, and floodlights indicate that it was and is a prison. I shudder. One more buzz and Chuck disappears into the building, followed by his minder. The door slams shut behind them.

The woman turns to me and smiles. "Welcome to Fernley," she says in a friendly voice. Somehow, it doesn't put me at ease.

She motions to our left, where a golf cart is waiting. I throw my bag into the back. She doesn't say a word as we drive the length of the runway, around the entire prison complex, and up a long paved path. Alice said it was large, but I'm still stunned at the size of this place. We pull up in front of an ornate building that looks more like a mansion than a prison. The other side of the complex is all electric fences and concrete yards. On this side though, there is a row of green trees, a patch of brilliant grass, a tennis court, and a pool. The woman hops out of the golf cart and grabs my bag.

Inside, the mansion feels like a resort hotel. A clean-cut young man stands behind a gleaming mahogany desk. He's in uniform—a double-breasted navy suit with absurd-looking epaulets.

"Jake?"

"Guilty as charged." I instantly regret my choice of words.

"I've got you in the Kilkenny Suite." He slides a typed sheet across the desk. "Here's your schedule for tomorrow, with a map of the grounds and amenities. Mobile service is extremely limited, so if you need to make a call, let me know and I can set you up here in the conference room." He sketches a map on a sheet of paper and then points the way to my room. "We're here 24/7, so don't hesitate to come down and ask for anything you might need."

"The key?" I ask.

"You won't be needing a key, of course. There are no locks in the luxury suites."

I want to ask what the hell I did to deserve a luxury suite, but I can tell that's not the sort of thing you're supposed to ask. This whole experience is beyond bizarre. If they'd led me away in handcuffs like Chuck, I'd be less freaked out than I am now.

The elevator has a chandelier. I glance up, looking for the camera.

There it is, mounted in a corner of the ceiling. I'm in room 317, at the end of a long hallway with red carpeting. The spacious room has a king-sized bed, a flat-panel television, and a view out over the tennis courts and swimming pool. With the lack of light pollution, I can see a billion bright stars. Guiltily, I realize it couldn't be any more different from Alice's experience here.

I lie on the bed and turn on the television. It takes me a few trips through the channels to realize that the entire complex is connected to a European satellite. Eurosport, BBC One through BBC Four, a documentary on the potato famine, a special on the Baltic Coasts, *Monty Python* reruns, and some giant slalom contest from Sweden.

I check the itinerary and realize I'm supposed to be in the lounge downstairs at ten tomorrow morning. After that, it simply says "meeting" from ten to noon, then lunch, then two more hours of meetings. I'd be more comfortable if they had included a line that said "return flight: three P.M."

I watch lame UEFA soccer for two hours before I finally fall asleep. Terrified of being late, I get up at six. Five minutes after I step out of the shower, there is a knock at the door. I open it to find a tray with French toast, a mug of hot chocolate with lots of whipped cream, and the *International New York Times*.

I want to explore the grounds, the whole complex, but I'm too jittery, so I just sit in my room. I wonder what Alice is doing right now. I wonder if she misses me.

At 9:44, I take the elevator down to the lobby, dressed in slacks and a dress shirt. The desk clerk hurries over with another mug of hot chocolate and invites me to have a seat. I sink into a plush leather chair and wait. At exactly ten, a man walks into the lobby.

"Gordon," he says, holding his hand out to me. He's medium-build, his hair black with gray at the temples. He's wearing a very nice suit.

I stand to greet him.

"Pleased to finally meet. I've read so much about you."

"I hope it was all good." I force a smile.

He winks. "There's good and bad in all of us. Did you get a chance to explore the grounds?"

"No," I say, regretting my hours in the room.

"Too bad. It really is a remarkable place."

Gordon is difficult to gauge, in temperament as well as age. He looks like a healthy fifty-five, but he could be much younger. His accent is Irish, but his tan tells me that he hasn't seen Ireland in quite a while.

We walk through a maze of hallways and up four staircases. At the top of the final staircase is a corridor with windows on both sides. The walkway, which goes on for about a hundred yards, appears to bridge two worlds. On one side, you can see only the resort portion of the complex—trees, grass, pool, driving range, something that looks like a spa. The resort area is bordered on three sides by a high wall painted top to bottom with an elaborate mural of bucolic beaches, sea, and sky. The wall is so tall that, from my vantage point, I can't see beyond the resort. On the other side, the view is the complete opposite: a sprawling prison complex, electric fences, guard towers, concrete inner courtyards, people in gray jumpsuits walking slowly around a dirt track. Beyond that, the desert stretches for miles. The prison is ugly and frightening, but the desert beyond is somehow more terrifying and forbidding. It's the sort of prison that you probably wouldn't escape even if the guards and walls all fell away.

Gordon punches a long code into a keypad and the door pops open. The plush carpeting and remarkable views give way to concrete walls painted institutional green. Gordon punches a code into another keypad and motions for me to step inside. Suddenly, a younger man in a gray uniform steps out of the shadows. I shudder, feeling his breath on my neck. We keep moving deeper into the concrete building. I walk several paces behind Gordon, and the younger man walks several paces behind me. Every hundred feet or so, we come to a new set of doors. Each time, Gordon enters a code and the door opens. Each door closes behind us with a loud electronic *clang*. It is as if we are on a journey deep into the heart of this cold building. With the sound of each closing door, I'm battling an increasing sense of hopelessness.

Eventually, we descend a steep staircase. I count thirty-three steps. At the bottom, we turn right, then left, then right. I try to memorize our turns, but we go on and on through more doors, more hallways. Is Gordon using the same code for every door, or has he memorized dozens of them? At this point, even if I had the codes, there's no way I could find my way out of the building. I'm trapped.

It occurs to me that I could die in here and no one would know. I tell myself that if The Pact wanted to kill me, they could have put a bullet in my head the moment I stepped off the plane; unless, of course, Gordon simply takes pleasure in the game—leading the rat farther and farther into the maze, until I die of terror and exhaustion.

I hear sounds up ahead. I glance right to another hallway, wondering what would happen if I took off running. There has to be an exit somewhere. As if reading my mind, Gordon asks, "Would you like a tour of this part of the facility?"

"I'd love one," I reply.

It appears to be the correct response. "Splendid. We can do it as soon as we get a few of our questions out of the way."

What questions? How will I possibly know the right answers? I imagine there are answers that lead to my release, and answers that lead to more dark hallways, more goons in suits.

One last door. One last code. And then Gordon, the uniformed guy, and I are standing in a small room, about ten feet by ten feet. The room is blazingly white. There is a table in the middle, two chairs, metal rings on the table. A plain manila folder sits atop the table. One of the chairs is bolted to the ground. One wall is covered by large black plate glass. A two-way mirror? "Have a seat," Gordon says, gesturing toward the restraint chair. I sit, trying not to focus on the metal rings directly in front of me. Upon my arrival, why did I allow myself to be lulled by the luxurious room and five-star service?

Gordon sits across from me. The other guy remains standing beside the closed door. "Jake," Gordon says. "Thank you so much for taking the time to help us with this inquiry."

I'm startled to hear my name. Members seem to have one name for each other: "Friend." So what does that make Gordon?

"Why am I here?" I say, trying to keep my voice steady.

Gordon rests his elbows on the table and temples his fingers in front of his face—a classic posture of disdain, signaling intellectual superiority.

"Inquiries are essentially a closer look we take at issues that have been brought to our attention. The issues arise in a variety of ways, and we investigate until some reasonably clear determination can be made."

Blah blah blah. Another thing I've noticed about The Pact is that they never just come out and say what they mean in clear and simple language. Everything is buried under a preamble of explanation, background, and hold-harmless clauses. I imagine a dictionary in some stuffy room, filled with phrases one must memorize and overblown words Orla and her cronies have made up. Throughout history, fascists and cults have spoken their own language—words meant to obfuscate, to hide the truth, but also to make members feel special by separating them from the general population.

Gordon opens up the folder in front of him and shuffles through the papers. "So I was wondering if you might take a few moments to tell me about JoAnne Charles."

My heart sinks.

"JoAnne Charles?" I repeat, trying to act surprised and detached. "I hardly know her."

"Well, let's start with what you do know, shall we? How did you meet?"

"JoAnne Webb, or JoAnne Charles, and I used to work together at university."

Gordon gives a slight nod. "Continue."

"We were both resident advisers during our sophomore year. We saw each other two or three times a week at RA meetings and training events. We became friends. Occasionally we met to discuss the rigors of the job, compare notes, or sometimes just pass along gossip."

Gordon nods again. Seconds pass. Clearly, he wants more. I know this tactic: A person in a position without power will keep talking just to avoid the awkward silence. I won't do it.

"I have all day," Gordon prompts. "Hours. Days. I have as long as we need."

"I don't know what you want from me. Like I said, JoAnne and I hardly know each other."

He smiles. The guy by the door shifts, his uniform rustling. "Perhaps you could tell me a little more about your time working together. I don't see how there could be any harm in that."

I consider. What will they do if I keep my mouth shut? I have no doubt Gordon would keep me in this room indefinitely. "Our junior year," I say, "we were two out of only four returning advisers, so we got to know each other better. We often saw each other at mealtimes or, on occasion, during social events."

"Did you eat meals together?"

"Sometimes."

"Would you say that you two were friends?"

"I suppose. But mainly I would describe our relationship as being that of work colleagues. Of course, living in close quarters, we came to know each other pretty well."

"Did you ever meet her family?"

I think back. "Maybe, I guess. But that was a long time ago."

The guy by the door is beginning to look impatient. This makes me nervous. "Is it possible that you met her family"—Gordon pauses while thumbing through the file—"during your junior year, when you traveled to Palos Verdes to enjoy Thanksgiving dinner at her family's residence?"

How the hell could he know that?

"Yes, that is possible."

"Did you visit her home after that?"

"Maybe. Like I said, it was a long time ago."

"Is it possible that you visited her family's home on five more occasions?"

"It's not like I kept a diary," I say.

He ignores the irritation in my voice. "Did you have a relationship with JoAnne?"

I look down at the table, the metal restraints. Why haven't they put me in the restraints? Are they meant as a threat? What is the answer that triggers the guy in the uniform to come over and force my wrists into the cuffs?

"A romantic relationship?" Gordon clarifies.

I shake my head. "No," I say emphatically.

"But you knew her pretty well?"

"Yes, I suppose I did. Many years ago."

"Before, you said that you hardly know her."

I glance at the two-way mirror. Who is behind the glass? And why do they care so much about my history with JoAnne? "People change a lot in twenty years. It is, in fact, true that I hardly know her now. After graduation, we both moved on to graduate schools in different states."

"And you never saw her again until you met up at Villa Carina?"

"Correct."

"Though it's possible you may have exchanged a few emails or letters?"

"I exchanged emails with a lot of people I knew in college. I didn't keep track."

"When you saw her at Villa Carina, you recognized her right away?"

"Of course."

"Were you happy to see her?"

"Sure, why not? JoAnne is—was—a great person. It was nice to see an old friend in a strange, unfamiliar situation."

"When did you see her after that?"

I try not to hesitate. In my mind though, I imagine someone behind the mirror studying my every move. Maybe they even have hidden electronic equipment measuring my heart rate and temperature, assessing my nonverbal cues. "It was at the quarterly party in Woodside."

"How did she seem?"

"She was with her husband, Neil," I say evenly. "They seemed very happy together."

"Do you recall what she was wearing?"

"A blue dress," I say, and instantly regret it. I know what he must be thinking: Why was I paying such close attention?

"And after that?"

"That was the last time I saw her." I say this last line with as much detached definitiveness as I can muster. I've committed to the lie, right or wrong, and now the only option is to see it through.

Gordon smiles, shuffles the papers, and looks up at the man in uniform. "The last time," he says, chuckling.

"Yes."

We sit in silence, my lie hanging in the air between us.

"Is JoAnne here?" I ask finally. Stupid, maybe, but I need to get in front of the questions.

Gordon seems surprised. "As a matter of fact, she is. Would you like to see her?"

Shit. Now that I've brought it up, it would seem suspicious if I didn't want to, wouldn't it? "Seeing as how I don't know anyone else around here, yes, I guess I would."

"Perhaps we could do a short tour," Gordon tells me. "Then we can get you on the early plane back to Half Moon Bay."

"Sounds good," I say, trying not to seem too eager. Does this mean I passed the test? Will I no longer need to do the two-hour session after lunch that was printed on my schedule?

The guy in uniform nods toward the two-way glass and the door opens. This time, the young guy leads, I'm in the middle, and Gordon follows. We pass through a couple of hallways, then step out a door to find ourselves in the exercise yard, surrounded on all sides by prison walls. I take a deep breath of the dry, warm air and blink in the sudden sunlight. There's a basketball court and dirt track, but not much more. An older blond guy in a blood-red jumpsuit sits on a bench at the far end of the yard. Seeing us, he stands at attention. The uniformed guy walks toward him.

Gordon gives a brief history of the prison as we walk across the yard. "This complex was built in 1983 for the state of Nevada," he recites. "It housed nine hundred and eighty medium- and high-security prisoners on average for thirteen years. The state of Nevada decided to contract out a large portion of its prison population during the early 2000s, which led to Fernley being shuttered. The location was too inconvenient and too expensive, and there were some unfortunate escape attempts that the inmates did not survive."

We've arrived at the door of another building. I look back to see the man in uniform standing with the guy in the jumpsuit. Not with him, exactly, but behind him. He appears to be putting the guy in handcuffs.

We pass through another door. Inside, a woman sits at a desk behind a plate-glass window. On the wall are dozens of CCTV monitors. She glances away from the monitors and nods at Gordon, then passes a bright orange badge on a lanyard through the slot under the window. Gordon takes the badge and thanks her. "Wear this," he says, looping the lanyard around my neck.

The woman flips a switch; a steel door swings open. Now it appears that we are in the heart of the prison. There are corridors to our right and left, and one in front of us. Each hallway extends up three levels, and I quickly count twenty cells per level. Although it's mostly quiet, random sounds tell me that not all the cells are empty.

"Do you want to try a cell?" Gordon asks as we walk through the cellblock.

"Funny," I say.

"It wasn't a joke."

In one cell, a man sits on his cot, reading The Manual. It is a sobering view. There's something incongruous about the Spartan cell, the blood-red jumpsuit, and the guy's nice haircut and well-manicured hands.

We arrive at a cafeteria. No one is at the tables, but I can hear the banging of pots and pans. The long metal tables and benches, all bolted to the floor, are clearly from the original prison. The smells seem out of place—I get a whiff of fresh vegetables, spices, grilled chicken.

"The food here is pretty good," Gordon says, again reading my mind. "It's all cooked by the inmates. This week, we're fortunate to have a gentleman here who owns a Michelin-starred restaurant in Montreal. He did a chocolate mousse yesterday that was unbelievable. If you stick around, you won't be sorry."

I have the distinct feeling that he's fucking with me. *If I stick around.* As if I have some choice in anything that happens to me here.

Suddenly, the kitchen noises subside. The only sounds are our footsteps on the polished concrete floors.

"Did you say JoAnne was here?" I ask nervously.

"Yes," Gordon says. "Patience."

We walk through another door and emerge into an octagon-shaped room. There are eight doors around a central area. Each door has a narrow slot in the middle. It occurs to me, horrifically, that we've arrived in some sort of solitary-confinement block. I listen for signs of life from within the cells. There is a single cough, then silence.

The therapist in me is not only horrified but incensed. How can they use solitary confinement? "Who's there?" I say, half-expecting to hear JoAnne's frightened voice calling back to me.

Gordon grabs my arm. "Relax," he says, but his grip is anything but relaxing. "Did anyone force you to be here?"

"No."

"Precisely. Every inmate in this building is like you. Like your lovely wife, Alice."

I shudder to hear her name coming out of his mouth. "No one is here against his or her will, Jake. All of our inmates understand their crimes and are grateful to have the opportunity for realignment in a supportive environment."

He steps over to the cell and leans down to speak through the slot. "Are you here on your own recognizance?"

For a moment, nothing. And then a male voice answers, "Yes."

"Are you being held against your will?"

"No." His voice is thin, tired.

"What is the nature of your stay here?"

More quickly this time, no hesitation: "Realignment due to repeat crimes of Emotional Infidelity." I can't place his accent. Japanese, maybe.

"And how is your progress?"

"Steady. I am grateful to have the opportunity to realign my actions within the parameters of my marriage and the laws of The Pact."

"Wonderful," Gordon says into the cell. "Do you need anything?"

"I have everything I need."

Shit. Can this be real?

Gordon turns back to me. "I know what you're thinking, Jake. I see the concern on your face. I can assure you that, while these cells may originally have been constructed for solitary confinement, we prefer to think of them as monastic rooms in which members who have gone far afield can reacquaint themselves, in their own good time, with their vows."

"How long has he been in there?"

Gordon smiles. "Does one ask the monk how long he has been in his monastic cell? Does one require the nun to answer for her devotion to her God?"

He places his hand on my arm again, gently this time. "Come, we're almost there."

We step through yet another door, and he points to the right, toward what looks like a waiting room. "That section is the holding area for pretrial. I believe your wife spent some time with us over there. She was extremely cooperative. An ideal visitor, really, to our facility. The courtrooms, pretrial meeting rooms, and attorneys are all down there. But that's not where we're going today."

He turns left, toward a set of double doors. While all of the other doors have keypads, this one is secured with a chain and padlock.

"This is our special wing for long-term pretrial. This is where we will find your friend JoAnne. Actually, this business with JoAnne is interesting, unexpected. Most of our visitors find that honesty helps move things along quickly. It's better that way for everyone."

Gordon spins the wheel on the padlock. The padlock pops open, and he noisily unloops the chain. Once we're inside, the door slams shut behind us. The motion sensor clicks and a spotlight comes on, shining down into the middle of the room, where a square platform rises out of the floor. Two concrete steps lead up to the platform. Around it are thick glass walls. One of the walls has a lock and a handle. Gordon stands on the top step, slips a key into the lock, and opens the glass door.

"You're free to go inside, Jake."

There, in the corner, pressed against the glass, beneath the harsh lights, someone is curled in a fetal position. I don't want to go inside. I want to turn, fight off Gordon if I have to, flee this horrible building. But I know instantly that I cannot. The door has locked behind us, the sound of it still echoing around the concrete walls.

I walk up the steps and into the glass-walled room. When I hear the door shut behind me, my stomach churns. There are no chairs inside this glass box. There is no bed. No blanket. Only a metal toilet in the corner and a cold, hard floor all around. The room beyond us is pitch-black. I know Gordon is there, outside the glass, but I can't see him.

"JoAnne?" I whisper.

She uncurls from her ball and looks up at me. She blinks, then shields her eyes, crying out. She must have been in the dark for a day or two, possibly longer. She is entirely naked, matted brown hair falling around her shoulders. Slowly, she moves her hands, peering at me from dazed eyes as if I have yanked her out of a very deep sleep. "Jake?"

"It's me."

She sits up, back pressed to the wall. She pulls her knees up to her chest, trying to cover her nudity.

"They took my contact lenses," she says. "You're a blur."

I look around the room for microphones. I don't see any, but what does that mean? I sense Gordon, just outside the box. Watching. Listening.

I sit down across from JoAnne, my back to the glass, hoping to provide her with some sense of protection from Gordon's prying eyes. "They asked me about you." I want to get my story out before she says something that could get us both into trouble. Of course, it's possible that she already told them about our meeting at Hillsdale. I tremble at the thought that they already know everything.

"I told them the truth," I say in a loud, clear voice. "How I haven't seen you since Gene's party in Woodside." She still seems groggy, so I'm not even sure if she understands what I'm saying. "I told them how you and Neil were so happy."

"I'm embarrassed," she says, blinking. Have they drugged her? "It's been twenty years since you saw me naked."

I am swept back to the memory of a sweet, blundering night in her dorm room. How awkward she had been.

I cringe. Why did she have to mention that? It contradicts everything I've said.

"You must be thinking of someone else." I sense that Gordon is parsing every word, scrutinizing every movement, and it dawns on me, with horrifying clarity, that my entire trip—the deceptively luxurious room, the disorienting journey through the prison maze, the interrogation, the glimpse of solitary confinement—has been arranged to bring me to this exact moment.

"I shouldn't be embarrassed by my nudity," she continues, as if she hadn't heard me. "That's what they want, but there's no reason for it." She unfolds her arms and lays her legs flat. Her feet are pointed directly at me. Her breasts are small, her body pale. Suddenly, she spreads her legs slightly. Involuntarily, my eyes flicker there. I blush and raise my gaze back to her face. She gives me a quick, strange smile.

Just then, I hear a rumbling, and the wall I'm leaning against begins to move. At first I think I must be imagining it. But then I see that the wall behind JoAnne is definitely moving. I scoot forward. So does JoAnne.

"Every hour," she says, "the room gets an inch smaller."

"What?"

"The room is shrinking. That's how unhappy they are with me. I will be a flat, naked pancake before they realize I've been telling the truth all along."

The coldness in her voice sends shivers through me. How can she be so nonchalant? Would they really do such a monstrous thing? Surely not. I think of the psychological experiments I read about in college, the experiments JoAnne and I talked about during late-night study sessions—experiments so cruel the subjects still experienced nightmares and fractured personalities years later. One of our professors even had us design hypothetical experiments in obedience. Back then, it all seemed so abstract.

"JoAnne, what do they think you're lying about?"

"They think I'm having an affair with you. Not just you—others too. Neil found a schedule on my phone. He misinterpreted it. He thought I was having a secret rendezvous at the Hillsdale mall."

"That's bullshit!" I say, too loudly.

"Isn't it?" she agrees. "How romantic. The Hillsdale mall. The irony is, he's worried that I'm fucking you, and his punishment is to send me away and have me put in a box, naked, with you. He's both paranoid and stupid."

Before I can reply, the door opens. Gordon stands just outside the glass, on the top step, looking angry.

"Are you going to be okay?" I ask JoAnne. A ridiculous question. Of course she is not going to be okay.

She hugs her knees to her chest again. "Don't worry about me," she says drily. "Haven't they told you? Everyone comes here of their own free will. We're all just salivating for reeducation. Really, they're doing me a favor."

She glares up at Gordon, defiant.

"Time's up," Gordon says.

I step out of the box and down the steps, and follow Gordon to the door. I glance back. JoAnne is now standing, facing me, palms pressed against the glass wall.

I grab Gordon's arm. "We can't leave her here."

But before I have a chance to say anything else, I feel something slam against the back of my knees. My legs buckle and I go down. My head slams against the concrete floor, and everything goes dark.

## 58

I COME TO ON A CESSNA, BUMPING THROUGH THE AIR. MY HEAD IS throbbing, and there is blood on my shirt. I have no idea how much time has passed. I look at my hands, expecting to see restraints, but there are none. Just an ordinary seatbelt looped around my waist. Who strapped me in? I don't even remember boarding the plane.

Through the open door of the cockpit, I see the back of the pilot's head. It's just the two of us. There is snow in the mountains, wind buffeting the plane. The pilot seems completely focused on his controls, shoulders tense.

I reach up and touch my head. The blood has dried, leaving a sticky mess. My stomach rumbles. The last thing I ate was the French toast. How long ago was that? On the seat beside me, I find water and a sandwich wrapped in wax paper. I open the bottle and drink.

I unwrap my sandwich—ham and Swiss—and take a bite. Shit. My jaw hurts too much to chew. Someone must have punched me in the face after I hit the ground.

"Are we going home?" I ask the pilot.

"Depends on what you call home. We're headed to Half Moon Bay."

"They didn't tell you anything about me?"

"First name, destination, that's about it. I'm just the taxi driver, Jake."

"But you're a member, right?"

"Sure," he says, his tone unreadable. "Fidelity to the spouse, loyalty to The Pact. Till death do us part." He turns back just long enough to give me a look that tells me not to ask any more questions.

We hit an air pocket so hard my sandwich goes flying. An urgent beeping erupts. The pilot curses and frantically pushes buttons. He shouts something to air traffic control. We're descending fast, and I'm clutching the armrests, thinking of Alice, going over our final conversation, wishing I'd said so many things.

Then, suddenly, the plane levels out, we gain altitude, and all appears to be well. I gather the pieces of my sandwich from the floor, wrap the whole mess back up in the wax paper, and set it on the seat beside me.

"Sorry for the turbulence," the pilot says.

"Not your fault. Good save."

Over sunny Sacramento, he finally relaxes, and we talk about the Golden State Warriors and their surprising run this season.

"What day is it?" I ask.

"Tuesday."

I'm relieved to see the familiar coastline out my window, grateful for the sight of the little Half Moon Bay Airport. The landing is smooth. Once we touch down, the pilot turns and says, "Don't make it a habit, right?"

"I don't plan to."

I grab my bag and step outside. Without killing the engines, the pilot closes the door, swings the plane around, and takes off again.

I walk into the airport café, order a hot chocolate, and text Alice. It's two P.M. on a weekday, so she's probably embroiled in a thousand meetings. I really need to see her.

A text reply arrives. *Where are you?*

*Back in HMB.*

*Will leave in 5.*

It's more than twenty miles from Alice's office to Half Moon Bay. She texts about traffic downtown, so I order French toast and bacon.

The café is empty. The perky waitress in the perfectly pressed uniform hovers. When I pay the check, she says, "Have a good day, Friend."

I go outside and sit on a bench to wait. It's cold, the fog coming down in waves. By the time Alice's old Jaguar pulls up, I'm frozen. I stand up, and as I'm checking to make sure I have everything, Alice walks over to the bench. She's wearing a serious suit, but she has changed out of heels into sneakers for the drive. Her black hair is damp in the fog. Her lips are dark red, and I wonder if she did this for me. I hope so.

She stands on her tiptoes to kiss me. Only then do I realize how desperately I've missed her. Then she steps back and looks me up and down.

"At least you're in one piece." She reaches up and touches my jaw gently. "What happened?"

"Not sure."

I wrap my arms around her.

"So why were you summoned?"

There's so much I want to tell her, but I'm scared. The more she knows, the more dangerous it will be for her. Also, let's face it, the truth is going to piss her off.

What I'd give to go back to the beginning—before the wedding, before Finnegan, before The Pact turned our lives upside down.

"Do you have time?"

"Sure. Can you drive? I can't see in this fog." She tosses me the keys.

I put my duffel in the trunk, get into the driver's seat, and lean over to unlock the passenger-side door. I pull back onto the highway. At Pillar Point Harbor, I turn toward the ocean. I park across the street from Barbara's Fishtrap, looking around to make sure we haven't been followed.

"You okay?" Alice asks.

"Not really."

The place is almost empty, so we take a table in the corner with a hazy view out over the water. She orders the fish and chips, and a Diet Coke. I get a BLT and a beer. When the drinks arrive, I gulp half of mine down in one sip.

"Tell me exactly what happened," she says. "Don't leave anything out."

But that's just the problem, isn't it? All the things I've left out.

I'm still trying to figure out how to tell her, mentally editing and revising my story. I'm not sure how I got to this point; I wish I had just told her everything from the beginning. Of course, all of my small decisions made perfect sense in a vacuum, but now, in hindsight, the parts don't entirely add up.

I tell her about how Chuck and I got separated after we arrived at Fernley. "They cuffed him and took him to a different building."

"Where is he now?"

"I don't know." I tell her about my luxurious accommodations.

"So you really weren't in trouble, then?" She sounds surprised.

The waitress brings our plates, and Alice digs into her fish and chips. Even though I'm still hungry, I pick at my food. "It's complicated."

"Were you or weren't you?"

"They wanted to ask me about JoAnne."

Alice's relaxed demeanor changes instantly. I can see anxiety forming; her eyes change; that telltale worry line between her brows deepens. As I mentioned, Alice's issues all fall into that complicated, dark area where insecurity, jealousy, and suspicion collide. When we first met, it would often come on swiftly and catch me off guard. It was a bad mixture. I would get angry or defensive, and my defensiveness would only heighten her suspicion. I told myself it was something we could get past once we were engaged, once she was certain of my love for her, my commitment. And since the engagement, and certainly the marriage, her episodes of jealousy have been less frequent. And when they do happen, I've been more intuitive. Usually, I see them coming, and I react in a way that deescalates the situation. Here, though, I'm not sure how to proceed.

"JoAnne from the dorm?" she says, setting her fork down beside her plate.

"Yes."

"Oh." I can sense her doing a million calculations in her head. The jealous Alice is so opposite from the regular, quirky, independent Alice. Even though I know both sides of her now, the transformation is always jarring. "The mousy one who cornered you at Draeger's?"

I nod.

"Why would they ask you about her?" She seems baffled. As I mentioned, JoAnne isn't the kind of person who stands out. Not the kind of person a wife would necessarily notice, or worry about.

"Later, at the second party, I talked to her again. She was obviously stressed about something. She was worried Neil or someone would see us talking, so I asked if we could talk later, somewhere else. I wanted to find a way out of The Pact for both of us. She finally agreed to meet me at the Hillsdale mall."

"Why didn't you tell me?"

"She was paranoid. She asked me not to bring you. She worried that if Neil found out that we were talking about The Pact, we'd all be in deep shit. She'd already spent time at Fernley; she didn't want to go back. And I remembered that she had bruises on her legs at the party . . . She seemed so disturbed. Terrified. Why would I drag you into that?"

Alice pushes away from the table and folds her arms. "After you first introduced us, I asked if you'd slept with her. You said no. Was that the truth?"

I should have prepared an answer to this question. But really, there's no way to make it look like I wasn't hiding something from her. "We might have dated a little. Back in college. It didn't work out, so after a few months we went back to just being friends."

"A few *months*? So you lied to me. Deliberately."

"I was so surprised to see her that night at the first party. It was all so out of context—"

"Sex is rarely out of context." Alice is angry now, tears rolling down her face. And yes, I'll admit it: Her tears make me angry.

"It was seventeen years ago, Alice! It was irrelevant." I look up and realize that our server is watching. We shouldn't even be talking here. We shouldn't say anything in public. I lower my voice. "What were you doing seventeen years ago? Who were *you* sleeping with?"

As soon as I've said it, I regret it.

"First of all, you know exactly where I was and what I was doing, because *I've told you.* This is not about what happened seventeen years ago; I don't give a shit about that. It's about what happened in the past few weeks. It's about you *lying* to me *now,* in the present." Alice falls silent, and I can see that something has occurred to her. "That's why Dave kept mentioning you and the Hillsdale mall." She shakes her head. "When I told you about it, you didn't say a word. You intentionally kept me in the dark."

Something flickers in Alice's eyes I've never seen before: disappointment.

"Look, I'm sorry. But I was desperate to see if there was a way out. And I knew that if I told you, you'd want to go, and it would be even more risky. You'd just gotten back from Fernley. I was trying to protect you." When I hear the words, I realize how feeble they sound.

"Don't you think that should have been *my* decision? Aren't we supposed to be in this together?"

"Listen, when I saw JoAnne at the mall, she told me some things that scared me. She said that there was a couple in The Pact before us— Eli and Elaine. Just weeks before we joined, they disappeared. Their car was found at Stinson Beach, and they haven't been seen since. JoAnne is certain they were murdered. By The Pact."

Doubt passes over Alice's face. "I'll admit their tactics are extreme, but murder is a little far-fetched, don't you think? Seriously."

"Hear me out. She said the one thing no one ever mentions is that The Pact has an alarmingly high rate of marriages ending in early death."

Alice is shaking her head.

"What about Dave?" I say. "He and Kerri were both married to other people when they joined the Pact."

"Coincidence. You can't base a huge conspiracy theory on one coincidence."

"Here's the important thing. JoAnne says we have to find a way to get off their radar. She thinks you're in danger. She thinks they like you, but they feel you need to be corralled, controlled. She said they don't know what to make of me."

"Did you meet her again after that?" Alice has unfolded her arms and is facing me directly. I imagine that this is something she does during her more difficult depositions. It makes me uncomfortable.

"She agreed to meet me in the same spot three weeks later, but she didn't show. When I left, I realized I was being followed."

"And you haven't seen her since?" Alice asks.

"No. Well, yes. She was at Fernley. But she wasn't there like me, or even like you. She was in a *cage,* Alice. A glass cage that was literally shrinking, with her in it."

Alice's face changes, and she laughs out loud. "You're not serious!" Alice is strange that way—she can switch in an instant from jealousy and anger to perfectly normal conversation. Her laugh is hard to read.

"It's not a joke, Alice. She was in serious trouble."

I tell her about the endless corridors, the locked doors. I tell her about the interview with Gordon. "They just kept asking me all of these questions about JoAnne."

"*Why* would they ask you about her, Jake? So help me God, if you fucked her again, we're finished. There's nothing you or The Pact or anyone else can do to make me stay—"

"I did *not* fuck her!"

But I can see it in her eyes: She doesn't entirely believe me.

I look over to the table next to us. A couple around our age are sitting with a bucket of fried shrimp between them. They're picking at the food, clearly tuned in to our conversation. Alice notices them too and scoots her chair closer to the table.

I tell her about the sole occupant of solitary confinement. I tell her about JoAnne's matted hair, her nakedness, her obvious fear. I don't leave anything out. Okay, maybe I don't mention JoAnne spreading her legs, but I tell her everything else. Alice's face registers confusion, then horror. And I can see we've moved past the jealousy, and now we're in this together again, Alice and me against something bigger.

She's sitting in stunned silence when her phone goes off. The vibration on the table makes us both gasp. Immediately, I fear that it's The Pact calling. Dave, maybe, or even Vivian.

"Just the office," Alice says, answering. She listens for a minute or more, then just says "Okay." She hangs up. "I have to go into work."

"Now?"

"Now." Nothing more. Before, she would have told me why. She would have confided in me about the case, complained about office politics. But instead, she tells me nothing. I can tell she doesn't like me very much right now.

When we get to the car, she asks me for the keys. She drives fast, making abrupt stops and rough turns. All the way home, through the tunnel, up past Pacifica and Daly City, I can tell that Alice is still trying to process what I've told her. She dumps me out front of our house, clicks the garage door open for me to enter, then heads to work.

I take a shower and change. When I open my overnight bag, I realize that my clothes smell like Fernley. It's a mix of desert air, cleaning fluid, and five-star cuisine. I turn on the TV, but I'm too wired to watch anything, too stressed about the tension with Alice. Things have never been this way with us before. I mean, we've had episodes, but not like this.

I throw on my coat and head over to the office. Huang frowns when he sees me. "Bad news, Jake. We lost two couples today. The Stantons and the Wallings called to cancel their appointments."

"For this week?"

"No. Forever. They both filed for divorce."

The Wallings don't surprise me, but I had real hopes for the Stantons. Jim and Elizabeth, married fourteen years, both super-nice, well matched. I sulk down the hallway, feeling the weight of failure. How can I save anyone else's marriage if I can't save my own?

# 59

The study that interests me the most is about the effectiveness of marriage counseling. Does counseling correlate with a higher or lower likelihood of divorce? In my own practice, I've seen mixed results, though it seems that the couples who persevere through at least eight to ten weeks of sessions tend to emerge with a stronger bond than the one they shared on the first day.

There's one interesting study from several years ago, involving 134 couples whose marriages were in serious distress. Two-thirds of the couples showed significant improvement following a year of therapy. Five years later, one-fourth of the couples had divorced, while one-third reported being happy together. The remaining couples were still together, though not necessarily happy. The deciding factor seemed to be whether both spouses really wanted to improve their marriage.

# 60

THAT EVENING, I TEXT ALICE ABOUT DINNER. I DIDN'T REALLY EAT anything at Barbara's Fishtrap, and I'm famished. Twenty minutes later, she responds, *Eat without me. I'll be late.*

Usually, that means she'll be home around midnight, so I hunker down in my office to take care of paperwork. Ian finishes with his last patient at eight, and I am left alone in the quiet office.

Sometime around eleven, I head out. The house is dark and cold. I turn on the heater and wait for the *whoosh* of air pushing through the old pipes, but nothing happens. I don't have the energy to start a fire or get something in the oven to warm the place up. The issue with Alice feels like a black cloud over me, and the Stantons' divorce makes it worse. I don't even want to think about The Pact. Certainly, there is trouble ahead. But at the moment, I don't have the energy to formulate a plan or even consider the next step.

I sprawl on the couch, exhausted. From the back bedroom, I can hear three bell tones—email arriving on Alice's iPad. Strangely, it doesn't make me worry about Eric the bass player. Why did I even look at that previous email? It all seems so stupid and insecure.

Still, I have to admit that it irritates me—Alice is treating me badly for a meeting I had with an old girlfriend, and yet at the same time her iPad is probably pinging with multiple emails from her old boyfriend. Of course, the jealous mind rarely interprets one's own actions in the same light as the actions of others.

I think about the Stantons and our nine meetings together. Therapy is unlike other human interactions, the calculations entirely different. In nine hours of serious, direct, unwavering discussion, you get to know a person deeply. I rarely heed my training to stay disconnected, simply an observer. No, with the ones I truly have hope for, I spend many hours thinking about how I can help them get to the place they need to be.

I think back on the sessions: What did I say, and what could I have said differently? Unfortunately, I remember it all, and so I'm able to critique my sentences, edit and revise them. Now that it's too late for the Stantons, I know what I should have said, the questions I should have asked.

When I went into therapy, I didn't realize what I was getting into. I wanted to help people. I only saw the upside of the job. I would take people at a point of trouble in their lives, and I would help them move incrementally toward a position of greater happiness. It seemed simple. What I didn't realize is that victories in therapy come slowly. They are spread out over many sessions—often many months, even years—and they are shrouded in various disguises. The defeats, on the other hand, come suddenly, without ambiguity and often without warning.

I don't consider the Wallings' divorce to be a defeat. They were already there when I first met them; they simply didn't recognize it. More important, divorce was the best choice for them. The Pact would disagree, but I know one thing for certain: Some people are not meant to be married. The Stantons, though, that's a true defeat.

I've dozed off when I hear the garage door open. I check my phone: 12:47. I get up and brush my teeth so I can greet Alice with a kiss, if she'll have one, but she stays in her car for a long time, listening to music, something loud with a bass beat. I can hear and feel it through the floor. Finally, she comes softly up the back stairs and into the kitchen. I can't tell if she is still angry, or merely tired. She glances at me, but doesn't really seem to see me. "I need some sleep," she says, heading for our bedroom. And that's it. I turn on the dishwasher, check the dead bolt on the front door, and turn out the lights.

In our room, Alice has already fallen asleep. I crawl into bed beside her. She is turned away from me, toward the window. I want to hold her, but I don't reach out. Still, I can feel the heat emanating from her body, and it fills me with longing. After everything that happened at Fernley, I want to be in my home, in my bed, with my wife. But what happened there has changed things between us. Or if I'm honest, it's not only what happened at Fernley. It's everything that led up to Fernley.

I stare at her back, willing her to wake up, but she doesn't.

So I'll just go ahead and say it: I feel like a failure. It's a rotten feeling. This is the first time in a long time that issues have mounted and the solutions haven't become apparent to me at the start. I'm caught off guard by my own inability to reason through the difficulties. Predictability is the consolation prize that comes with getting older. The older you get, the more experience you accumulate, the easier it becomes to know instantly, in so many different situations, what the future will hold. In my teens, everything was new and vibrant and mysterious, and I found myself constantly surprised. And then I reached the age where surprises became more rare. And though life is perhaps less exciting when you can predict what will happen next, I somehow like it better that way.

Now all that certainty has vanished.

## 61

I T'S A WEDNESDAY, SO I DON'T GO HOME FOR LUNCH. I PRETEND THAT I'm too busy with work, preparing for my one-on-one with Dylan, the high school freshman with depression. The reality, of course, is that I don't want to be at home when the messenger shows up. I don't want to have that awkward conversation while my eyes see the dreaded envelope. I don't want to sign the delivery slip, I don't want to be responsible for deciding the way forward. Most of all, I don't want to face the troubles ahead. I realize it's immature, but I just can't do it today.

The sit-down with Dylan goes poorly, and it worries me. Are there no clear answers for Dylan right now, or is it me? Still, trying to break this spell, I leave at a normal time, and I pick up some fresh greens and chicken on the way home. Other therapists laugh at the power-of-positive-thinking movement from the 1970s, but I'm not so quick to dismiss its effectiveness. Optimistic people are happier than pessimistic or cynical people—dumb but true, even if sometimes you're only faking it.

At home, I'm relieved to discover there's nothing from the messenger. I dive into the comforting routine of making dinner. I'm listening for Alice's car, but I'm also keeping an eye on the phone. From the bedroom, I hear the ping of email on the iPad. At seven thirty-five, just when the chicken is out of the oven, the bread is sliced and on the table, and the wine bottle is open, I get a text from Alice.

*Working late, eat without me.*

I wait up. She doesn't show. It's after one in the morning when I finally go to bed. It's after two when she quietly slides in next to me. Her body, in her thin T-shirt and underwear, is so warm and nice. When I roll over and put an arm around her, she stiffens. At six, when I awake, she is gone.

I'll come right out and say it. I'm terrified that I'm losing my wife.

At the office, I brace myself for a long day. Three couples in the morning, and the Thursday group of teenagers in the afternoon. The teenagers are combative. Like animals on the savanna, they sense weakness instantly and rarely have qualms about moving in for a quick attack.

The session with the Reeds, Eugene and Judy, at nine, goes surprisingly well. At eleven, the Fiorinas arrive. Brian and Nora are my youngest clients, thirty-one and twenty-nine. Usually, marriage counseling is the wife's idea, but not in this case. They've been married for just nineteen months, and the cracks have already begun to appear. Brian got my number from an old client he plays tennis with. Nora was resistant at first but agreed to do it as a favor to her husband. In our first session, they told me their story: They met online and married quickly. Nora is from Singapore and had immigration problems, and if they hadn't gotten married, she would have had to return home. They're both in tech, although when we met, Nora was still looking for a new job after losing her H-1B visa. Her troubles with finding a job have wreaked havoc on her confidence, and her lack of confidence seems to be eroding their marriage.

This morning, Nora is in a feisty mood. I can tell they had a fight in the car outside my office or on the ride over. Brian looks bone-tired. "I'm not sure why we're doing this," Nora begins, plopping down in the big chair.

Brian sits on the couch, arms folded, leaning into the corner, clearly not open to venturing a response. Nora is ramrod straight, her hair pulled back too tight.

"Why *are* you here?" I ask quietly.

Nora looks frustrated. "I guess because it was scheduled on my calendar."

"That's it?"

"That's it."

Brian rolls his eyes.

And then it's quiet for a minute. A minute can feel like a long time, but sometimes that's what a session needs. Like a run on the beach, sometimes in a therapy session a minute of silence serves as a release valve—tension slowly leaking out, anxiety working its way to the top before evaporating.

"Do you see value in marriage?" I ask. "Do you want to be married?"

Nora glances at her husband. Brian rustles to life. His expression tells me he's surprised by my question, and not necessarily happy.

"I feel," Nora says, measuring her words, staring only at me, "that being alone might be easier. No responsibility, do what I want, eat what I want, go where I want, no questions, no need for answers. Simple."

"Yes, that would be simple," I agree. I leave a little more silence. "But is simple always best?"

"Of course," she says without thinking. And then she glares at me, as if she's playing a game of checkers and has just been kinged.

"There's a song I like," I say, "by Mariachi El Bronx. I was listening to it this morning. The chorus is about how everyone wants to be alone, until they find themselves alone." I quickly pull up the song on my iPod and play it; the soft melody changes the mood in the room.

Nora seems to be contemplating the lyrics.

"Simple is easy," I say. "I'll give you that. No trouble. No complications. But you know what? Humans are complex. Yes, we like simple, we like easy, we don't like problems. It's relaxing to live a simple life, without complicated relationships. I'm drawn to it myself. Sometimes I just want to be alone, at home, on the couch, eating cereal, watching television."

Brian is leaning forward now. We've been meeting for five weeks, and I've probably spoken more words today than in all of their previous sessions combined.

"But you know what?" I say to Nora. "Sometimes I need complicated, I need complex. It's interesting. It challenges me. Easy rarely achieves anything grand, and sometimes I want something grand."

Nora appears to be softening. Her shoulders have relaxed. Her expression has gone from angry to neutral.

"Do you like Brian?" I ask her.

"Yes."

"Does he treat you well?"

"Of course he does."

"Are you attracted to him?"

Nora smiles for the first time. "Yes."

"What's not to love?" Brian says, patting his overgrown stomach, and they both laugh.

And that's when I know they'll be okay.

# 62

ANOTHER FULL DAY GOES BY WITHOUT ALICE CALLING, EMAILING, or texting. We've reached that dreaded marital stage that usually doesn't come until years after the wedding. We're living like roommates, not lovers. Sure, we share a bed, but we're never awake at the same time.

It's already dark when I pick up my phone and text, *Dinner?*

*Will be late.*

*You have to eat.*

*I have Wheat Thins.*

*Can I bring you something?*

Long pause. No response. *I'll be out front at nine,* I text.

Longer pause. *OK.*

I pack sandwiches, chips, drinks, and brownies in an insulated bag. I arrive early, so I pull into the loading zone beside Alice's office building and just sit in the dark, listening to the radio. KMOO is doing the album caravan, and tonight it's *Blood on the Tracks.* Of course. It's one of the greatest albums of all time, yet I wish they'd chosen something else. Something happier. Marriage is difficult. Dylan understood that.

As the opening bars of "Simple Twist of Fate" come on the radio, Alice opens the passenger door and slides into the front seat.

"*Blood on the Tracks*?" She laughs. "How apropos."

I hand her a sandwich and a bag of SunChips. I give her the choice of Peroni or Diet Coke, and she takes the latter. She digs into her food like a small wild animal. We don't speak, just eat, listening to the music.

"I would've preferred *Planet Waves*," I say.

"Of course you would." Then she sings a few lines from "Wedding Song." Her voice, even when she's angry with me, is so pure and pleasing. But then she transitions from the brilliant, happy "Wedding Song" into singing along with Dylan, who's now moved on to "Idiot Wind."

She looks at me. So much in a look.

She finishes her sandwich, balls up the used paper, and stuffs it into the bag. "Vadim has been working for me nonstop for the past three days."

"I'm not surprised. Vadim has a crush on you."

"I know. But listen, he's been working for *me*, on a personal research project."

"Shit, Alice. You didn't tell Vadim what's going on with The Pact, did you?" I can almost feel my blood pressure rising. Dylan is singing about gravity pulling us down.

"Of course not. I just asked him about Eli and Elaine. Here's the thing, Jake. He's checked every major database, public records, LexisNexis, Pacer, Google, the news, everything. He's called friends, the best hackers, and you know what he found? Nothing. There is no missing couple named Eli and Elaine. There have been no marriages between anyone with those names over the past five years. Not in San Francisco, not in California. There aren't any couples with those names who've lived in the Bay Area during that time either. There was no disappearance at Stinson Beach. Eli and Elaine don't exist."

"That doesn't make sense." I'm struggling to process what she's telling me. Why would JoAnne make that stuff up?

"There's more. Dave's first wife died after a nasty battle with cancer. At Stanford, with Dave standing by her side. Sad, not mysterious. You told me that his current wife, Kerri, had been widowed under mysterious circumstances. But her first husband, Alex, died of liver disease.

At Mills-Peninsula Hospital in Burlingame. Also sad, but certainly not mysterious. I think your pasty ex-girlfriend is full of shit."

I think about what she's telling me. Dylan is still singing, his pointed words about love gone wrong filling the car, and it's not helping things.

"Damn it. Why would she lie?"

"Maybe she just wanted to get close to you. Maybe it was some fucked-up kind of test. Maybe she's working for The Pact. Or maybe—ever consider this, Jake?—she's completely fucking off her rocker."

I replay all of my encounters with JoAnne, trying to recall some tell, some clue, that she was making it up.

"Maybe Neil is behind it," I reason. "Maybe he told her lies to keep her in line or something."

Alice leans back against the door. It's almost as if she wants to get as far away from me as possible. "You just can't let go, can you, Jake? You're convinced that JoAnne is some quivering victim in need of your help."

"Vadim could be wrong."

"Vadim knows his stuff. He worked for three straight days. If he says Eli and Elaine don't exist, they don't exist."

A terrifying thought occurs to me. "What if Vadim is in on it, Alice?"

"Seriously?"

"Okay, you're right. Shit. I just don't get it."

"Maybe The Pact isn't killing people. And more important, maybe it isn't really The Pact you're so scared of."

"What the hell do you mean by that?"

"I mean exactly what I said, Jake." The tension crackles just beneath Alice's words. She's still so angry. "Is it possible you're really just afraid of being married to me?"

"Alice, our marriage was my idea."

"Was it?"

For a second, I'm stunned. Immediately, I wonder what the story of our marriage would sound like if she were telling it.

"You may have been the one to pop the question, Jake, but I've been the one carrying the heavy load. Every time you fight The Pact, to me it sounds like you're trying to get out of this marriage. Everything you've done, every little clandestine conversation with JoAnne—it sounds like you're having second thoughts, like you want your old life back, like you want to be *free*. And then you tell me this insane story about her naked in some shrinking cage."

"Are you accusing me of making it up?"

"No. Crazy as it sounds, I believe you found her in a glass cage. I think that The Pact is capable of all sorts of minor monstrosities. But I'm not so sure that the participants aren't willing. I've been to Fernley, remember? And it was bad, I'll grant that. Awful, really. But I put up with it because I wanted to be a better wife, and I genuinely believed they could help me do that."

"They threatened your career!" I shout. "They threatened mine!"

"Maybe those threats were real. Maybe they weren't. Either way, they're not murdering couples at the beach. They're not crushing the regional director's wife between walls of glass. I think what you're committing is a Crime of Interpretation."

"What the hell is that supposed to mean?" And I'm suddenly in free fall. I feel as if I don't know my wife. Because those words she just used, that phrase—*a Crime of Interpretation*—isn't that straight out of The Manual?

"You're the therapist. What would you think if someone came to you with that story? You made out like it was so horrific, but when I picture you in that cage with her, I can't help thinking that you *liked* it. That it *turned you on*."

"No," I protest, but the word doesn't sound convincing.

"And I also think it was what *she* wanted. I think she lured you there, as part of some sick, stupid game, and you played right into it."

I feel as if I'm going to vomit. "Alice, she was in pain. It wasn't a game."

"She's manipulating you, and you can't even see it. Or maybe you don't want to see it."

"You're so off base, Alice. What is wrong with you?"

In the firehouse down the street, the alarm goes off. It's so loud we both cover our ears. Seconds later, the fire engine rips past, sirens wailing. It passes so closely that the rush of wind shakes the car. Then the engine is gone.

"When you asked me to marry you, what did you expect?" Alice's voice is chillingly quiet. "Did you think it was going to be all happy times, flowers and rainbows? Did you think it was going to be all *Planet Waves* and no *Blood on the Tracks*? Is that what you thought?"

"Of course not."

"I went to Fernley, I wore that fucking collar. I stood there in front of that judge, I took his lecture, and I accepted his sentence. Do you know why?"

I'm not sure which is more devastating—the anger in her voice, or the sadness. "Do you know why, Jake? Do you know *why* I sat there with Dave all of those afternoons? Do you know *why* I wore that fucking bracelet? Do you know what I was thinking when they dragged me all the way out to the desert? Do you know what I was thinking when they put the chains around my ankles, or when they took all of my clothes, or when they gave me a lice bath, or when that big fucking female guard stripped me down and said she needed to search me?"

"A strip search? You never told me. . . ."

Side one of *Blood on the Tracks* comes to a conclusion. Although I can't see it and I can't hear it, I know that Alice is crying. Finally, she says, "I did it for you, Jake. I want this marriage to work. I'm not afraid of commitment. I'm not afraid to do whatever the fuck needs to be done to keep us together. I did it for *us*."

The DJ comes on. He's talking about the album and Dylan's fiery relationship with his wife, the magical beginning, "Sad-Eyed Lady of the Lowlands," the ups, the downs, the passion, and eventually the rumored ending. It was three in the morning, Dylan in the studio with his band, not having been home for days, when his wife appeared out of nowhere, slipping into the darkened booth, standing in the back, and not even the producer was aware of her presence. How she stood there, just watching. Eventually Dylan saw her, and he started playing a song he had written for her earlier that day, strumming the guitar, staring intensely across the room, right into her eyes—singing those words, a brilliant stew of intense devotion, bitter venom, and everything in between. When the song ended, she slipped out the side door and that was it, she was gone.

"What do you want me to do?" I ask Alice.

Alice swipes her tears away. It's strange to see her crying. I think the tears embarrass her.

"I want you to do exactly what you want to do."

"Yes," I say. "But what would make you the happiest?"

"I want you to commit to this marriage, Jake. To *me*. If that means making your peace with The Pact, then that's what it means. If you are serious about me, about our marriage, then push forward, take the bad with the good. I want to know that you love me, Jake, I want to know that you are with me. I want to know that you are prepared to do whatever it takes."

It's quiet, save for Dylan's strumming. Alice puts her hand on my thigh. "Is that too much to ask? It's serious adult shit. Are you ready for that?" She gives a sad little laugh.

I take her hand in mine. Her fingers are cold, so different from her usual warmth, and it makes me think of how her hands might feel when she's old. And I know that I want to be with her then. I want to know what her voice sounds like when she's eighty. I want to know how she looks when her dimples turn to wrinkles, or how she smells when she's sick, or the look in her eyes when she can't remember the name of someone she's always known. I want all of it. Not because I need to possess her, as I once thought, but because I love her. I love her so much.

I power on my cell and pull up Vivian's name. Vivian answers on the first ring. "Friend," she says.

"Hello, Friend. I'm sorry to bother you so late."

"No need. I'm always here for you and Alice."

"I need to confess something."

"I know," Vivian says, "I'm glad you called." It doesn't really register, at first, what she's saying.

"Actually, a couple of things."

"I know," she says again. "Take a day for yourself. Get your things together. Spend some time with your wife. Can you be at your home on Saturday morning?"

"Saturday?" I say, looking at Alice. She is staring at me, pleased. She nods. "Why don't I just meet you at the Half Moon Bay Airport?"

"That won't be necessary," Vivian says. "They would prefer to meet at your house. Good night, Friend."

I have a sensation—is it real or imagined?—of someone watching. I look up at the building, the light shining in Alice's office. Someone is standing in front of the window, hands in his pockets, looking down at us—Vadim.

## 63

I REACH FOR ALICE. OF COURSE SHE'S ALREADY GONE. IN THE KITCHEN, there's the usual chaos of coffee and empty yogurt containers. But I feel stronger today. Nervous yet strangely calm. Last night, Alice and I made love. I can still smell her on my skin.

As I shower and dress for my eight o'clock appointment with the Chos, I think about JoAnne. After last night, after everything Alice said, even thinking about JoAnne feels like a betrayal. But how can I not? I replay our conversations in my head. Her fear seemed palpable; I can't recall even a single false note. In hindsight, I understand that she had given me a few nonverbal signals in the past. That night at the Woodside party, she walked away from me. Was she trying to stop me from asking questions? Or was she trying to protect me from Neil, from The Pact?

Or was it that she was trying to protect me from myself?

I think of JoAnne in the glass cage. Her tangled hair. Her bare legs, spreading open. I think of Alice's accusation—that all of it turned me on. And even as the guilt rushes over me, I get hard. Making love to Alice last night, I was thinking only of Alice. Mostly, I was thinking only of Alice. Yet in the midst of it, the image flashed through my mind, just for an instant: JoAnne, naked and vulnerable in the cage, beneath the spotlight. Her bare skin against the glass. Her arms reaching up to cover her imperfect breasts, then falling to her sides, as if she was daring me to look. Last night, I opened my eyes and stared at Alice's face, trying to push away the image of JoAnne, even as I was entangled in my wife's arms.

"I know you," Alice said, in a hard, throaty voice that didn't sound like the Alice of our wedding, the Alice of our home, the Alice of our life. It sounded like Alice from the band, years ago, before I knew her, the voice I've heard in the angrier, harsher songs, the ones she must have sung in black eyeliner and torn fishnets, the songs that were equal parts fury and lust. "You want to fuck her," Alice said. And then she came.

Yes, there's that. My complicated, beloved Alice.

## 64

W HEN I GET HOME FROM WORK ON FRIDAY NIGHT, A FIRE IS burning in the fireplace and Alice is almost finished making a complicated dinner.

"I thought we should do something special," she says, "for your last supper." And then she laughs. A genuine, sweet, real laugh. She hasn't been in such a good mood in months. She hands me a cocktail, Bailey's on the rocks. "I made your favorite. Sit."

The old Alice is back. No mention of last night, no mention of the bizarre thing she said while we were making love. And I begin to think I imagined it. That my subconscious really is fucking with me on a supremely cruel and unusual level.

The big dinner, though, the special attention, leave me tense, worried about what tomorrow might bring. Alice tries to reassure me. "It will be fine. It's your first offense. Okay," she admits, "maybe not entirely fine. You're looking at a pretty extensive indictment: Omission of Facts with Partner, Dishonesty with The Pact Apparatus, and Unsanctioned Meetings with Nonspouse Pact Member."

"Don't forget Crime of Interpretation."

And that's all we say about The Pact. After dinner, we head to the back balcony to enjoy the ocean breeze before stepping back inside to our comfortable bed. Sex is long, nice, and somehow feels different. More loving. Although we've been married now for quite a while, and we've had our share of fun in the bedroom, there is something this time that feels unique, even momentous.

I can't describe how I know, but I do: In her own way, and without ambiguity, Alice has finally consummated our marriage.

# 65

ON SATURDAY MORNING, I WALK DOWN TO NIBS ON THE CORNER and order a bag of scones—lemon chocolate chip for me, orange ginger for Alice, and two random ones for our visitors. I figure it can't hurt. I grab a large hot chocolate and a newspaper. Alice was still asleep when I left home, so I sit down and try to calm my nerves. I open the newspaper and start to read. One minute becomes ten, then fifteen, then twenty. I am dreading going home and facing whatever comes next. What if I were to fold my newspaper up, grab my hot chocolate, walk out the door, and head east—away from our house, away from The Pact, away from our future?

Instead, I head home. I turn the corner, expecting to see the black Lexus SUV in the driveway, but it's empty. Inside, I put on a pot of coffee for Alice. When the smell doesn't wake her, I strip and climb into bed next to her. Without a word, her body slowly forms to the contour of mine. Her lips touch the back of my neck. Her warm breath feels so good on my skin. I have made the right choice, I decide. I drift off to sleep in her arms.

Later, the house smells of bacon. I wander into the kitchen in my boxer briefs to discover Alice at the stove in her underwear and old Sex Pistols T-shirt, transferring bacon from her grandmother's cast-iron pan to a plate lined with paper towels.

"You should have some protein; you might need it." Buried deep in her tone, I sense an odd giddiness. Although she would likely deny it, Alice seems to find some pleasure in my predicament.

"I brought you a scone," I say.

She points to a plate full of crumbs. "I already ate it. But I'm still hungry."

We both eat ravenously. Under the table, Alice touches my foot with her own.

"I guess we better both put on some pants and brush our teeth," she says. But as I'm getting my clothes out of the closet, she drags me to bed. I don't know what's gotten into Alice. All I can figure is that she's turned on by my willingness to put myself through the rigors of The Pact. Eventually, with both of us showered and dressed, the kitchen clean, and my belongings organized, we wind up on the couch. Alice with her guitar on one end, and me, nervous, on the other end.

Alice, fiddling with the guitar strings, begins playing Johnny Cash's "Folsom Prison Blues." I close my eyes and lean my head back. I hear the ping of Alice's email somewhere in the house.

Seconds later, her phone rings on the coffee table. She ignores it. The violence of the song she sings unnerves me.

Her phone rings again.

"Aren't you going to answer?"

"It can wait."

She works her way into an old favorite by the Mendoza Line. "Anyway," she sings with a wry smile, "I was never interested in your heart and soul. I just wanted to see you, and make love on parole."

Again, the phone rings. "The office?" I ask. She shakes her head. She plays for a minute longer, a nice instrumental, and then the phone rings once more.

She groans, sets down her guitar. "Hello?"

Someone on the other end of the line is speaking fast and loud.

"Are you sure? Can you send it to me? I haven't looked at my email today. Are you at your desk? I'll call you back." Alice hangs up the phone. She doesn't say anything. Instead, she jumps up, hurries into our bedroom, and returns with her laptop.

"Putting out fires?" I ask.

She doesn't answer. She clicks through a bunch of buttons, her eyes on the screen. "Shit," she says. "Fucking shit." As she turns the laptop toward me, I hear a car pull up in the driveway. And then, the rattle of our garage door opening. How did they get the clicker? I glance out the window. The big black SUV is nosing into the garage. With Alice's car blocking the way, they can get the SUV only halfway in.

"Read it," Alice whispers urgently.

A car door slams.

I grab the laptop. It's an article from an alternative newspaper in Portland. "NorCal Couple Still Missing, 107 Volunteers Search South Coast Beaches."

Footsteps on the front stairs. A rap on the door.

I scan the article quickly.

Eliot and Aileen Levine's Saab 9-2x was found in the parking lot near Stanton Beach 100 days ago. Friends described the couple as happy and loving, avid hikers and bikers, with a passion for the ocean.

The knock at the door grows more insistent. *Bang bang bang.*

"One second!" Alice yells, though she isn't moving. She's watching me, eyes filled with terror.

While it was not unusual for the couple to go on long ocean kayak trips, they had not mentioned to family or friends an intention to travel from their Northern California home to the Oregon coast.

*Bang bang bang.* A voice from the porch: "Jake, you need to open the door."

"Coming!" Alice calls.

In fact, credit card records indicate the couple had spent the previous evening at a hotel near Hopland, California, and had reserved plane tickets for a trip to Mexico during the days after their disappearance.

I close the computer and hit the power button. JoAnne had the details wrong. It was Eliot and Aileen, not Eli and Elaine. Stanton Beach, not Stinson Beach. That's why Vadim didn't find it sooner. "Shit. What are we going to do?"

I can hear the doorknob jiggling. Alice reaches forward and puts her arms around my neck. "God, Jake, I'm so scared. You were right. How could I be so naïve?"

We hear footsteps on the side stairs.

"We have to do something!" she urges, grabbing my hand and yanking me up from the couch.

More jiggling of the doorknob, and then it's all a moot point anyway, because the front door swings open. Alice whispers in my ear, "Just act normal." I give her a quick squeeze of the hand.

It's the pair who took Alice to Fernley. Just as Declan comes through the front door, Diane comes in through the kitchen.

"I didn't really expect to be in this home ever again," Declan says.

Alice and I stand side by side, holding hands. "Was it really necessary to pick the lock?" I ask, trying to sound in control.

"I didn't pick it," Declan answers. "I just jiggled it a little. You might want to invest in a new doorknob."

Diane comes to stand in front of us as Declan walks through the house, looking into each room, checking to make sure that it is just me and Alice. When he rejoins us, I see he's taken my phone from the bedroom. Alice reaches for her phone on the coffee table, but he's faster. Declan puts both phones on the mantel, out of our reach.

"What are you doing?" As I step toward him, I feel Alice's body tighten.

"Don't worry. You'll get them back."

Alice lets go of my hand. "I'll get you some coffee," she says, her voice amazingly even.

"No thank you," Declan says. "Why don't we all have a seat?"

Alice and I sit side by side on the sofa. Declan takes the chair. Diane goes to stand by the front door. Alice reaches for my hand.

"Look . . . ," I begin, although I have no idea what I'm going to say. I'm hit with the dizzying realization that, at this moment, I have no cards to play.

Declan shifts in his chair, and his jacket pulls slightly to the side. That's when I see the gun tucked into a holster beneath his jacket. I feel nauseous.

Alice grips my hand so tight it hurts. I know she's trying to send me some private message, but I have no idea what it is.

"I'm ready to go," I say.

I have one goal at this moment: get Declan and Diane out of our home, away from Alice. I'll do whatever they ask.

"Do you remember how this works?" Declan asks.

"Of course," I say. I try to sound nonchalant, fearless, although I'm terrified.

"Hands on the wall, feet back, legs spread." Alice won't let go of my hand. I turn and look at her. "Sweetheart," I say, unwrapping her hand from mine, then brushing my fingers against her cheek. "I'll be fine."

Then I do as he asks.

As I'm standing there, hands to the wall, Declan kicks my legs farther apart. I remember that day at Fernley, when someone kicked my legs out from under me, and I realize with sickening clarity that it was Declan. As I begin to fall, he catches me and slams me back against the wall.

"Don't!" Alice cries.

"Resisting will only make it worse," Diane says.

Declan's hands move roughly up and down my body. Every instinct tells me to fight, but he has a gun. Diane no doubt has one too. I have to get them out of here, keep Alice safe.

"Why wasn't he sent a directive?" Alice asks desperately. "He would've shown up at the airport. There's no need for force. He's agreed to comply with everything."

Declan's hands continue probing my body, and I get the feeling he's enjoying this too much—his control, my vulnerability. "Good question," he says. "I was wondering the same thing. Jake, did you piss someone off?"

He steps back and I turn to face him. "I don't know."

"Someone is very unhappy with you," he says. "Our orders on this one don't leave a lot of wiggle room."

Declan gives Diane a nod. "Hands out," she commands.

"I'm begging you—"

"Alice," I say sharply. "It's okay."

Of course it isn't okay. Nothing is okay.

Alice stands there, weeping silently.

Diane pulls a straitjacket out of her black canvas bag. As she slides it onto my outstretched arms, I have a feeling of utter hopelessness. Diane starts buckling and snapping things. I get a whiff of stale coffee on her breath, and I catch a glimpse of us in the hallway mirror. In that moment, I hate myself. My weakness. My indecision. Everything I've done has led us to this moment. Surely, at some point, I could have made a different choice, taken a different turn. When we got the box from Finnegan, we should have said no. That was an option then. To simply return the gift. Or when Vivian came to our house that first day and placed the contracts in front of us, we could have refused to sign. I shouldn't have arranged a secret meeting with JoAnne. I shouldn't have asked so many questions.

If I had made different choices at any of those crucial junctures, then Alice would not be standing here, terrified and crying.

Diane pulls the final strap between my legs and fastens it to a buckle halfway up my back. She is behind me now, and so is Declan. I can't see them, but I can hear chains rattling, and I feel Diane sliding them through loops around my waist, then leaning down to attach the chains to a pair of restraints that she clicks around my ankles.

I can't move my arms. I can barely move my legs. Alice is sobbing.

"I appreciate you two being so cooperative," Declan says. "Diane and I were both happy to have drawn this assignment."

It occurs to me that Declan may not even be in The Pact. Is this merely a job for him?

Diane is fishing through the canvas bag.

"Is there anything you two want to say to each other before we go?" Declan asks.

Alice doesn't hesitate. She runs to me and gives me a long, soft kiss. I can taste the saltiness of her tears when she kisses me. "I love you so much," she murmurs. "Be careful."

"I love *you*." I hope that my words convey all of what I'm feeling. I long to hug her, feel her in my arms. I wish I could backtrack to fifteen minutes ago, just the two of us together, Alice singing. If only we had checked the email when it dinged, if only she had answered the phone the first time it rang, maybe we could have escaped. Maybe we would be on 280 by now, speeding south, away from here.

How unforgivably stupid we've been. How innocent and naïve.

Then I see the fear in Alice's eyes, and I suddenly know there is more, and it is not good.

"This can't be necessary," Alice protests. Her voice trembles.

Hearing her fear makes it all much more scary.

"I'm afraid so," Declan responds. "I'm sorry." It actually sounds like he means it. "This is written into the order. Not sure why, but it is. I need you to open your mouth wide for me."

"No," Alice whispers.

But I think of the gun, and I do what he says.

"Wider, please."

I feel Declan's hands pull something over my head. A ball gag is forced into my mouth, straps pulling it tight at the edges. As I bite down, I taste metal and dry rubber.

Alice is watching, eyes blank. Declan is fiddling with straps and buckles. Then something comes down over my eyes and I realize I'm wearing blinders, like a horse being fitted for the racetrack. I can see directly in front of me, but nothing on either side. I focus entirely on Alice. I try to speak to her with my eyes. Then something else comes down over my head—a black cloth. I can't see a thing.

With each step, each descent into the madness of this process, I am struck anew by what I'm losing. Just days ago, I wished we could go back to how we were before—Alice and me, together, happy. Five minutes ago, I wished I could hug her. Sixty seconds ago, that I could speak to her. And now I wish desperately just to see her again. I feel her hand pressing against my chest, through the thick canvas of the straitjacket, but that is all. I'm drowning in the darkness. It is hushed for a moment, just the sound of Alice's breath, her weeping, and her voice saying urgently, *I love you so much.* I try to focus on her voice, I hold on to it in my mind, fearful that they will take this too from me, this one last tether to sanity, to Alice.

And then the pressure on my chest—Alice's hand, that comforting presence—is gone, and I am being led through the kitchen—I can smell the bacon, feel the floor change from hardwood to tile. We are going down the back stairs.

"Jake!" Alice implores.

"Stay here, Alice." Diane stops to answer her. "This is Jake's punishment, not yours."

"When will he be back?" she wails. There is no control in her voice now, no calmness, only desperation.

"Your job now, Alice," Diane says, "is to go about your business as if everything is normal. Go to work. Above all, if you want to see your husband again, don't speak to anyone about any of this."

"Please don't . . . ," Alice pleads.

I want to tell her so many things. But my tongue is immobile, my teeth jammed against the metal and rubber. My mouth is dry, my eyes sting. All I can manage is a guttural garble. Five syllables in my throat—*I love you, Alice* is what I mean to say.

Declan is pushing me roughly into the SUV. All hope drains from me.

As we pull away, I can't see her but I sense her. I imagine Alice standing there, weeping, willing me to come back to her.

What have we done? Will I ever see my wife again?

## 66

I CAN FEEL THE CAR MAKE A RIGHT TURN ONTO BALBOA. I CAN TELL from the sound of cars idling around us that the next turn is at a light, so it must be Arguello. I want to convince myself this is only a bad dream, but the chains bite into my ankles and the taste of rubber in my mouth is sickening. I need to try to figure out our route, commit it to memory.

We drive for some time before we come to a halt, and I know from the noise that we're in Bay Bridge traffic. Then I can feel the bridge under the wheels. I can sense a change in the light in front of my face; then, without warning, the black cloth is lifted. I see the back of Declan's head in the driver's seat, Diane's profile. A partition rises between the backseat and the front seat. From the darkness of the car, it's obvious that the windows must be blacked out.

We start moving, more rapidly this time, and there is the rumble of the Yerba Buena Island tunnel. I sense a quiet movement beside me. I struggle to turn my head. In the shadows, I'm startled to discover a small woman sitting beside me. She's in her fifties, I think. Like me, she's wearing a seatbelt over a straitjacket, although she is not in head restraints. How long has she been staring at me? She gives me a sympathetic look. The sympathy is mostly in her eyes, but there is also a rigid smile, like she's trying to convey that she understands what I'm feeling. I attempt to smile back, but I cannot move my lips. My mouth is so dry, it hurts. To be polite I should look away, perhaps, but I don't. The woman looks wealthy—the well-done injections, the diamond earrings—but her glossy hair, mussed in spots, betrays some sort of a struggle.

I lean my head back clumsily, constrained by the straitjacket. I think of Alice.

And then I think of the kids. It's not that I have this overwhelming sense that my patients can't live without me. But for all the talk of adolescent resilience, teenagers are also fragile. What would it do to them if their therapist suddenly vanished? The most elemental difference between my teenage clients and the married couples is this: The adults arrive convinced that nothing I can say will change anything, while the teenagers believe that at any moment I might utter some sort of magical sentence that instantly wipes away the fog.

Take Marcus from my Tuesday group. He's a sophomore at a magnet school in Marin. Marcus is an instigator, combative, always looking to get things off the rails. At our last meeting he asked me, "What is the purpose of life? Not the meaning—*the purpose?*" It was a tough spot for me; once he threw down the challenge, I needed to respond. If my answer missed the mark, I would expose myself as a fraud. If I refused to answer, I would look like a poser who was of no use to the group.

"Difficult question," I replied. "If I answer, will you tell us what *you* think the purpose of life is?"

He jiggled his right leg. He wasn't expecting that. "Yes," he replied reluctantly.

Experience, time, and education have taught me how to read people and situations. I generally have a decent sense of what someone will say or how they will react, even why people do the things they do, and why certain situations lead to certain outcomes. Yet somehow, when I least expect it, I discover a hole in my knowledge. What I don't know, perhaps what I haven't even considered, is this: What does it all add up to, what does it mean?

I looked around the circle of teenagers and I gave it my best shot:

"Strive to be all good, but know that you are not," I said. "Try to enjoy every day, but know that you will not. Try to forgive others and yourself. Forget the bad stuff, remember the good. Eat cookies, but not too many. Challenge yourself to do more, to see more. Make plans, celebrate when they pan out, persevere when they don't. Laugh when things are good, laugh when things are bad. Love with abandon, love selflessly. Life is simple, life is complex, life is short. Your only real currency is time—use it wisely."

When I was finished, Marcus and the others were all staring at me, looking stunned. No one spoke. They had no response. Did this mean that I was right, or that I was wrong? Probably both.

As I sit here in the dark SUV with the stranger, I think of those words I offered to the kids. Here I am, in a terrifying situation of which I cannot begin to predict the outcome. I have loved with abandon, but have I truly loved selflessly? How much of this precious currency—time—do I have left? Have I used it wisely?

## 67

HOURS PASS, AND I TRY DESPERATELY TO STAY AWAKE. WE MUST be somewhere in the desert. I can taste the dust in my mouth. My tongue is swollen under the gag, my lips painfully cracked, my throat parched. It's difficult to breathe. I'm dying to swallow, but I can't work the muscles in my throat.

From the bumps, I can tell we've turned off the highway. Drool has run from my mouth, down the straitjacket, and onto my leg. I'm embarrassed. I turn my head painfully to the right. The woman beside me is sleeping. Her cheek is bruised and cut. Whoever doesn't like me apparently isn't all that keen on her either.

Suddenly, the partition between the front and back seats lowers. The sun blasts through the windshield and I squeeze my eyes against the blazing light. The woman rustles beside me. I move my head to look at her, hoping to communicate something with my eyes, hoping for some connection. But she is staring straight ahead.

In the distance, I see the facility rise from the desert heat.

At an imposing iron gate, we wait for a uniformed guard to check our papers. I can hear him on the phone in the guardhouse, making a call, announcing our arrival. The gate opens and we drive through. As I hear it roll closed behind us, I calculate whether it is too high for me to climb. And, if I could, how long would it take? What would they do if I tried?

Then I think of the glass hallway I walked through on my first visit to Fernley: the resort on one side, the vast desert on the other. Escaping this place would be like swimming from Alcatraz. Once you're out, how do you survive? The desert is too remote, too unforgiving. Without water, I'd be dead within hours. What is a better way to die: in a prison, at the mercy of your captors, or alone in the desert?

We drive through a second gate. Eventually, we park exactly where I got off of the plane last time. This time, though, I'm the one standing on the yellow line, looking tired and apprehensive. The woman stands beside me.

A gate buzzes open. A short guy in a black uniform yells, "Move. Walk on the line!" We shuffle up the narrow, fenced-in corridor, both struggling to stay on the yellow line that leads the way. The chains around my ankles dig into my skin, forcing my steps to be short. The woman moves quickly—her ankles must not be shackled—and I struggle to keep up.

At the end of the yellow line, we reach the building entrance. The door swings open and we enter. Two women in uniform take the woman off to the left. Two men flank me on each side, leading me the opposite direction. We go into an empty room, where they unshackle my waist and ankles. Immediately, I feel lighter. When they remove the straitjacket, my arms are numb. Maybe the gag will be next. I hope so. I'm dying to lick my lips, to taste a sip of water.

"Take off your clothes," one of the guys says.

Soon, I'm standing here completely naked, save for the contraption around my head. My lips are numb, and I feel drool against my chin.

The two guys are staring at me, a little fascinated.

The pain in my mouth is so severe, I don't even register the proper humiliation. I just want this thing off. I point to my mouth, make a pleading gesture with my hands. I motion that I need to drink.

Eventually, the shorter guy pulls some keys from his belt. He fiddles with a lock at the back of my head. When the gag slips free, I gasp. Tears of relief sting my cheeks. I struggle to close my mouth but cannot.

The tall guy points. "Showers are through there. Take your time. When you're done, put on the red jumpsuit. Exit to the rear."

I step through a door. There are five sinks on the left, five showers on the right, a bench in the middle, no doors, no curtains. I go over to the middle shower. Part of me believes that the water won't turn on, that this is just a cruel psychological prank.

I turn the knob. Miraculously, water pours down. I shiver as the icy water hits my skin. I lift my head and gulp it down, mouthful after mouthful. Abruptly, the water goes from frigid to scalding. I jerk back. Then I piss into the drain and watch the dark yellow swirl through the steaming water and vanish.

I pump the plastic soap dispenser, and pearly pink liquid spits into my palm. I scrub off the grime of the drive. The water is tepid now. I wash my face, my hair, everything. I stand under the spray, eyes closed. I want to lie down and sleep for an eternity. I don't want to get out of the shower, I don't want to put on the jumpsuit. I don't want to go through the door. Every door I go through is just another door I will have to go through to escape this hell, if that's even possible.

Eventually, I turn off the water and step out of the shower. A red jumpsuit and a pair of white underwear hang on hooks on the wall. Beneath the clothes is a pair of slippers. I put on the underwear and jumpsuit. The fabric is oddly comfortable, just the way Alice described. The suit fits me perfectly. The slippers are too small. I put them on anyway and step through the door.

I find myself in a narrow room. The woman I traveled with is standing in front of me, next to a chair, wearing a blood-red jumpsuit identical to mine. Block letters on the front spell out the word PRISONER. There is a tall table next to the chair. With its elegant marble top it looks out of place. In the center of the table is a wooden box. I shudder to think what it contains.

The woman reaches up and pats at her hair self-consciously. Her skin is still damp from the shower, but her hair is dry. "There's no way out," she says.

She's right. There are no other exits. I turn back toward the door I came through, but it has already shut. I think of JoAnne in the shrinking glass cage and begin to panic. I move the handle, but it won't open. We're trapped.

I turn in a slow circle, surveying the room.

"Please sit," the woman says tentatively. When I don't move, she repeats, "Please." Her eyes are red, and I can tell she's been crying.

I walk over to the chair and sit.

"I'm sorry," she says.

"Why?"

She's quiet for a minute, and then she begins to sob.

"Are you okay?" I know the question is absurd even as I ask it, but I want her to know that I understand how she's feeling.

"Yes," she says. It's clear that she's struggling to regain her composure, her dignity. She opens the box and begins rummaging around. Hearing the sound of metal on metal, I feel queasy.

"What's in there?" I ask, afraid of the answer.

"They gave us a choice," she says. "One of us needs to walk out of this room with a shaven head. They said I could decide. They said that if there was a single hair remaining, they would shave both of our heads and something worse."

"You've decided?"

"Yes. I'm sorry."

A shaved head. I can live with that, no problem. The more disturbing question is why they're putting us through this. If they're giving her a choice, they're likely to give me one too. What will my choice be?

## 68

As the razor buzzes over my scalp, I think of Eliot and Aileen. JoAnne had called them Eli and Elaine. Maybe the Portland paper had the names wrong. Maybe JoAnne did. Either way. Is it possible that I misheard? Our ears often hear what they expect, rather than what is said.

I remember another couple who disappeared while kayaking in the ocean. It happened somewhere north of Malibu, a couple of years ago. They were considered missing for weeks, until their two-person kayak was found with a jagged bite in the hull, bits of shark teeth still embedded in the fiberglass.

What if someone from The Pact read that story and considered it a plausible narrative for a couple like Eliot and Aileen? What if Dave's wife's cancer was also just that—a plausible scenario?

I think of the 107 people searching the shores of Oregon for signs of Eliot and Aileen's disappearance. That's the number the newspaper article gave: 107. I think of them all walking the length of the long beach in single file, heads bent, searching for clues buried in the sand. If I disappeared, would 107 people show up to look for me? I'd like to think so, but probably not.

The newspaper article was from three months ago. I wish I'd had time to search for the update. Did the friends give up? Or are they still out there looking? If I disappeared, how long would they look for me?

## 69

ALL OF MY HAIR IS GONE, BUT THE WOMAN CONTINUES TO RUB her hands over my scalp, searching for anything she might have missed. She stops every now and then to pick up the razor, rub in some lotion, shave a real or imagined follicle. She seems obsessed, terrified of unknown consequences. Her hair is coiffed in the tasteful manner common to well-to-do women of her age—expensively bobbed, blond but not too blond, highlighted in a way that draws attention to her attractive cheekbones. I sense that she spends a lot of time on it each morning. I can understand why she made the choice she made. Still, the thoroughness with which she shaves my head seems almost cruel.

Stepping back, she says, "It looks perfect."

The guilty always find a way of rationalizing their behavior, making it sound as though they've done you a favor.

From the intercom speaker in the ceiling, we hear a woman's voice. "Well done. Now, Jake, it is your turn to choose."

I knew it was coming. Still, my body tenses.

"We have two holding cells," the voice says. "One is dark and cold, the other is bright and hot. Which would you like?"

I look at the woman. I sense that she has a husband who always allows her to choose—chocolate or vanilla, window or aisle, chicken or fish. Fortunately, I am not her husband. As she begins to open her mouth to tell me which she would prefer, I say, "Light and hot."

"Good choice, Jake."

The door swings open and a lighted path leads us down a hallway and into a common area with eight cells. The intercom comes on again: "Jake, please step into cell thirty-six. Barbara, cell thirty-five."

So that's her name. Barbara and I look at each other, but neither of us moves. "Go on," the voice says.

Barbara steps toward her cell, stopping just short of the door. It's dark inside. Barbara reaches out and clutches my hand as if I might somehow save her. "Go ahead," the voice says. Tentatively, she lets go of my hand and inches inside. When the door slams shut, Barbara lets out a frightened yelp. I walk resolutely into the other cell, acting braver than I feel. The fluorescent lights are painfully bright, and the temperature must be close to a hundred degrees. The door slams behind me.

There is a narrow metal bed attached to the wall. One sheet, no pillow. A toilet hangs from the wall. A worn copy of The Manual sits alone on a single shelf. I ignore the book and lie on the bed. The lights are so bright that I have to lie facedown with my head buried in the sheet.

Hours pass. I sweat, I fidget, I don't fall asleep. From the cell next door, I hear Barbara scream twice, then nothing. I survey my cell again, my eyes still trying to adjust to the blinding light. I'm so thirsty, but they haven't brought water. If all goes wrong, I tell myself, I can drink the water in the toilet. It would probably last for five or six days. And then what? I try not to think that far ahead.

## 70

I CAN'T SAY FOR SURE, BUT I THINK A DAY PASSES BEFORE THE DOOR opens. I feel the hot air from my cell rush out into the common area. My jumpsuit is soaked in sweat. I get off my cot and step out of the cell. The cool air makes me dizzy.

The door to the other cell has also opened. Barbara emerges, holding both hands over her face to protect her eyes from the light. I feel guilty for choosing the dark cell for her. I rest a hand on her shoulder, and she whimpers. We have been given no instructions, but I see an exit sign up ahead. I lead her down the corridor and out the exit. I feel like a rat in a familiar maze, following the mandated path, my free will no more than a fiction.

Barbara has opened her eyes now, although it is clearly painful for her, and she walks close behind me, clutching my hand.

"Where are we going?" she whispers.

"Is this your first time?"

"Yes."

"Every door leads to another door. I figure we just keep going. When they want us to stop, we'll know. If it helps, just count. That way, at least we'll know how long we walked."

"One Mississippi," she says. "Two Mississippi, three . . ."

I walk slowly but deliberately. Just as I expected, when we reach the end of each hallway, a door opens, then closes behind us. Is it all controlled by sensors? Or is the impeccable timing the work of someone watching the cameras?

Barbara is at 1,014 Mississippi when we reach two glass doors. Both have a plastic sign inscribed with the words PUBLIC DEFENDER. The voice emanates from overhead. "Barbara, now it's your choice. For your attorney, would you like David Renton or Elizabeth Watson?"

I barely know my fellow prisoner, but I am certain whom she will select.

"David Renton," she says without hesitation.

Both doors open to reveal a desk with someone standing beside it. Barbara goes to the left, toward the man, and I step right, toward the woman.

Elizabeth Watson—tall, thin, and pale—looks like a mannequin in a navy suit. At first, she doesn't move, and I sense she is sizing me up. My clothes and slippers are drenched in sweat—I imagine it's not an appealing sight. The room is heavily air-conditioned, and I begin to shiver in my damp clothes. My attorney motions me to the chair opposite the desk. Before taking her seat, she casually pushes the window open to let in some hot desert air.

"Freezing in here," she mutters. "I grew up in Tallahassee. My mom kept our house at a constant sixty-five. Can't stand air-conditioning."

I'm stunned by her candor. She's the first person I've met at Fernley who has ever revealed anything about herself.

She swivels her chair and opens her big leather purse.

I realize this isn't actually her office. There are no pictures or personal belongings of any sort. Up close, I can see that her suit is wrinkled, a crease along the right side, maybe from a suitcase, a stain on her left sleeve. The purse is filled to the brim. She must have just flown in, unexpectedly summoned.

She places three beverages on the desk: Diet Coke, Icelandic water with essence of raspberry, and iced tea. "Your choice," she says with an empathetic smile. I imagine her grabbing the bottles in a rush on her way out of a fancy law office. Unlike Declan and Diane, Elizabeth Watson is likely a member of The Pact. Perhaps she did something wrong once or twice, and now on occasion she flies in to represent her "Friends."

I reach for the water, and she takes the iced tea for herself. "So," she says, leaning back in her chair. "First offense, right?"

"Yes."

"The first time is the worst." She opens a file on her desk.

As I guzzle the water, Elizabeth begins reading the paperwork. "They haven't filed charges yet. That's unusual. They want to talk to you first."

"Do I have a choice?"

Elizabeth glances out the window, across the shimmering desert. "Not really, no. We still have a few minutes. Hungry?"

"Starving."

She rummages through her purse and pulls out half of a sandwich, wrapped in blue wax paper, and pushes it across the table. "Sorry, it's all I have. It's good, though, turkey and Brie."

"Thank you." I eat the sandwich in four bites.

"Want to call your wife?"

"Really?" It seems too good to be true.

"Yes, you can use my cell." She pushes the cellphone across to me and says quietly, "We always register our cells when we get to Fernley." She puts air quotes around the word *register,* warning me my call might not be exactly private. It seems she really is on my side. But then, maybe this is just another sick game, another test. Maybe she's playing good cop.

"Thank you," I say uncertainly. I pick up the phone. I'm desperate to talk to Alice, but what will I say?

Alice picks up on the first ring, her voice a breathy, frightened "Hello."

"It's me, sweetheart."

"Oh my God. Jake! Are you okay?"

"I got a haircut, but other than that, I'm fine."

"What do you mean, a haircut? When are you coming home?"

"I'm bald. And unfortunately, I don't know when I'm coming home."

The bald part doesn't even seem to register. "Where are you?"

"With my attorney. I haven't been charged yet. They want to interview me first."

I glance up at Elizabeth, who seems engrossed in my file. "How's Vadim?" I ask quietly.

"Working hard," Alice says. "He found more paperwork."

Elizabeth looks up at me and taps her watch.

"I have to go," I say.

"Not yet," Alice says. I can hear that she's crying. "Whatever you do, don't tell them anything incriminating."

"I won't," I promise. "Alice? I love you."

I hear a hand on the office doorknob, quickly hang up, and slide the cellphone across the desk to Elizabeth. The office door opens. Gordon, the guy who questioned me on my first visit to Fernley, stands there in a black suit, holding a briefcase. Beside him is a different guy—bigger and rougher than his partner last time, with a tattoo of a serpent snaking up his massive neck. "Time to go," Gordon says.

Elizabeth stands, comes around the desk, and places herself between me and Gordon. I like her more already. "How long will the interview last?" she asks.

"Depends," Gordon says.

"I'd like to sit in on it."

"That won't be possible."

"Damn it, I'm his attorney. Why does he even have an attorney if I can't be there for the interview?"

"Look," Gordon says impatiently. "Just let me do my job. When I'm finished, I'll bring him back. Deal?"

"Will it be an hour? Two hours?"

"That's up to our friend here." Gordon grabs me by the elbow and pulls me toward the door. Elizabeth starts to follow us, but Gordon glances back, snaps his fingers, and says, "Maurie, handle this." Serpent guy stands in the doorway, blocking Elizabeth's exit.

We walk through more long corridors. Eventually Gordon punches a code into a keypad and we enter a windowless room with a table and three chairs. I can feel Maurie breathing behind me.

"Sit," Gordon says, and I obey. He sits across from me, setting his briefcase on the table between us.

There is a metal hoop affixed to the table. "Hands," Maurie says.

I place my hands on the table. Maurie threads handcuffs through the hoop and then clicks them tightly onto my wrists. Gordon pulls a red folder out of his briefcase and opens it. It's stuffed with papers. Are all of those about me?

"Is there anything you want to talk about before we get started?" he asks.

Before Alice showed me the newspaper article, I'd planned to just lay it all out in the open, tell them the truth, 100 percent, and take whatever came my way. Now I'm not sure.

I shouldn't ask the next question, but I do. Because I have to know. "Is JoAnne okay?"

"I'm very surprised that you would ask that." Gordon frowns. "Why are you so concerned about JoAnne? Have you learned nothing?" He glances at Maurie. "He's apparently learned nothing."

Maurie grins.

"I ask," I say, "because last time I saw her, you had her trapped, naked, in a shrinking chamber."

"We did," Gordon says amiably, "didn't we?"

He flips through the file, then leans forward, so that his face is inches from mine. "So, I understand you want to make a confession."

I don't respond.

"This might jar your memory." He slides a photograph across the table. Maurie leans up against the door, bored. The photo is black and white, grainy, yet it is impossible to deny what I'm seeing.

"Let me ask you again," Gordon says, "something I asked you the last time we met. Do you recall meeting with JoAnne in the food court at the Hillsdale mall?"

I look down at the photo. It appears to have been taken from a CCTV security video. I nod.

"Okay," he says. "Now we're getting somewhere. Could you characterize your relationship with JoAnne?"

"We met in college. We worked together. For a very brief time, we were lovers. After graduation, I didn't see her until my wife, Alice, and I attended our first quarterly dinner with The Pact in Hillsborough, California."

"And then?"

"I saw her at our second Pact party, in Woodside, California. A week later, at my request, we met for lunch at the food court in the Hillsdale mall in San Mateo. We ate hot dogs on a stick and drank lemonade. We talked."

"About what?"

"The Pact."

"And what did JoAnne say about The Pact?"

"I was having some concerns about whether it was a good fit for my wife and me. JoAnne reassured me. She said it had been very good for her marriage." I've rehearsed this line in my head a hundred times, yet when I say it, it sounds forced.

"What else?"

"We agreed to meet a second time, but she didn't show."

"And then?"

"And then, as you know, I saw her here." I try to rein in the impatience in my tone. I remind myself Gordon holds all the power here.

"Did you tell your wife about these meetings?"

"No."

"Why not?"

"I don't know."

"Because you intended to sleep with JoAnne?"

"No." I say it emphatically.

"You were just meeting her to talk about old times? To enjoy the delicacy known as hot dogs on a stick? For the incredible ambience at the Hillsdale mall food court? Did you not try to seduce her?"

"No!"

Gordon pushes his chair back and stands, hands on the table. Maurie is beginning to look a little more interested in the conversation. "Did you not suggest that you should rekindle your relationship?"

"Of course I didn't."

"Did you suggest a meeting at the Hyatt hotel?"

"What the fuck? No!"

He comes to stand beside me and places a hand on my shoulder, like we're buddies again. "Here's the difficulty I'm having with you right now, Jake. You have this little story you want to tell. You're determined to stick with it. I get that. Self-preservation and all. But our sources have confirmed that you had sex with JoAnne Charles in the Hyatt hotel in Burlingame, California, on March first."

"What source? That's insanity!"

Gordon sighs. "We were making such nice progress, Jake. I had high hopes. I thought we could be out of here by lunchtime." He sits down again.

"I did not sleep with JoAnne Charles." As the words come out of my mouth, I realize that it sounds wrong.

"But you did. You've already confessed!"

"Seventeen years ago! Not recently. The thought hasn't even crossed my mind." Of course, that isn't true. The thought has definitely crossed my mind. Fuck. JoAnne, naked, spreading her legs, that weird defiant smile on her lips. How could the thought not cross my mind? But is that a crime? I never would have acted on it. Never.

"Who can know a man's thoughts?" Gordon asks. The timing is uncanny. Yet I know it's just a tactic. The Pact wants me to think they're inside my head. But they can't be inside my head. Can they?

"Jake," Gordon says, almost crooning my name. "I'm going to ask you something extremely important. I want you to think about it. I don't want you to answer right away. Would you agree to testify against JoAnne in order to make this all go away?"

I already know the answer, but I delay just to make it appear that I'm considering his offer.

Finally, I simply say, "No."

Gordon blinks as if I've just slapped him. "All right then, Jake. I don't understand it, given our information, the *source* of our information, but I respect your decision. If down the road, you have a change of heart, just let them know that you want to talk to me."

What the hell does he mean, given the source? He's implying that JoAnne was the one who said we had sex at the Hyatt. But what reason would JoAnne have for saying that? She could only have said it under terrible duress. I think of the shrinking cage. Torture may elicit answers, but it rarely elicits the truth.

"I won't have a change of heart. I met JoAnne Charles one time in a mall food court. The rest of what you are saying is a lie."

Gordon gives me a dismissive look. Then he stands and exits the room. Maurie follows.

I sit with my hands chained to the table. I can hear air hissing through the vent overhead. The room grows steadily colder. I'm so tired, so hungry, so cold, I can't even think. I wish I could talk to Alice. I put my head down on the table, and immediately the light switches off. I lift my head, and it goes on again. I try it several more times. Every time, the same thing. Is there a sensor somewhere, or is someone fucking with me? Finally, I lay my head down and sleep.

Later, I wake to utter darkness. How much time has passed? An hour? Five? I lift my head from the table and the light comes on. The room is cold. The handcuffs have begun to dig into my skin. There are a few dried drops of blood on the metal table. There's a mossy taste in my mouth. It's possible that I've been asleep for a long time. Was I drugged?

More time passes. The boredom is its own kind of torture. I think of Alice back in San Francisco. What is she doing? Is she at work? At home? Is she alone?

The door swings open. "Hi, Maurie," I say. He doesn't respond. He unlocks the handcuffs and I lift my hands from the table. They feel heavy, not my own. I move my fingers, rub my hands, shake them out. Maurie grabs my arms, roughly pulls them behind my back, and hand-cuffs me again.

He leads me down the hallway and into an elevator.

"Where are you taking me?"

No response. He seems nervous all of a sudden, even more nervous than me. I remember the Düsseldorf study: When frightened or pan-icked, humans release a chemical through their sweat that sets off certain receptors in the human brain. I can smell Maurie's anxiety coming off of his skin.

The elevator door closes. "You got a wife, Maurie? Kids?"

Reluctantly, his eyes meet mine. A slight shake of the head.

"No wife?" I repeat. "No kids?"

Another subtle shake of the head. And I realize he's not responding to my question. He's warning me.

The elevator takes us down five floors—*ding, ding, ding, ding, ding.* My empty stomach turns; my resolve weakens. I am forty feet below the desert floor, a hundred miles from anywhere. If there were an earthquake, if this place collapsed, I would be buried, forgotten forever.

We leave the elevator. Maurie too seems to have lost some of his resolve, because he doesn't bother to grab my arms. He walks and I follow. He punches a code into a keypad and we enter a room where another guard is standing—a woman, about forty-five, bleached-blond hair in an old-fashioned style. She doesn't look like she's a member of The Pact. Employment in the desert must be difficult to find. Maybe she's a former prison employee, from before this place shut down.

The door slams shut behind us. Maurie unlocks my handcuffs, and then the three of us just stand there. Maurie looks at the woman. "Go on," he says.

"No, you," she says.

I get the feeling this is the first time they have done this, whatever it is, and neither of them wants to take charge. Finally, the woman tells me, "I need you to take all of your clothes off."

"Again?"

"Yes."

"Everything?"

She nods.

I slowly remove my slippers, thinking. Maurie gave me that nod of warning in the elevator—not an unfriendly nod, I'm sure of it, more like a conspiratorial one. These two both seem jittery. Could I convince them to let me go—while it's just the three of us? No Gordon. How much do they get paid? Could I offer them money?

"Are you from Nevada?" I ask. I pretend to have difficulty with the top button on my jumpsuit, stalling for time.

The woman glances at Maurie. "No. I'm originally from Utah," she says. Maurie gives her a scolding look.

"Hurry it up," he says.

I unbutton the jumpsuit and let it fall to the floor. The woman looks away. "Where are you from?" she asks, clearly uncomfortable with my state of undress.

"California." I stand here in the prison-issued boxers. "Would you be willing to help me?" I whisper.

"Enough," Maurie hisses. I know I'm crossing a line. I sense he could erupt into fury at any moment. Still, I'm running out of options. "I have money," I say. "A lot," I lie.

I can hear the beep of numbers being punched into the keypad on the other side of the door. The blond woman shoots Maurie a glance. Shit, she's as nervous as he is. The door swings open and a tall, stout woman enters. She looks like an old-time prison warden, the real deal, like she could gleefully crack my skull open with her fist. "Guards," she says, her voice unexpectedly soft, studying her clipboard, "we need to pick it up." She looks at me. "Buck naked. Right now."

I shrug off my underpants and cover my groin with my hands. What an awful feeling, to be naked among the clothed.

The warden glances up from her clipboard. My nudity neither surprises nor interests her. "Take him to twenty-two hundred," she tells Maurie and the blond woman. "Quick. Get him into the apparatus. Everyone's waiting."

Shit. That can't be good.

The blonde, clearly terrified of the warden, pushes me forward. We walk down the hallway and enter another room. In the center is a table made entirely of plexiglass. An attractive woman stands beside the table. Although she too holds a clipboard, she wears a crisp white shirt and white linen pants, nice leather sandals—not the usual uniform. Her hair is a strawberry-blond bob. She must be special somehow. Maybe she's one of the Friends.

Her eyes roam over my body. "Get on the table," she says.

"Are you kidding me?"

"No." Her eyes are cold. "Maurie can show you an alternative, but I assure you it's much worse."

I look over my shoulder at Maurie. Shit. Even he looks scared.

"Look," I say. "I don't know what kind of medieval—"

The woman's hand comes up so fast, I don't even have time to avoid it. She smashes the clipboard into my face. My gaze goes blurry. "On the table, please," she says evenly. "You need to understand that there are many of us, one of you. You can give in to our requests, or you can resist, but either way it's going to happen. Your level of resistance merely equals the level of your pain; the outcome is the same otherwise. It's a simple equation: Resistance equals pain."

I shudder and climb onto the table, feeling profoundly vulnerable. There's a foam neck rest at one end, and beside it a leather strap. There are other straps on the table too, wooden blocks at the bottom. The blond woman is looking at the ceiling. Maurie is watching the woman in white, apparently awaiting orders.

The plexiglass is cold against my bare skin. My head aches, and I feel a trickle of blood on my face. Where yesterday I longed to be free of the straitjacket, now I long for anything to cover my nakedness and humiliation.

The blond woman arranges my head on the foam, then tugs the leather strap across my throat and disappears from view. I feel my arms being strapped into place—Maurie. His grip is powerful, but he is surprisingly gentle. Then I feel the straps across my ankles. It must be the blonde. After strapping me in, she pats my foot. Such a maternal gesture. I fight back tears. Why are the two of them acting this way? What do they know? Is this the kindness before the slaughter?

I'm staring up at the ceiling, immobile, chilled. All I can see are ugly fluorescent lights. The room is hushed. I feel like a frog strapped down in a high school biology class, waiting to be dissected.

There are footsteps—it sounds as though a couple more people have entered the room. The woman in white is standing over me now. "Close it in," she says.

A large plate of plexiglass moves over me. My heart is beating so hard, I can hear it. I wonder if they can. I try to move, to resist, but it's no use. The sheet of plexiglass looks heavy. "No!" I shout, panicked.

"Calm down," the woman in white says. "This won't necessarily hurt. Remember the equation."

I close my eyes and tense up, waiting for them to drop it, crushing me. This could all be over soon. A horrific death. Is that what this is? An execution? Do they plan suffocation, or worse? Or is this more of the same—fear tactics, mental cruelty, empty threat?

The plexiglass hovers six inches above me.

"Please," I plead, disgusted by the weakness in my voice.

What would it say in the news? *Man disappears while kayaking.* Or maybe there would be no news. Maybe it would be a routine medical ailment. *Man dies of liver failure. Aneurysm.* There is no limit to what they could say, no one to contest their story. Except Alice. God, Alice. Please leave her alone.

But they won't leave her alone. They'll marry her off. Who will they find for her? Someone whose spouse has met a similar fate?

Neil, I think. What if this is all an elaborate ploy, devised by Neil, so that he can be rid of JoAnne, married to Alice? Bile rises in my throat. Then, the glass lowers.

# 71

I WAIT FOR THE PRESSURE OF THE GLASS, BUT IT DOESN'T COME. I HEAR a drill, and I realize that they are fastening the piece just above me on all four corners. My frantic breathing fogs up everything, and soon I can't see.

The drilling stops, and it is quiet. One of the women counts, "One, two, three, four." I feel myself being lifted. And then I am upright, suspended inside the plexiglass, arms by my sides, legs slightly spread, feet standing on the wooden blocks, head facing forward. In front of me, a blank white wall. I can sense the others behind me, but I can't see them. I feel like an organism trapped between slides, waiting to go under the microscope.

The floor shudders beneath me, and I realize that the plexiglass structure is on wheels. I squeeze my eyes shut and force myself to breathe. When I open them, I see that I am being rolled down a narrow hallway. People walk past us, glancing at my naked body. Some pass to the front, others pass behind me. I am rolled into a freight elevator, the heavy doors close, and we rise. I'm not sure if the woman in white is still with us. Or the blond woman. It seems my handlers are standing behind me.

"Maurie?" I say. "Where are we going? What's happening?"

"Maurie's gone," a voice replies. A male voice.

I think of Alice's face just before they pulled the blinders on. I think of her hand on my chest when I wore the straitjacket, how the release of that reassuring pressure was such a jolt. How, in the past few hours, my life has been turned on end. Everything has been taken away from me, piece by piece.

I want to weep, but I have no tears. I want to scream, but I know now that my screams will change nothing.

I hold my breath just long enough to clear the plexiglass in front of my eyes. As the elevator doors open, I realize that we are in a cavernous room. I remember this room from my first visit to Fernley: the cafeteria.

I hear footsteps receding, and I am left here alone, staring straight ahead through the fogged plexiglass.

I listen, but don't hear anything. I try to move but can't. After a few minutes, I can't feel my legs, then I can't feel my arms, then I close my eyes. I am nothing more than my detached thoughts. I have lost my will to fight.

It occurs to me now, at last, that this was their plan: to strip me of my bravado, to strip me of all hope.

Time passes. How much time? My thoughts drift to Alice, to Ocean Beach, to our wedding. To the image of her there in our garage with Eric, singing.

I try to push away the thought. But I can't. How silly of me, this jealousy at this moment. The truth is, when I'm gone, if I'm gone, she won't be free to be with Eric, even if she wants to. She'll still be at the mercy of The Pact and their random decisions. Probably for the rest of her life.

I long for voices, or even just a sound. A scrap of music. What I'd give to see Gordon right now. Or Declan. Or even Vivian. Just another human being. Anyone. Is this the very definition of loneliness? It must be.

At some point, I hear the elevator open. Relief floods through me. There are voices—two, maybe three—and the floor begins to vibrate. Something heavy is rolling toward me. I keep waiting for it to come into view, but it doesn't. Then the voices fade down the hallway. The elevator dings again, more voices, and again something rolls down the hallway.

An upright plexiglass contraption, just like the one I'm in.

Inside it, there is a female figure. Brunette, medium build; like me, nude. The glass in front of her face is fogged, so I can't make out her features. They wheel her into place diagonally across from me. Footsteps move away from us, voices fading. The elevator. More voices. Another plexiglass structure. I can't see it, but I can hear it.

There are three of us now. Sensing that we are alone, that all of our handlers are gone, I gather my courage and speak. "Are you both okay?" I ask quietly.

I hear the woman's sobs.

And then, to my right, a man's voice: "What do you think they'll do to us?"

"It's your fault!" the woman cries. "I told you we'd get caught!"

"Shh," the man warns, and it dawns on me that she is talking to him. They know each other. "What's your fault?" I whisper.

A voice comes over the loudspeaker: "Will the inmates please refrain from discussing their crimes?"

An older man in a white cook's uniform passes between us. "Well, you three have sure gotten yourselves into a pickle," he says, looking directly at me. Then he walks away.

A minute later, the elevator dings. As another plexiglass cage slides past me, I see a naked woman, her back to me, her hair gnarled and greasy. I think it can only be one person. The guards spin the plexiglass around, and in an instant she is facing me, six feet away. The woman is pale and thin. She looks like she hasn't seen the sun in weeks. Fog covers the area where her eyes are, so it is moments before the glass clears and she sees me. No, it is not JoAnne. What have they done with JoAnne?

I hear the rumble of many footsteps. In an instant a long line of prisoners in red jumpsuits and employees in gray uniforms are streaming into the cafeteria. Then, all at once, I understand the point of this whole horrific exercise. The four of us are positioned in such a way that everyone has to walk between us to get to the food line. I try to make eye contact with the woman across from me, but her eyes are squeezed shut, tears trickling down her cheeks.

The line stops. I hear the rattle of trays and silverware, workers barking orders. The line backs up as more prisoners pour in—how many? How can so many Friends have gotten on the wrong side of The Pact?

Soon, the line is stationary in front of us. Most of the people are just looking down, avoiding eye contact, though others—first-timers?—seem fascinated, horrified. One man, twenty-something with black hair and perfect teeth, is even smiling. He seems cruelly amused. Others just seem bored, passing time, eating another lunch at Fernley. As if they've seen it all before.

At first, I avoid everyone's eyes. Out of shame, humiliation. But then it occurs to me that if this is the end, I want to force them to look at me. To see me. To know that tomorrow, this could be them. If I can end up here, any Friend can end up here.

The crowd is about half men, half women. The red jumpsuits can't hide the fact that nearly everyone is well groomed, probably well-off. Not your usual prison population. I wonder what crimes brought them here. As the crowd increases, the line doubles in on itself, and triples. It's so crowded that some are pressed against my plexiglass prison, only the clear pane separating them from my nude body. The noise intensifies, and I am filled with rage and disappointment. I want them to do *something*. Anything. I want them to rise up against The Pact.

How is it that we have all allowed this to happen to us?

A woman with auburn hair, an elegant streak of gray at the temple, smiles at me. She glances around to see that no one is watching, then quickly she kisses the plexiglass where my mouth is. She says something, though I can't hear her over the din. *What?* I mouth. She mouths the words back to me, slowly: *Don't give in.*

At least I think that's what she says. *Don't give in.*

## 72

BACK IN THE HOLDING CELL, BACK IN THE RED JUMPSUIT, BACK ON the thin mattress. I try to fall asleep, but it's too bright and too hot. There is nothing to do in here, nothing to read except The Manual. I refuse to touch it.

My mind drifts. For some reason I think of one of my patients, Marcus, the one who asked me the purpose of life. He's writing a paper about Larsen B, a sheet of ice the size of Rhode Island that sat on the edge of Antarctica. In 2004, after nearly twelve thousand years of strength and stability, Larsen B cracked, fragmented, and went hurtling into the ocean. Twelve thousand years, yet it only took three weeks to disintegrate. Scientists aren't sure why, though they suspect that it was a monumental confluence of events—a changing water stream, a hotter sun, ozone depletion, and the usual summer cycle of twenty-four hours of light—that did Larsen B in. The warm water stream caused some tiny cracks, and then the hot sun melted the thin top layer. The droplets rolled down, slowly working their way into the cracks, which then expanded until the entire structure weakened. Finally, in a matter of minutes, a catastrophe that had seemed inconceivable for twelve thousand years suddenly became entirely imminent.

Then I think of my new clients the Rosendins. Darlene and Rich have been married for twenty-three mostly happy years. Nice home, decent jobs, two kids, both in college. Everything was great until about six months ago, when Darlene did a couple of dumb things. In the grand scheme of life, her infractions weren't huge, but in the weeks since then a domino effect began, anger and distrust, and the entire marriage has crumbled. I admit that it left me a little pessimistic about marriage. You hold things together every second of every day, then one time, just for an instant, one person loses concentration, lets go of the thread, and the whole thing unravels.

## 73

"READY TO TALK?"

I stand stiffly and follow Gordon and Maurie out of the cell, down the hallway, and into the interview room. This time, they don't secure me to the table. Maybe they can tell I'm too exhausted to fight.

Gordon sits there, staring at me across the table. Maurie takes up his position at the door. He won't meet my eyes.

"So," Gordon says. "Can we find some common ground? Have you had some time to think?"

I don't answer. I'm not sure there's anything I can say. When I was wheeled into the cafeteria, it felt as though I'd opened the door to a rabbit hole that led to hell. I was ready to make it all right—for JoAnne and for me, for Alice—but then when the stranger mouthed those words, it gave me the strength to stand my ground. *Don't give in.*

"This isn't really about you," Gordon tells me. "JoAnne is a tricky one. Would it interest you to know this isn't her first Crime of Infidelity? Neil has asked me to get to the bottom of it." This is the first time anyone at Fernley has referred to someone in authority by name; that can't be good. Does it mean he's planning to eliminate the witness?

"Look, Jake, I understand you're in a predicament here. You feel that you can't help me solve the problem without incriminating yourself." Gordon stands and moves to a mini-refrigerator in the corner. "Drink?"

"Yes. Please."

He places a plastic bottle in front of me. Icelandic water again—blueberry and mint.

"You seem to have serious resolve, Jake. So, I've been giving it some thought. We have two ways to go. Either I break your resolve—which is a lot of work for me and not much fun for you—or we find a way out of this whereby you can help me solve my problem, but we do it in a manner that allows you to walk away relatively unscathed."

"After the shit you just put me through, I don't trust your definition of unscathed."

"Trust me. That was nothing."

"Is this normal?"

"Is what normal?"

"I thought The Pact was supposed to be about fostering successful, healthy, long-lasting marriages. Where do interrogation and torture fit into a healthy marriage?"

Gordon sighs. "Here's where we're at. I've been asked to solve the problem with JoAnne. Usually, in most cases, I confront the adulterer, she pleads guilty, faces the judge, takes her medicine. The couple moves on. Simple. A marriage is a remarkably resilient thing. I've seen marriages withstand horrible, devastating blows, and somehow they bounce back. It's uncanny. Most of the marriages turn out to be even stronger once the ordeal is over. Do you know why that is?"

I refuse to answer.

"When the offending partner accepts the consequences of his or her actions, Jake, it returns balance to the relationship. It brings back stasis. It eliminates the noise, resolves the problem, and starts the relationship anew. Balance is the key. Balance is the fuel that powers a successful marriage."

While it sounds like a rehearsed speech, it does have a ring of truth. I remember saying something quite similar to my patients.

"Most couples can't bring balance back to their relationship on their own. That's what I'm here for."

"So," I ask, "what is it exactly you need?"

"Because JoAnne has refused to fully confess, this is one of those extremely rare instances where I have been forced to intervene."

"Have you ever considered the possibility that there is simply nothing to confess?"

Gordon sighs again. "The first day my team ran surveillance on JoAnne, she lied to Neil. She snuck out of the house and met you in the food court. For years, I worked for a foreign intelligence service. My subjects were professionals; they knew how to cover their tracks. That was difficult. This is not."

"Have you considered the possibility that JoAnne isn't cheating on Neil? That she was meeting me just as a friend?"

"In situations like this, I've found that the suspected spouse is always cheating. That will be the outcome here as well. It is simply a matter of how we get to that inevitable outcome."

"I can't lead you there. Because it didn't happen."

In an era of Big Data and plentiful information, it's always possible to find evidence to support any point of view, whether it is right or wrong. I think of the run-up to the war in Iraq, yellowcake uranium in Africa, atrocities in Kurdistan—the tidal wave of evidence, both true and false, that leads nations to the decision to go to war.

Gordon gives me a pained smile. "Here's my suggestion. You testify that JoAnne made some sort of overt act or statement that indicated she was interested in pursuing a sexual relationship with you. You don't have to say anything more. You don't have to incriminate yourself. We can just leave it at that. You can plead to some unrelated, minor offense, accept the judgment, and move on with your life. Quite simple. Won't you at least do it for Alice?"

When I don't answer, he scowls. "Look, I'm doing everything I can to help you, Jake. I'm out on a limb here, and you don't seem to appreciate it. You probably don't know that there is an auxiliary handbook that addresses The Pact's implementation requirements. It's not for members but for enforcement personnel like myself, and it guides me in carrying out my responsibilities. This is an unusual circumstance, however, in that it involves an executive's wife. In the interests of expediency, Neil arranged for us to have an expanded array of techniques. Each time we implement a new technique, we need an order from the judge. I've already obtained that authority. I can't share with you the specific set of techniques that have been authorized, but I can tell you that they're something you don't really want to experience." His face is turning red. "If this is all about some sort of misguided altruism, I assure you that JoAnne won't want to experience them either."

"You're saying that the only way for me to save myself and JoAnne is to lie. But if I do lie and give you what you want, how do I know that the punishment for JoAnne won't be even worse?"

"I guess you'll just have to trust me."

I look up at Maurie, hoping for some sort of guidance, but he's studying the floor.

"One of the hard-and-fast rules, Jake, is that you can only be held here for six days without being charged. Once you are charged, we get a week to prepare for the hearing. You can request more time, but I cannot. Do you understand why I'm telling you these things?"

"No."

"It means we must come to an understanding during the next three or four days. I will need to escalate things quickly, which I don't like— and I know you won't. In my previous work, I could take my time, hold someone for weeks on end. I could get to know them, mete out punishments slowly, and ensure that when we reached an understanding it was firm and truthful."

"Look, I have not had a relationship with JoAnne Charles in many years. No matter how many times you ask me the question, the facts won't change. I'm not an adulterer."

We glare at each other. Clearly, we've reached an impasse. I can't see a way out. "Can I call my wife?"

"Yes, maybe that would be a good idea."

Gordon pulls a phone out of his back pocket. I recite Alice's cell number and he enters it. He puts me on speakerphone.

I don't know where she will be; I realize I don't actually know what day or time it is.

"Hello?"

Alice's voice, after everything that's happened over these past few hours, is almost more than I can take.

"Jake? Is that you?"

"Alice."

I can hear office sounds in the background, then a door shutting and quiet. "Jake, are you hurt? Where are you? Can I come to get you?"

"I'm still at Fernley. I'm not with my lawyer right now, and I'm not alone. I'm in an interrogation."

I hear her frightened intake of breath. "What did the judge say?"

"I haven't seen a judge yet. They just keep asking me questions. They want me to say things. Things that aren't true."

A long silence. More doors shutting, elevator, then street noise. Finally, Alice says, "Just tell them whatever they want to hear."

"But what they want to hear is a lie, Alice."

"Jake, for me, for our marriage, please give them what they want."

With that, Gordon clicks the speaker off. Maurie leaves the room and the door slams behind him.

"Are you ready to have that conversation now?"

"I need to think."

"Wrong answer," he says, standing so fast his chair topples over. "Time's up." He stalks out. The light goes off. I'm in the dark, confused, uncertain, and I feel like I can still hear Alice's voice echoing off of the walls.

Minutes pass before the lights come on. A mustached man in a black uniform walks in. He looks like a cross between a plumber and an accountant. "Looks like you're our first guinea pig for this one." He's holding a black canvas bag. "I apologize in advance. I would say, 'Let me know if this hurts,' but I'm fairly certain it will."

The plumber clicks two metal bracelets around my wrists. Then he leans down, pulls my pant leg up and clicks two on my ankles. I'm relieved when he stands to go, but then I sense him behind me. He pushes a rubber ball into my mouth, securing it in place with a strap. "Nice to meet you, Jake," he says, then leaves the room.

By the time Gordon returns with a laptop, my mouth is dry, my jaw aching. "This is four on the escalation levels," he informs me. "I'm sorry it had to get to this." He taps a few buttons on his computer, then looks up. "These things around your wrists and ankles, as I think you might have guessed, are electrodes."

I hadn't guessed.

"I've set the program for one hour. Every four minutes, one of your limbs will receive a shock. The program is random, so you won't know which one until it happens. Okay?"

No. Not okay. Drool dribbles around the rubber ball and down my chin.

"Sorry about the headgear. It's to protect your teeth and gums. Anyway, it's set to start in four minutes. I can't stop it now, even if you wanted to talk."

I shake my head and try to speak through the bit, but my tongue is useless.

"See you in an hour," Gordon says. "We'll have a chance to talk before we get to level five."

"Please." It's what I'm thinking, and I try to say it, but the word is mangled, unintelligible.

The lights go out. For a few minutes, nothing happens. Maybe it's all an empty threat. Maybe Gordon doesn't know how to work the damn program. Then out of nowhere, an electrical shock zings my right ankle. The pain buzzes straight up my leg and spreads through my body. I smell the stench of burning hair. It hurts so much, I scream, or try to. Slobber drools down my face. I taste rubber. I'm breathing heavier. I don't know if the buzzing in my brain is from the shock or from fear of the next one.

I'm sweating profusely when the second shock hits my other ankle. More burning hair, more screaming. I've never felt anything this painful. I've never even imagined this much pain. My jumpsuit is drenched in sweat and piss, I have nearly bitten through the rubber in my mouth. Thirteen to go.

After shock number six, I black out. I come to in horror as the next shock bolts through my body. The room is filled with the stink of burning flesh, urine, and shit. My head is on the table, my brain empty of anything except the searing knowledge of this pain.

When Gordon finally returns, I'm ashamed by how relieved I am to see him.

Maurie enters the room after Gordon. This time, his eyes meet mine. I see something there—is it horror or pity? Or disgust?

Gordon casually pulls out a chair and sits down. He sniffs the room and grimaces. "Don't be embarrassed, Jake, by your loss of control over bodily functions. Just a natural reaction, I assure you. Should we move on to level five?"

I realize he has done this before. I imagine that it always ends the same.

I shake my head as hard as I can, but I can't be sure it's moving at all. "Nnnnnnn," I mumble, gagging on a foul mixture of spit and rubber.

"What?"

"*No!*"

He smiles, genuinely delighted. "Okay, then. Good choice."

Maurie opens the door a crack and mutters something to someone I can't see. Seconds later, the plumber is back, and he removes the head-gear. He starts to unlatch my wrists, but Gordon stops him. "Let's hold off on that for now."

The plumber doesn't respond. Instead he just packs up his things noisily and leaves.

Gordon takes out his iPhone and sets it almost tenderly on the table between us. He takes a clean white towel and wipes the sweat off of my face. "Better?" he asks.

I lick my lips. I taste metal, rubber, and blood.

"You probably want to go clean up," he says.

I barely manage a nod. My body is still shaking. My bladder has been emptied. I am mortified and miserable, sitting in my own piss and shit.

"Soon," Gordon says soothingly. "I promise."

Even though I know it's all some sick game to him, something in me responds to the kind note in his voice. I want desperately to believe that it's real.

He sets a legal pad beside the phone. "Just answer yes or no," he says, tapping the record button on the phone. He reads from the legal pad. "Did you have a previous sexual relationship with JoAnne Charles?"

"Yes."

"Did you see her at a Pact party approximately two months ago?"

"Yes."

"Did you see her again a week later?"

"Yes."

"Did you conspire to meet with her secretly at the Hillsdale mall?"

"Yes."

"Did you meet her at the Hillsdale mall?"

"Yes."

"Did you buy her lunch?"

"Yes."

"Did she make sexual advances to you?"

"Yes," I mumble.

"What?"

"Yes," I say more clearly.

"Did you have sex with her?"

"Recently?"

"Just answer the question."

"Yes, I have had sex with JoAnne Charles."

"Please repeat that." Gordon pushes the phone closer.

"Yes, I have had sex with JoAnne Charles."

"Did you have sex with JoAnne Charles at a hotel in Burlingame, California, on March seventeenth?"

I look into his eyes, trying to voice the words he wants to hear. Level five. What does that mean? My mind races. Is this just another trick? If I confess, will they use my confession as the rationale for sending me wherever they sent Eliot and Aileen? Worse, will they play the confession for Alice? Will they turn my precious wife against me? What is more dangerous? A false confession, or the truth?

I know one thing for certain: *I cannot lose Alice.*

Finally, I say, "No."

Anger flares in his eyes. He turns to the computer and hits a few quick keys. He hands me the towel he used to wipe my face. "You may want to bite down on this."

"Please, don't," I plead.

He looks at me and grins. "Thirty seconds," he says. "Did you sleep with JoAnne Charles at the Burlingame Hyatt?"

I'm sweating; my mind is blank. Before I can answer, I feel the electricity sizzling through my body. I topple off my chair, moaning, and hit the floor. The cuffs dig into my wrists.

"Thirty seconds," Gordon says.

I lie here, not even sure if I'm still alive.

"Fifteen."

My brain is on fire.

"Ten."

I'm staring at something on the floor. A shoe. Gordon's shoe.

As the current shoots through my left leg, up to my chest, I flop around on the floor. I smell my skin burning. I look up at Maurie, begging him with my eyes but unable to utter a single world. He winces and looks away.

I'm under the table now, blood streaming down my arms from the cuts in my wrists. I notice for the first time that the wall behind me is mirrored. Who's watching?

The current shuts down. Someone uncuffs my hands. I lie in my own fluids, motionless, stunned. I want to die. The thought shocks me. I would rather die than suffer through that again.

"Help me," I whisper.

## 74

How long have I been lying here? An hour? A day? The door opens.

"Enough," Neil says.

"Not now," Gordon says. "We're so close."

"Come with me," Neil says. I think he means me. I try to move, but I can't. But then Gordon follows him out of the room. "Help," I say once more.

"You're going to have to help yourself," Maurie says. He walks out the door, closing it softly behind him. I understand now, with a sinking certainty, that Maurie will do nothing for me. No one here will do anything for me. They will only stand by and follow orders.

For the longest time, I hear nothing.

Finally, the door opens again. Elizabeth Watson seems harried. Then she sees me on the floor and exclaims, "My God, what have they done to you?"

She helps me up, grimacing. I'm embarrassed by the stench in the room, the stains on my clothes. She reaches into her bag and hands me a bottle of water. I'm insanely thirsty, but I can barely get my hands around the bottle. I struggle to get the top off, and Elizabeth takes it from me gently and unscrews the lid, holds the bottle to my lips. After I've drunk the entire thing, water dribbling down my chin, she hands me a new jumpsuit, a pair of white underwear folded neatly on top. "I'm so sorry, Jake. You can get cleaned up now. Follow me."

I stumble down the hallway, no doubt leaving a trail of filth behind me. She stops in front of a door marked SHOWERS. I go in and stand under the warm water. I stay under the water for a long time, until it turns cold. I put on the clean clothes.

Outside the bathroom, Elizabeth stands waiting. She pulls a packet of peanut butter M&M's out of her bag and pours a few into my palm. I'm so hungry, but when I bite down on the candy, my whole face aches. She doesn't say a word until we are in her office and the door is closed.

"Relax," she says, pointing to the chair.

I collapse into the chair and close my eyes. I hear Elizabeth pull the blinds down, lock the door, turn on some music. Tears for Fears is singing "Everybody Wants to Rule the World." I will never hear this song the same way again.

When she turns the volume up and pulls her chair over to me, I realize the music is to drown out her voice, to counteract any microphones.

"You were hard to find." She's whispering. "They wouldn't tell me where they'd taken you. I started looking around, making phone calls. Finally, I had to file a paper with the judge requesting an injunction. When they kept stalling, I knew it had to be bad, whatever they were doing to you."

I give her a look to say *You have no idea.*

"The judge unsealed their brief requesting enhanced techniques. I read what they'd been given permission to do." She squeezes my hand. "I'm so, so sorry."

"Can I please go home?" My voice sounds like a stranger's.

"Sorry to say we're not there yet. They have painted you in a very negative light. Because of some irregularities in their request, however, we may have some openings."

I'm still trying to figure out Elizabeth Watson. She is dowdy and impossibly thin. Her confidence tells me she has been a real lawyer for a long time.

"Do you work here?" My jaw hurts. My whole body hurts.

She gives me an odd look. "No."

"Are you a member of The Pact?"

"Yes. Eight years. My partner and I live in San Diego."

She moves in closer, her mouth only inches from my ear. "We're not supposed to talk about this. I'm here for a Trust Infraction—because I didn't have the proper level of trust in my partner."

"And this was your sentence? Representing me in their kangaroo court?"

"Yes, first offense, I pled out and agreed to do twelve days. Normally, I do trial work for a defense firm in Century City. You're in very good hands. I'm very, very expensive," she says; then, smiling, "but free for you."

Elizabeth Watson smells like hazelnut shampoo. The aroma is comforting. With all my heart, I want to put my head in her lap and sleep.

"My wife is an attorney too," I say.

I imagine Alice in our home, dressed in her flannel pajamas. She is drinking coffee, reading, sitting at the table, watching the door, waiting for me. I don't regret marrying her. Even now, even today, even with the buzz bouncing around my body, the pain in my head. For better, for worse. Definitely worse. I don't regret it.

I close my eyes again. Alice. I dream of Alice.

I dream of our honeymoon. I dream of the wedding. I dream of the trip to sell her father's house, the ring I carried around in my pocket. When it first arrived, it seemed like just a glorified rock on a metal band, a simple object—pretty, I guess, but insanely overpriced. On the flight, though, and during the days afterward, the ring seemed to take on a kind of magic. I thought about the power it held, the spell I could cast by slipping it on her finger.

I saw the ring as the talisman that would make Alice mine. It seemed so simple. Now I see my plan for what it was: naïve and somewhat devious.

When I open my eyes, Elizabeth is back at her desk, making notes on her legal pad. She catches me watching her and smiles. "These twelve days were supposed to be easy. And the first ten were. Everyone pled, everything was straightforward. I got them all the best deal I could, and for the most part, they were all very thankful." She taps the pen on her pad. "And now this."

"Sorry. Can I call my wife?"

She scribbles something on the legal pad and holds it up for me to read. *Bad idea!* She crumples the paper, then touches her ears. Someone is listening.

The music is still on. Now it's Spandau Ballet.

She comes to sit by me again, and leans in to speak quietly. "This judge is a shithead. He's from the bench of the Second Circuit. I can't imagine what the fuck he did to wind up here. I've read his decisions. He likes compromise, he likes people who are trying to work things out. We really need to plead to something."

"Anything to get me out of here."

"In your marriage, Jake," she says, "what have you done wrong?"

I think for a minute. "Where should I start?"

# 75

THE WEEK BEFORE I MET ALICE, I RENTED A HOUSE AT SEA RANCH, a coastal enclave three hours north of San Francisco. It was a gift to myself for finishing my final internship, a grueling year at the clinic. Online, I'd selected a tiny cottage up in the hills—no bedrooms, just a loft with a galley kitchen.

On the drive up, I stopped at the bookstore in Petaluma, the pie shop in Sebastopol, bought groceries in Guerneville, then made my way up the twisting coastal highway, going faster than I should where it hugged the cliffs high over the Pacific. I was supposed to pick up the keys and sign the papers at a rental place next to a biker bar in Gualala. When I arrived at the office, though, it was empty. I sat there, reading real estate magazines, until a pale-skinned young woman finally showed up. It was a Tuesday in winter, and it seemed as if they hadn't rented a house in months.

As the rain started to come down, she began searching for my keys. After twenty minutes and several apologies, she confessed there had been a mix-up. The cottage I had reserved had been fumigated the day before. She gave me the keys to a place called Two Rock, provided directions, then sent me on my way. As I was walking out the door, she said, "I have a hunch you might like this place."

Five miles down a highway lit only by the full moon and a crisp array of stars, I turned down a dark road, shadowed by eucalyptus trees. The road turned into a driveway, and the driveway turned into a compound. A grand house right on the ocean was flanked on each side by guesthouses. Just inside the gate, there was a bocce court, and around the side there was a luxurious hot tub and a sauna house that smelled of cedar.

It should have been a glorious celebration of my recent success to have seven thousand square feet all to myself. But it was cold and empty, and it made me feel, for the first time in my life, entirely alone.

The living room, facing the ocean, had a massive wall of windows. A telescope sat in the middle, and a bookshelf held a stack of books on the migration routes of whales. I spent the next morning staring through the lens, waiting to see the telltale sign, a blowhole moving slowly up the coast. I did not.

The hollow sound of that rented house, the huge television echoing down the empty hallways, the endless waves crashing on the rocks, kept rattling around my brain throughout the beginning of my relationship with Alice. The memory of the empty house at Sea Ranch made me want her more. It made me want to have her there when I got home from work. It made me want to have her there to do things with on the weekends. It made me want her in my bed. It made me want her more than I had ever wanted anyone.

## 76

ELIZABETH IS SHAKING MY SHOULDERS. "IT'S TWO MINUTES TO SIX, Jake."

"Morning or evening?"

"Evening."

"We have a court date for tomorrow at nine A.M.," she tells me. There are papers all over the desk behind her. "They're going to take you back to your cell now. They'll return you two hours before court."

There is a knock at the door. Elizabeth watches as two guys in gray uniforms pass chains through my belt loops, then connect them to restraints around my arms and legs.

"Don't worry, Jake," Elizabeth says, noting my embarrassment. "We've all been there."

Back in my original cell, the lights appear brighter, and I notice that the heat has been turned up. Inside, there's still only the flimsy sheet and the worn copy of The Manual. The heat is like a sauna. In an hour, my new jumpsuit is drenched. Eventually, a tray appears through the slot in my door. A bowl of macaroni and cheese and two bottles of Icelandic water. Truffle mac and cheese. My jaw still hurts, but I can tell from the tiny portion that the chef must work in a very fancy restaurant. It's delicious.

The following morning, I wait for what seems like hours until my door opens, and a guard leads me to Elizabeth's office. She has another clean jumpsuit—this one yellow—and a bottle of water waiting for me. As I stand in the corner, changing out of my clothes, she keeps reading her computer screen and typing.

I sit in the chair and wait. After a while, she looks up. "We may finally have a deal, Jake. Hungry?"

"Starving."

She makes a call, and minutes later a woman in uniform shows up with a tray of toast, juice, yogurt, bacon, and scrambled eggs. Obviously not the same chef as last night. I take my time with the food, savoring it.

Downstairs, the courtroom is just like the real thing—a jury box, a place for a stenographer, a prosecutor on one side, Elizabeth and me on the other, a few observers chatting in the pews. As we take our seats, the chatter subsides. Then a female bailiff announces, "All rise, court is now in session."

The judge emerges from a side door. He has silver hair and thick glasses and is wearing the traditional black robe. He looks like an actor playing a judge on TV. He takes his place in front of the courtroom without speaking. His clerk hands him a file.

As he reads the paperwork, we sit in silence. I tug at the neck of the yellow jumpsuit. It's cut the same as the red ones, but the fabric is different. Scratchy. I wonder if it's been specially engineered to make defendants uncomfortable in court. While we wait, the prosecutor, a stern guy in a business suit, keeps glancing down at his cellphone.

Finally, the judge looks at me. He takes a minute to size me up. "Hello, Friend," he says.

I nod in response.

"Morning, counselors," he says. "I understand that we have come to an agreement, a plea to two counts."

"Yes, Your Honor," the prosecutor says.

The judge picks up the file and drops it back down on his desk dramatically. "This is an alarmingly thick file," he observes.

The size of my file. What could possibly be in it? Alice and I have only been married for six months. Have I really been such a terrible husband? Is my list of crimes so vast?

"Yes, Your Honor," the prosecutor agrees. "There were some issues that needed to be sorted out."

"Given the seriousness of the file," the judge says, "a plea to two counts, albeit a Felony Three, seems surprising, no?"

"Well . . ." The prosecutor squirms.

"I would expect a plea to at least a few more charges. Did our defendant's counselor get the best of you? I must say, I'm surprised."

I glance over at Elizabeth. Her expression remains unreadable.

"Your Honor," the prosecutor says, "in this highly unusual case, I believe that the plea is fitting."

The judge doesn't speak. He flips through the file again. Except for the shuffling of papers, it is hushed in the courtroom. I get the feeling everyone is terrified of the judge. And I realize that, despite his robe and the bailiff and all the usual trappings of the justice system, this court is far from ordinary. Even the attorneys are afraid. At any moment, they might find themselves sitting right where I'm sitting, defending themselves against false allegations, answering for crimes they may or may not have committed.

Finally, the judge tucks the papers back in the folder. He takes off his reading glasses and looks down at me. "Jake, you're a lucky man."

Why don't I feel like a lucky man?

"Last week, our defense attorney was an ambulance chaser from Reseda. I doubt he would have been able to orchestrate the same outcome for you that Ms. Watson has." The judge seems slightly frustrated but resolved. Then he says, "Please stand."

I stand, and beside me Elizabeth stands too.

"Jake, you have been charged with one felony count of Possessiveness, section nine, unit four, paragraphs one through six, and one misdemeanor count of Seeking Anti-Pact Propaganda, section nine, unit seven, paragraph two. You have the right to a jury trial among your peers. How do you plead?"

I glance at Elizabeth. She whispers in my ear.

"Guilty, Your Honor," I say. "On both counts."

"Do you understand that with this plea you do not have the opportunity to appeal should you have a change of heart following the sentencing?"

"Yes. I understand."

"Are you familiar with The Manual's teachings relating to possessiveness?"

"Yes."

"How would you define possessiveness?"

"Manifesting a desire to control your partner."

"Would you agree that appropriately describes your behavior?"

"Yes, Your Honor. One of my original intentions when I proposed marriage may have been rooted in this desire."

"You are aware, also, that seeking information online to vilify or otherwise cast aspersions upon The Pact is a crime that we cannot tolerate, for the health of The Pact and for the good of your marriage?"

"I understand, sir."

"Okay, Jake. I will accept your plea. You have been found guilty of one count of Possessiveness, as defined in nine, four, one through six. As you know, that is a Felony Three. You have also been found guilty of one count of Seeking Anti-Pact Propaganda, as defined in nine, seven, two. Misdemeanor Four. Both are serious crimes. In mitigation, this is your first offense; you have willingly acknowledged and pleaded guilty to the offenses. Your sentence is as follows: six months of weekly consultations with a certified Pact mentor selected by your regional coordinator, one year availability for participation in our long-distance counseling program, the customary hundred-dollar fine, a three-month moratorium on Internet use with the exception of email, and four days at Fernley as time served."

*Time served.* That means I'm getting out. Relief makes my knees buckle.

But then he continues: "Because I'm uncomfortable with the size of your file and the accusations contained within, and because something in my gut tells me you are at risk to become a repeat offender, I am also going to order the following suspended sentence: one year home moni-

toring, one year mobile incarceration level one, and thirty days at Fernley, to be served consecutively. Although I have suspended this sentence
for now, let it stand as motivation each day to follow the correct path. If
at any time it comes to my attention that you have begun questioning
The Pact, if I discover that you've been pursuing further conversations or
conducting similar inappropriate research into past or present enemies
of The Pact, you'll find yourself right back here. And I assure you, Jake,
the punishments to which you've been subjected will seem, in hindsight,
like child's play."

I look straight ahead, trying not to show my fear. Inside, my heart is
sinking. Will I never be free?

"Jake," the judge continues, "I don't know the truth regarding the
accusations contained in your file, and I'm not going to ask you. To be
blunt, your attitude disturbs me. The Pact and your marriage are one
and the same. Without respect and submission, there will be no success.
You have been a member for only a short time, so I have shown lenience.
But as you can see, my leniency has a limit. The Pact exists above us, with
no man rising higher. Make your peace with The Pact. Do it now—not
five years from now, not ten years from now—for your own good. We're
not going anywhere. Look around you. The walls of this institution are
strong; the influence of its people are stronger. The Pact casts a shadow
wider than you know. Most of all, we have a complete and unwavering
belief in the rightness of our mission. Find your position within The
Pact, find your position within your marriage, and you will find your
own daily reward."

"Yes, Your Honor."

The judge whacks his gavel, stands, and departs.

Elizabeth and I collect our things and wait for the courtroom to
clear. When the stenographer has finally packed up her machine and
departed, I turn to Elizabeth. "What is 'mobile incarceration level one'?"

"That's something I'm going to have to find out." She looks grave
and deeply concerned. "I don't know what you did, or who you pissed
off, but you need to make it right. If you wind up back here, I don't
think anyone will be able to help you."

I find myself standing alone with Elizabeth in the hallway in front of the courtroom. One wall is lined with black-and-white photographs of Orla. She poses above a rugged coastline, in front of a cottage obscured by fog. The other wall is lined with black-and-white photos of couples on their wedding day. Important people. Surely, none of these people knew, when these photos were taken, what they were getting into.

Elizabeth's phone vibrates. She looks at a text message. "Your plane is ready," she says, leading me toward yet another door.

The light of the outer room blinds me for a few seconds, and then I realize we are at the very place where I entered this nightmare. Fernley suddenly reminds me of the rides I loved when the carnival came to the fairgrounds: part tunnel of love, part funhouse, all terrifying. A guard hands me a sealed plastic bag containing my meager possessions.

"This is where we part," Elizabeth says.

I sense she wants to give me a hug. Instead, she takes a step back. "Safe travels, Friend."

I step inside the men's room, quickly shed my jumpsuit, and put on my street clothes. On my way out, I pass a mirror. The view is startling. I glance behind me, half-expecting to see a bald stranger, but then I realize that the alien in the reflection is me.

I walk out of the bathroom, still not completely convinced they're going to just let me go. But the double front doors open for me. I head down the long hallway toward the runway. I'm tempted to run, but I don't want to give the impression that they've made a mistake. When I get to the final gate, I can see a Cessna—my plane, I hope—sitting on the runway.

I turn the handle on the gate, but it's locked. I glance at the security camera, but nothing happens. Time passes. Being trapped at the locked gate makes me increasingly nervous.

A larger plane touches down on the runway and comes to a stop near the Cessna. The noise of the plane engine dies down, and a door slowly opens. A van rounds the corner and pulls up next to it. The van door slides open, and two young women in matching navy dresses step out. Not women, really. They don't look a day older than seventeen. Their uniforms are tighter and shorter than the ones everyone else wears. I sense they're some kind of special welcoming party.

I see a golf cart on the horizon, moving toward us. The driver is female, and the passenger is a man in a suit. A foot in a prison slipper emerges from the van. The hem on the red jumpsuit gets caught on the door and slides up, revealing a bare ankle. I'm not sure how, but I know it is JoAnne.

Two thin arms emerge, shackled at the wrists. Then a head, covered in a black hood. The two young women take her by the arms and guide her toward the larger plane. As JoAnne hobbles across the tarmac, the black hood swivels in my direction. Can she see me? I am horrified, mesmerized, watching her shuffle toward the awaiting plane. Did I do this to her?

She struggles up the ramp and disappears into the plane.

The golf cart comes to a stop just beyond the gate. The man gets out and stands, his back to me, just a foot away. Expensively tailored suit, Italian shoes. For a minute, no one moves.

Finally, the man in the suit turns. Neil.

"Hello, Jake," he says, pulling a key ring out of his pocket. "Did you enjoy your stay?" The ring holds a single key.

"Not entirely."

"Next time, Jake, we won't be quite so hospitable."

The key glints in the sun, sending splinters of light across his suit. The fabric has an unpleasant sheen. His forehead has clearly been injected with Botox many times. I can't imagine what JoAnne ever saw in him.

He looks directly into my eyes. "When a rule is broken," Neil says, "the price must be paid. It is only then that balance is restored, equality returns, and the Pact, like a marriage, can move on." He puts the key in the slot but doesn't turn it. "Things are seriously out of balance, thanks to you. You and Alice are out of balance, JoAnne and I are out of balance, and more important, The Pact is out of balance."

Neil turns the key and the gate slides open.

"I will not rest until balance is restored. Understand?"

I don't reply.

There is something in his voice, something familiar. "You'll find the plane is well equipped." Then from behind me, I hear him say, "Dr Pepper, Jake?"

In my mind, I complete the exchange, the way I always do: *That sounds good.*

And that's when it hits me, why he seemed so familiar that day at the Woodside party. Back in college, I never knew his name; I always thought of him as "the jumper on Sproul." JoAnne married the boy she talked down from the roof. She married the boy she saved. What would Freud say?

And why, then, did she tell me she had met Neil after a car accident? Why did she lie to me?

I walk steadily toward the Cessna, watching JoAnne's plane as it taxis down the runway and rises into the air. It disappears into the shimmering desert heat.

## 77

THE CESSNA'S WHEELS SHUDDER ON THE RUNWAY IN HALF MOON Bay. I grab the Ziploc bag, thank the pilot, and stumble down the stairs.

In the café, still groggy, completely starving, I sit down at a table in the corner. The waitress in the retro uniform slides a menu in front of me. "The usual?" she says in a friendly voice.

"Sure," I reply, surprised that I've been here enough times to have a usual.

She returns with French toast and a side of bacon.

When the food is gone, I turn on my cellphone. It takes a while to kick in. When it does, I notice there's a new icon on the main screen. It's a small blue *P*. I try to delete it, but nothing happens. It disappears for a second, then returns. There are a handful of texts and several voicemails. I don't look at any of them. Instead, I dial Alice.

"I'm home," I tell her before she even has a chance to say hello.

"Are you okay?" I hear the sounds of her office in the background.

"I seem to be."

"I'll be there in thirty minutes."

Outside, I find a spot on the bench. The planes circle overhead. A black Chevy Suburban is parked at the corner of the lot.

I hear the distinctive rumble of Alice's old Jaguar as it turns off of the highway. She pulls up beside me and leans over to open the passenger door. I grab my Ziploc bag and slide in beside her. She runs her hand over my bald head, gives me a sympathetic look, and then pulls out of the parking lot and back onto the highway.

The Chevy edges out of the parking lot and turns onto the highway behind us.

Alice is wearing her favorite wrap dress, the one that shows her small waist, her beautiful hips, and just a hint of cleavage. As we move into the tunnel, pointed toward Pacifica, I slide my hand under the hem and rest my palm on her bare thigh. She feels so warm. I remember precisely how I got to where I am. This wonderful marriage, this terrible nightmare, all began with that touch—the surprise of warmth, the smoothness of her skin.

I see the SUV in my side view mirror, and I hear Neil's voice in my head: *I will not rest until balance is restored.*

Alice's iPhone rests on the console between us. A small blue *P* in the top corner blinks off and on.

## 78

URING THE CAR RIDE HOME, ALICE DOESN'T ASK QUESTIONS, and I don't offer up my story. I'm not quite ready to share what I've been through, and I sense she isn't quite ready to hear it. Still, after she pulls into the driveway and leans over to give me a kiss on the cheek, I'm hurt when I realize she isn't coming inside. I need so badly to be with her right now.

"So sorry," she says. "Big court date tomorrow. I'll be home late."

After being apart for a while, it takes time for a couple to reconnect. I tell my patients this. In movies and literature, there's such a fascination with couples who are meant to be together, the idea of Mr. or Mrs. Right. But, of course, none of that is true. For some people there are many Mr. Rights. For others, there are none. Like atoms, the fact of couples coming together is based more upon timing and circumstance than magic.

Of course, there is magic too. Like atoms, couples can only combine if there is attraction, some sort of logical connection, chemistry producing a reaction. When two people are apart, though, even the strongest bonds inevitably dissipate, so it is necessary to rediscover the connection, rebuild the bonds.

Several years ago, I did an internship with the Veterans Administration. One of my first patients was Kevin Walsh. He had joined the reserves as a way to pay for college but was surprised to get deployed to the Middle East. One tour led to two, two to three. When he returned to San Francisco, to his wife and two kids, Kevin said he felt like he was stepping into someone else's life. The kids were well behaved and fun, the wife was pleasant and attractive, but he couldn't escape the feeling this life wasn't his, that it was a life chosen by a different man and he was an impostor trying to make it work.

I wander around our home, becoming reacquainted with our things, our life. The place is a mess. Clearly, Alice didn't expect me home today. In the garage, her studio has been rearranged—two chairs, two amps, two guitar stands facing each other. A worn piece of sheet music lies on a table. I pick it up and scan the page futilely, as if the bars and notes might contain some secret code to Alice. But it is a bizarre, impenetrable language.

I'm worried. Less for myself than for Alice.

Back upstairs, I see the house with fresh eyes: two plates in the sink, two forks, two empty wineglasses on the floor beside the couch. I feel sick. I go to the window and scan the street for the black SUV, but it isn't there. I peer up at the streetlight. It has always been there, rendered invisible by its mundane presence. But now I notice three small boxes on top. Were they there before?

What has happened inside the house while I've been gone? More important, has The Pact been watching? Of course they have. How can Alice be so reckless? If The Pact comes and takes her away again, it will change her forever. She might be more faithful, she might be more obedient, but that's not what I want. I want Alice. Beyond that, I want Alice to be Alice, good and bad. Finally. Is this love?

I call the office to let them know I'm back. Huang is surprised. "Where have you been, Mr. Jake?"

"Here and there. I got a haircut."

A notebook lies open on the couch. All of the guitars and speakers are scattered around the house. The Teac four-track is set up on the breakfast room table, another notebook beside it, song titles scribbled.

On our bed, I find a wrapped present with my name on it. A compact disc.

I slide it into the player on the bedside table, turn the power on, pull the headphones over my ears, sit on the bed, and press play. It's Alice singing, accompanied by guitars, keyboards, drums, and at one point even a set of children's percussion instruments. There are several background voices, but those are also Alice. The songs are beautiful and moody.

Track five is a duet. Alice is joined by a man's voice. It's another relationship song, a relationship that sounds familiar, and I realize that it's about Alice and me, though somehow foreign. It's the story of us, as seen through Alice's eyes. The male voice sings my lines, certainly better than I ever could. The intimacy between the two voices makes the song deeply disquieting. The intake of breath before each line, the sort of thing that gets removed in the final edit, makes me feel as though I am right there in the room. I try to distance myself, to hear it as it would sound to an outside party, to someone who is not in love with Alice, but it's not possible.

I remember the day on the stairwell, when Eric knew I was there but Alice did not. I think of the look he gave me. There was a challenge in his eyes, though maybe I read it all wrong. Maybe what I was seeing, instead, was compassion for me, or pity—because he knew something that I did not.

I listen to the disc all the way through, and then I start over again. Like the room in the garage, it feels as though I am peering into a part of Alice that I have imagined but never actually seen.

The musical portrait she paints of me is nuanced, occasionally forgiving, and brutally honest.

For so long, I held on to Alice so firmly, keeping her directly in my sight, looking only at the parts I wanted to see. I encouraged those qualities I loved in her, coaxing them forward, subconsciously hoping that if I ignored the other parts, they would recede and fall away. Of course, in my absence those parts have been flourishing. Yes, Alice has been becoming Alice again, her full and maddeningly complex self. I close my eyes, listening to her voice.

At some point, I hear a noise in the kitchen. I slide the headphones off. Alice is home. I wander down the hallway and find her high heels kicked off on the living room floor. I smell chicken, garlic, a hint of chocolate. I take in the moment, which feels perfect and welcome, until a vague sense of dread edges in. I look out the window and check for any suspicious cars parked on the block.

Alice is standing at the stove in pajamas and a Lemonheads T-shirt, frying mushrooms in butter, a wooden spoon in one hand, a beer in the other. The pan sizzles, and a slight smokiness fills the air. I slide my arms around her waist.

"Well, look who's returned from the dead," she says.

I murmur into her ear, "I loved your songs."

She turns to face me, and I take the glass and the spoon out of her hands and put them on the counter. I pull her away from the stove, into the center of the kitchen. We stand there, locked in a kind of slow dance. At first, she is stiff, her hands perched on my shoulders, back slightly arched, as if she's unwilling to give in to this moment, and to me. Then her body relaxes. She leans her head on my shoulder, moves her hands down my back, and pulls me close. I can feel her breath through my shirt. "Sorry about some of the lyrics."

I can tell she wants to say something else. I just hold her and wait. "And the rest of it," she says, sighing. "I'm sorry for the rest of it."

Which sounds like a confession, at once alarming and a relief. If this happened between clients, I'd congratulate them on the breakthrough. I'd tell them that honesty is good, honesty is the first step. Of course, I would also warn them that, now that the truth was out in the open, things might get worse before they got better.

"You be you," I say, and I mean it, I think.

Alice jumps up and puts her legs around my waist, and I am holding her entirely. We haven't done this in so long, and I'd forgotten how light she feels, wrapped around my body.

# 79

I T's SURPRISING HOW QUICKLY ALICE AND I RETURN TO OUR PATTERNS.
I catch up at work, and she returns to her new case. But she leaves for
the office a little later each day and comes home a little earlier. And
when she's home, I rarely catch her with the briefcase open, reviewing
legal things, doing research. Instead, before we retire to the couch and
click on a new episode of *Sloganeering*, she spends an hour or so on her
laptop, inside Pro Tools, headphones on, mixing, tweaking, reviewing
the songs for her new album.

We don't talk about the days I was gone, what happened at Fernley
or what happened here in the house. It is as if we have reached some
silent agreement. Although the judge sentenced me to mobile incarceration, there was no further explanation. I waited for the bracelet, but it
never came. I can only assume that they're watching me more closely
than ever. Maybe the house is bugged. Maybe there is a device in my car.
Or maybe it is all some cruel psychological game: the not knowing is its
own kind of prison.

Slowly, my hair begins to grow back. The longer it grows, the more
Fernley seems like a distant nightmare.

At work, I return to my regular patterns, my clients, the teenagers, the married couples. I slowly start to wrap things up with those who are ready. Therapy, like all long conversations, has a beginning, middle, and end.

At home, I treasure the happiness we've found these past few weeks, the stability, the security, the warmth. I can see it in Alice's eyes: She is happier. I imagine she is surprised to have found a hidden path that has let her merge the different sides of her personality. It feels as though we are slowly building our relationship, unique and different from all others, a marriage not unlike the ideal described in The Pact.

And yet my mind, like a computer calculating pi forever in the background, is still desperately trying to find a way out of The Pact. I sense Alice is doing the same.

Last night, I saw a dark SUV up the corner. The day before, Alice spotted a Bentley across the street. We both know that change is coming, that something has to be done, but neither of us mentions it.

## 80

ON TUESDAY, ALICE RECEIVES WORD THAT THE KEYBOARD PLAYER from her old band Ladder has been killed in a motorcycle accident on the Great Highway. He was in his early forties and had a wife and twin daughters in preschool. Alice once spent two years with him in a van, on the road touring, so the news hits her hard.

An impromptu benefit has been planned at Bottom of the Hill on Saturday night. I suggest maybe she should go alone, but she insists that I come with her. When I get home from running errands on Saturday, I catch a glimpse of her in front of the bedroom mirror, and I barely recognize her. Her hair is crazy, her makeup extreme, the black minidress, fishnets, and Doc Martens unlike anything she has worn in years. She looks great, but her ability to transform so swiftly back into the creature she once was makes me uneasy.

I struggle with my own clothes, finally settling on jeans and an old white button-down. We look entirely mismatched, like a couple heading out on an ill-conceived first date set up by friends who don't know either of us well. Alice is nervous about being late. We finally squeeze into a parking spot six blocks away, and we run-walk all the way to the club.

Inside, Alice is swallowed up immediately by a crowd of old friends, acquaintances, and fans. I stand back and watch.

The music starts. It's a strange mishmash of musicians playing all of the old favorites. Green Day is there, the keyboardist from the Barbary Coasters, Chuck Prophet, Kenney Dale Johnson, others who look vaguely familiar. The crowd seems to be enjoying it. It's a mix of sadness and joy, people celebrating their friend's life, still stunned by his death. The music is good, and I can tell the musicians are putting their hearts into it. Still, it has been many years since I've been to a club like Bottom of the Hill, so it's not long before my ears are ringing. I scan the crowd, but I don't see Alice.

I grab a Calistoga at the bar and find a spot against the wall in the back, in the dark. As my eyes adjust, I realize that there are three other guys against the back wall, two of them also drinking Calistoga, all three wearing white button-downs and jeans, all three around my age. Probably A-and-R guys.

When did I get old?

It happens slowly, but rarely with ambiguity. In restaurants, the waiter places the check beside you. At work, in meetings, when a difficult decision arises, others look to you first for direction. A tint of gray at the temples, the obvious signs: a house, a car that's paid for, a wife instead of a girlfriend.

A wife. I finally spot Alice, talking with people I don't recognize, a crowd between us. Despite the complications, I'm so happy with my choice, and I hope she's happy with hers.

Eventually, the noise becomes too much, so I get my hand stamped and step outside. The fog feels good on my face. I watch the cars moving up Seventeenth Street.

"So I hear you're a therapist."

I turn to see Eric Wilson standing beside me. I see now what I didn't notice that day in our garage—probably because I was so focused on Alice. He no longer looks like the young, good-looking bass player from that photo out front of the Fillmore. His hair is a little greasy, and he has bad teeth.

"Yes," I say. "And you are a bassist in a band." It comes out more derisive than I mean for it to, or maybe not. The fact is, I have nothing against bassists in general. Just this bassist.

He pulls out a cigarette and lights up. "By night," he acknowledges. "During the day, I'm a professor at Cal. Biology. Didn't Alice mention that?"

"No, she didn't."

"It's not unprecedented. The guy from Bad Religion teaches at UCLA."

"Interesting."

"Yeah, we're co-authoring a paper on the green turtles of Ascension Island. *Chelonia mydas*. Ever heard of them?"

"No."

Through the wall, I can feel the vibrations of the music inside. I want to go back in, but more than that I want to punch Eric Wilson in the face. It's a fairly new sensation. What would happen, I wonder, if I were to simply put my more rational nature aside, just for once, and act on instinct?

Eric must have just come offstage, because he has sweat running down his neck. I'm reminded of a recent article from *JAMA,* a piece about how women are often attracted to their future mate by the smell of his sweat. The theory is that women look for a man with unique-smelling perspiration because it implies a difference in genes, a better prospect for immunity in their children, a better chance for the family line to endure. Immortality, all in the smell of sweat.

"These giant green sea turtles," Eric says, "are born on Ascension Island. Then, they spend their lives far away, enjoying different waters, exploring, swimming off the coast of Brazil and things like that. But you know what?" Eric has turned to face me, so close I can feel his breath on my face.

"I imagine you're going to tell me."

"When it's time to settle down, time to have a family, they return to who they are. Can you imagine that? When the time to get serious comes—and trust me, it always does—wherever they are, whoever they think they've become, they put it aside, and they swim, and they swim. Sometimes, thousands of miles. They shed their current life without a moment's hesitation. They return to that beach on Ascension Island, give up all pretense, and become exactly who they are, exactly who they were."

Eric finishes his cigarette, drops it on the ground, and grinds it under his boot heel.

"Nice seeing you, Jake," he says.

I watch him walk away, the back of his shirt streaked with sweat.

Later, Eric is onstage with his band. It's hard to look at him. It's hard not to think about him in my house, eating off our plates, drinking from glasses we got for our wedding.

Eric calls Alice up to sing. She appears from the side of the stage, and the volume of the applause surprises me. She perches on a stool beside Eric. They start with a popular song from their old band, then move into one of the songs from the CD she gave me.

I watch them up there onstage together, sitting so close, and I shudder. When we first met, Alice was inching out of music, already on a different path. It wasn't clear where the path would lead, but it was obvious that she'd given up her old life and was determined to move forward to a new adventure. I worried that one day she would discover this new adventure, of which I was a part, to be nothing more than a tangent she was ready to discard as she returned to her former life.

At times, I tried to distract her from returning to that life. I encouraged her to take the job at the law firm, I bought her the first designer suit she ever owned. It was stupid, maybe even manipulative, but I was scared. I wanted to keep her.

What I didn't fully understand was that Alice isn't a simple idea, she isn't an unbendable object, an unchanging showpiece. Yes, I knew she was complex, I didn't need a degree in psychology to see that. The first day I met her, I was reminded of the Walt Whitman lines *Do I contradict myself? Very well then, I contradict myself. I am large, I contain multitudes.*

No, I recognized Alice's complexity from the beginning. What I didn't grasp was that Alice is a growing, evolving organism. So am I. I want to believe that we are not like the green turtles of Ascension Island, that we have evolved beyond the basic patterns of the natural world. I want to believe that it isn't possible for Alice to go back to being the person she was before I met her. I want to tell Eric that he's wrong about my wife. The trip through law school, through her career, into the depths of our marriage, hasn't just been a side trip from which she can emerge and step back onto the intended path of her life. Our marriage is not a misguided adventure, as much as Eric Wilson would like it to be.

And it occurs to me that this is the very essence of what I love about Alice. She contains contradictions, she contains multitudes. She embraces every stage of her life, learning from each one, carrying her experiences with her, nothing left behind. Intuitively adapting, becoming a different, more complex version of herself with every passing year.

I expected marriage to be a door that we went through. Like a new house, you step into it, expecting it to be an unchanging space to inhabit. But, of course, I was wrong. Marriage is a living, changing thing that you must tend to both alone and together. It grows in all sorts of ways, both ordinary and unexpected. Like the tree outside our front window, or the kudzu that lined the backyard of Alice's father's house the night we got engaged, it is a living thing of contradictions—simultaneously predictable and baffling, good and bad—growing more complicated each day.

Then Alice turns to face Eric, as if she is singing directly to him. They sing the duet, and the whole place grows hushed, mesmerized by them together up there onstage. They're face-to-face, knees touching. Her eyes are closed. Doubt seeps in. The worry that used to exist only at the edge of my consciousness, held at bay by my optimism and the blindness of my love, is now a black fog in my brain.

Is that why she wanted me here tonight—so I can see what has happened between her and Eric? Is this her way of telling me that our marriage has run its course? I try to steady myself for the moment I may have to walk out of the club alone.

## 81

Oₙₑ of the questions I ask couples in therapy is "Do you still believe that you have the capacity to surprise each other?" The answer, too often, is no.

I wish I could come up with an easy formula for inserting surprise back into a marriage. That simple change could be the salvation for so many marriages I've seen. The Marriage Defibrillator, I'd call it. A good, stiff shock to revive the system.

Seeing Alice in the black minidress and Doc Martens is a surprise. But what happens onstage isn't. Watching her sing with Eric, I think I can see the end of our story.

As it turns out, I'm wrong. When the night is over and almost everyone has left, I'm standing outside again—worn out, troubled, confused by what I've witnessed—when she steps out of the club.

Her mascara is messed up, and I can't tell if it's from the heat of the bar or she's been crying. But here she is, holding on to me tightly. "Too much whiskey," she says, her words fuzzy and slow. "I'm gonna need to lean on you."

On the drive home, Alice surprises me again. She flips down the passenger-side visor, peers into the mirror, grimaces. "Should have worn waterproof mascara. Some of us got to talking about him right at the end. We were telling stories about our last tour. I laughed so hard I cried."

When we reach Fulton Avenue, the long stretch of empty road descending toward the beach, she powers down her window. Waves of fog glow under the streetlights. "Mmm," she says, sticking her head out the window. "Smells like the ocean."

And I am struck by a memory of a night just like this one, years ago, when we were newly in love. A cruel kind of déjà vu. Things were simple then. Our path forward seemed clear.

After a moment, I ask, "Ever heard of the green turtles of Ascension Island?"

"That's random," she says, snapping the mirror shut. She doesn't look at me.

It's after three in the morning when we retreat into our bedroom. The curtains are open and I can see the moon rising over the Pacific Ocean. Alice is sloppy drunk, but we have sex anyway, because she wants to and I want to. I want to reclaim what is mine, what is ours.

I lie awake, Alice sleeping noisily beside me. There's hope for us yet. Or is there? I think of turtles swimming endlessly south across the Atlantic Ocean. More important, though, I think of The Pact, this hole we have fallen into, my mind in the background frantically still calculating, trying to figure a way out.

At 9:12 A.M., I notice that I've slept straight through the alarm. It's a gentle alarm—David Lowery of Cracker singing "Where Have Those Days Gone." The clock lies sideways on the floor beside the bed. Alice is asleep beside me, a little drool and tangled hair the only evidence of her wild night.

I realize that I've woken up because of banging next door. The walls seem to be shaking, and at first I think it's the neighbors. Our neighbors are a friendly elderly couple, and I've always liked them, but they have been known to host all-day mah-jongg games.

Then it dawns on me that the noise is coming from our front door.

"Alice," I whisper. "Alice?"

Nothing.

I shake her shoulders. "There's someone at the door!"

She flips over, pushing hair out of her eyes. She blinks against the light. "What?"

"There's someone at the door."

"Ignore it," she groans.

"They're not going away."

Abruptly, she's fully awake, sitting up. "Fuck."

"What should we do?"

"Fuck fuck fuck."

"Get dressed," I say. "Quick. We have to get out of here."

Alice jumps out of bed, pulls on her dress and boots from last night, and throws on her trench coat. I tug on my dirty jeans, a T-shirt, and sneakers.

More banging. "Alice! Jake!" The doorknob rattles. I recognize the voice. Declan.

We race out the back door and down the stairs into the yard. It's freezing. The neighborhood is blanketed in fog, a chill breeze drifting in from the ocean. I help Alice over the back fence and into the next yard, and I hastily follow. We move quickly through the grid of rectangular yards, over tottering wooden fences. At one point, we have to climb a bottlebrush tree to get over a high fence. Finally, at the corner of Cabrillo and Thirty-ninth, we slip through a gate and out onto the sidewalk.

In the distance, I can still hear Declan shouting our names. His partner must be in the SUV by now, trolling the Avenues, looking for us.

I pull Alice behind a bank of recycling cans. I check my pockets: $173, phone, house keys, wallet, credit cards. Alice is shivering, pulling her coat tight around her body. She looks at me, panic in her eyes. Leaves are stuck to her coat, sticky red petals from the bottlebrush tree.

"Which way do we go?" she asks, petrified. I don't have a clue.

## 82

WE HEAD EAST ALONG FULTON, STAYING CLOSE TO THE TREES, then slip into Golden Gate Park at Thirty-sixth Avenue. We wade through dense fog, hurrying past Chain of Lakes Drive and deeper into the overgrown paths. I hear the sound of many voices up ahead, and it occurs to me that today is Bay to Breakers, San Francisco's annual road race that traverses the city from the Embarcadero to the beach and features an odd mix of Ethiopian four-minute milers, families, nudists, and drunk guys in cheerleading costumes bringing up the rear.

The event must be at least half over, because when we cross Kennedy Drive, the racers are all in costume, some walking, many carrying drinks. Alice turns to me, a look of shock and relief on her face. There's no better place to get lost than Bay to Breakers. We watch the runners go by— a dozen M&M'S costumes, a groom being chased by a bride, an all-female version of the 49ers' offensive front line, and a throng of regular slow-moving runners, all trying to grit out the final stretch of the 7.46-mile course. A guy dressed as Duffman, pushing a cart filled with kegs of beer, hands Alice and me each a full cup.

"Cheers," he says.

We sit on the grass and sip our warm beers. We are both silent, trying to figure out our next move. Alice points to twenty guys and girls dressed as Kim Jong-il. She almost smiles.

"When do you think we can go home?" I ask.

"Never," she says.

She leans into me and I put my arm around her shoulders.

The sun comes out, and Alice spreads her trench coat across the damp grass and lies on top of it. "I haven't been this hungover in years," she moans. She closes her eyes, and within a minute or two she's asleep. I wish I could do the same. But the crowd is beginning to thin, and we don't have much longer.

I pull out my phone and fish around for ideas on where to go next. The blue *P* flashes in the corner of the screen. I quickly do a search for car rental companies, then power down the phone. I search around in the pockets of Alice's coat for her cell, but she must have left it behind.

"Come on," I say, shaking her awake. "We have to get moving."

"Where?"

"There's a Hertz rental not too far from here."

We start the long walk toward Haight, moving against the thinning crowd.

"What if they don't have a car?"

"They have to have a car," I say.

With Alice's rumpled coat and my dirty old shirt and ripped jeans, we don't stand out among the drunken morning Bay to Breakers crowd. We trudge east through the park toward the Panhandle, finally arriving at the intersection of Stanyan and Haight. We stop at Peet's and order a hot chocolate and a large Americano. We use both of our bank cards at an ATM to withdraw the maximum daily limit of cash. Outside Hertz, she plops down on the curb, drinking her coffee, trying to wake up.

When I pull up alongside her in an orange convertible Camaro, the only car they had available, she smiles.

We weave through the city, over the Golden Gate Bridge, and north through Marin County. We stop at an electronics store in San Rafael and buy a new SIM card. Back on the road, Alice pulls the old SIM card out of my phone and tosses it out the window. When we hit Sonoma, she tilts her seat back, closes her eyes, and soaks up the sun. I love that she hasn't even asked where we're going.

I turn on KNBR and listen to the Giants game as long as the signal will last. It's 4 to 2, and Santiago Casilla is trying to close out the ninth when the reception finally fades. We drive down 116, along the Russian River, and out toward the ocean. At Jenner, where the river finally meets the Pacific, I pull the Camaro in to the Stop & Shop.

Inside the store, Alice goes to the restroom while I stock up on gas station food. In the car, she pops open a bottle of vitamin water. She downs the whole thing, then peers into the bag. "Chocodiles!" she squeals.

The road past Jenner is a narrow ribbon edging the high cliffs. It's a scary drive but gorgeous. I haven't driven this stretch of Highway 1 since the week before Alice and I met. So much has happened since then. Who is this man fleeing his life in an orange Camaro, with a beautiful, confusing, unshowered woman munching Chocodiles in the passenger seat?

In Gualala, I pull into a grocery store parking lot. We buy milk and bread, a few things for dinner, some hoodies and shorts for both of us. A mile down the road, I park in front of Sea Ranch Rentals. "Sea Ranch!" Alice says. "I've always wanted to stay here."

The same pale-skinned girl who rented me the compound last time is sitting behind the desk, reading a paperback copy of *The Crying of Lot 49*. She glances up as I walk in. "You again," she says, though I can't imagine she actually remembers me. "Don't love the new haircut," she says. "Reservation?"

"No."

She sets down the book and swivels toward the computer. "How long?"

"I don't know. A week?"

"I have the same one you got last time," she says. "Two Rock." She really does remember me. "I never forget a face," she says, as if she's reading my mind. That's uncanny, I think. Or is it? I shake off the thought, though I glance down quickly at her ring finger. She's not even married.

"I don't think I can afford it."

"I'll give you the returning family discount. You're returning with your family?"

"Does my wife count?"

I hear someone moving around in the room beside us.

The girl picks up a pencil, writes *$225/nt,* and slides the paper across the desk for my approval. I nod and give her the thumbs-up. It's surely several hundred dollars less than the lowest posted rate. I put a credit card on the counter. "Can you just hold on to this and run it when we check out?" I ask quietly.

"Can you leave it spotless?" she whispers.

"Like we were never there."

She slips the credit card into an envelope, seals it, and hands me a clear plastic bag with the keys and directions. I thank her.

"If anyone asks, I was never here."

"Ditto," she says.

"I'm serious," I whisper.

"Me too."

## 83

WHEN I PULL DOWN THE ROAD AND INTO SEA RANCH, ALICE leans up in her seat, gazing out at the ocean. The wood-and-glass houses get bigger and nicer as we head west toward the cliffs. When I pull into our rental compound, Alice punches me on the shoulder and says, "Holy shit!"

I unlock the door, and she runs into the living room and looks out to the ocean through the floor-to-ceiling windows. I turn on the heater. The place looks and smells the same. Sea air and eucalyptus, a hint of cedar from the sauna.

"Strip," I say.

Without asking why, she peels off her dress. "Underwear too," I say. She steps out of her underwear and stands there naked. I kiss her—overwhelmed with relief that we're here together, safe—pick up her dirty clothes, and go upstairs to start a load of laundry. When I come back downstairs, Alice is sitting in a chair next to the telescope, wrapped in a blanket, staring out at the ocean.

"Maybe today is the day," she says dreamily. I know what she's looking for. What she's always looking for, whenever we're on the coast.

Later, I'm in the kitchen, preparing the rock cod and asparagus we bought in town, when a scream startles me. I race to the living room, expecting the worst, expecting to find Declan and his friend. But when I get there, Alice is looking through the telescope and pointing toward the ocean.

"Whales, Jake! Whales!"

I look out into the vast expanse of gray sea, but I see nothing.

"Whales!" she shouts again, motioning me to look through the telescope.

I peer into the eyepiece, but all I see is calm blue waves, a rocky shoreline, a freighter way off in the distance.

"Do you see them?"

"No."

"Keep looking." Alice has plopped down in the chair and is flipping through the Lyall Watson book on whales.

I pan left, I pan right. Nothing. One more time, but I still can't see anything. Then I do. Two spouts slowly moving up the coast. It is nothing, just water flying into the air, yet it gives me chills.

## 84

THE NEXT MORNING, EARLY, I LINE UP FOR PASTRIES AT TWOFISH bakery. The last time I was here, the doors opened at eight, and everything was gone by eight-fifteen. I arrive early and walk away with a morning bun, a blueberry scone, a chocolate chip muffin, coffee, and hot chocolate. I remember the pall of loneliness that descended upon me during my first trip here, when I ate my morning bun in the cavernous kitchen of the huge, empty house.

When I get back, Alice's showered hair is damp, her face lovely without makeup. We sit eating our pastries, looking out over the ocean, saying nothing.

We lounge about all day, both of us reading books from the eclectic collection in the master bedroom. At three, I finally manage to pull Alice away from her Norwegian mystery so we can go for a walk up the coastline. We look like some other couple in the ill-fitting clothes we bought at the local grocery store. Alice's hoodie bears the seal from Cal State Humboldt, along with the university's unofficial weed logo; mine says KEEP BACK 200 FEET.

About five miles up the coastline path, we find a bench, and I turn on the phone with the new SIM card: no blinking P. We both leave messages for our offices—rushed excuses about how we're going to be out of town for a while. I feel bad for the couples I'm supposed to be meeting and especially bad for my weekly teenager group. I know I'm letting everyone down, but there's no way around it.

"Crash and burn," Alice says, hanging up. It's hard for her, I know. If and when we go back home, Ian and Evelyn and Huang will welcome me with open arms. Cutting out on a corporate law firm in the middle of a huge case is a different story.

In the evening, I fry the rest of the rock cod while Alice finishes her book. Later, on the deck, looking up at stars, I'm amazed at how quickly the two of us have adapted to this beautiful new location, the relaxed pace of coastal life. It occurs to me that we could live here, we could so easily settle into this rhythm.

Beside me, tilted back in her Adirondack chair, Alice seems truly relaxed for the first time in ages.

"We could afford a place here," I say. "Easily, if we sell our house in the city."

"You wouldn't get bored?"

"No. Would you?"

She glances at me, surprised, it seems, by her own realization. "No. It would be good."

That night, I sleep soundly, the waves crashing in the distance. I dream of Alice, the two of us in a cottage overlooking the ocean. There isn't much to the dream; it's more just a feeling of happiness and security. I wake and take in a deep breath—the cold sea air fills my lungs. It hits me then: a strong, certain belief that it is truly possible for us to create something new, something entirely different.

When Alice and I were getting married, my only concern was how I was going to integrate this wonderful marriage into the framework of our lives. Lying in bed, it occurs to me that the old lives are no longer necessary—for me at least—and I can live on the marriage alone, whatever it is, however it develops. What happened in the past seems irrelevant. For the first time, I know that Alice and I will grow together, our marriage will evolve in ways I may or may not understand. For the first time, I know that we will be all right.

I roll over in bed to kiss Alice, to tell her my dream, to describe this overwhelming sense of optimism that I have, only to realize that she's gone.

She must be in the living room, at the telescope, looking for her whale friends.

"Alice?" I call.

Nothing.

As I swing my legs out of bed, my feet come to rest on something hard and cold. It's my phone, lying upside down on the floor. Immediately, I am overcome with fear and dread, but then I remember the new SIM card. There's no way they could have tracked us. I pick it up and realize that in the fall from the nightstand, the phone must have turned itself on. There are twenty-eight text messages waiting, nine voicemails. Then, in the upper right-hand corner, I see the blinking blue *P*.

## 85

I BOLT OUT OF BED, STILL IN MY UNDERWEAR, AND RUN DOWN THE hall. A million questions race through my brain. How long has the phone been on? How long has the little blue *P* been flashing, betraying our exact location? And how is it even possible? We'll have to leave. I need to pack our things right now, load up the car, get as far away as possible. There's only one road out of Sea Ranch, and the only way to go is north, toward Oregon, because if we go south we'll surely cross paths with Declan as he makes his way up the coast.

Still, part of me believes that as soon as I turn the corner, I'll see Alice in her chair, curled in a blanket, peering through the telescope. She'll mock me for racing around the house like a madman in my underwear. She'll call me over to her, and I'll pull her up from the chair and tug her back to bed. We'll make love.

Later, we'll have another long walk along the coast. We'll drink a whole bottle of wine. We'll sit in the sauna, sweating out all the pain and fear.

But she isn't at the telescope. There are the massive windows, the path down to the ocean, the waves, the dark clouds sweeping south down the coast; no Alice.

I hear a sound in the kitchen, and I take a shaky breath, relieved. She's making coffee, trying to figure out the house's newfangled machine.

But no, she's not in the kitchen. There's a coffee cup on the counter, nearly full, still steaming. Next to it, the Lyall Watson book is open to a page about blue whales. The page is ripped. A gash stretches from the top right corner to the bottom, almost severing the page from the book.

Surely it's nothing. So many guests have been through this house, so many kids have pawed at that book.

What's that smell? The oven is on, and I open it to find a tray of burning cinnamon rolls. My heart rate triples. My gut heaves. I grab a towel, pull out the pan, and slide it onto the counter.

What did I hear? A bumping sound.

I open the cutlery drawer and pull out a knife. It's a chef's knife, German steel.

I wander through the breakfast room, gripping the knife, but Alice isn't there either.

More noise. It came from the garage, I think. Shuffling, feet against the floor. Maybe she went out to get something from the car and forgot about the rolls. That's what I tell myself.

I head farther down the hallway of the cavernous house, toward the garage. Another sound, but no, it isn't the garage. It's coming from the mudroom that separates the house from the guest cottage.

I move more cautiously now, clutching the knife. My heart hammers. Something isn't right.

"Alice?"

No response.

"Alice?"

The noise is definitely coming from the mudroom.

Shuffling again, then a scraping sound, then nothing. Just the ocean, the waves crashing. Why won't she answer me?

Then I hear a door opening. I'm pretty sure it's the side door, from the mudroom to the outside.

I know where I have to go now. Whoever it was has gone out the door, and I need to get there before he disappears. That's what I'm thinking, for a couple of stupid, foolish seconds.

But as I turn the corner toward the mudroom, I see Declan. He seems so much larger than I remember. Behind him, at the door, is his partner Diane. She is not alone. She's shoving someone in front of her. Even with her hands tied behind her back, a black bag over her head, I know, of course, that it is Alice. She's barefoot, wearing only the T-shirt she slept in last night.

"Friend," Declan says.

I lunge toward him with the knife.

"Hey." His huge arm flashes in front of me, and suddenly the knife is on the floor, my right arm twisted painfully behind my back. A trickle of blood seeps through a tear in Declan's shirt. He touches the gash, surprised. "Not a good way to start, Jake. I'm not hurt, but you've really pissed me off."

"Alice!" I shout, thrashing.

The door of the mudroom closes, shutting me off from Alice.

"Now, Jake," Declan scolds. "You know you shouldn't have done this. I've always treated you with respect." His fist is digging into the small of my back. I try to move my arm, but his grip is relentless. I reach back to punch at him with my left arm. He releases his fist from my back, grabs the elbow of my left arm, and yanks so hard I scream in pain, flailing wildly.

"It was a stupid thing to do, Jake. Running away like this. Why would you think you could escape The Pact?"

He kicks my legs out from under me and I crumple onto my knees. For a second, I want to explain to him my dream, the feeling it gave me, the promise of starting over.

"Jake, seriously, don't push me. I've had a long night cleaning up other people's messes, and a tough drive—I'm not in the mood."

"Please take me instead," I say.

Declan releases my arm and I struggle to get up. My face is at the level of his waist, and his jacket is pulled back. I can see the gun in its holster. If I could just get the gun.

"That's not how it works. Open your fucking eyes to what's going on." He sounds more exasperated than angry. "And don't worry," he adds, walking away. "Your time will come."

Outside, I hear a car door slam.

"What is she accused of?" Ashamed to ask, but I have to know. "At least tell me that."

Declan opens the door, then looks back at me. He seems almost pleased to deliver the news: "Adultery in the First Degree."

The words are swirling through my head as he walks out into the fog. "You're not the law!" I shout, stumbling after him. "None of you are! You're just a fucking cult!"

He doesn't even turn to acknowledge me. Declan gets into the driver's seat of the black SUV, slams the door. The engine turns. Through the tinted windows, I can barely make out Alice in the backseat, hooded. I pound on the driver's side window. "I'm calling the police!"

Declan powers down the window. "You do that." He smiles, pure disdain. "Tell my friends at the department I said hello."

"You're bluffing."

"Believe that at your own risk." Declan winks. "Eliot and Aileen thought the same thing." The window powers up. I drop to my knees in the sand as the vehicle makes its way up the road, turns onto the highway, and vanishes.

I am left kneeling alone in the cold, in my underwear. Utterly useless to my wife and to myself.

Alice. Oh, Alice.

Until the moment I saw Declan, I didn't know for certain that my wife had been unfaithful. Yes, the signs were there, so I suppose I knew, but I shoved my suspicions aside—the two wineglasses by the couch; the two plates in the sink.

Somehow, when we escaped through the backyard that morning, I assumed The Pact had come for me.

*Adultery. First-degree.*

Suffering under the sudden crush of loneliness, a new feeling overtakes me. A new certainty. Despite all of this, I need to save Alice. I need to figure out how to do that. I am all she has. Whatever she has done, she is still my wife.

## 86

I'M SORE AND BRUISED, BUT NOTHING IS BROKEN. I PICK UP THE landline and dial 911. But there's something wrong. A recorded voice intones, "Your call is being redirected."

Moments later, a male voice comes on the line. "Is this an emergency?"

"I need to report a kidnapping," I blurt.

"Friend," the voice says. "Are you certain?"

I slam the phone down. Shit.

I dress, throw our meager belongings into the car, toss the burned cinammon rolls into a trash bag, and quickly wipe down the kitchen counters. It feels important to keep my promise. I leave no signs that we have been here, no signs of the new life that only an hour earlier seemed so possible.

When I turn in the keys at the office, the girl doesn't seem surprised to see me. She's wearing a *Sloganeering* T-shirt. The TV is playing behind her.

"I have to check out early," I say, placing the keys on the desk.

"Right." She pulls my card out of the envelope and runs it, then hands it back to me. "Next time, I have a different place for you. It's a talent I have. I match people with places. The more I know you, the easier it is. That place seemed right, but it wasn't. Give me another chance."

"Okay." But all I can think is that I'm out of chances.

## 87

Back home, packages are piled on the doorstep. For the first time, I notice weeds growing through cracks in the sidewalk. When did we let things go? I'm reminded of the photos of Jonestown, before and after, a strange utopia so swiftly and completely swallowed up by the jungle, gone and nearly forgotten. I think of Jim Jones, his makeshift throne, and the sign above it: *Those who do not remember the past are condemned to repeat it.*

The house is freezing. At this moment it seems that all I have left of our marriage is this: our little house in the Avenues. I must restore it to order. I must not let it be reclaimed by the elements. In a fever of activity, I clean, organize, bring in the mail, run the dishwasher, fold the laundry. I'm terrified that this thing that Alice and I are building together will be swept away, overtaken by a jungle we can't possibly hope to control.

When order is returned, I set about with the real work—the only work that might bring Alice and me back together.

Online, I do a search. I locate a small island off the coast of Ireland. Rathlin. I chart a course. I buy a series of airline tickets, far too expensive, then grab my passport from the safe, throw things into a suitcase, and call a cab.

On the way to the airport, I power on my phone. The *P* is there again, blinking. A text message from an unknown number links to SFGate. On the home page, buried between the opening of a new restaurant and a tenants' rights dispute, is the headline "Local Musician Missing." I shudder, my thumb hovering over the headline.

I click through to the article.

Former Ladder bassist Eric Wilson was reported missing on
Monday night after his car was found abandoned at Ocean Beach.
He was last seen early Sunday morning after a memorial show at
Bottom of the Hill for former bandmate Damian Lee. A search
has been under way at Kelly's Cove, where Wilson often surfs.

The article lists each of his bands and albums. And because the Ladder album was his most successful, it mentions Alice by name. There is a comment from one of his biology students, who had no idea he was a musician, and one from a former bandmate, who had no idea he was a professor. There is a video of Ladder performing twelve years ago, Alice at his side. I don't watch it. His parents and sister have flown in from Boston to help with the search. I nervously read the article two more times, as if more details might magically appear. But there is nothing.

Should I feel sad that he is missing? Should I feel anything other than relief?

I think of Eliot and Aileen. What had JoAnne said? "They just disappear without a trace."

## 88

A T THE AIRPORT, FLIGHTS ARE BACKED UP DUE TO WEATHER ON the East Coast. I find myself hopping across the country. SFO to Denver to O'Hare to EWR to Gatwick to Northern Ireland. When I finally arrive in Belfast, hungry and stiff, I'm not sure what day it is. I'm desperate for news of Alice. Is she in a dark cell or a bright one? Is she handcuffed? Is she being interrogated? What is her punishment? Does she have a good attorney?

The line at customs feels endless. Businesspeople in suits all seem in a hurry to get to some important meeting. A customs agent with a spattering of freckles takes a long look at my passport, then back up at my face. "Difficult flight, then, sir?"

"Long."

She looks back at the passport. "That's a fine Irish name you've got."

It's true. My family is Irish. We ended up in San Francisco four generations ago when my great-great-grandfather, a streetcar driver with a drinking problem, killed a woman in this very city. He fled to the United States on a steamer to avoid prison. Until now I've never been here. I guess you could say I'm finally returning to the scene of the crime. Maybe it's still part of me, that genetic predisposition for murder.

The freckled border guard flips my passport to the final page, and then with a definitive thud leaves a large red stamp. "Welcome home," she says.

I find an ATM and take out a wad of cash. Outside, I step into a taxi and head toward the train station. I take off my watch to sync it to the local time. Before putting it back on, I turn it over to read the simple inscription: TO JAKE—WITH ALL MY LOVE. ALICE.

My brain is spinning, my body exhausted. The morning bustle, the congestion, and the traffic don't help. At the station, I realize that getting to my destination will be more complicated than I had expected. A train will only take me part of the way, if I could even get a train. But the station is blocked by a picket line, more than a dozen workers holding signs declaring, OFFICIAL DISPUTE.

I walk over to the hotel Malmaison. The receptionist is a puffy guy in a wrinkled suit. I ask about the train and he responds with a long, convoluted explanation. As far as I can understand, I'm in Northern Ireland at a bad time. The buses are on strike, the trains are on strike, and there is apparently some major soccer tournament just getting started.

"Do you like football?" he asks.

"Um . . ."

"Neither do I. If you wait until noon, I can give you a ride as far as Armoy." He hands me a paper that appears to be a ticket of some sort. "Free English breakfast, if you want." He points toward a sad, cavernous room that looks like an abandoned elementary school cafeteria. Immediately, a waiter is on me, insisting on pouring some weird brown tea. I thank him, then head up to the buffet with a plastic plate.

There are bowls of sweaty eggs, skinny sausages, and a few unidentifiable casseroles, piles of thin white toast. I force down two boxes of something called Fruity Sugar Surprise soaked in skim milk. I watch the tourists, soccer fans, and English honeymooners—mostly young, glowingly happy—juggling cameras, maps, and umbrellas. I envy them.

At noon the guy from the reception desk taps my shoulder. We climb into a car so small our arms touch every time he has to shift gears.

He talks all the way to Armoy, though I only catch about half of it. He's going to his ex-wife's house to pick up his son to take him to a birthday party. The son is ten and they haven't seen each other in a month. He says he would've driven me all the way to Ballycastle if he weren't already late. His ex-wife will be angry, the kid will be mopey, he has to hurry.

Armoy is a nothing town, just a blip on the road. It's ten kilometers to Ballycastle, he tells me. He suggests a taxi if I can find one, but I tell him I'm going to try walking. He starts laughing. "This is Northern fucking Ireland—it'll rain four times before you get there, and that's the easy part. The wind alone may fucking blow you back to Belfast."

Out front of his ex-wife's house, we go our separate ways. I walk twenty or thirty feet, but I turn back and peer through the hedge to see him walking up to the door. The ex-wife answers, a pretty woman who looks bone-tired. Of life, maybe; of him, certainly. Even from a distance, I can sense the sad, complicated ball of love and hate that she presents him with at the front door. The kid, tall and lanky, tremendously dumb haircut, darts outside to hug him, and I turn away.

A mile into the walk, on schedule, the rain comes down in icy sheets that soak through my coat before I can pull a windbreaker out of the bag. I push forward into the wind, against the spray of the passing lorries. I'm freezing, but the rain wakes me up; it's the slap in the face I need.

By the time I enter Ballycastle, my clothes have gone from drenched to damp, but now the rain starts up again. I trudge straight down to the terminal, hoping to catch the ferry to Rathlin. The doors to the building are locked, the parking lot empty. At the end of the dock, three fishermen are unloading something from a boat. They seem oblivious to the freezing rain. I ask about the boat to Rathlin. All three stare at me as if I have just arrived from another planet. Their responses come back in a language I don't understand. Seeing my confusion, the captain explains patiently that the ferry to Rathlin is part of the transportation strike. "I hope you're not in a hurry," he says.

Fuck.

I head back into the center of town. I can't help thinking it's a pretty place, even in this relentless rain, with its brightly colored buildings and green cliffs overlooking the sea. Alice would love it here. I find a travel agency, but it's closed. I duck into a pub, the Dog & Shoe. The place is packed. As I step through the door, twenty different conversations stop abruptly and every head turns my way. A second later, just as abruptly, the din resumes. Years ago, I gave a talk at a conference in Tel Aviv. Afterward, I remember wandering around the town alone. Each time I walked through the door to a café or restaurant, all of the talk would cease, and all heads would turn toward me. Instantly, they would all do the same calculation, conclude that I was not a threat, and continue on with their discussions.

I find a dirty table in the corner by the fireplace. I drape my wet coat on the back of my chair and let my eyes adjust to the darkness before heading up to the bar. I'm dying for a Diet Coke to take the edge off my exhaustion, but all they have is beer, lots of beer.

"Is there any way out of town?" I ask the bartender.

"Not until the strike ends."

"Can't I hire a water taxi?"

He shakes his head, apparently amused by my ignorance.

I order a Harp and return to my seat to contemplate my next move. I turn on my phone, surprised that it works. I bought a new cell at the airport in San Francisco. The phone was cheap, but the two-year plan cost an arm and a leg. It was a small price to pay for something without a blinking blue *P.* I had all the calls from the old number forwarded to this one, just in case Alice calls.

She hasn't.

I stand and face the room. "I need to get to Rathlin," I say loudly. "It's urgent." There's a prolonged silence, then a chair scrapes back. A compact, muscular man strides over to me. "No boats," he says. "When we strike, we strike."

"It's a matter of life and death," I plead, but I am met with blank, angry stares.

Outside, the rain has stopped. I hurry back to the marina, where a couple dozen abandoned vessels knock about in the wind. A lone fisherman sits on a boat, untangling a line.

"I'll pay you five hundred pounds to take me to Rathlin," I say, pulling the stiff new bills out of my wallet.

He assesses me for a minute. "Make it a thousand."

I step onto the boat, pull out another five hundred, press the bills into his palm.

He glances at my wrist. "And the watch."

"It's from my wife," I say.

"Taking you across won't make me too popular around here," he says. He goes back to his fishing line.

Reluctantly, I undo the clasp and slip off the watch. I glance at the inscription one last time. He fastens it onto his wrist and admires it for a second before pointing me toward a rickety bench at the stern. "Grab a jacket, Friend. Might get rough."

## 89

I F BALLYCASTLE WAS SMALL, RATHLIN IS TINY. FROM WHAT I CAN TELL, it is home to a rooming house, a pub, a café, a gift shop that doubles as a post office, and a mile of empty coastline.

I walk over to the rooming house. "Crowded?" I say to the teenage boy behind the desk.

"Just you."

For an extra nine pounds, I get a room with a window looking out over the sea. It's a shared bathroom, but apparently I'll only be sharing it with myself.

"I was wondering if you could direct me to—"

"Orla knows you're here," he says. "She'll call for you when she's ready."

Before I respond, he has already turned back to his game. I go upstairs, pace in my small room, and stare out at the sea. There is no cell service.

Anxious, I go for a walk. The beach is empty in both directions. The sea here looks astonishingly similar to the beach where Alice and I take our weekly walks. The waves are treacherous, and the fog reminds me of home. It's dark when I get back to the rooming house, and there is no message awaiting me. The boy is still watching soccer.

The following morning, more impatient, I linger in the lobby. "It's extremely important that I see Orla," I insist.

"Look, sir," the boy says, "things in Rathlin don't move the way they do in San Francisco. No need to stand around. I'll find you."

I wander the island. I hike up the hills, among the sand dunes, over the slippery rocks. I find the one spot on the island with cell service—and yet there is still nothing from Alice. I stare out at the ocean, exhausted and depressed, wondering if I have lost my wife forever.

That night, I wake in a panic from a nightmare in which I'm swimming through a turbulent sea, trying to get to Alice, but she is always just out of reach.

And then, finally, on the third day the boy hands me a parchment envelope. My name is written in elegant cursive across the front.

I go up to my room, sit on the bed, and take a deep breath. My heart is racing. Inside the envelope, I find a map of the island. A blue X marks a spot toward the north end. Written on the back of the map are the words *Ten A.M. Walking shoes required.*

I lie awake all night. At dawn, I dress warmly, plow through an English breakfast, and trek to the far end of the island. Where the X is on the map, I find only a bench overlooking the ocean. The sea is steel-gray. Beyond the bench, a trail leads westward along the cliffs. I'm more than an hour early, so I sit. I do not see anyone or anything in any direction. Slowly, the fog moves in and swallows me up. I wait.

Later, I hear movement and glance up to see a woman standing over me.

"Friend," she says. "Walk with me."

## 90

ORLA IS TALLER THAN I EXPECTED, HER SILVERY-WHITE HAIR cropped short, her outfit plain. My anger at her nearly chokes me, and I'm ready to hate her, to hate this thing she created, this ugly conspiracy that has caused Alice and me so much harm. There are so many things I long to say to her—statements of opposition, of critique, a long, scathing monologue.

Yet I know that I must tread carefully. I know that with Orla, as with many of my patients, the confrontational approach will not work. I want to lash out at her, to scream—but it would get me nowhere. It would only make more trouble for Alice. Shouting implies threat, and Orla is not a woman who will respond to threats. In order to achieve my goals, I must be as calm as she is, and more calculating.

We walk in silence. In the beginning, I keep an eye on her, waiting, ready for the dialogue to begin, waiting for the words to turn poisonous. Her silence is maddening, and it's difficult to resist the urge to empower her by filling it with my own words.

"I like to walk," she says at last. "It allows me to think clearly. Do you believe, Jake, that you are thinking clearly?"

"I'm thinking more clearly than I have in months."

She doesn't reply.

Eventually, we crest a hill, and I see a wide cottage blending into the grassy landscape below. The house is instantly recognizable. Its combination of reclaimed wood and walls of glass brings me back to the photographs lining the hallway outside the courtroom in Fernley. Is Alice there in the courtroom? Has she looked at those photos the way I did, desperate to be in a different place? Is she safe?

Orla glances at me, and the expression on her face makes me wonder if I spoke my thoughts aloud. "Friend," she says as we make our way down the hill, "we have much to discuss."

I'm surprised by the size and simplicity of the home's interior. Yes, it is impeccable, with its polished concrete floors and magnificent views, but it somehow manages to feel modest. The furniture is sparse and white. I expected something more—a world headquarters, a command center, video monitors, smart boards, a building filled with administrators, sycophants, and acolytes.

There is none of that. In fact, as far as I can tell, it's just the two of us.

"Make yourself at home, Friend."

She slips off her walking shoes and disappears. I pace the room, impatient for her to return. I parse the contents of the bookshelves, looking for some clue to Orla's character. I find the collected works of Yeats; William Dean Howells's brilliant marriage novel, *A Modern Instance;* collections by Joan Didion, Cynthia Ozick, and Don Carroll; signed first editions of *1984* and *Catch-22*. On the top shelf, Romney Schell's *At the Disco* stands beside Michal Choromanski's *Jealousy and Medicine*. My gaze falls on a tattered spine, and I do a double-take: Stanley Milgram's *Obedience to Authority: An Experimental View.*

And there are photos. A picture of Orla, a man who is perhaps her husband, Ali Hewson, and Bono. Orla with Bruce Springsteen and Patti Scialfa. A younger Orla with Tony Blair and his wife, Cherie. Bill and Melinda Gates. A blurry black-and-white of Orla with the late James Garner and his wife, one with the Clintons. Jackson Pollock and Dolly Parton with their respective spouses. Scattered among the books and photos are a few knickknacks. I pick up a Breitling watch with a red 5 on the front and turn it over to find an insignia that might not be popular with all of the residents of Rathlin.

I browse with a boldness that surprises me, yet even this time alone in her house feels orchestrated. If Orla didn't want me to look at her things, would she have brought me here?

In the kitchen, I find a metal container of ten different spatulas, all different types and colors. I'm turning the purple silicone one over in my hands when Orla returns. "I was trying to see where it was made," I say. "Believe it or not, I collect spatulas."

"I know."

I drop the spatula back into the container.

"That one is from a design shop in Copenhagen. Richard and I were there nearly a decade ago, and the color caught my eye. I didn't say anything, but somehow he noticed. A few months later, it mysteriously appeared in our kitchen."

She moves to the counter and hits a button, prompting a touch screen to rise from a hidden compartment. "When the architect gave me the keys to this house, he told me it was designed to go better with music. I'm not sure I understand why, but I've come to think he was right." Alfred Brendel's rendition of "Für Elise" emanates from hidden speakers throughout the house.

Orla takes a bottle of wine from a cabinet. "It's a special bottle," she says, "a gift from a member. I've been wanting to open it, but I guess it's still a bit early."

"It's night somewhere," I say.

She opens the bottle and pours the wine. It is a pinot noir, mossy and dense.

"Please, have a seat," she says, leading me into the living room.

"I'm not sure I can drink red wine on your white couch."

"Don't be silly."

"Seriously, one sneeze and Alice and I will be bankrupted."

Orla almost smiles, and for an instant I catch a glimpse, I think, of the real woman behind the measured responses. "You would be doing me a favor. I despise that sofa." She swirls the wine in her glass and sips, closing her eyes to savor it.

I place my glass on the coffee table and sit. Orla slides into the leather chair next to me. She moves like a much younger woman, tucking one foot underneath her, holding her glass high and straight.

"I've come to talk to you about Alice."

"Of course you have," she says serenely.

"One week ago, my wife was kidnapped. Dragged away, terrified, half-dressed."

Orla looks at me directly. "I am sorry, Jake. I will be the first to admit that excessive force was used."

Her reaction takes me by surprise. I assumed she would admit nothing, apologize for nothing. "She's at Fernley?"

"Yes. But in the hotel wing."

I think of the comfortable bed, the view, the room service. I imagine Alice there. And yes, I admit, I remember Declan's words—"Adultery in the First Degree"—and I imagine her with nothing to do but contemplate our marriage. Then, guiltily, I picture her in one of the solitary confinement cells, or worse.

"Why should I believe you?" I demand.

"Your wife has a powerful ally in Finnegan," Orla replies, unfazed. "I will tell you the details later. But first, humor me. I've been waiting for so long to talk to you." Clearly, she will talk about Alice when she's ready and not a moment sooner. I can almost hear Alice's warning in my head: *Play nice.*

Orla leans slightly toward me and I can sense that she is sizing me up. "Allow me a question. Assuming that five hundred years from now the planet is still here and mostly the way we know it, do you think marriage will exist?"

"I really don't know." I'm impatient with this nonsense. "Do you?"

"Not how it works. I asked you first."

I think for a moment. "Deep down, our one true goal is immortality," I say. "The only way to achieve immortality is through procreation. When a couple remains together, particularly within the legal construct of marriage, the offspring have the greatest chance of survival, and thus the individual has the greatest chance at immortality. The question of children aside, I believe that most people have a strong desire to have a life partner."

"I imagined you would say exactly that."

Orla is gazing at me intently. I'm not sure if she has complimented or insulted me.

"Can I tell you a story?" Orla asks.

I have a feeling she's about to give me some version of the narrative I heard that first day, when Vivian showed up at our house with the contracts we so naïvely signed, the contracts that sucked us into this nightmare. I remind myself that, despite her warm hospitality and the seemingly instant rapport, this frail, silver-haired woman is a wolf in sheep's clothing. Or more accurately, a wolf in fine linen.

"My parents were poor," Orla says. "My father worked in a coal mine in Newcastle; my mother was a seamstress. While they provided a supportive home for my sister and me, they never gave us any advice. They had opinions, but their opinions were without conviction or clarity. When it came to the big things—religion, politics, work—I had to find my own way. I don't blame them. Our world is growing at such a rapid pace, how can any of us be equipped with the right tools to pass on to the next generation? The world today is not the same one my parents grew up in—it's not even the same world in which I grew up.

"I've become concerned that the modern world is evolving in a way that might leave marriage behind. This has a great deal to do with globalization and the sharing economy."

"What does globalization have to do with the death of marriage? What does any of it have to do with this brutal system you've created?"

She sits back, eyebrows raised, apparently surprised by the anger in my tone. "Marriage is inefficient!" she proclaims. "The whole construct is a model of wasted resources. The wife often stays home to care for the children, or even a single child, abandoning the career she worked so hard for, losing years of creative output. Beyond the wasting of talent, think of the physical waste. For every home, there are so many redundancies. How many toasters do you think there are in the world?"

"I have no idea."

"Seriously, just guess."

"Ten million?" I say impatiently.

"More than two hundred million! And how often do you think the average household uses its toaster?" Once again, she doesn't wait for my answer. "Just 2.6 hours per year. Two hundred million toasters are sitting unused, statistically speaking, more than 99.97 percent of their active lives."

She sips the last of her wine, rises, and goes into the kitchen, returning with the bottle. She pours more for me without asking, then for herself. "The world wants to conserve resources, Jake. People are waking up to the fact that we don't need all of these toasters; we don't need the small family units and their selfish, self-contained homes. Evolution always rewards efficiency. Modern marriage and the single-family unit are simply not efficient."

There is something slightly mad about her passion for the subject. Of course there is. Without madness, how could The Pact exist?

"So you're saying we should move away from marriage?" I'm stunned. How can I reason with someone who so blatantly contradicts herself?

"Not at all! I am not an economist, Jake—thank God! This is what I believe: Efficiency is not always good. What is easy, what is even good, for that matter, is not *always* good. Why do I believe in marriage?" She stands in front of me. "Because it is not easy. Because it challenges us. It challenges *me* to bend my ways, to consider other points of view, to get beyond my own selfish desires."

"Let me get this straight. You believe in marriage because it's *difficult?*"

"Maybe it is difficult, but that's beside the point. What matters is that marriage creates a platform for understanding. It enables you to put yourself inside the thoughts and needs of your partner, to truly explore the essence of another person."

Orla is moving around the room now. "This understanding is an empowering point of departure for creativity and thought beyond what is available to the single, self-interested being. Humans too often drift toward repetition, toward doing what is safe and easy over and over. Marriage challenges that tendency. The Pact, as you know, grew out of the failure of my first marriage. I saw what marriage could be, but I knew that most marriages, like mine, were powerless to achieve it. I wanted strict rules that would strip away the selfishness."

"It all sounds noble in theory. But what I've witnessed, Orla, is far from noble."

She seems agitated at the mention of her name. She turns. "You are here to ask me to allow you and your wife to leave The Pact. Is this correct?"

"Yes."

She stares at me, saying nothing.

"You must know, the very fact that I have to ask is absurd." I stand to face her, lowering my voice to a near whisper so she has to come closer to hear me. "You believe your mission is noble, that The Pact is pure—yet you run the organization like the cruelest kind of cult."

She takes an audible breath. "Do you not want a successful marriage, Friend? Do you not want a life together with Alice? Do you not want to challenge yourself?"

"Of course I want all of those things! Why the hell do you think I've come all this way? I want Alice back—the way she was before we started living in fear. I want our *life* back. We were so happy before you waltzed in and turned everything to shit."

"Were you?" Orla smiles. She seems to be enjoying herself. I want to wrap my hands around this woman's neck and squeeze.

"Yes, Orla. We were. I love Alice. I would do anything for her. *Anything*."

It occurs to me that I have never said this to anyone. And in an instant, I wonder if it only became true at this moment, when I uttered it aloud. Yes, I wanted Alice for my own, but maybe I did not love her enough.

"Then why are you giving up?"

"I'm *not* giving up on my marriage! I'm giving up on The Pact. You're clearly a very intelligent woman. I refuse to believe that you don't understand the difference. Please explain to me how surveillance, threats, and interrogation lead to any of the grand goals you've described. You speak like a barrister, but you rule like a tyrant!"

A phone rings somewhere deep in the house. Orla glances over at the clock. "Sorry," she says. "Have to keep the lights on, you know." She walks away and disappears into the back of the house. I pace for ten minutes, fifteen, expecting her to come back. She doesn't.

What to make of Orla? I was certain she'd be charismatic, unbending, a leader in the mold of Jim Jones or David Koresh. But she isn't like that at all. In fact, she seems thoughtful and almost gentle. She seems open to new information, willing to assimilate new ideas and actively seek opinions contrary to her own. If I could bottle this thing she has, I would give it to all of my patients, but first I'd save some for myself.

Of course, this is probably just an act. Is it a coincidence that her phone rang at precisely the moment I challenged her on The Pact's ruthless tactics?

I find myself staring at a picture above the mantel. Orla and her husband stand between two other couples—Meryl Streep and Pierce Brosnan with their respective long-term spouses. Do all of these famous people really consider her to be a friend? I wonder. Or have they too been caught in a web from which they can't escape? How many interrogations have been recorded? What secrets would escape if they dared break free?

A tall man walks into the room, a Scottish terrier at his heels. The man looks tired, his sleeves rolled up, his boots scuffed. All this time, I thought Orla and I were alone. Where did he come from?

"Hello, Jake," he says, extending his hand. "I'm Richard. This is Shoki." Richard is ten or fifteen years older than Orla, shaggy, good looking in a tweedy, rumpled way. The dog remains alert by Richard's side, staring at me.

"Orla is eager to continue your conversation, but it will have to wait."

"Listen, I've been waiting long enough. I just want my wife back—"

"Unfortunately," Richard interrupts, "that's something you'll have to discuss with our fearless leader." He gives me a wink, as if we're in on this together. "I'm sure she'll be with you again very soon. In the meantime, Altshire is a guesthouse we have at the south end of the property. You'll be quite comfortable there. Follow the path south for six hundred meters, turn right at the lone tree, and continue until you see it."

"Look, I don't know what kind of game you're playing here—"

The Scottish terrier growls. Richard, close behind me, reaches over my shoulder to unlatch the lock and places a hand firmly on my back. "She's sick, you know."

My first thought is of my wife, and I panic. "Alice?"

He steps back. "No, not Alice. Orla."

The relief makes me dizzy. "I . . . I didn't know," I stammer.

He gives me a quick, sad look, though his hand on my back continues to motion me out the door. "I'm glad I got the chance to meet you, Jake. Orla has spoken of you and Alice with great admiration."

The door closes behind me and a gust of cold ocean wind blows straight through my coat. I can hear Shoki barking inside the warm house.

The air is wet and the fog is thick. I can't see a cottage in the distance. Is this another trap? Is this some code in The Pact, shorthand for dealing with a problem? "I haven't seen Jerry," one member might say; another would respond, "They sent him to Altshire"; and both would know that the individual had been tossed from the cliffs of Rathlin, his body smashed upon the rocks and swept into the sea, floating north past the Faroe Islands, off into oblivion.

## 91

BURIED IN THE FOG AND BUILT INTO THE SIDE OF A GRASSY HILL, Altshire is a smaller version of Orla's house. The door requires a full lunge with my shoulder to jar it open. The place is spartan. One bedroom, one bath, a sitting room, a tiny kitchen. It's freezing and a little musty. When I turn on the faucet, the water comes out brown and grainy. There's no food in the cabinets, only bottled water in the refrigerator. I open the windows, shake out the sheets.

In a metal shed outside the cottage, I find a half rack of wood and an ax. I haul some of the wood into the yard and go at it with a vengeance, chopping until my arms are on fire and my back is aching. Dazed and spent, I stare at the pile of chopped wood. Eventually, I go inside, close the windows, and start up a fire in the woodstove. What now?

How long does Orla intend to keep me here? Is this hospitality or another prison? Did Eliot and Aileen also stay at Altshire before they disappeared?

I keep hoping to hear Orla at the door, but she doesn't arrive. I make the long walk back to the boardinghouse to retrieve my things. At the grocery store, I purchase the essentials, cram them into my backpack, and quickly return along the path to Altshire, racing the sunset, dreading being lost in the darkness, in the foggy cold. I keep looking at my cellphone, waiting for service to kick in.

In the cottage, I turn on the lights and make myself a sandwich, but I have no appetite. Orla never arrives.

Around midnight, I scavenge blankets from the closets, go back outside to fetch the ax, stash it beneath the bed. Lying awake on the hard mattress, watching the shadows on the ceiling, I think of my great-great-grandfather, the one who killed a woman in Belfast before fleeing for America. Each one of us becomes so used to the person we think we are. In our minds, we carry a vision of ourselves, naïvely certain of our own moral boundaries, what we would and would not do.

## 92

IN THE MORNING LIGHT, THE PLACE LOOKS DIFFERENT. THE FOG HAS lifted and I can see the ocean through the picture windows. I start up the fire again, the warmth quickly filling the cottage, and bathe as well as I can in the tiny lukewarm shower.

A guest book lies beside the sofa. I flip to the beginning. November 22, 2001, Erin and Burl enjoyed their tenth anniversary in the cabin. I flip ahead. April 2, 2008, Jay and Julia were in town for a book signing. They saw three foxes and it rained nonstop for a week.

October 4, no year: *I recorded three songs while my beautiful wife cooked the longest, most complicated dinner on record. Feeling whole again, ready to write a new album. Finally met the young lawyer from the copyright case. Spoke again with Orla. We all agreed she will be perfect. Finnegan.*

Perfect for what? I shudder. Finnegan. The source of all this turmoil. If only Alice had never met Finnegan. Rereading the words, I feel as if I am traveling back in time. I briefly entertain the magical notion that I could simply rip out the page, toss it into the fire, and undo the damage of the past few months. I try to imagine what it would look like—a marriage without The Pact. And it occurs to me that, of course, I have no idea. Alice and I have known marriage only as it exists inside the confines of The Pact. The intensity of our love, the passion of those nights with the bracelet, the Focus Collar, my fierce need to protect my wife—all of these things exist within The Pact.

I remember those first days, when I worried that marriage would not be exciting enough for Alice. I cannot deny that The Pact has challenged us. It has brought us uncertainty and, yes, excitement. In battling a mutual enemy, Alice and I grew incredibly close. But it has also nearly broken us.

In the bedroom, I notice a small television and a neatly arranged library of DVDs. I put in *Crimes and Misdemeanors*. Two hours later, I'm antsy, filled with nervous energy, but I don't leave the cottage for fear of missing Orla. I fill the kitchen sink with soap and warm water and dump all the clothes I'm not wearing into the sink to soak, then hang them around the woodstove to dry. All day I pace and wait.

I read the guest book back to front. More entries from Finnegan, cryptic thank-you notes from several of the couples whose photographs grace Orla's shelves.

In the afternoon, I hear a knock at the door. Orla is standing there in her rain gear and tennis shoes. I motion for her to come in, but she takes a step back. She seems to be reassessing me.

"Walk?" she says.

I grab my windbreaker and head outside to find that she's already a hundred yards up the path. She certainly doesn't seem ill. As I come up beside her, she doesn't say a word. We walk for a long way, not speaking, and turn in the direction of her house only when the rain starts blowing sideways.

Inside, she gives me a towel to dry my hair and leaves the room. When she returns in fresh clothes, she's holding a glass of wine for herself and hot chocolate for me.

"Perhaps I should ask what's in it," I say, waving away the proffered mug.

She ignores my sarcasm. "Have a seat."

She settles into the leather chair. There is no mention of the time that has passed since our discussion. Time seems oddly elastic in her world. I sense that there is something else going on in her life—the illness Richard mentioned?—but when she speaks she seems completely focused.

"I really do like you, Friend."

"Is that supposed to make me trust you?"

She waves her hand in the air, as if this is a matter of little importance. "Not yet, but you will. You've had time to think?"

"Yes," I say, suddenly understanding the time alone at Altshire, the long wait at the rooming house. Nothing has been left to chance.

"And you still believe The Pact is not the appropriate avenue to a successful marriage for you and Alice?" She says this bluntly but without judgment.

"You told me a story. May I tell you one?"

She nods.

"As a child, I had a vague, idealized sense of what marriage should be. It was some goofy amalgamation I'd handpicked from my parents' marriage, what I read in books, what I saw on TV or in the movies. It wasn't realistic, and even if it was, it would have been the architecture of a marriage for a different time. As I got older, this unrealistic notion became a barrier, blocking me from moving forward in relationships. I simply couldn't picture any of the women I'd dated in the context of this idealized marriage."

"Go on," she says, listening closely.

"When I met Alice, though, something clicked. All at once, this idealized notion began to fade away, and with it the burden of having to get everything just right. I knew that if I wanted to keep her, I would have to abandon my preconceived notions of marriage, to let it develop naturally. When she accepted my proposal, Alice and I made the unspoken decision to move forward blindly, feeling our way, trying to discover what worked for us. Then, when The Pact intervened, I guess we were both relieved to have some direction. Maybe it was laziness on our part. It was as if you were offering us a clear road map at a time when we were standing lost in some vast, uncharted territory."

Orla says nothing.

"The Pact has many good ideas—Alice and I will give gifts to each other forever, thanks to you, and we'll always take trips together. I also love the idea of surrounding oneself with others who are deeply committed to marriage. And I will grant you this: There was a time, after Alice's first visit to Fernley, when she started coming home earlier from work, paying more attention to our home life. It may surprise you to know that, despite the hell Alice and I have been through, I can see how The Pact as you originally envisioned it has a good heart. I embrace the idea that is the very foundation of The Pact ideology."

"And what idea is that?" Orla seems fascinated by my response.

"Balance. The Pact is about bringing balance and fairness to a marriage. Let's face it, at different points in a marriage one partner may need the other more than they are needed. Most of the time, isn't one partner giving more than he or she is receiving—more love, more resources, more time? The roles may change, but the imbalance remains. I like that The Pact works hard to nudge the relationship closer to that exquisite balancing point. As a marriage counselor, I know through painful experience that most marriages fail when the balance becomes too out of whack to be made right."

There are voices in some other part of the house. Orla frowns.

"Don't worry about them," she says. "Just operational stuff."

"My issue with The Pact," I continue, measuring my words, "is the methods it uses. Your goals should be achieved with a gentle, guiding hand, not an iron fist. There is simply no justification for the things you do. The violence is barbaric. I can't for the life of me understand why you allow it."

"The Pact is guided by an elegant set of ideas. The iron fist is only a small part of it."

"But you can't separate the two," I say angrily. "Threat equals fear. When you instill fear in your members, you can never know whether their marriages are truly successful or they're just following rules because they're afraid of the Draconian punishments."

Orla stands and walks to the window. "Each day, Jake, nearly all members of The Pact live productive, creative lives made richer by supportive marriages and a community of like-minded individuals. More than ninety percent of our members have never seen the inside of places like Fernley or Kettenham or Plovdiv."

Kettenham? Plovdiv?

"Instead, they enjoy contented lives, close to that ideal of the perfect balance."

"But what about the others?"

"Honestly? The minor inconvenience of some, or in rare instances the major debt paid by a few, is justified if it provides an effective example, a cautionary tale to help the others maintain better marriages." Her back is to me. Outside the window, a fog bank moves swiftly over the ocean. "I know your background, Jake. I've read your graduate thesis. There was a time when you might have passionately defended our tactics. Can you deny it?"

I cringe. During graduate school and the years that followed, I was fascinated by some horrifically cruel studies, like the Stanford Prison Experiment and the Milgram Experiment, as well as lesser-known experiments out of Austria and the Soviet Union. Although I chose to pursue a path of therapy defined by compassion and personal choice, I have to acknowledge the ruthless conclusion of my thesis: Individual obedience is sometimes required to serve the greater good, and fear is an extremely effective tactic to elicit obedience.

"Call me what you will, Jake, but the statistics indicate that even among Pact members, whose marriages are far more successful than the general population, those who have spent time at our correctional facilities report even greater intimacy, greater happiness, over a longer period of time."

"Are you listening to yourself? This is textbook propaganda!"

She crosses the room and sits again. Not in the chair but on the couch, right beside me, so close our thighs and arms are touching. The murmur of voices in the background has faded.

"I've been closely following your progress, Jake. I know what happened to you at Fernley. I will not apologize for our use of consequences, but I will admit that your case was handled harshly. Far too harshly."

"Do you know they put me through an hour of electric shock? That they just sat there and watched while I writhed on the floor in excruciating pain? I honestly believed I might die at Fernley."

She winces. "I'm deeply sorry about that, Jake. You don't know how sorry. The past few months, I've ceded too much control to a powerful few. Things slipped past my attention."

"That's no excuse."

Orla closes her eyes, takes a soft breath. I realize that in this moment, she is in physical pain. When she opens her eyes, she looks at me directly, unflinching.

What an idiot I've been. The clipped hair, the sunken cheeks. Bruises traveling the length of her veins. This woman is dying. I feel so stupid for not having noticed it before.

"The board acted reprehensibly, Jake. We are instituting new regulations to ensure that enforcement officers can refuse to comply with unjust orders. As for leadership, there will be changes—"

"Where are they now?" I cut in. "Neil, Gordon, the members of the board? The judge who approved the interrogation techniques used against me? Whoever approved Alice's kidnapping?"

"They're undergoing reeducation. After that, we'll have to decide if there is still a role for them in The Pact. There's a lot of work to do, Jake. I am proud of The Pact, and despite this recent spot of unpleasantness, I receive new evidence daily that convinces me of its efficacy. The Pact is about marriage, yes, but it is so much bigger. There are nearly twelve thousand Friends around the world. The best of the best. The smartest, most talented people. Every one handpicked, rigorously vetted. But there will be more, mark my word. I have no clear vision of where The Pact might go, but I want it to grow and thrive. Marriage may not last forever. But as long as possible, I want to fight for it. As you point out, Jake, all marriages need to evolve. So does The Pact."

She walks to the counter and fiddles with the controls. Music fills the house. "Has The Pact made mistakes? Have I made mistakes? Yes. A thousand times yes! Yet I am still proud of trying. Friend, perhaps we come at things from opposite sides, but we meet in the middle. We want the same thing. We do the best we can, and we either succeed or fail. Neither outcome is to be feared. Doing nothing, Jake, that is what terrifies me."

I walk over and stand directly in front of her. I put my hands on her frail shoulders. I can feel her bones through the thin fabric of her sweater. My face is inches from hers. "All your theory," I say, "all this talk. It means nothing to me. Are you so blind you can't see that? Alice and I want out."

She winces in pain, and I realize that I'm squeezing her shoulders tightly. I let go and she steps back, startled but unyielding.

A young woman in a gray linen dress appears, whispers something into Orla's ear, hands her a green folder, then disappears. And that's when I hear other voices in the back of the house, men's voices, at least three of them. What do they plan to do with me?

"I know that you and Alice have been tested. It was necessary."

I remain still, though my mind is racing.

"Some didn't see you and Alice in the same way that Finnegan and I did," Orla says, watching me carefully. "They didn't understand your potential."

"Potential for what?" I ask, confused. What game is she playing now?

"I have been a questioner all my life, Jake. I rarely take things at face value. It is a quality I admire in you too. Doubt is a useful tool, so much more desirable than blind belief. Your doubt has made your journey through The Pact infinitely more difficult, yes. But it has also made me respect you. Believe me when I say that you have enemies, but I am not one of them."

"What enemies?"

I think back to the first party, in December in Hillsborough. Everyone was so friendly, so welcoming.

Orla stands there, studying me. Behind her, the vast and roiling sea. It is as if she is waiting for me to complete a complex math problem in my head, to see what she has seen all along.

"Perhaps it's better if you just read the documents." She hands me the green folder. The file is heavy. It has a faint smell of decay, as if it has been unearthed from a musty warehouse.

I look down and see that there is a name on the cover: JOANNE WEBB CHARLES.

Orla has left the room. I am alone with the file. For a long time, I don't open it.

## 93

THE FIRST PAGE CONTAINS A PHOTO FROM MANY YEARS AGO. JoAnne as I knew her in college, relaxed, tan, and happy.

Page two is her résumé, both professional and personal—no unfinished degrees, no MBA, no job at Schwab. In no way does it resemble the story she told me that day in the food court. Instead, a PhD in cognitive psych, with honors, but then an abrupt end to a postdoc she was pursing at a prestigious university in Sweden, followed by marriage to Neil.

There's a photo of Neil and JoAnne on their wedding day, holding hands against a brilliant desert background. On the following page is a photo of Neil with another woman. Below the photo, the typed words *Neil Charles. Widowed. Pictured with first wife, Grace. Cause of death: accidental.*

What the fuck? I read the caption three times, not wanting to believe it.

The next page contains a clipping from a Swedish newspaper, along with a translation. The article announces a seven-figure settlement in a lawsuit against JoAnne Webb and the Swedish university. The plaintiffs in the suit were volunteers from a psychological experiment that had gone horribly awry. Reading the details—so cruel yet so familiar—I feel sick to my stomach.

The following pages contain an unpublished draft of an academic article, co-authored by JoAnne, on the correlation between fear and desired behavioral changes. A footnote has been highlighted: *Subjects who show little or no fear for their own safety can usually be persuaded to act in direct conflict with their own moral code when they witness a friend or loved one in danger of violence.*

I flip through the file, shaking. The final sheaf of papers is stapled together with a red cover, the words *Report on Subjects 4879 and 4880* scrawled across the front.

These pages are not typed. Instead, they are in JoAnne's familiar handwriting. *Met 4879 at the Hillsdale mall. Audio file attached. Responses to my questions and comments reveal disloyalty to The Pact.*

I shudder and turn the page. *Glass Cage Experiment,* JoAnne has written at the top. *4879 shows continued disloyalty to The Pact while exhibiting strangely detached tendencies. Seemed to be horrified by my predicament but at the same time clearly took some pleasure from it.*

I'm fighting the urge to vomit. JoAnne wasn't the subject of the Glass Cage Experiment; I was.

I turn the page. *Infidelity Report: Subject 4880.* My hands begin to sweat.

Clipped to the page is a grainy photograph of a man walking up the stairs of my house, carrying a guitar. Even though his back is to the camera, I know exactly who it is.

*Witnessed non–Pact member, identified as Eric Wilson (see attachment 2a), visit home of Subjects 4879 and 4880 while Subject 4879 was at Fernley. Wilson arrived at 10:47 P.M. on Saturday night and departed at 4:13 A.M. on Sunday morning. Music was heard from within the house during the entire night.*

There was music throughout the night. Five to six hours is Alice's ideal span of time for a serious rehearsal. Any less, she insists, and it's impossible to get deep into the music; any more and it stops being productive.

I look up to realize that Orla has silently returned. She's sitting in the chair across from me, drinking her wine, staring.

"I have to know," I say. "The charge against Alice, Adultery in the First Degree. Was it based solely on this report?"

Orla nods.

The truth hits me: Alice wasn't sleeping with Eric. Yes, Eric was in my house. Yes, it looked as though Alice was unfaithful. But simple facts, taken out of context, do not always point to the truth. He wasn't screwing my wife—they were rehearsing. How stupid I've been. How wrong I was to doubt my wife.

I shake my head, disbelieving. "Why would JoAnne do this?"

"The Pact has become unexpectedly wealthy, incredibly strong. There are those who desperately want to lead. When Neil and JoAnne learned of my illness, they saw an opening. They envisioned themselves at the very head of The Pact. But those who strive to lead rarely make good leaders."

Orla hesitates. "Now I have to decide what to do with them." A sly smile crosses her face. "What would you do?"

As I mentioned earlier, there is always a shadow that hovers between the person we want to be and the person we are. In our minds, we carry a vision of ourselves, naïvely certain of our own moral boundaries. I want to be that person who embodies the ideal of doing something good, rather than doing nothing at all. But good and evil are complicated, aren't they? And doing something, anything, is so much more difficult than doing nothing at all.

I respond without hesitation, without even a shred of doubt. When I am finished, Orla takes a sip of her wine and nods.

## 94

A T THE AIRPORT IN BELFAST, I PLUG MY PHONE INTO THE WALL
and wait. Staring out at the wet runway, I consider my next step.
The phone finally beeps, the power comes on, and there, in the
corner, is the blinking blue *P.*

There are emails and texts whizzing past. I've only been gone for
seven days, yet my old life seems impossibly distant. I scroll through the
texts and emails, searching for one from Alice. I'm surprised to discover
that my old life is still there, waiting for me. There are texts from Huang,
Ian, and Evelyn. Dylan has started a new play—he'll be Hook in *Peter
Pan*—and wants me to save the date for opening night. Isobel writes,
*Conrad took me to this new Buddhist bakery that makes the most amazing
bread. We made French toast. Here's the secret to life: It's all in the bread.*

Finally, buried among the others, several screens down, is Alice's
name. The feeling of relief is physical, as if a tight band around my chest
has snapped, allowing me for the first time in so long to really breathe.
I click on the message, hoping for news, something to go on. It is from
two days ago, when I was still at Altshire. *When are you coming home?*
That is all. I can almost hear her voice.

I text back, *On my way, are you OK?* but there is no response. I call. Her phone rings and rings.

The flight from Belfast to Dublin is bumpy, from Dublin to London crowded, and the night spent at Gatwick cold and uncomfortable. Finally, the plane touches down at SFO. Walking through the clean, gleaming terminal, I'm exhausted. My pants hang so loose on my waist, I must have lost ten pounds since I was last here. I move resolutely through the airport, hoping not to run into anyone I know. At the bottom of the escalator, I pull my hood up over my head and push my way through the crowd.

I think I hear my name being called, but when I glance back I don't see anyone I know. I keep moving. Outside, as I'm walking toward the taxi stand, I hear my name again.

"Friend," says a familiar voice.

I turn, startled. "What are you doing here?"

"The car is this way." Vivian tugs gently at my arm.

"I'd rather take a cab," I insist.

"Orla called me." Vivian is smiling. "She wanted me to make sure you're completely comfortable."

Vivian leads me to a gold Tesla parked at the curb. It's not a model I've seen before—probably a prototype. The driver is up and out of the car, placing my bag in the trunk. His tailored suit barely disguises the fact that he's excessively large and muscular. He is behind me now, the rear door to the car open. I glance longingly at the line of people up ahead stepping into an endless stream of yellow taxis. Vivian motions me into the car. "Relax. You've had a long journey."

There on the seat beside us is a basket filled with bottled water and pastries. She leans forward between the seats to say to the driver, "We're all set."

Vivian reaches into the console and hands me a cup of hot chocolate. Then she settles back into her seat. As the driver negotiates the airport gridlock, I take a sip. It's rich and minty. I take another sip. Then I notice that Vivian is leaning toward me, her hands outstretched, ready to take the cup.

Suddenly, I am profoundly sleepy. The flights were so long, the trip and these past few months so draining. I struggle to keep my eyes open—where are we going? I need to know that I am headed home.

"Go to sleep," Vivian says soothingly.

"You're taking me to Alice, right?" I say to Vivian, but she's fiddling with her phone. Her face blurs.

The driver angles toward 101 North. There's a metallic taste in my mouth, and I feel dizzy. I try to stay alert until the 80 split, where one route leads toward our house by the beach and the other leads over the bridge and eastward into the mountains, but the sweep of the road beneath us is hypnotizing.

## 95

I N MY DREAM, I GO UP THE FRONT STAIRS, FISH THE KEY OUT OF MY bag, let myself in.

"Alice?" I call, but there is no response.

On the kitchen table, there is a note. It is written in electric-blue crayon, and at the bottom she has drawn a picture of us in front of our house, a bright orange sun shining down from above. I love her optimism. I can't recall the last time I saw the sun shining through the fog of our neighborhood. At the bottom, she has clipped a single ticket.

Then I am no longer in our home. I am standing in line outside Bottom of the Hill. By the time I walk through the door, the show has started. Alice is standing front and center, leading the band through one of her new songs. The lights are low. A waitress slides up beside me and hands me a Calistoga. She holds her tray at her side and leans back against the wall next to me. I feel her bump against my shoulder, then another bump. It's jarring. I turn to look at her, but instead I see the tinted windows of the Tesla. My head is so heavy, my mind so groggy. I want to keep dreaming. I'm not ready to turn the page.

I will myself back to sleep, I will myself back to that music club. I will Alice back onto the stage.

"She's amazing," the waitress says, her eyes on Alice, "isn't she?" And then she's gone.

A bump on the shoulder, light streaming through the tinted windows, Alice's voice almost a whisper, fading. Where am I? Reluctantly, I open my eyes just a sliver. Why am I not home yet?

Another bump. The car is swaying back and forth. We're on a dirt road, dust swirling, obscuring the view. The sun is so bright, blinding, really, even here behind the tinted windows.

Sun? I realize that we are nowhere near Ocean Beach; we are nowhere near San Francisco. In our neighborhood, the sun is not scheduled to shine for at least another three months.

Dust rises around the car, a thick cloud enveloping us. The heat, the intense glare, the flatness of the landscape, the absence of color. It feels as if we are traversing one of those massive valleys on the planet Mars. Am I still sleeping?

Something is wrong. Very wrong. I jerk to my right, expecting to see Vivian. I will demand answers, I will demand to know where we are, and more important, where we are going. But then I realize that I'm in the back of the car, alone. A glass partition now divides the front and back seats. I shade my eyes from the relentless glare of the sun. Through the glass, I can barely discern the outline of two heads in the front seats.

I panic. I feel so stupid. Again. So naïve. Trusting Orla. Trusting her kindness and her reason. How could I have been lulled into believing her?

I don't want Vivian to know that I'm awake. I scan the backseat. There's nothing of use. Just the bag of scones, and a gray woolen blanket that someone has placed over me, now tangled around my legs. I look for the window controls. They aren't on the door but on a central panel, attached to the side of the console. Slowly, barely moving my body, I reach toward the buttons. I have no plan. I just want to get out. I need to escape.

My outstretched finger reaches the switch labeled REAR LEFT. I'm about to press it when it occurs to me that perhaps I should press the other one, REAR RIGHT. Although it would be harder to make a jump across the backseat before climbing out the window and sprinting through the dirty, barren landscape, I figure that's my best chance. If

I jump out this side, the driver will catch me in a matter of steps. If I jump out the other side, it will be up to Vivian in her three-inch heels to initiate the chase. Yes, I can outrun Vivian, I am certain.

I reposition my body, sliding across the backseat, quietly pushing the blanket off of my legs, my finger near the window control. I think for a second or two, reviewing my incredibly limited options, and it occurs to me that this unlikely escape is my only real choice. To save myself, to save Alice. Is she even still alive?

In a single motion, I push the button and lurch toward the window. I will dive headfirst. It will hurt, but somehow I will roll, stand up, and run.

Then this happens: nothing. The windows are locked. Desperate, I pull up on the door handle, positioning my body to drop and roll, but still nothing. All of the rear controls have been disabled. I'm trapped.

## 96

THE TESLA COMES TO A STOP. THE CLOUDS OF DUST OUTSIDE THE window take forever to subside. I can't see anything. I hear the driver's-side window purr down, the mumble of voices.

Then I hear the clatter of a gate opening, and I feel the tires of the car rising up onto concrete. My heart sinks. I no longer need to look out the window to know where we are. Fernley.

What have they really done with Alice?

As we drive through the gate, the guard in his gray uniform peers inside the car to get a look at me. I shudder, hearing the second gate opening up ahead. The car sweeps forward and the gate closes behind us. Inside the compound grounds, we skirt the runway, taking the long way around. Above, there is the hum of a Cessna coming in low for a landing. The plane pulls in just ahead of us.

The Tesla parks behind the plane, waiting. A man is being led from the Cessna. Something about the way he stands, the uncertainty in his posture, tells me this is his first time here. Two guards take him from the landing strip and usher him into the fenced breezeway that leads toward the massive structure.

I'm staring at the prison, the horror of it sinking in, when the car door opens. I look up to see my driver. Heavyhearted, I step out, using my hand to shield my eyes from the sun. He motions me into the front seat of a golf cart. His hand goes to his pocket, and I instinctively recoil, but he pulls out a pair of Ray-Bans and hands them to me. They fit perfectly.

A uniformed man is in the driver's seat, red-haired and absurdly tall, his pale face burned from the desert sun. He glances at me nervously, then faces forward. Vivian slips in behind us. I twist to confront her, but she smiles, her face calm. The smile only makes things worse.

"Where's Alice?"

Neither the driver nor Vivian says a thing. Something about Fernley demands this behavior, like church, the principal's office, or something far worse.

The golf cart speeds around the side of the building, down a long narrow passageway that leads underneath the complex. The tunnel is damp and cold. The cart is moving so fast that I have to reach out and grip the bar in front of me. I consider leaping, but where would I go? After a time, we come to rest at a loading dock. A well-dressed man with silver hair stands waiting for us.

"Friend," he says, reaching out to shake my hand. I meet his eyes but say nothing, leaving my hand by my side. I hate this relentless game— the polite handshakes and cordial greetings, every civil transaction masking some unspoken horror.

The two of us walk up along the loading dock and through a locked door. Vivian is gone, but the tall guy seems to be hovering somewhere behind us.

We enter a hallway that leads to a stairwell. The stairwell leads to another hallway, then that hallway leads us through a laundry area, the air thick with steam. Seeing us, the workers all stop what they're doing and stare. Up more stairs, down other hallways, through more locked doors, all with complicated keypads, each door in the maze slamming shut behind us.

The place is empty, hushed, save for the slamming doors and the echo of our shoes. The man is not speaking to me. I imagine that my refusal to shake his hand only made things worse.

But before, when he called me Friend, he seemed so flustered when I did not respond. How can one learn how to play the game when the rules are always changing?

We go through a labyrinth of stairwells into the belly of the building. At one point, we travel through a noisy boiler room, then through a series of storage rooms and up four flights of stairs. Sweat pours into my eyes, blurring my vision. The trip is so long that it becomes almost absurd. The air seems thin, and I struggle to catch my breath. I'm reminded of that first day here, following Gordon. Even before I knew where he was taking me, I realized that escape was impossible. Throughout, my guide says nothing.

Finally, a series of locked doors, a mantrap, and a metal detector lead into the longest hallway I've ever seen. The concrete floors give way to plush carpet, and dazzling light flows in from many windows. I lift my hand to shield my eyes against the glare. Behind us, I can still hear the quiet footsteps of the tall man's size-fifteen shoes. As we walk, I become aware of a room at the end, a door standing open.

The hallway is so long, the sun through the high windows so blinding, that at first I think I've imagined the blaze of red at the far end, standing there in the open doorway. A woman. We are moving toward her. My heart pounds. For an instant, I freeze at the telltale movement, a way she has of holding her elbows as if she is cold. It is all so familiar, my eyes must be tricking me.

But as the distance between us closes, I realize that it is, in fact, exactly who it seems to be.

## 97

I WALK THROUGH THE OPEN DOOR. SHE IS STANDING THERE JUST IN-
side the room, utterly still, wearing a formal red dress cut to show off
her pale shoulders. Her hair is pulled tightly to one side, wound into
an elaborate knot. She seems so polished, her makeup more pronounced
than I'm used to, her nails perfectly manicured in a deeper red, her
jewelry—a single strand of pearls I've never seen before and small, shiny
earrings—impeccable. As I get closer, she doesn't say a word.

"I imagine you two would prefer some time alone," my escort says.
He meets my eyes, looking nervous, before walking out of the room,
shutting the door behind him. I realize that we must be in the hotel
wing. The room contains a king-sized bed, an elegant desk, a window
overlooking the desert.

I open my mouth to speak, but no words come. As Alice stands before me, beautiful, I am speechless with happiness and relief.

How long has she been in this room, waiting for me?

Overwhelmed, I reach out and pull her toward me. She slides her
arms around my waist and nestles in close. She sighs deeply, and I understand that she too is relieved. I hold her tightly, feeling the warmth

of her body, her head on my shoulder. She feels good, but there is this: She doesn't seem entirely like Alice. Maybe it's the hair, the makeup, the dress; I'm not sure. I step back for a second. She looks wonderful but different. It is the same Alice, yes, but dressed for a different role, a role in a theater production I've never seen.

"I went to Ireland," I say. "I went to find Orla."

"And you came back."

Hearing her voice, I realize this is not a punishment. I have not been led to my doom. Orla was indeed telling the truth.

"We could still make a run for it," I say.

Alice smiles sadly. "In these shoes?"

She kisses me, long and soft, and for a moment I almost forget where we are.

But then I hear voices, and I pull away. Paranoid, I glance at the corners of the ceiling, looking for a telltale light. I listen for the buzz of equipment. I gaze at the strip of light under the door, looking for signs of movement. I go to the window and look past the ivy-covered fence to the immense desert beyond. Nothing but sand and scrub for miles. It all seems so unreal—for a moment, I am mesmerized by the orange sun hovering over the desert.

When I turn to face the room, Alice is standing before me, naked, the red dress pooled around her feet. Sunlight pours through the window and I stare at my wife in wonder. I see how pale she is, how thin. I wonder if the mark on her ribs is a bruise, days old, or just a trick of the shadows.

I walk to her. She reaches out and unbuttons my shirt, unbuckles my belt, runs her fingernails over my chest. I touch her face, her breasts. Her skin beneath my hands is so warm. I've missed her so much.

As my wife pulls me toward her, I cannot help but wonder if this beautiful moment is a dream. Or worse, is it a performance?

For a split second, I have a vision of a small room, video monitors, someone in a drab gray uniform watching us, listening. Alice steps away from me. I watch her move toward the bed. She lies back on the white sheets and opens her arms. "Come here," she commands, the expression on her face impossible to read.

## 98

I ROLL OVER, REACHING FOR MY WIFE, AND REALIZE WITH A SHOCK that the bed beside me is empty. I jolt up, panicked. But Alice is there, sitting in the chair at the end of the bed, watching me. She is back in the red dress, but her makeup has faded and her careful hairdo has come undone. She looks like herself again.

I ask the question I've been avoiding. "Did they hurt you?"

Alice shakes her head. She comes over to sit beside me. "They had me in solitary for two days, maybe longer, then I was moved to this room, no explanation. I've been free to roam the grounds as I please." She gestures toward the window. "But where would I go?"

I get out of bed and am reaching for my clothes on the floor when Alice says, "Look in the closet."

I slide open the door. There, on velvet hangers, are an impressive suit, a crisp linen shirt, and a Ted Baker tie. On the floor is a shoe box containing shoes of Italian leather. "When I came out of the shower this morning," Alice says, "all of my clothes were gone. This dress was hanging in the closet. A woman came in to do my hair, makeup, and nails. When I asked her what it was all about, she told me she wasn't at liberty to say. She seemed nervous."

I pull on the white shirt, the pants, the jacket. It all fits perfectly. The shoes also appear to have been custom-made for me.

Alice takes a small velvet box from the desk and opens it to reveal two gold cuff links in the shape of the letter *P*. I hold out my wrists, and she pins them on.

"What now?" I ask.

"I have no idea. Jake, I'm scared."

I approach the door, half-expecting it to be locked from the outside. But the knob turns and the door opens. As an afterthought, I grab a large glass bottle of water, a futile weapon. Together, we step into the empty hallway.

## 99

STRANGE TO FIND US TOGETHER IN THIS PLACE. STANDING HERE with my wife, I can almost pretend that it is just the two of us. I can almost pretend that we are not surrounded by concrete, barbed wire, and an endless desert.

We begin walking toward the elevators. I hear voices, but I can't tell where they're coming from. Then a door opens as we pass and a man steps out. Tall, wearing a dark suit and red tie. And though I am startled to be face-to-face with him, in some way it makes perfect sense.

"Hello, Friends."

I nod. "Finnegan."

He looks first at Alice, then at me. His gaze is intense, but I do not look away. "There is something Orla would like for you to see."

With that, Finnegan pulls the door wide open to reveal a narrow, windowless room. Alice leads me in, and I feel Finnegan's hand on my back urging me forward. Along one wall is a dark curtain. Finnegan draws back the curtain to reveal a long window, looking onto a chapel of some sort, lit by a grand chandelier.

The place is packed. There is a buzz of chatter, an expectant electricity permeating the room. People hold full champagne flutes, but no one is drinking. It is as if they are waiting for something. Strangely, when the curtain parts, no one glances in our direction.

"They can't see us," Alice observes.

There are faces I recognize but many more I don't. I look for Neil, JoAnne, Gordon, everyone from the black-and-white photos lining the wall of the marble courtroom. I remember staring at each of the portraits, waiting for the judge to hand down my sentence. For a moment, I wonder where they are. But then I think I understand.

Finnegan stands by silently as we watch the crowd. After a minute, he touches a button and yet another door swings open, revealing only darkness. Alice takes a trembling breath and leads me into the unknown, her fingers entwined through mine.

I feel a hand on each shoulder and turn to see that it is Finnegan's wife, Fiona. She wears the same green dress she wore on the day of our wedding. She and Finnegan silently fall in behind us.

Candles line the walls of the narrow corridor, flickering in the darkness. Behind us there is only the sound of feet moving across the floor. A moan echoes down the corridor from up ahead. We are not alone. My heart starts beating faster, I feel sweat running down my arms, my back. Beside me, though, Alice seems at peace; eager, even.

As we walk, the sounds intensify—a chain rattling, something struggling in an enclosed space. The breathing becomes louder, the echo of more chains, something pulling or perhaps stuck. A motion sensor clicks, dimly lighting the way in front of us. I glance to my right and see a tall, familiar structure. I freeze, only to realize that it's just inches from me. And then a figure comes into view—standing between sheets of plexiglass, arms and legs outstretched and shackled. A Focus Collar forces him to stare straight ahead. As we move past, another motion sensor clicks and a spotlight blazes down upon the structure for a second, maybe two. Through the fog of condensation on the glass, the face becomes clear. For a moment, I lock eyes with the judge, the man who approved my interrogation. His eyes betray no emotion. And then he is plunged into darkness once again.

I turn to Alice, only to realize that she is looking to the other side, more plexiglass, another installation. A woman. I remember meeting her at one of the parties, remember seeing her in the corridors of Fernley: an esteemed member of the board. Her hair is matted, her face shiny with perspiration.

Alice pauses before her, mesmerized.

One by one, we pass the towering, living installations. One by one, motion sensors click on, briefly illuminating the prisoners' faces. Their expressions are impossible to read. Is it fear? Is it shame? Or something else—an understanding that justice has been achieved? That no one is above the laws of The Pact? Its mission must be served. Balance must be restored, no matter what.

As Finnegan and Fiona follow us a few paces behind—each stopping to look, then moving on—the hallway is filled with flashing lights. Members of the board, alone in their glass frames, shackled, each a witness to his or her own fall from grace. Specimens for study, as I once was. Subjects under a microscope. Only the terror in their eyes and the persistent clatter one prisoner makes, struggling against the firm restraints, remind us that this is life, not art.

I remember the moment when Orla asked me what penalties should be meted out to those who abused their power, those who subverted the goals of The Pact for their own desires. I do not regret my answer.

Good and evil are complicated. Who we are, and who we think we are, are rarely one and the same.

Perhaps Orla and I, The Pact and I, are not as different as I once thought.

Up ahead, there are two final installations, set apart from the others and surrounded by candles. As Alice and I move between them, I focus my gaze in front of me. I do not need to look; I know who is there. On my left, I sense Alice's hand reaching toward the thin plexiglass frame that separates her from JoAnne. As the motion sensor clicks and the light shines down, I hear the brush of Alice's fingers sliding along the glass.

## 100

A T THE END OF THE CORRIDOR, WE TAKE A SHARP TURN RIGHT, then right again. In the darkness, I try to get my bearings. I have the feeling that we are returning to where we started, every step leading us deeper into the prison. And then a light flickers and Orla comes into view. She is standing beside a tall candelabra, clad in white, watching us, waiting.

When I pause, Alice tugs me forward gently. She moves without hesitation, her hand so warm, so right. It all seems incongruous—this inertia, this momentum, propelling us forward.

We stand before Orla. The candle flame carves shadows across her pale face. To her left is a closed door, painted gold. To her right, another closed door, this one painted white.

"Hello, Friends." She leans forward to kiss Alice on the cheek, then me. She is even more frail than when I saw her just days ago. Her voice is weak, her skin sallow. "Perhaps now I have earned your trust," she says.

I nod.

"And you have earned mine." She gestures toward the gold door on her left. "Step closer. Listen."

I put my ear to the door. Alice does the same. On the other side, there are voices. Dozens of voices, all talking at once. Glasses, faint music—the sounds of a party. I realize we have somehow been led back behind the chapel.

Alice looks down at her red dress, as if for the first time she understands its purpose.

"On the other side of that door are forty of our most esteemed, most trusted members," Orla says. "They have no idea why they have been summoned here."

I look at Alice. She doesn't seem afraid. Far from it. She looks intrigued.

"I have taken The Pact as far as I can," Orla continues. "And now it is time for me to let go. I cannot leave this earth without knowing that The Pact will be taken care of, that it will evolve and grow."

Alice remains motionless beside me. Orla is watching her carefully, and it occurs to me that Orla knew from the beginning exactly how this was going to end.

"In one hand, a leader holds kindness, and in the other, discipline. I have seen that you are capable of finding this balance." She steps closer. "Jake, Alice, with all my heart, I believe you are the ones to lead The Pact into this new chapter. However, in order to be a great leader, one must be willing. One must accept the responsibility without hesitation, without regret."

Orla places one hand on my shoulder and the other on Alice's shoulder. "That is why I am giving you a choice. If you step through the gold door, all of the resources of The Pact will be at your disposal. You will be able to shape it as you see fit. I will stand with you in that chapel, we will stand with Friends, and I will announce you both as our new leaders."

"And the white door?" Alice asks.

Orla coughs violently, sagging against me, clenching my arm. I feel the surprising strength of her fingers through my suit jacket as I reach out to steady her. Seconds later, she recovers, and she seems to stand taller than before, as if she is summoning all of her strength.

"My dear Jake, my dear Alice, as you know, no one in the history of The Pact has ever been allowed to leave. Never. However, given the significance of what I am asking of you, it is only fair to allow you to choose. The white door is an exit. If you walk through it, your obligations to The Pact will cease immediately. But know this: step out that door and no one will come to save you. No one will come to save Alice. You will be completely on your own. Live or die. Alone."

I look at Alice, regal in her red dress. Her eyes are shining, her face expectant. I try to figure out what she is thinking—my wife, who is always determined to win. My wife, who contains multitudes.

I imagine walking through the gold door. I can see us moving through the crowd, hands brushing our arms, our backs. I imagine the well-dressed couples, their devotion, that collective embrace. I imagine the hush falling over the crowd as Alice and I step forward, lift our glasses into the air, and utter a single, powerful word: "Friends."

Alice grasps my hand, and in that moment I know. For better, for worse, she is with me. She pulls me in close and I feel her breath against my neck as she whispers in my ear. Words of encouragement and, yes, something else. Words meant just for me.

I place my hand on the knob and turn.

## 101

We step out into the desert night. There are millions of stars, more than I've ever seen. The lawn beneath our feet is green, still damp from the sprinklers. A hundred yards on is the chain-link fence, eight feet tall, covered with ivy.

Alice slips off her heels and tosses them onto the grass. "Now," she whispers. We sprint toward the fence. There are no sirens, no flashing lights, just the soft pounding of our feet on the grass.

At the fence, we rip away a cluster of ivy to find a foothold. Side by side, we climb. Despite her days at Fernley, Alice is still strong from her morning sessions at Ocean Beach, and it only takes her a few seconds to scale the fence. We drop down on the other side, onto the cool desert sand. We collapse into each other's arms, laughing, giddy with our new-found freedom.

It takes us several seconds to catch our breath. They are letting us go.

We both stop laughing. I look into Alice's eyes, and I know what she is thinking. Are we really on our own?

I imagine a highway far off in the distance, black under the moon, reflecting yellow stripes to point the way home. But I can't see a highway.

Giant cacti dot the landscape. The desert stretches on endlessly. There are no lights from distant towns, no sounds of civilization.

We have only the bottle of water I brought from the room. We'll have to make good time before the sun comes up and the heat sets in. We begin running, away from Fernley, toward the highway that must be there—somewhere—but the sand is soft and deep, and soon we slow to a jog, then a labored walk. The hem of Alice's dress drags in the sand.

Eventually, we reach a packed-dirt trail and begin walking along the flat surface, dotted with sharp pebbles. I give Alice my shoes and continue on in my socks. A light arcs across the sky, then another, and another. "A meteor shower," Alice says. "It's beautiful." We each take a sip of water, careful not to spill a drop.

We walk for a long time. My legs ache, my feet are numb. I'm not sure how much time has passed when I notice that Alice has slowed and she is panting. Where is the highway? The stars have disappeared, the moon barely visible as night gives way to twilight. I unscrew the cap from the bottle and urge her to drink.

Alice takes a cautious gulp, then hands me the bottle and drops onto the rocky path. "Let's just rest for a minute," she says. I take a sip of water, carefully screw on the cap, and sit beside her.

"There will be a road somewhere, a gas station," I say.

"Yes, there has to be."

She puts her fingers on the back of my neck. I kiss her, long and soft, noticing with alarm that her lips are rough and chapped. A terrifying thought crosses my mind: Have we made the wrong choice? But when I reluctantly pull away, I realize that Alice is smiling.

This is the wonderful, complicated woman I married. The woman who lay beside me on the beach during our honeymoon on the Adriatic. The woman who stood in the lobby of the Grand Hotel, dancing slowly around me, singing in full voice the entirety of Al Green's "Let's Get Married." The woman who sat in front of me at the pool on a warm night in Alabama, gazing at the ring I offered, and simply said, "Okay."

I see in her a resolute determination to move forward, not back, a determination to embrace this strange journey, this marriage, and all of the surprises it holds. A determination to see it through to the end. For better or worse.

Here in the desert, I understand now what I should have seen a long time ago: Our love is strong. Our commitment is solid. I do not need The Pact to hold on to my wife. Yes, marriage is a vast, uncharted territory, and nothing is certain. Still, we will find our own way.

Suddenly, the sky fills with dazzling light as the enormous sun lifts over the horizon. I can hear the wind sweeping across the valley floor. Waves of heat begin to emanate from the earth. Minutes pass and we sit here motionless, transfixed. We are so tired, and there is so far to go. My mind is blank. The relentless sun and the dry air of this strange desert landscape seem to have washed away everything in my life that came before.

Soon, the desert will shimmer with unbearable heat and the sand will be scorching beneath our feet.

"Friend," Alice says, standing. She reaches for my hand, and with surprising strength she lifts me up. Together, we begin walking.

# ACKNOWLEDGMENTS

I wish to thank my longtime agent and friend, Valerie Borchardt, as well as Anne Borchardt. You are both amazing.

Thanks again to my brilliant editor, Kate Miciak, for her vision and infectious enthusiasm. Thanks to Kara Welsh for supporting this book, and to the wonderful team at Penguin Random House: Julia Maguire, Kim Hovey, Cindy Murray, Janet Wygal, Quinne Rogers, Susan Turner, and Jennifer Prior.

Thanks to Jay Phelan and Terry Burnham for their thoughts and writings on gift-giving. Thanks to Bill U'Ren, of course. Thanks to Ivana Lombardi, Kira Goldberg, and Peter Chernin for believing in this story. Many thanks to the publishers and translators around the world who embraced this book; I hope to meet you someday. Thanks to Jolie Holland and Timothy Bracy for the lyrics.

The great Leonard Cohen used to address his audience with the word "Friends." Much of this book was written with the album *Live in London* playing in the background.

Thanks to Kathie and Jack for a thousand small graces. Thanks to Oscar for his insights on plot. Above all, thanks to Kevin for more than two decades of unexpected gifts, including this one.

# THE
# MARRIAGE
# PACT

## MICHELLE
## RICHMOND

A READER'S GUIDE

## QUESTIONS AND TOPICS FOR DISCUSSION

1. In general, what do you think motivates people to join cults such as The Pact? What motivates Jake and Alice in particular?

2. Jake and Alice are drawn into The Pact because it seems fine from the outside, and also because they feel it would be impolite to refuse Finnegan's gift. Have you ever found yourself drawn into something seemingly innocent only to discover that it was not what it seemed?

3. Are there any Pact rules that you find appealing or that you think could strengthen a marriage?

4. Though Alice and Jake both enjoy their work, Alice has the more demanding job, and Jake takes on more of the household responsibilities. Jake comments at one point that marriages are always slightly out of balance and that The Pact's goal of restoring balance to relationships is noble. Do you agree that most marriages go through periods of imbalance? What makes relationships imbalanced? And is it even possible for two people in a relationship to find a perfect balance?

5. How does Jake and Alice's relationship change over the course of the novel?

6. Do you think Jake and Alice's marriage will last forever? Why or why not?

7. Is Alice right to be angry with Jake when she discovers he hasn't been forthcoming about his meetings with JoAnne? Is his excuse—that he wanted to protect Alice—a fair reason for his lies of omission?

8. Discuss the punishments The Pact imposes on Alice for failing to give her marriage adequate attention. Though their methods are extreme, can you justify the principle behind The Pact's rules?

9. How do Jake and Alice's family histories and previous relationships inform their choices over the course of the novel? Were there choices they made that you strongly agreed or disagreed with?

10. Jake worries that Alice has given up too much of her true self in her marriage to him. In what ways does marriage require us to change who we are or to leave behind a valuable or essential part of ourselves?

11. What surprised you the most in the novel?

12. How do you feel about the choice Alice and Jake make at the end? Is it the right choice? Why or why not? Given that situation, what choice would you have made? Do you think you and your spouse would agree on what choice to make?

13. Would you ever be tempted to join an organization like The Pact?

MICHELLE RICHMOND is the *New York Times* bestselling author of the novels *The Year of Fog, Golden State, No One You Know,* and *Dream of The Blue Room.* She received the Palle Rosenkrantz Prize for the best crime novel published in Denmark for *The Marriage Pact,* which has been sold in thirty languages. Her story collections include *Hum,* winner of the Truman Capote Prize for Short Fiction and the Catherine Doctorow Innovative Fiction Prize, and *The Girl in the Fall-Away Dress,* winner of the Grace Paley Prize. A native of Mobile, Alabama, she lives with her husband and son in Northern California.

michellerichmond.com
@michellerichmon

## ABOUT THE TYPE

This book was set in Garamond, a typeface originally designed by the Parisian type cutter Claude Garamond (c. 1500–61). This version of Garamond was modeled on a 1592 specimen sheet from the Egenolff-Berner foundry, which was produced from types assumed to have been brought to Frankfurt by the punch cutter Jacques Sabon (c. 1520–80).

Claude Garamond's distinguished romans and italics first appeared in *Opera Ciceronis* in 1543–44. The Garamond types are clear, open, and elegant.

# Chat.
# Comment.
# Connect.

Visit our online book club community at
Facebook.com/RHReadersCircle

## Chat
Meet fellow book lovers and discuss what you're reading.

## Comment
Post reviews of books, ask—and answer—thought-provoking
questions, or give and receive book club ideas.

## Connect
Find an author on tour, visit our author blog, or invite one of
our 150 available authors to chat with your group on the phone.

## Explore
Also visit our site for discussion questions, excerpts, author
interviews, videos, free books, news on the latest releases,
and more.

**Books are better with buddies.**
Facebook.com/RHReadersCircle